D0949250

Sharon Sala is a native of Oklahoma and a member of Romance Writers of America. She is a *New York Times, USA TODAY* and *Publishers Weekly* bestselling author of eighty-five-plus books written as Sharon Sala and Dinah McCall. She's also a seven-time RITA® Award finalist, Janet Dailey Award winner, five-time National Readers' Choice Award winner, four-time Career Achievement Award winner from *RT Book Reviews* and four-time winner of the Colorado Romance Writers Award of Excellence. Visit Sharon's website at sharonsala.net, or go to harlequin.com for more information on her titles.

Books by Sharon Sala

The Chosen
Missing
Whippoorwill
Capsized
Dark Water
Out of the Dark
Snowfall
Butterfly
Remember Me
Reunion
Sweet Baby

Sharon Sala

The Way to Yesterday
&
Shades of a Desperado

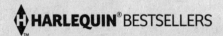

HARLEQUIN® BESTSELLERS

Recycling programs
for this product may
not exist in your area.

ISBN-13: 978-0-373-40114-7

The Way to Yesterday & Shades of a Desperado
Copyright © 2015 by Harlequin Books S.A.

The publisher acknowledges the copyright holder
of the individual works as follows:

The Way to Yesterday
Copyright © 2002 by Sharon Sala

Shades of a Desperado
Copyright © 1996 by Sharon Sala

This edition published by arrangement with Harlequin Books S.A.

For questions and comments about the quality of this book,
please contact us at CustomerService@Harlequin.com.

Printed in U.S.A.

CONTENTS

THE WAY TO YESTERDAY

During my lifetime
there have been many people who've
made promises to me. Some have been diligent
in keeping the pledges they made, while others
swiftly forgot or ignored the fact that they'd
once given their word.

I want to dedicate this book to
three very special people who have been
forever faithful to me in this respect.

First, to my agent, Meredith Bernstein.
Thank you for your honesty and your constancy
and your belief in what I do.

Next, to my editor, Leslie Wainger.
Thank you for trusting me enough to let me
tell my stories my own way.

Last, but not least, to Dianne Moggy.
Thank you for taking me in at MIRA Books
and letting me stretch my wings and fly.

Three ladies who are, to me, the epitome of class.

Thank you for your presence in my life.

Chapter 1

"I'm sorry Ms. O'Rourke, but your friend had to cancel your luncheon appointment. She said to tell you that the school called. Her daughter is ill and she had to go home. She tried to reach you at your office but you'd already left. May I seat you at a table for one?"

Mary Faith O'Rourke shook her head. "No, thank you. I won't be staying," she said softly, and walked out of The Mimosa without looking back.

It wasn't as if she'd wanted to come. For the past six years she hadn't wanted to do anything but die, and today was no exception. Exactly six years ago today, her husband and child were killed in front of her eyes.

Her friends worried about her, and in the back of her mind, she appreciated their kindnesses and sincerity. But they simply did not understand. Oh, they knew what had happened, but they didn't know the details or the guilt with which Mary lived.

Yes, she had been standing in her front yard when her husband had backed out of the driveway with their baby in the car. And yes, she had heard, before she'd seen, the police car come careening around the corner in pursuit of another vehicle. And yes, she had yelled at Daniel—screaming for him to stop. But they didn't know that the reason he'd been leaving the house was because they'd had a fight, or that the last words they'd spoken to each other had been in anger. They would never understand how insidious guilt was, or that she had tried so hard to die along with them when the three cars had collided and then burst into flames. Watching Daniel and their baby daughter die in that fire had destroyed her spirit. Now, she was just waiting for her body to catch up.

She glanced at her watch. It was a whole hour before she had to be back at work at the dress shop across town and since food was the farthest thought from her mind, she started to wander the streets.

It had been years since she'd been in this part of Savannah, but her friend had been insistent, raving about the renovations that had been done and the new businesses that had sprung up afterward. Mary had to admit that the place looked good. Old cement had been removed from the sidewalks, revealing a herringbone pathway of ancient, red bricks. Trees lined the curbs on both sides of the street, laying down a wide swath of shade for the shoppers who were on foot. Dainty trellises covered with climbing ivy and bougainvillea partially hid the tiny alleys between the buildings, giving the area an old-world appearance.

Mary walked and looked, but without really seeing. As she stopped at a crosswalk, waiting for the light, she overheard the conversation between the two women in front of her. Three children had gone missing from Savannah schools over the past six weeks, the latest only the day before yesterday. With no clues as to what had happened to them, Mary could only imagine the parents' fears. She knew the meaning of loss and of mind-numbing fear, and she felt guilt that she had prayed for the children's safe return without actually believing it would happen. The truth was, Mary had lost her faith in God and humanity.

She continued to walk, absently window-shopping without interest in buying. It wasn't until later when she stopped in front of a jewelry store to look at the window display that she realized she was lost. Curious, rather than concerned, she turned around, intent on searching for familiar landmarks, when the store across the street caught her attention.

The name over the doorway intrigued her. Time After Time. But when she realized it was an antique shop, pain hit her with the force of a fist to the gut, leaving her weak and motionless.

Before she and Daniel had married, antiquing had been one of their favorite pastimes. She loved old cookbooks and tiny treasures that were often overlooked by the true collectors. But that was back when they had still been happy, when his family hadn't known she existed. She shuddered. God. How many times in the past six years had she relived those last moments of their lives? Remembering the fights was like being stabbed repeatedly in the heart, and always because of the same thing.

His parents hated her, and she hadn't known how to make him understand. She couldn't forget the sounds of her baby's shrieks, echoing above their own shouts, and feeling the guilt of knowing that she was frightened by their anger and harsh words.

She had known Daniel was frustrated with everything, including her constant tears and her inability to get along with his family. She had lived in fear that he would get fed up with her and leave, then knowing if that happened that her world would come to an end. And it had happened, but not as she'd expected. She had feared that he would leave her, but not that he would die in the process.

A car sped past in front of her, shattering her concentration.

God...how much longer do I pay penance before you put me out of my misery?

As usual, she got no answer to the question. Weary all the way to her soul, she started to turn away, barely missing a young boy on a bicycle as he came flying around a corner. In reflex, she jumped off the curb to keep from being hit and when she turned around, realized she was halfway across the street on her way to the antique store.

Longing for a connection with the man that she'd loved and lost, she started toward the store, hesitating only briefly as she reached the door. When she stepped inside, she paused and took a deep breath. The scent of well-oiled wood and ancient books mingled with the faint layer of dust on the jumbled-up counter. To a true antique buff, it was like waving free money in front of an addicted gambler.

Telling herself she was a glutton for punishment, she let the door shut behind her. As it did, a small bell jingled from somewhere overhead. At the same moment, her gaze caught and held on the old man behind the counter.

She hadn't seen him at first, but when the bell sounded, he'd looked up and the movement had caught her eye. He was tiny and stooped and looked as old as the jumble of artifacts in the store. He had a tube of glue in one hand and a pair of tweezers in the other. She could just see the corner of a picture frame on the table in front of him and supposed he was trying to repair something that had broken.

"I'm just looking," she said.

He nodded and then returned to his task.

A slight shift of relief moved through her when she realized he wasn't going to follow her around in the store, trying for the hard-sell approach. She and Daniel had always liked to browse on their own.

Her nose wrinkled slightly in reaction to the musty odors as she moved toward the back of the store. The farther back she went, the more narrow the aisle became. Finally, she found herself holding the skirt of her dress against her body to keep from sweeping the dust off an assortment of old tables and chairs.

Despite her initial nervousness in coming inside, she quickly lost herself in what Daniel used to call her "search mode." She shopped from instinct rather than a skill of knowing true antiques, and her purchases had always reflected that. She bought because she liked a piece, rather than due to any value it might have. In all those precious years with Daniel, her favorite purchase was still a small fluted vase for which she'd paid the huge sum of fifty cents. It was barely big enough to hold a single sprig of honeysuckle, but its fragility reminded her of a kinder, gentler time and place. If she closed her eyes, she could still see the laughter on his face when she'd crowed with delight at the find.

Determined to proceed, she jutted her chin and pushed past the dusty jumble toward a single counter at the back of the room.

There, in the middle of the mess, was a small glass case filled with an assortment of jewelry. The padlock on the case was rusty, which went rather well with the thick layer of dust on top of the glass. Determined to look inside, she took out a tissue and gave the dust a quick swipe. The moment she did, she knew she wanted to see more.

She turned and called out to the old man up front.

"Sir…I'd like to see the jewelry inside this case. Do you have the key?"

She heard the sound of chair legs scooting against wood and then the squeak of a drawer opening and closing. A few seconds later, the old fellow emerged and started toward her.

Mary tried not to stare, but there was something so compelling about his face that she couldn't look away. It was a mixture of age and grief and a knowing that comes with having outlived too many friends and family.

He stepped past her without speaking, removed the tiny

padlock with surprising ease, then opened the case. For a moment, their gazes met and Mary felt as if someone had caressed her face. But then he blinked and the notion passed.

"Thank you," she said. "I'm interested in those rings. Do you mind if—?"

He walked away without bothering to comment and Mary shrugged. It was obvious from the dusty contents of the store that he didn't sell much, and if his behavior with her was normal, it was a wonder someone hadn't stolen him blind.

She dug into the display, soon realizing that most of it was junk, although the rings were another matter. Eagerly, she glanced through the lot, fingering them gently and sorting through the array, trying on one, then another. A few minutes later, convinced she'd seen all there was to see, she started to close the case when she noticed a tattered piece of lace stuffed in the corner of the case. Curious, she picked it up, then gasped in delight when a single ring tumbled out in her hand.

The band was silver, etched with an elaborate series of engravings that were reminiscent of a twining ivy and set with a single, clear blue stone. Blue topaz, she thought, and turned it toward the weak, yellow glow from the single bulb hanging from the ceiling. The light caught and held in the stone like an ember coming to life. She turned it in her hand, admiring the workmanship and wondering what it cost when she realized there was an inscription within. She squinted, trying to read the elaborate script and only with some effort finally discerned what was there.

I promise you forever.

Her eyes filled with tears. There was no forever.

Thinking of the man who'd first given this ring to his love, she clutched it in her fist and then closed her eyes. Daniel's face slid through her mind and without hesitation, she slipped the ring on her finger.

Just because it was there.

Just because the promise was forever.

Within seconds, her finger began to burn. She jerked back in shock and yanked at the ring, trying to pull it off but it wouldn't come. She cried out, both in fear and in pain. As she did, the little old man suddenly appeared before her.

"Oh my God…oh my God…Sir, please help me. I can't get this—"

He smiled and the pain disappeared. Again she felt as if someone had just kissed the side of her face. She held up her hand, but the old man just nodded, as if in understanding. Although his lips never moved, Mary thought she heard him tell her it would be all right. Before she could argue, a sudden wave of dizziness sent her reaching for a dusty old highboy to steady herself.

"I don't feel so good," she muttered, and knew she should have eaten lunch after all.

A faint shift in the air almost took her breath away, then the pressure in the room began to expand. Even though she knew she was standing still, it felt as if she'd started to turn. Around…and around…and around…the chairs and the tables, the dusty pictures on the wall began to move backward, like a carousel in reverse. Everything in the room began to turn, taking Mary with it. She wanted to close her eyes, but she was afraid if she did she'd fall off the world. The old man's image began to waver before her eyes, as if he'd suddenly lost substance. A sudden chill filled the air, and panic struck Mary dumb as the old man disappeared. She stared in disbelief at the place where he had been standing.

The scent of dust and camphor was thick around her as was another, less potent, but still definable scent: the scent of lavender and dried rose petals. She heard crying and laughing, then a single, thin high-pitched wail and knew it was her own. Something within her snapped and she felt herself falling.

When she came to, she was standing at her kitchen sink.

The smell of baby formula was thick in her nose and she could hear her baby crying in the next room.

Oh God...not this. Not again.

Gritting her teeth, she felt herself turn, knowing that Daniel would be standing in the doorway as he'd been before—looking at her as if she was a stranger and not the woman he'd made a child with—not the woman he'd taken as his wife. She heard herself saying the same words and wanted to scream. She knew what she would say because she'd heard it every night for the past six years. Was this her punishment for still being alive when everyone she loved was dead? Was she doomed to replay her last moments with Daniel and Hope forever? Would this nightmare never stop?

"Isn't her bottle ready yet?" Daniel asked.

Mary turned toward the sink where the bottle was warming in a pan of hot water. She yanked it out, shook a few drops on her wrist to test for temperature and started past him when he stepped in her way.

"I'll do it," he said, and took the bottle out of her hands.

Mary felt his rejection as plainly as if he'd slapped her in the face. She turned and stared back at the room. The sink was full of dirty dishes, and there was a pile of laundry in the floor just inside the laundry room in need of washing. The scent of burned bacon from breakfast was still strong in the air, and she needed to mop the floor. In the next room, she heard the low rumble of Daniel's voice as he soothed their baby girl, then heard Hope's satisfied gurgle as she began feeding from her bottle. Her shoulders slumped. She was a failure. Everything she tried to do went wrong.

From their first date, she'd known he was the man she wanted to marry. His Irish charm had worked magic on her too-tender heart and their first kiss had turned her knees to jelly. She'd loved him without caution and gotten pregnant for her abandon. She had to admit that he'd never wavered when she'd told him she was carrying his child. He had seemed elated and had quickly asked her to marry him that very same night. But his family, which had kept her at arm's length from the start, was furious. As they were certain that she'd gotten pregnant just to trap their only child into marriage, their cool behavior toward her had changed to an underlying hate. And they were so good at it—never maligning her or making snide remarks when Daniel was in earshot, always waiting until she was on her own. The sheer force of their will was eating away at her sanity and causing friction between Daniel and her. He didn't understand, and she didn't know how to tell him without sounding like a tattle tale, so she kept her pain inside and let the infection of it spill out into their personal lives.

In the other room, Daniel looked down at his daughter's face, marveling at the perfection in such tiny features and felt his heart twist into a deep abiding ache. He'd had no idea that love such as this even existed. He had been certain that the love he felt for his Mary Faith was perfect and all-consuming and then he'd seen Hope being born. The bond had been instantaneous and he had expected their child to cement their love even more. To his surprise, Mary had begun to pull away—keeping her emotions to herself in a way he didn't understand. She rarely left the house and when she did, seemed to scuttle through the errands like a crab seeking shelter, relaxing only after they were home again.

As for his parents, she had completely withdrawn from them and he didn't understand why. It seemed the only time she was even slightly comfortable was when it was just the three of them, alone at home. She had to understand that his parents needed to be a part of Hope's life, too. After all, they were her grandparents. He knew that Mary had grown up without any family of her own, and would have thought she'd be elated to share his. But it was just the reverse. Daniel wanted to believe that her reluctance to be with his family was nothing more than needing to recover from giving birth. But Hope was three months old now and things weren't getting better. They were getting worse. He went to bed with a knot in his belly and woke up the same way. Without knowing why, he was losing his wife, and it scared the hell out of him. And because he was so afraid, his fear often came out in anger.

He heard Mary banging pots in the kitchen and sighed. He wasn't fooled. She did that to cover up the sound of her tears. He looked down at their baby, his heart full to breaking and felt like crying himself. They'd made this baby with so much love—where had it gone?

Mary squirted a dollop of dishwashing liquid into the sink, filled it with hot water and put the dishes in it to soak for a few minutes as she went to start the laundry. Her back ached. Her head throbbed. But it was her heart that hurt the most. Last night she had turned to Daniel in her sleep and awakened as he rolled over and shrugged out of her grasp. She knew it was only a matter of time before he told her he wanted a divorce. She couldn't really blame him. He didn't know what was going on between her and his family and she didn't know how to separate his love for her from his love for them. It was all a horrible mess.

She shoved a load of Hope's baby clothes into the washer, added laundry detergent and started the machine, then went back to the dishes in the sink. Without thinking, she plunged her hand in the water and at once, felt a sharp, piercing pain.

"Ooh!!" she cried, and yanked her hand back. It was dripping blood.

"Mary! What's wrong?" Daniel called.

"Nothing," she said, then grabbed a hand towel and quickly wrapped it around her slashed finger before dashing toward the bathroom.

* * *

Daniel looked up from feeding Hope in time to see Mary bolt through the living room and then down the hall. Hope was almost through with her feeding and already half-asleep. Concerned, he laid her down in her bassinet and then went to see what was going on. He walked into the bathroom just as Mary started pouring alcohol over the wound.

"My God!" he cried. "Honey…are you all right? What happened?"

"Obviously, I cut my hand," Mary snapped.

Her anger sideswiped him, leaving him frustrated and hurting. And because he hurt, he lashed back.

"I can't win with you, can I?" he muttered, yanked the alcohol bottle out of her hand and began ministering to her himself. "No matter what I say, it's wrong." Then he peered a bit closer, assessing the cut. "I don't think it needs stitches, but maybe we should go to the emergency room… just in case."

"We can't afford a trip to the emergency room," she said. "Just give me some Band-Aids. They'll do just fine."

Daniel froze.

Mary felt sick. Daniel looked as if she'd just slapped him. But if she went, Phyllis O'Rourke would find out and she would find a way to say something hateful about the money an emergency room visit would cost. She couldn't face another one of Phyllis O'Rourke's tirades. He didn't know that his mother had been sniping at Mary for weeks about the fact that her son was having to work too hard on his own and that she should be doing her part by going back to work, too. No matter how many times Mary had tried to explain that she and Daniel had made the decision together that she should stay home with their child, it never seemed to matter. Phyllis blamed Mary for everything wrong in Daniel's life.

Mary sighed. "Daniel…I'm—"

Hope started crying. Daniel took a deep breath and momentarily closed his eyes, as if trying to make himself calm. When he looked up, Mary actually flinched and took a step backward. That hurt him most of all. Dear God! Did she actually think he would strike her?

Hope's wails increased.

Suddenly, he snapped.

"Damn it all to hell, Mary Faith. That does it! I am taking you to the emergency room. We'll drop Hope off at Mom's on the way. No need exposing her to God knows what. And when we get home, we're going to talk. I don't know what's wrong with us…but I am sick and tired of being shut out of your life. Do you hear me?"

"No!" Mary cried, and clutched his arm. "Please don't take Hope to your mother's house. I don't need to go to the emergency room. It'll be fine. See…it's almost stopped bleeding."

Daniel ignored her and kept walking toward the living room to get their baby.

Mary followed, still begging him to stay, but her pleas fell on deaf ears. She watched in horror as Daniel got a fresh bottle from the fridge, packed the diaper bag and then picked up their crying baby. Almost instantly, Hope's crying stopped, but now Mary was in tears.

"I won't go!" she cried. "You can't make me."

Daniel turned, staring at her as if she were a stranger.

"Fine," he said. "Stay here. But I'm still taking Hope to Mom's and when I get back, we're going to talk."

He strode out of the house, put Hope in the baby seat in the back of their car and strapped her in, ignoring the fact that Mary had followed him out into the yard, still begging him to stay.

The moment he laid Hope down, she began to cry again. But Daniel couldn't let himself focus on her tears. Her diaper was dry and she wasn't in pain. She just liked to be rocked to sleep and he'd laid her down a bit too soon.

"Hush, baby girl," he said softly. "You're okay. You're okay. Grandma Phyllis will rock you back to sleep when we get to her house."

He closed the back door and then turned to get in when Mary grabbed at his arm.

"Daniel...please! Don't! You don't know what you're doing to me."

He frowned. "To you? Damn it, Mary Faith! Don't you know what you've done to me? To us?"

Panic began to rise.

Mary stepped back, watching in horror as Daniel got into the car and closed the door.

Her heart began to race—her stomach turned. She didn't want to be here again. She knew what was going to happen. She'd seen it every night in her sleep for the past six years.

Oh God...wake me up before the crash. Please...I don't have the strength to see it again.

Daniel started the car. Mary stood, frozen to the spot, listening to the sound of her daughter's shrieks. Daniel put the car in gear and began backing down the drive. Mary could already hear the sound of an approaching siren, but Daniel couldn't hear for the baby's cries.

Oh God...oh God.

The brown sports car suddenly appeared, careening around the corner and fishtailing as the driver tried to maintain control.

Oh God...oh God.

The police car came seconds later, sirens at full blast—lights flashing.

And Daniel is looking at me, not behind him.

Suddenly, Mary bolted, screaming as she ran, and threw herself on the hood of the car. Daniel hit the brakes and then put the car in Park just as Mary slid off the hood.

His heart was in his mouth as he bolted from the car.

Dear God…if Mary had fallen beneath the wheels he would never forgive—

Suddenly, he became aware of the sirens and spun in shock, just in time to see the sports car spin out of control. A heartbeat later, the police car broadsided it and the cars exploded in a ball of flame.

Without thinking, he slammed the car door to keep flying debris from hitting Hope and threw himself over Mary's prone body.

Mary was in shock. The dream! It wasn't the same! It wasn't the same. Overwhelmed with relief, she started to cry. Thank God. Thank God. Maybe this meant she was starting to heal. Even if it was just a dream, she'd given herself a happy ending.

"Mary, darling…are you all right?"

Daniel's weight on her back felt wonderful, as did the sound of his voice in her ears.

"Yes, Daniel, I am now."

He pulled her to her feet and then held her tight, pressing her face against his chest as he stared at the two cars engulfed in flames.

"If you hadn't stopped me, we would have—"

"Don't say it," Mary begged, and put her hand to his lips. Then she moved from his arms to the car, opened the back door and lifted her screaming daughter from the seat. "It's all right, punkin…it's all right," Mary crooned. "Mommy's got you now. You're going to be just fine."

Daniel watched the two most important women in his life walk back in the house, then got in his car and pulled it back up the drive, away from the flames. Already, he could hear more approaching sirens. The neighbors must have called the police. It was just as well. He'd been too shaken too think past his own family's safety.

With one last regretful glance at the cars and for the demise of both drivers, he hurried back into his home and found Mary in the rocker, singing softly to their daughter as she drifted off to sleep.

Without talking, he went into the kitchen, stood at the sink and stared down into the bloody water for a moment, then pulled the stopper. As the water began to drain away, he saw the knife at the bottom of the sink that had cut Mary's hand. Cursing softly, he laid it on the counter, refilled the sink with clean water and soap, and did the dishes. He could still hear Mary singing, but Hope was no longer crying. At least she was happy because now he felt like crying. He'd come so close to killing both himself and Hope.

Bracing himself against the top of the washing machine, he closed his eyes and dropped his head.

"Thank you, Lord," he muttered, then took the clean clothes out of the washer and dropped them into the dryer before grabbing the broom and sweeping the kitchen floor.

A short while later, he had finished with the morning chores. He went into the living room to check on Mary and found Hope asleep in the bassinet and Mary asleep on the sofa. Pain wrapped itself around his heart and squeezed. Not much, but just enough to remind him of what he'd almost lost. Then he picked Hope up from the bassinet and carried her into the nursery down the hall, covered her up with her favorite blanket and closed the door. She would sleep for at least an hour, maybe more.

He went back to the living room, gazed down at his wife's thin, pale face and then at the blood seeping from beneath the bandages on her finger and sighed. She probably needed stitches, but what was done, was done. He got a small towel and wrapped it around Mary's hand, then covered her with an afghan. She needed to sleep worse than she needed stitches, and he needed to think.

Chapter 2

Mary woke with a start, then sat up in fright. Hope's old bassinet was in the living room, her finger was throbbing, and it was almost noon. She wouldn't stop to let herself even wonder where that bassinet had come from or why her finger was wrapped up in a bandage and towel. The last thing she remembered was walking into an antique shop. How she'd gotten home was beyond her and why she was on the sofa instead of in her bedroom was beside the point. She had overslept and her boss at the dress shop was bound to fire her.

Thinking she would immediately call in to the store, she bolted to her feet, frantically searching for the phone, but it wasn't in its usual place. Then she saw the stroller by the front door and Daniel's jacket on the back of a chair and went weak with relief.

The dream.

She was still having the dream, and as long as she slept, Daniel and Hope were still alive.

She looked in the nursery. The baby wasn't there, but when she walked back in the hall and heard the soft rumble of Daniel's laughter and a high-pitched baby squeal, it made her smile. Following the sounds to the small patio beyond the kitchen, she found Daniel in a chaise lounge under their shade tree, holding Hope against his chest. She was on her back, her arms and legs beating the air as she gazed upward into the treetop.

She combed her fingers through Daniel's thick, dark hair, relishing the feel of it against her palm, and then leaned down and kissed the side of his cheek.

"You shouldn't have let me sleep so long."

He looked up and smiled. "Why not? You needed it, honey. Besides, where else would I rather be than with my girls?"

Mary conscience tugged. If only she believed that he meant it.

"Really, Daniel? Do you really mean that? In spite of...I mean, things haven't been..."

"Come sit by me."

She hesitated, then when he moved his feet to give her room, she sat. She glanced at Daniel and then focused her attention on Hope, laughing at the baby's antics, unaware that Daniel was watching her and not their child.

Except for being thinner and paler, and a little the worse for a constant lack of sleep, she was the same pretty woman she'd always been. Hair the color of caramel taffy framed a small, slender face. Sometimes he thought her eyes were blue. Sometimes they almost looked green. But he could always see the tenderness of her spirit looking out at him from within. Only now, Daniel was trying to understand where her uncertainty had come from. Before they'd married, he'd never seen her down or second-guessing herself. Now she seemed to do nothing else.

"Mary?"

She looked up and the expression on his face was a bit frightening.

"What?" she asked, and then caught herself holding her breath as she awaited his response.

"What's happening between us?"

Her shoulders slumped. "Nothing."

"It's not nothing," he said gently.

"You're right. It's me. I'm sorry. I don't know why I'm so mean and hateful." Her chin trembled. "I don't mean to be."

"You aren't mean or hateful," he said. "And it's not you. It's something else, isn't it?"

Tell him. Tell him how much Phyllis hates me.

"I don't know what you mean." She was saved from having to talk further as the phone began to ring. "I'll get it," she said, and ran for the back door, leaving Daniel with a heavy heart and unanswered questions.

A few moments later she peeked out the back door.

"It's Phyllis. She wants to talk to you."

Daniel looked at Mary. That sick, nervous expression was back on her face.

"Tell Mom I'll call her back later, okay?"

Mary nodded and then went back into the living room and picked up the receiver.

"Phyllis, he's outside with Hope. He said he'll call you later."

"You're lying. You didn't even tell him, did you?"

Mary's stomach knotted. "Of course I'm not lying. He said he'd call you back."

"I don't believe you," Phyllis snapped.

The phone went dead in Mary's ear. She replaced the receiver and then slumped where she sat. Leaning forward, she rested her elbows on her knees and covered her face, trying to regain her composure before she went back outside. But when she stood up and turned, Daniel was standing in the doorway.

Mary flinched, wondering how much of their conversation that he'd heard.

"I was just coming back out," she said, and made herself smile.

"Hope's wet," he said.

"I'll change her," Mary said, took her from Daniel's arms and escaped into the nursery.

Daniel's eyes narrowed thoughtfully as he watched her go. He hadn't heard the conversation, but he'd heard the panic in her voice. What the hell was going on? Better yet—why wouldn't she tell him?

He followed her into the nursery and slipped an arm around her shoulders as she fastened the last tab on Hope's diaper. Just for a moment, he felt her hesitate and then lean back against his chest, just as she'd done so many times before. His heart quickened. He couldn't remember the last time she'd let her guard down like that.

"Are you okay?"

The deep rumble of his voice, as well as the gentleness of his touch, was almost her undoing. She wanted to tell him now, in the quiet of their daughter's room, but then he took hold of the hand that she'd cut and placed a tender kiss in the palm of her hand.

"How about we give this poor little hand a rest? I'll make us some sandwiches for lunch and tonight we could order in. We'll have an early dinner…maybe watch a movie. It's been a long time since we've done anything for us."

She laid Hope in her crib and then turned, unaware that the shimmer in her eyes was a dead giveaway of her emotions.

"I'd love that. You choose the food. I'll choose the movie."

He grinned. "As long as you don't make me watch *You've Got Mail* again, you've got a deal."

Mary made a face. "But I like Meg Ryan and Tom Hanks."

"I do, too, but I've seen that movie enough already to last me a lifetime."

"Then how about *Sleepless in Seattle?*" she asked, fully

aware that her two favorite actors also starred in that movie, as well.

He growled as he swung her off her feet.

"You pick the food. I'll pick the movie," he bargained.

"Chinese."

"Lethal Weapon."

They laughed in unison and then walked out of the room arm in arm. For now, the tension between them had been shoved aside in the joy of the unexpected reunion.

Less than an hour later, the doorbell rang. Daniel was in the act of slicing tomatoes for their lunch.

"I'll get it," Mary said. The smile was still on her face as she opened the door, but when she saw the expression on Phyllis O'Rourke's face, it was all she could do to be civil. "Phyllis...what a nice surprise. Please, come in."

"Where's Daniel?"

"In the kitchen making sandwiches for our lunch. We'd love to have you join us."

Phyllis glared. "Isn't it enough that he works all week as a lawyer? Must he come home and feed himself, too?"

Mary's stomach began to knot. She held up her bandaged hand to add to a hasty explanation.

"I cut myself this morning. He's only helping—"

"It's always something with you, isn't it?" Phyllis said, and physically pushed Mary aside as she strode into the house.

Mary staggered, then steadied herself by grabbing onto the small table in the hall. Sick at heart, she turned around and saw Daniel standing in the doorway. The look on his face was somewhere between disbelief and fury.

"Mother?"

Phyllis turned, her expression full of indignation.

"I called you about an hour ago, did you know that?"

"Yes, Mary told me. Didn't she tell you that I would call you back when I had time?"

Phyllis looked as if she'd just been drop-kicked. She glanced at Mary and then back at her son.

"Well…yes…I suppose she mentioned it, but you didn't call and I needed…" She took a deep breath and started over, refusing to admit she'd been wrong. "Your Aunt Evelyn is in town. She and Hubert are coming to dinner tonight and I want you to come."

Daniel looked at his mother, then at Mary, who was still clutching the hall table as if it were a lifeline. Suddenly, things were beginning to make sense.

Mary braced herself, waiting for Daniel to accept and knowing that she would have to endure a night of misery when they went. But Daniel surprised her by refusing.

"Sorry, Mom," then he walked past Phyllis and put an arm around Mary and gave her a quick hug. "We've already made other plans."

Phyllis's lips went slack. If he'd slapped her, she wouldn't have been more surprised. She glared at Mary, convinced that the woman was, somehow, at the bottom of Daniel's refusal.

"But Evelyn hasn't seen your daughter and there's no telling when they'll be back in town."

Ignoring the whine in his mother's voice, he tightened his grip on Mary.

"Hope isn't just *my* daughter, Mother, she's *our* daughter, and I'm sorry we can't come. Tell Aunt Evelyn we'll send her some pictures, okay?"

Mary was in shock. She still couldn't believe what was happening or what had caused it, but it was all she could do not to giggle with relief.

"Want to stay and have lunch with us?" Daniel asked. "It's not much. I'm not as good a cook as Mary, but she cut her hand pretty badly this morning and I'm filling in. I still think she should have gotten stitches, but she thought otherwise. Anyway, it's only canned soup and sandwiches, but I slice a pretty mean tomato."

Phyllis wouldn't look at Mary and couldn't meet Daniel's gaze.

"No…I'd better not. Since I'm having company tonight, there are a dozen things I need to do." She smoothed a hand down the front of her dress and then lifted her chin and made herself smile. "Thank you for the invitation, though. Maybe some other time."

"Give our love to Hubert and Evelyn," Daniel said.

"Yes…yes, I will," Phyllis muttered. "They're going to be disappointed."

Daniel chuckled. "Then maybe next time they'll call ahead and let people know they're coming."

Phyllis didn't bother to comment as she let herself out of the house.

The moment she was gone, Daniel took Mary by the shoulders.

"Mary…"

She sighed, then looked up.

"Talk to me."

"What is there to say?"

"You can start by telling me how long she's been treating you like this."

Mary's chin trembled, but she wouldn't let herself cry.

"Since the day she found out I was pregnant and we were going to get married."

"No way!"

"Oh, but yes."

"Why didn't you tell me?"

Suddenly, Mary's chin jutted mutinously. "And say what? That your mother thinks you would never have asked me to marry you if I hadn't gotten pregnant?"

"That would have been fine for starters," he muttered.

"I couldn't," she said, then pulled out of his grasp and turned away.

"Why the hell not?"

She answered, but the words were spoken so softly, he couldn't hear what she said.

"What did you say?"

She pivoted sharply, her voice rising in misplaced anger.

"Because I wasn't sure but what it might be the truth."

Daniel was momentarily speechless, unable to believe the words that had come out of her mouth.

"You can't be serious!"

She stood her ground without answering.

Daniel tried to draw a deep breath and choked on tears instead.

"My God, Mary Faith…how can you doubt me like that?"

Mary's lips trembled as her eyes welled.

"Oh, baby…don't," Daniel begged. "Please don't cry."

He pulled her close; his hands shaking as he tunneled his fingers through her hair, then rocked her where she stood.

"I promise you will never suffer another indignity from my family and I apologize for being blind to what they've been doing. Trust me. It won't happen again. I love you so much, sweetheart, and losing you would kill me."

"You can't lose me," she whispered. "And I love you, too, Daniel. Forever."

"Okay, then," he said softly, then gave her a kiss so tender that it stole her breath away.

"Are you real hungry?"

Mary tilted her head, meeting his gaze with a smile.

"Not for food."

"Thank God," he muttered, and swept her off her feet and into his arms. "Now if Hope will just stay asleep for a little while longer…"

Mary leaned her cheek against his shoulder as he carried her down the hall to their bedroom.

"It's been a long time," she said softly, as he laid her down on their bed.

"Too long," Daniel said softly, and began unbuttoning his shirt.

The last thought in Mary's head was a small prayer that this dream would not end.

It was three o'clock in the morning when the phone rang. Daniel jerked in his sleep and then reached for the receiver before he was fully awake, not wanting it to ring again for fear it would awaken Hope.

Mary sat straight up in bed, listening as Daniel answered.

"Hello? Mom! What's wrong? What? Slow down...slow down...you're not making any sense."

Phyllis took a deep breath and then started to cry.

"Oh, Daniel...it's gone. Everything is gone!"

"What's gone, Mom?"

"Our home. Our car. The clothes. All of my pictures."

Daniel swung his legs to the side of the bed.

"What are you saying?"

"The house caught on fire." She choked on a sob. "Everything is gone."

"Are you and Dad all right?"

"Yes, but—"

"Where are you?" he asked.

"Across the street at Bob and Julia's. Hang on a minute, will you? Your father is trying to tell me something."

"Yes, sure," he said, and wiped a shaky hand across his face as he began to visualize the enormity of the loss. It was the house he'd grown up in, and there was nothing left but memories.

Mary clutched Daniel's arm, her voice taut with anxiety. "What happened?"

"Mom and Dad's house burned down."

"Oh no! Are they all right?"

He nodded.

"Go get them. They belong with us."

Daniel sighed. Hearing Mary say what he'd already contemplated was a huge relief. After what he'd witnessed earlier, he'd feared the last thing Mary would stand for was having his parents under her roof.

"Thank you," he whispered, and then turned back to the phone. "Mom?"

"I'm here," she said. "Mike wanted me to tell you which motel we'll be at."

"No motel, Mom. We want you here. As soon as I get dressed, I'm coming after you and Dad."

Phyllis hesitated. She wasn't sure if she was ready to face her daughter-in-law under such intimate circumstances.

"Are you sure?" she finally asked. "I mean, your wife might not—"

"Her name is Mary, Mom, and it was her idea first. Not mine. I'll see you soon."

Phyllis heard him disconnect and then replaced the receiver. She knew Daniel. When he set his mind to something, there was no turning him back. She looked at her husband.

"Mike, go wash your face. Daniel is coming to get us."

Mary dashed into the spare bedroom as Daniel pulled out of the driveway. It would take him about twenty minutes to get across town to where his parents lived, then another twenty or so to get back. It would give her just enough time to put clean sheets on the spare bed and find some fresh clothing for Phyllis and Mike to put on. Her hands were shaking as she began her duties, trying to imagine the heartbreak of losing forty years of accumulated possessions and memorabilia.

Then suddenly she froze. She still had all the worldly possessions. It was her loved ones that were really gone.

In that moment, she felt herself trying to surface from the indulgence of this fantasy. Before it could happen, Hope let out a wail and Mary began resubmerging, pushing away the fear and returning to the dream—because it was safer—and because it was where she wanted to be.

She blinked, then looked up. The bedroom was still the same and Daniel's winter clothes were still hanging in the extra closet. With a sigh of relief, she pulled the last pillow slip onto the pillow and dropped it in place, making sure that the bed was turned back in an inviting manner, then bolted out of the room toward the nursery.

"Mommy's coming, honey. Don't cry."

She'd taken a coffee cake out of the freezer and had it thawing on the cabinet. Hope had been changed and fed and Mary was in the act of laying out a clean nightgown and pajamas when she heard Daniel's car in the driveway. With a last look at the bedroom to assure herself that everything was in place, she hurried to the front door. They were just coming up the steps as she opened the door to greet them.

"Phyllis...Mike...thank goodness you're both all right."

She took Phyllis by the hand and pulled her into the house. They were red-eyed and soot-stained and the smell of smoke was all about them.

"I'm so sorry," she said softly, then gave Phyllis a quick hug before moving on to Daniel's father. "Mike, tell me you're both okay?"

"As good as could be expected, I guess."

Mary nodded then her gaze moved to Daniel, as if seeking his approval.

"I've given your father a pair of your clean pajamas and you two can sort through other clothes later." Then she turned to Daniel's mother. "Phyllis, you'll find a clean nightgown at the foot of your bed beside Mike's pajamas. There are clean towels in the bathroom as well as shampoo and a hair dryer. Please use anything you need. When you've both had a chance to clean up, come to the kitchen. I've made some hot chocolate and there's coffee cake to go with it."

Mike O'Rourke seemed to go limp with relief, as if he'd been holding himself together by sheer will alone.

"Thank you, dear. We appreciate you and Daniel having us here and we'll try not to be a bother."

"Family is never a bother," Mary said.

Guilt rode hard on Phyllis's conscience as she let Mike lead her down the hall toward the guest room. She paused in the hallway and looked back. Daniel was standing in the shadows with his arms around his wife, holding on to her as if his life depended upon it—and she was holding him back—her head buried on his chest, her hands fisted in the fabric of his jacket. Quickly, she turned away, unwilling to admit that the fresh set of tears in her eyes were because of them, and not the loss of her home.

"Come on, Phyllis," Mike said. "You shower first."

She took a deep breath and lifted her chin as she walked into the room, quietly closing the door behind her.

Daniel gave Mary a swift kiss and then followed her into the kitchen. It was warm and comforting and smelled of chocolate and cinnamon. He took one look at the table set for four and hugged her again.

"You are a saint," he said quietly.

"No, Daniel. Just a woman fighting for a place in your world."

"You are my world, Mary Faith. You and Hope matter more to me than anyone or anything else."

She pulled back and looked at him then, her shy smile almost childlike.

"I know that…at least…I know that now. I'm sorry I doubted you."

"Forgiven," he muttered, and slanted a hard kiss across

her mouth before he turned her loose. "Is there anything I can do to help?"

"I couldn't find the marshmallows for the hot chocolate. Do you know where they are?"

"Nope, but I can look."

"Thanks," she said, then fluttered nervously toward the cabinet. "I just want this to be nice for them."

He frowned. "I don't know that they actually deserve this, but I appreciate it, just the same."

She turned, her hands clutched against her middle.

"Daniel, please. Don't say anything to them about…well, you know. They've suffered a traumatic loss. Let bygones be bygones, all right?"

"Fine, but I'd better not hear one critical remark out of my mother's mouth or they'll be looking for that motel after all."

She smiled. "Thank you."

"Don't thank me yet," he muttered.

"The marshmallows, please?"

"Oh. Yeah. Right."

About a half hour later, Mike and Phyllis emerged from the bedroom, freshly showered and shampooed and wearing clean clothes. Daniel was waiting in the living room, watching Mary sleeping on the sofa. When he heard the door open, he arose, then pulled the afghan a little higher over her shoulder before he went to meet them.

"Where's Mary?" Mike asked.

Daniel pointed toward the sofa. "Asleep. She doesn't get much rest these days and Hope's already had her up once tonight. I thought it best to let her sleep."

Phyllis peered over the sofa and stared at the thin, pale face of the woman who'd married her son. Even from here, she could see dark circles of fatigue beneath her eyes and felt a quick spurt of remorse. She remembered how hard it had been to be a mother for the first time and how exhausted she'd been. Fortunately, she'd had her mother and older sister nearby who'd been of tremendous help and support. She looked at Mary again. Mary had no one.

As Daniel and Mike moved into the kitchen, she turned away and followed them, well aware that she had Mary to thank for her present safety and comfort.

"What's all this?" Phyllis asked, as she entered the kitchen.

Daniel took the pot of hot chocolate from the stove where Mary had been keeping it warm and began to pour it into their mugs.

"Cinnamon coffee cake, freshly warmed in the oven, and hot chocolate," he said, as the warm, sweet scent filled the room. "Mom, will you cut the cake?"

Reluctantly, Phyllis picked up the knife and thrust it through the cake. It parted tenderly beneath the blade in perfect slices.

"It looks wonderful," Mike said.

Daniel beamed. "It tastes even better. Mary's a really good cook."

Phyllis served up the slices, then sat down in her chair. The horror of what they'd just endured had been lessened by the warmth and comfort of this home. Up until she'd walked into the kitchen, she hadn't been able to get the smell of burning wood and smoke from her nostrils. Now all she could smell was hot chocolate and cinnamon. She was clean and safe and everything they'd lost could be replaced.

Then she looked at Daniel, watching the animation on his face as he talked to Mike about his plans for the future and knew there was one thing she'd almost lost that was irreplaceable—her relationship with their son.

"How's the cake, Mom?"

Phyllis blinked, then made herself smile and take a bite.

"Very good," she said, although the guilt she was feeling threatened to choke her. "I wonder if this is from a mix."

"Nope. It's out of one of her old cookbooks. She collects them, you know. One of her favorite things to do is to prowl antique stores for cookbooks, although she hasn't had a chance to do that for quite some time now. Hope is a pretty demanding little squirt."

Mike chuckled. "Then she takes after you, boy. I well remember how many nights you kept your mother and I up. You had your days and nights turned around for a good four months. I used to tease Phyllis about finding a way to return the merchandise."

Daniel laughed. "Yes, that's the thing about having a family. You'd better be darn ready to give up every indulgence you once enjoyed."

"It's fine if you've had a hand in the decision to be a parent," Phyllis said.

The smile froze on Daniel's face.

"Mother, I'm going to chalk that up to the stress you were under tonight. But I better not ever hear you say another denigrating word to Mary or about her...do you understand?"

Phyllis paled. "I didn't—"

"Yes, you did," Daniel said. "And Mary didn't tell me. I heard you myself, remember?" Then he looked at both of his parents and sighed. "She didn't get pregnant...*we* did. And I couldn't have been happier. I have been in love with Mary almost from the first date. I'd already put a down payment on an engagement ring when she told me she was pregnant. It didn't change anything I'd planned except the date."

Phyllis looked stunned. "But you never said...I didn't know that—"

"Mom...I was twenty-six and long past telling you everything that went on in my life. The fact that I introduced you to Mary on our second date should have been warning enough that I was serious. How many other girls had I brought home before her?"

Phyllis frowned. "None."

"I rest my case."

She looked at Mike and then sighed. "And I apologize. I was wrong."

"Fine...but I'm not the one who deserves the apology, am I?"

Phyllis stifled a groan. The last thing she wanted to do was face her daughter-in-law with this guilt. But she'd already lost a lot this night. She didn't want to lose what was left of her family as well.

"I'll tend to it tomorrow."

Daniel gave her a cool look. "And I hope with more meaning than you just implied."

Phyllis had the good grace to blush.

Chapter 3

Mary woke up on the sofa with the first rays of morning sun shining in her eyes. The last thing she remembered was sitting beside Daniel and—

Oh lord! Mike and Phyllis were here!

She sat up with a jerk and then jumped to her feet. What must they think?

When she dashed into the kitchen and found it neat and gleaming, she groaned. Another mark against her. Phyllis would find a way to insinuate how Daniel had to do all the work. She pivoted quickly and started down the hall, expecting the doors to open and see accusing fingers pointed in her direction. Instead, she was met with the soft, but familiar, sounds of muted snores from the spare bedroom.

Thankful that her in-laws were still asleep, she peeked into her bedroom. Their bed was empty and she could hear the shower running. Daniel was up and getting ready for work. His diligence at the law office was starting to pay off and she knew he didn't want to give anyone an excuse to deny him a future partnership.

With a small sigh of relief, she moved across the hall to the nursery and pushed the door inward. Hope was lying on her back, waving her arms at the Mother Goose mobile hanging over her crib.

"Good morning, pretty girl," Mary whispered.

The baby turned toward the sound of her mother's voice and started to squeal.

Mary laughed as she picked Hope up and then laid her down on the changing table.

"A dry diaper and a warm bottle, in that order, little lady. How does that sound?"

Hope squinched her face into a tiny grimace and squeaked in disapproval when Mary began unsnapping the legs on her one-piece pajamas.

"Oh, it can't be all that bad," Mary crooned, as she deftly cleaned the baby and fastened a new diaper in place. "I'll hurry. I promise. Okay?"

A couple of snaps later and Hope was good to go. Mary picked her up, cradling her against her chest as she walked out the door, cherishing the feel of baby curls under her chin as well as the satin-smooth texture of Hope's delicate skin.

She met Daniel in the hall, and to her surprise, he was wearing sweats and a T-shirt, rather than his usual suit.

"Daniel, you're going to be late."

"I'm staying home today. I've already called in."

Mary felt a small surge of panic. "Is that okay?"

He knew her fear stemmed from more than worry about his job, but there was nothing much he could do other than what he'd already done.

"It's more than okay," he said. "They were very sympathetic to what happened to Mom and Dad. I had no pending court cases and the paralegal is still gathering research for that brief that's due next week, so my work will not suffer." Then he wrapped his arms around Mary and Hope and gave both of them a quick kiss. "Besides, I'd rather spend the day with my two best girls than go sift through the constant mess of our judicial system."

Mary nodded, but the frown on her face stayed in place as they walked toward the kitchen.

"You shouldn't have let me sleep last night. What must your parents have thought?"

"That you were exhausted and that you make damned good coffee cake."

She paused. "Really?"

He smiled and took Hope out of her arms. "Yes, really. Now go heat up Miss Thing's bottle. I'll feed her while you make us some coffee, okay?"

Mary's heart swelled with love as she handed the baby to Daniel. Their dark hair and stubborn chins were so identical it was almost comical.

"Okay, and I think I should start breakfast. Your parents probably have a lot to deal with today and won't want to be delayed."

"Honey...take it easy," he said. "My parents are still asleep and there are no deadlines to be met. Not in this house. Not today."

She smiled and nodded, then took a bottle out of the refrigerator and began heating it as Daniel sat down in the window seat. Bracing his long legs against the other side of the window frame, he laid the baby down in his lap. When she stretched and then began kicking him in the stomach, he laughed. It occurred to him as he watched Mary busying herself at the sink that he was quite possibly the luckiest man alive. He thought back to yesterday—to all the turmoil that had been in their lives and how close he'd come to killing himself and Hope. If Mary hadn't thrown herself on the hood of the car, he wouldn't have stopped, and if he hadn't stopped, he would have backed right into the speeding driver and the police cruiser that was in pursuit. As it was, two men had died horrible deaths, and they'd been spared.

It was still difficult for him to accept that his mother had been so mean to Mary. What was even worse was that

Mary had been afraid to tell him. He tickled the little roll of fat under Hope's baby chin and then looked up at his wife.

"Mary?"

The tremor in Daniel's voice made Mary turn abruptly, thinking something was wrong with Hope. But the baby was momentarily pacified by the sunlight coming through the trees outside the window.

"What?"

"I love you."

Emotion hit her like a fist to the gut.

"Oh, Daniel…I love you, too."

"You have nothing to worry about. Do you understand?"

Mary sighed, unaware that her shoulders slumped slightly in relief. But Daniel saw it and knew that his decision to stay home today as a buffer between his mother and his wife had been wise.

"Yes, I understand," Mary said, then lifted Hope's bottle out of the water and dried it off before testing a few drops on her wrist. "It's ready," she said, and brought it to him.

Daniel lifted his mouth for a kiss, which she happily supplied, then groaned softly when he refused to relinquish the connection.

She knew what he wanted and the thought of lying beneath his beautiful hard body made her ache. But with their unexpected houseguests just down the hall, what they both wanted was definitely not going to happen. Finally, it was Mary who pulled back.

"Daniel…we can't," she whispered. "Your parents…"

He frowned as he took the bottle and poked it into Hope's eager little mouth.

"I know. I know," he muttered. "But this won't be forever and when they're gone…"

She hugged the thought to herself as she turned back to the task at hand, which would be making breakfast.

"What sounds good this morning?" she asked.

"You," Daniel muttered. "But I'll settle for bacon and eggs."

She grinned and combed her fingers through his hair in a gentle, loving manner.

"And biscuits?"

He rolled his eyes in pretend passion. "Oh yeah." Then he added. "Better double the recipe. They're Dad's favorite, too."

"What about your mother?" she asked. "If she doesn't care for them I can make her some—"

He frowned at the nervousness once again in her voice.

"Mary Faith, you do not worry about what my mother likes or dislikes again, do you hear me?"

"Yes, but—"

"No buts, sweetheart. She will be thankful for whatever we serve and you will not suffer her disdain or criticisms again."

Mary was too moved to answer. Instead, she took a large bowl from the cabinet and began assembling the ingredients for the biscuits. By the time Mike and Phyllis were up, she was dishing up the scrambled eggs and taking the biscuits from the oven.

"Man, oh, man," Mike said, as he entered the kitchen. "A guy could get used to waking up to food like this."

Daniel eyed the slight shock in his mother's eyes and took no small amount of satisfaction in answering.

"I already have," Daniel said. "Mary is a super cook." Then he handed the baby to his mother. "Morning, Mom. Here, say hi to your granddaughter and see if you can get a burp out of her while I help Mary get the food to the table."

Phyllis was torn between jealousy and devotion. It had been years since she'd gone out of her way to fix breakfasts like this, and the comment Mike had made went straight to her conscience. But the smiles of delight on her granddaughter's face rechanneled her focus. She settled the baby on her shoulder and began patting her back as she took a seat at the breakfast table. As she sat, she watched and she listened, and not for the first time since their arrival, began to wonder if she could have been wrong.

"Mary."

Mary jumped at the sound of her mother-in-law's voice, then turned abruptly, almost dropping the load of clean bath towels she was carrying.

"Yes?"

Phyllis sighed. The anxious expression in Mary's dark eyes was nobody's fault but her own. She reached for the towels.

"Let me help do that."

"No, please," Mary said. "It's just a load of laundry. I can do it."

Phyllis frowned. "I'm well aware that you're capable, girl, but it's your third load, and frankly, I haven't seen you sit down since breakfast. Besides that, isn't your hand still sore?"

Mary glanced down at the bandage on the finger she'd cut yesterday.

"Well, yes, but it's healing."

Phyllis took the clean laundry from Mary's arms.

"We'll fold them on your bed, okay?"

Reluctantly, Mary followed her into the bedroom. When Phyllis dumped the towels on the bed, Mary took a deep breath and moved to the opposite side. For a few minutes, they worked in silence. It wasn't until the last washcloth had been folded that Phyllis laid it aside and then sat.

"Mary, there's something I want to say to you."

Mary flinched. The last thing she wanted was another confrontation, but with Daniel and his father gone to the insurance agency, she was all alone. She gathered up the stack of clean towels and carried them into the bathroom, then put them away. When she turned around, Phyllis was standing there with the hand towels and washcloths.

"Thank you," Mary said, and put them into the linen cabinet beside the towels.

Phyllis nodded. "You're very neat," she said, eyeing the even rows of linens inside the cabinet.

"Thank you. I suppose it comes from living in foster homes."

"What do you mean?"

Mary shrugged. "Well, I never knew how long I would be allowed to stay, so always having my things neatly together made it simpler to pack when social services moved me."

Phyllis frowned. "You never knew your parents, did you?"

"I remember my mother," Mary said. "At least, I think I do. But I was so small when they took me away." Then she turned, looking Phyllis square in the face. "She didn't give me away, you know. She died of cancer."

Phyllis sighed. "You've had a difficult life, haven't you?"

"From your standpoint, I suppose so. But I never knew anything else." Then her expression softened. "But now I have Daniel and Hope. They…and you and Mike…are my family now." Then she took a deep breath, needing to get the rest of this said before she chickened out. "I know you and Mike wanted better for Daniel. But I love him. So much. And I would never do anything to hurt him or make trouble for him. He and Hope are my life."

Phyllis felt like a heel. "Yes, I can see that," she said. "I've not been fair to you and I'm sorry." Then she turned away and walked back into the bedroom.

Mary hurried after her. "It's okay," she said. "Really."

Phyllis turned. "No, dear, it's not okay. I've been horrible to you, but given time, I will make it right. I hope you forgive me?"

Mary's eyes welled. "Oh, Phyllis, thank you," she cried,

and impulsively threw her arms around her mother-in-law's neck.

Phyllis hesitated briefly, then returned the embrace.

"It's me who should be thanking you," she said softly. "You have a generous heart, my dear. Daniel and Hope are lucky to have you."

Lucky to have you...lucky to have you...lucky...

A car horn blared, followed by a burst of angry curses and then the squealing of tires on pavement.

Mary jerked.

Reality and fantasy were beginning to separate within her mind and all she could think was *not yet. Not yet.* But no matter how desperately she tried, she couldn't hold on to the dream. Her head was spinning, her legs weak at the knees.

"Daniel," she moaned.

But there was no answer, only the smell of old wood and dust. In that instant, she knew it was gone. She opened her eyes.

The antique shop. She was still standing in the antique shop and Mike and Phyllis O'Rourke hadn't spoken to her since the day of the funeral six years ago.

In that moment, what had been left of her spirit died, too. There was nothing in her life but an emptiness that all the jobs and all the busy work would never fill. The only people who'd ever loved her were dead and she wanted to be with them.

With a shuddering sob, she stared down at the ring on her finger. The engraving—*I promise you forever*—was a joke. Hating herself and life in general, she tore it off and flung it back into the case. There was no such thing as forever.

"No more," she muttered. "I can't do this...I don't want to do this. Not anymore."

She turned, only to find the old man staring at her from the end of the counter.

"I don't want the ring. I put it back," she muttered, and pointed in the general direction of the case. "I have to go." But her feet wouldn't move. She seemed helpless beneath the compassion of his gaze. Her eyes filled with tears. "You don't understand. They're dead, you know. They're all dead but me."

Then her composure broke and she started to cry.

Love doesn't die.

Mary stared. Although she'd heard the words, his lips had not moved. When he started toward her, shuffling his tiny little feet on the dusty, planked floor, she wanted to run, but he was blocking her only exit.

"Don't," she muttered, although she didn't quite know why she said it.

He'd made no move to harm her and had yet to say a word. When he reached in his pocket, she caught herself holding her breath. But when he pulled out a neatly ironed linen handkerchief and laid it in her hands, she felt shame that she'd feared him.

"Oh God," she moaned, and bent her head.

At the same time, she felt a hand at the crown of her head and then the old man was stroking her hair, as he might have a child. Mary shuddered as she lifted the handkerchief to her face and wiped away tears. What had she been thinking, behaving this way in front of a stranger? When she looked up, he was gone. The only proof she had that he'd been there was the handkerchief she was holding.

"Lord," she muttered. "I probably embarrassed him horribly."

She laid the handkerchief aside and started to weave her way through the narrow aisle, anxious to be away from this place. She'd been crazy to come in here to begin with. All it had done was remind her of what she'd lost. She wouldn't let herself think about why the dream had been different this time, because it didn't really matter. Her reality was a living hell and *it* hadn't changed.

The front door was open and she headed for it like a moth to a flame.

Out.

She needed out.

Away from the memories.

Away from the pain.

She fixed her gaze on the rug of sunlight spreading across the threshold and told herself that if she didn't breathe until she passed it, all the pain would go away. It wasn't the first time she'd played such a mind game with herself, but she was brought up short from escaping when a curly-haired little girl burst into the building.

"Mommy! Mommy!"

The brutality of the moment stopped Mary short. In her mind, it was but another bit of proof as to how perfectly cruel life could be. If Hope hadn't died—

"Mommy! Where are you?" the little girl cried.

Mary swallowed past the knot of misery in her throat and stepped out of the shadows and into the light. No matter how much it would hurt her, the child was obviously lost and afraid. But the words never came out of her mouth. When the child saw her move, the frown on her face turned to joy.

"Mommy! Mommy! We're ready to go! Daddy's going to buy us all ice cream and I want banilla with starberry sprinkles."

Shock spread across Mary's face as she stared at the approaching child in disbelief. Then over the child's shoulder, she saw the sunlight on the floor suddenly shrink as a man appeared in the doorway. At first, she saw nothing but a big, dark silhouette, but then he spoke and the sound of his voice grabbed her heart.

"There you are," he chided, and took the little girl by the hand before she could go any farther.

Mary struggled to take a breath. *Damn you, God...you took my reasons for living and left me behind. Now you want my sanity, too?*

The man looked up at Mary and grinned.

"Hey, honey. Did you find anything you can't live without?"

Mary moaned and took a short step backward. *Why was this happening?* That had always been a running joke between herself and Daniel when they used to go antiquing, but this wasn't funny.

Then the man moved past the doorway and further into the store. When Mary saw his face she started to shake. Black hair, blue eyes and that square jaw with a slight dimple in his chin. *Daniel? Oh God...Daniel.*

"Mary...darling...are you all right? You look a little pale."

He reached for her, steadying her with a hand to the shoulder, then he cupped her face.

She looked up in horror. She could feel his fingers on her skin. This wasn't possible. She took a deep breath and closed her eyes. PTSD. That's what it was. Post-traumatic stress disorder, brought on by her foray into antiques. When she opened her eyes, he would be gone. All of this would be gone. But when she looked he was still there, leaning closer now, and she could feel his breath on her face.

"Daniel?"

He smiled. "Definitely not the Easter Bunny," he teased.

She fainted in his arms.

"Mary...darling...can you hear me?"

Mary moaned. "Make it go away," she muttered.

Daniel frowned. "Make what go away?"

"The dreams. Make them all go away."

He shook his head slightly, ignoring her rambling remarks as he continued to dab her forehead and cheeks with a dampened handkerchief. Before he could answer her, Hope slid between them and put a hand on her father's arm.

"Daddy, what's the matter with Mommy?"

"I think maybe she just got too hot."

His daughter's voice trembled slightly. "Is she going to die?"

"No, baby…oh no! Mommy's fine. See! She's waking up right now."

Mary found herself focusing on the sound of their voices and wondered when she looked, which dream she would be in—the one from her past or the one from the future. The urge to scream was uppermost in her mind, but what was happening was inevitable. She was losing her mind. It was the only explanation for the fact that she kept slipping in and out of a fantasy. She shouldn't be surprised that it was finally happening. She was having a nervous breakdown. End of story. Curious as to what she'd see next, she opened her eyes.

"See," Daniel said. "I told you she was okay." Then his voice deepened as he caressed the side of her face. "Sweetheart…how do you feel?"

"Crazy," she muttered. "How about you?"

He chuckled and then winked at Hope. "I think the worst is over. At least your mother's sense of humor is firmly in place."

"Help me up," Mary muttered.

Daniel stood, then put his hands beneath her arms and pulled her upright.

"Easy," he warned. "You might still be dizzy."

Mary swayed momentarily, then slowly gained her equilibrium.

"Okay?" he asked.

She took a deep breath and then nodded.

"Mommy?"

Mary's stomach knotted as she looked down at the little girl.

"I don't have to get banilla ice cream today," Hope said.

Mary frowned, then remembered something being said about vanilla ice cream with strawberry sprinkles.

"That's very sweet of you, but I'm all right."

"Oh goody," Hope cried. "Ice cream will make you feel better, too."

Daniel slid an arm around Mary's waist and turned her toward the door.

"Hope, can you carry Mommy's purse for her, please?"

"Yes. I always carry it when Mommy's arms are full of groceries," she said, then picked up the shoulder bag Mary had dropped and slung it across her shoulder.

Mary fought the urge to laugh, but she was afraid if she started, she wouldn't be able to stop. Maybe she should tell someone what was happening. Then she discarded the thought. After all, who would believe her?

As they started out the door, she paused and looked back, but the old man was nowhere in sight. That figured. She'd probably imagined him, too.

When the sunlight hit her face, she squinted and ducked her head against the glare. And because she did, she missed the fact that she was being led to a waiting car. When they paused, she looked up, her eyes widening at the big, white Cadillac Daniel was unlocking.

"I walked here," she muttered.

Daniel frowned and ran his hand through her hair.

"What are you doing?" Mary asked.

"I was checking for a bump. You're not making a lot of sense right now and might have a slight concussion. I thought I caught you before you hit the floor, but I could be wrong."

"I didn't hit my head," she said. "I just lost my mind."

Hope giggled. "Mommy's funny."

Mary let herself be seated in the car and then watched as Daniel put Hope in the back seat. Without thinking, Mary turned around, got up on her knees and buckled the little girl into her booster seat. It wasn't until she had turned around and was reaching for her own seat belt that she realized what she'd done. It had been so natural. Something she'd done without thinking. Something she'd done a thousand times before. She pulled the sun visor down and then looked at herself in the attached mirror. Ignoring her pallor, she stared, trying to find the madness in the woman looking back. But all she could see was a slight expression of shock.

Then her gaze slid past her own reflection to the child behind her as Daniel got into the car. He reached for Mary's hand and gave her fingers a slight squeeze.

"Honey…are you sure you're up for this ice cream stop?"

"I have no idea, but we'll soon find out."

"It's not that important," Daniel said. "Hope won't mind."

"But I will," Mary muttered. "In fact, I'd say we have to go. I can't wait to see what happens next."

Chapter 4

Daniel was more than a little distracted by Mary's behavior as he drove through the Savannah streets. Even though it had been overly warm inside the old store, it wasn't like her to faint. When he came to a main intersection and stopped at the red light, he reached across the seat and threaded his fingers through hers.

"How are you feeling?"

Her eyes widened as she stared down at his hand and then he heard her take a deep shaky breath.

"Mary Faith...what's wrong?"

Mary didn't know what to say. She was convinced that this was nothing more than an extension of her other fantasy. The dead do not come back to life, but she'd never had a dream this real. If she only had a choice, she would choose this insanity rather than go back to the loneliness and misery of her life. And therein lay her dilemma. If she voiced her fears, would it make all of this disappear? The fact that she could actually feel Daniel's hand on hers was an unbelievable facet to this dream. To lose it—and him—again, would break what was left of her heart.

She managed a smile and opted for safety.

"I'm fine," she said. "Stop worrying."

Daniel grinned. "Now that's asking the impossible and you know it. I always worry about my girls." His voice softened and lowered so that only Mary could hear. "You're my heart, Mary Faith. If you hurt, then so do I."

Mary's eyes welled with tears. Impulsively, she lifted his hand to her lips and kissed the palm before cupping it to her cheeks.

Daniel groaned softly, then glanced in the rearview mirror before winking at Mary.

"Your timing could be better here. I want to ravish you madly and we're in the middle of a busy intersection with way too much company."

The heat in his eyes made Mary's toes curl. Suddenly, she remembered the feel of Daniel's kisses and the pounding thrust of his body between her legs. She bit her lower lip and then looked away.

Crazy. That's what she was. Stark, raving mad.

"Mommy, are you sick?"

The quaver in Hope's voice was enough to get Mary's attention. She turned around quickly, making sure the child could see her smile.

"No, darling, I'm all right. I think I just got a little too hot, okay?"

Hope nodded, but her big eyes were still dark with worry.

Daniel glanced in the rearview mirror. Her panic was obvious and catching. He knew just how she felt. When Mary had gone limp in his arms, his heart had almost stopped. She was the center of their world. He winked at Hope in the mirror and then asked, "Are you still up for vanilla ice cream, honey, or are you going to try something different this time?"

The change of subject was exactly what Hope needed.

"I'm still having banilla," she announced. "But when we get to the ice cream store, can I have my ice cream in a cone instead of a cup?"

Hope's innocent question shifted Mary's focus into the everyday business of parenting so smoothly that she answered before she thought.

"May I, not can I," Mary said, as she turned to Hope, then somehow knew she'd said that very thing a dozen times before.

Hope sighed. "Oh yeah…I forgot. May I have a cone?"

Mary knew she was staring, but Hope's expression was so like Daniel's she couldn't look away. Was this what Hope would have looked like if she had lived, or was this just a wider crack into insanity?

"Mommy…may I?" Hope persisted.

Mary blinked, as if coming out of a trance.

"What? Oh…uh…yes, you can have the cone but we'll have them put a little marshmallow in the tip of the cone like before, okay? Then when the ice cream starts to melt, it won't leak."

"Yea!" Hope cried, and settled back in her seat as Daniel accelerated through the intersection.

Mary felt herself nodding as she turned around, but her heart was hammering in her chest. With a near-silent moan, she leaned back against the seat and closed her eyes.

Like before? Where in hell had that come from?

Almost an hour later, they were on their way home. Hope was asleep in the back seat of the car and the taste of praline and pecan ice cream was still on Mary's tongue as Daniel turned right.

"Where are we going now?"

Daniel frowned. "Home."

"But this isn't the way to our house."

Daniel's frown deepened. The confusion on her face was real. Once again, he knew he should have ignored her resistance to a checkup and taken her straight to the emergency room. Something wasn't right.

He pulled into the circle driveway and parked beneath the portico, then turned to face her.

"Honey, we've lived in this house for almost three years."

Mary's eyes widened as she stared at the brick two-story house and the tall white columns bracing the roof of the portico. Then she closed her eyes and took a deep breath before she was able to face him.

"Isn't that silly of me? For some reason I was thinking of our old house over on Lee Street."

Daniel leaned across the seat and felt her forehead, as if she might have a fever.

"I still think you need to see a doctor."

Panic shifted, then receded. "And I think we need to get Hope in bed," she said.

Before Daniel could argue, Mary was out of the car and opening the door to the back seat. Gently, she unbuckled Hope from her booster seat and took her in her arms.

"I'll carry her," Daniel said.

"No, you get the door," Mary said, certain there were no keys to this house in her purse.

Daniel sighed, then shook his head and quickly did as she asked.

The shaded rooms were cool, a welcome respite from the sweltering heat of afternoon. But Mary's relief was short-lived when she realized she had no idea where her daughter's room was supposed to be. She stared up at the circular staircase and wondered if she could bluff her way through, but the worry was taken out of her hands when Daniel took Hope from her arms.

"You're not carrying her up those stairs," he muttered. "In fact, you need to take a nap, yourself. Come on, honey. I'll unload the groceries and put them up. I want you to rest."

Mary followed Daniel up the stairs, not because she particularly wanted to sleep, but because she needed to see the layout of the house without making a complete fool of herself.

As she watched him laying Hope on the bed in her room, she couldn't help but wonder about this constant confusion. This was *her* dream. So why didn't she just know this stuff?

She backed out of Hope's room into the hall and then turned around, staring blankly at the series of closed doors. As she stood, certain things began to emerge. The door directly across from Hope's room was a bathroom, decorated in three shades of blue. She didn't know how she knew it, but she was positive she was right. When she opened the door and peeked in, her heart skipped a beat. Just as she'd thought it would be.

Quietly, she backed out and then walked a few feet down the hall to the first door on her left. This was the spare bedroom. She closed her eyes, picturing what was behind the door. Immediately, she focused on a pink and gold comforter on a four-poster bed. And she knew that, in the corner, there was a matching armoire she and Daniel had found on an excursion to Atlanta two years ago.

Taking a deep breath, she looked in. It was there, just as she'd envisioned. When she closed the door she was smiling.

Okay, I've been making this too hard. It's still my dream. It can be any way I want it to be.

Daniel was coming out of Hope's room as she turned around.

"Why aren't you in bed?" he asked.

"Because I was waiting for you to tuck me in, too."

Breath caught in the back of Daniel's throat. The invitation in her voice was impossible to miss. He caught her up in his arms and carried her across the hall, toed the door open with his shoe and then kicked it shut behind him.

Mary knew before she looked that there would be a king-size brass bed and that the room was decorated with the colors of autumn. When Daniel laid her down, she felt, before she saw, the handmade quilt on their bed. As the familiar softness cushioned her back, she kicked off her shoes and reached for Daniel. There was no way to know how long this fantasy would last, and she didn't want to waste a moment.

A hungry glint fired in Daniel's eyes as he sprawled across her. Tunneling his fingers through her hair, a low moan rose from his throat as he centered his mouth upon her lips.

In desperation, Mary clung to him. It had been so long. But before she could remove her clothes, Daniel drew back with a groan.

"Oooh, baby, hold that thought. I've got to get the groceries in out of the heat."

He rolled away from her and then got off the bed. Before she could think, he was out of the room and on his way down the stairs.

Mary turned over on her belly and buried her face in the pillow in mute frustration, then moments later, sat up in bed.

The furnishings in the room were almost opulent, but had a comfortable, lived-in look about them that almost seemed familiar. Her gaze fell on the closet and suddenly, she bounced off the bed and ran toward it. As her fingers curled around the doorknob, she caught herself holding her breath in nervous anticipation. Slowly, she pulled the door open then stepped inside and turned on the light.

Daniel's clothing was hanging on the right in a neat and orderly manner, from suits, to sport coats to casual slacks. Blue jeans were folded and stacked neatly on a built-in shelf as were an assortment of T-shirts. A row of shoes was on the floor beneath the clothing and a small rack of neckties hung from the back of the closet door. Just as she would have expected it to be.

When she looked to the left, all the air went out of her lungs in one breath, as if she'd been punched in the stomach. An entire wardrobe of women's dresses, blouses, skirts and slacks—and in her size—were hanging on the rack.

Okay...so I'm dreaming in detail and color...and with sensation. So what? I've already accepted the fact that I'm losing my mind.

She stepped out of the closet and then turned off the light. Immediately, her gaze moved to the door Daniel had left open. She walked into the hallway and then into the room where Hope was sleeping.

For whatever reason and for however long this fantasy would last, she not only had Daniel back, but she had her daughter, too. The bond she'd had with the baby seemed nothing but a distant memory as she stared down at the six-year-old girl in disbelief. The longer she looked, the tighter the ache grew within her chest. Quietly, she tiptoed to the side of the bed, smiling at the one-eared bunny tucked beneath Hope's chin, and pulled the covers back over the little girl's shoulders. Then, reluctant to lose the connection, she lifted a stray lock of hair away from Hope's face, then leaned down and brushed her forehead with a kiss and as she did, felt as if she'd done it countless times before. Her heart swelled as she watched the little girl's eyelids fluttering in sleep.

This is my baby.

She watched her for only a few moments, then, afraid her presence would wake Hope up, she went back to the bedroom she shared with Daniel. For a few moments, she stood in the doorway, staring at the room and the feelings it evoked. Finally, she took a deep breath and began taking off her clothes. Seconds later, she was in the bathroom and stepping beneath the warm water jetting from the showerhead. It could only be symbolic, but she had a sudden urge to wash away every remnant of her old, sad life.

Daniel's heart sank when he saw the empty bed, then he heard the shower running and smiled. With a quick glance over his shoulder to make sure the door to Hope's room was still closed, he shut the door to their bedroom and then turned the lock. Mary had strewn her clothes on the foot of the bed. He added his to the pile and then headed for the bath.

The water was warm on Mary's skin as she closed her eyes and turned her face to the jets, but when she heard the shower door open then close, her breath caught in the back of her throat. Suddenly, Daniel's hands were tracing the length of her back, then around, cupping her breasts and pulling her back against his body.

"I love you, Mary Faith."

Tears welled against Mary's eyelids. To hear these words and to feel her husband's touch after all this time was staggering. Why and how this was happening was no longer of concern to her. If this was madness, then so be it. God knew it was better than what she'd had.

She turned in his arms, her heart pounding, her body weak with longing. With a soft, desperate moan, she threw her arms around his neck, relishing the roughness in his kiss.

Reluctantly, Daniel stepped back and began touching her all over, as if to assure himself that she was truly okay.

"You scared me today," he said softly. "When you went limp in my arms, my heart almost stopped."

Mary didn't want to think or talk about anything that had to do with before. All she wanted was Daniel.

"Make love to me, Daniel. I need to feel you on me…in me…I've been so lost."

Daniel turned off the water and then pulled her out of the shower and into their bed, his need to be with her driving caution completely out of his mind.

Mary had a few brief moments of cognizance as Daniel laid her down and then took the phone off the hook. After that, there was nothing left in her head but a series of mind-numbing images.

The slight drip of a faucet in the other room.

The beads of water still on Daniel's hair and the shuttered look on his face as he beheld the woman beneath him.

The sound of her own heartbeat loud in her ears.

The flare of Daniel's nostrils as he slid inside her body.

The shattering of her thoughts when he began to move.

The curl of need deep in her belly.

The building heat.

And then ultimately, the blinding insanity of release.

They lay wrapped in each other's arms, their hearts still pounding, their muscles weak and lax. But the unity that Mary had remembered was still there—even stronger than before.

Daniel had his arms around his wife, and when he rolled onto his back, he took her with him. Now, Mary lay with her cheek against his chest, feeling the strong, even heartbeat beneath his ear and closed her eyes.

Heaven. Sweet heaven to know this again.

"Love you, Danny."

He couldn't remember the last time Mary Faith had called him Danny, but the sound of it on her lips made him smile.

"Ah, baby...I love you, too," he said softly and held her a little bit tighter.

She sighed with pleasure.

Somewhere within the next few minutes, Daniel felt her go limp and knew that she slept. Carefully, he slipped out from under her and covered her with a sheet. Aware that Hope's nap wouldn't last much longer, he hurried into the bathroom and cleaned up the mess that they'd made, then dressed. Pausing beside their bed to look at his sleeping wife, he felt a familiar tightening in his chest. For all these years, it was still the same feeling he'd had the first time he'd seen her. She was the anchor to his world.

As he watched, a slight frown creased the middle of her

forehead. Impulsively, he leaned down and brushed a kiss across her lips and as he did, the frown disappeared.

"Yeah, baby…I know. That's what you do to me, too," he said softly, and then closed the door behind him as he left.

It wasn't until much later that he remembered what she'd said just before he'd taken her to bed—something about being lost. But it didn't make sense. There hadn't been a day in the almost seven years of their married life that he hadn't known where she was.

Mary woke with a start, her heart pounding, her body covered in a sweat of panic.

Alone. She was alone.

"No," she moaned, and bolted from the bed.

She didn't want to be awake. She wanted back in the dream.

Yanking on her clothes with shaking hands, she tore out of the room. It wasn't until she reached the head of the staircase that she realized she was still in the house from the dream.

She stood, her legs shaking, trying to still a racing heart as the sounds of childish laughter floated up the stairs.

Hope? Was that Hope?

Without caution, she bounded down the stairs, following the sounds of her daughter's laughter and then found both Hope and Daniel in the kitchen having cookies and milk.

The moment Daniel saw her, he got up from the chair and went to her.

"Hey…look who woke up," he said, and then nuzzled her neck, whispering a more intimate welcome that only she could hear. "Ooh, lady, you look like a woman who's been had."

Mary went limp with relief, clinging to his embrace and trying not to weep.

"I wonder why," she said, cherishing the hard, hungry

kiss that he slanted across her lips. Then she stepped out of his arms and peeked around at the table. "Hey, you! Did you save me any cookies?"

Hope giggled and pointed to the neat pile of raisins on her plate.

"Only the raisins."

Mary stared at the plate. "You don't eat raisins?"

Hope rolled her eyes. "Mommy...we never eat the raisins, remember?"

Mary stumbled to the table and then slid into a chair beside her daughter. She knew her voice was shaking, but there wasn't a damn thing she could do to hide what she was feeling.

"Yes...I *do* remember. We always give them to Daddy, don't we?"

Hope giggled. "Yes, and we pretend that—"

"...they are pills to grow hair on his chest," Mary added.

Daniel gave a pretend growl, popped the handful of raisins into his mouth, then thumped his chest with both fists. Hope shrieked with laughter and Daniel loped around the kitchen like a monkey on the run.

Mary watched the pair's antics without comment, making sure that she was nodding and smiling in all the right places, while she struggled to understand. This was nothing like a dream. She distinctly smelled oatmeal and raisins and the scent of fresh-brewed coffee, and there was something else about the moment that she couldn't get past. The longer she sat, the stronger her sense of déjà vu.

The vague scent of meatloaf was still in the air as Mary hung up the dishtowel and then dried her hands. At first, it had been awkward, delving into cabinets in search of bowls and pans, looking for spices, trying to find dishes with which to set the table for a meal. But the longer she'd worked, the more comfortable she'd become. By the time the food was cooked and ready to serve, she was on a roll. More than once during the meal, she felt a little like she'd felt as a child playing house, pretending that everything was real. But she'd never tasted pretend meatloaf as good as what had come out of the oven, or felt as much joy from the dolls that would join her for tea parties as she did with this man and this child. She felt like Alice, who'd fallen down the rabbit hole. For some reason, up was down, and down was up, and the faster she ran, the later it got.

But confusion paled in comparison to the love on Daniel's face and the sound of her daughter's laughter. Even now, the faint sounds of their voices in the other room made her want to cry. She couldn't count the number of times she had dreamed of such an evening. Giving the kitchen a last, satisfied glance, she decided that beggars should not be choosers and moved toward the other room where her family waited.

"Mommy!" Hope cried, and bounced up from the sofa where she'd been sitting to launch herself at Mary's legs. "I want to watch *101 Dalmatians*...please, please!"

Mary braced herself for the impact and then laughed when Hope's arms wrapped around her knees.

"You're going to be watching Mommy fall if you don't turn me loose," she said.

Hope giggled, then started dancing around in a little circle, still pleading her case.

Mary's first instinct was to never say no to the child that she'd lost, then looked to Daniel for support.

"Hey, kiddo," Daniel said. "Tomorrow is a school day. You need to get a bath and get in bed. You know the rules."

Hope's lower lip jutted, but she didn't argue.

Mary knew that a crisis had been averted and breathed a small sigh of relief.

"Come on, honey...you can use some of my bubble bath," she said, and then took a deep, shaky breath as an image flashed through her mind. Her—in the boutique section of

Savannah Square—buying freesia-scented bubble bath and body powder. *God...how did this keep happening?*

"Yea!" Hope squealed, and headed for the stairs.

Daniel stood, then circled the sofa and took Mary in his arms.

"You sure you're up to this?" he asked. "You insisted on making dinner and doing the dishes, even after what you went through this afternoon."

Mary leaned against him, remembering the power of their lovemaking and suddenly shivered.

"Cold?" he asked.

She made herself smile. "No...just an unexpected case of goose bumps."

Daniel scooped her up in his arms and buried his nose beneath the nape of her neck.

"You like goose bumps? I can give you goose bumps."

She clung to him, thrusting her fingers through his hair and offering her mouth to his kiss. Again, the touch of flesh to flesh was like lightning—shocking and heated.

"Those will do for starters," Mary whispered. "I'd better hurry or Hope will have dumped the whole bottle of bubbles into the tub like last time."

Daniel rolled his eyes and then grinned. "Yeah...I remember. I smelled like flowers for a whole damned week."

"No, you didn't," Mary said. "It was only more like two days." The hair on the back of her neck suddenly rose. The line between reality and fantasy was blurring more with every passing hour.

"I stand corrected," he said, and then razed her mouth with one last kiss as he cupped her backside and pulled her hard against the juncture of his thighs. "Feel that?"

Mary closed her eyes, giving herself up to the pure animal attraction between them.

Reluctantly, Daniel finally turned her loose, then lifted a stray lock of her hair from the corner of her eyes.

"You sure you don't want me to help Hope with her bath?"

"I'm sure," Mary said.

"Okay...but later, you have to help me with mine."

She laughed. "We've already done that once today."

Daniel smirked. "Cleanliness is next to godliness, Mary Faith. Would you have me become a heathen?"

"You already are," she said, and then headed up the stairs to find her daughter.

Chapter 5

It was twenty minutes after three in the morning and Mary had yet to fall asleep. Her eyes were burning with fatigue, her body trembling from the strain of trying to stay awake. Daniel's arm was across her shoulders, holding her firmly in place against the curve of his body. It would have been so easy to just close her eyes and let go, but the fear of losing what she had was too strong. This had become her reality. Going back to the emptiness of her other life would kill her, and that's what she feared would happen if she let herself sleep in this one.

Daniel shifted where he lay and then sighed. She felt his breath against her cheek and clung to him in desperation. Moments passed. Moments in which she remembered the scent of her freesia bubble bath emanating from Hope's skin as she helped her into her nightgown, and the heartbreaking sweetness of her daughter's good-night kiss on her cheek.

Mary stifled a sob as another thought surfaced. What if she had nothing to fear? Maybe she was already dead. Maybe this was heaven. If so, then there was no danger in going to sleep.

Yes! That must be it! Back there in the antique store when she'd started to get dizzy, she must have been dying!

The fact that Daniel and Hope had been there to greet her should have been her first hint, because she'd never had dreams like that before.

Suddenly, the urge to look at this world anew drove away her exhaustion. She'd been looking at all of this wrong. It wasn't exactly what she'd thought heaven would be like, but who was she to quibble? With the people she loved best, it was perfect.

Careful not to awaken Daniel, she slipped out of his grasp and tiptoed from the room, anxious to see Hope again.

She was there in her bed, sleeping soundly, with that same old one-eared rabbit clutched tight beneath her chin. The urge to take Hope in her arms and never let her go was overwhelming. Instead, Mary straightened her covers and forced herself to walk away.

She paused for a moment in the hall, thinking of going back to bed and lying in the comfort of Daniel's arms. But the relief she was feeling wouldn't let her sleep. Not yet. Not now. She needed to see the house again, without the fear and confusion she'd had before.

Her steps were light as she moved down the staircase, her gaze curious and accepting as she studied the shadows made by the nightlight at the foot of the stairs. The carpeted floors in the living room were soft beneath her feet. The scent of bougainvillea was faint, but familiar. She turned toward the hall table and saw the vase of fresh flowers, then moved toward it, touching the clusters of tiny blooms with her fingertip, then bending to inhale the perfume.

A brass ship's clock on the mantel over the fireplace began chiming out the hour. The sudden noise within the silence of the room sent her spinning about. Sensing she was no longer alone, she looked up the stairs. Daniel was standing at the top, looking down at her in the darkness.

"Mary...are you all right?"

His presence was so real, so strong. There was no more

doubt. She sighed, and as she did, gave up the last of her reservations. This now was her truth.

"Yes, darling, I'm fine."

"What are you doing down there in the dark?"

She hurried up the stairs and into his arms, relishing the comfort of his embrace.

"Oh…I just had a bad dream. I needed to make sure that everything was all right."

"Next time you wake me and let me be the one to chase away the ghosts. Okay?"

"Okay."

"Now that's settled, come back to bed. The alarm clock will go off before you know it."

Mary laughed softly to herself. Alarm clocks in heaven? Who would have known?

Hope downed the last of her milk and started to leave the table when Mary caught her and quickly wiped the milk mustache from her upper lip.

"Mommy…I've got to hurry," Hope wailed. "I don't want to be late for school."

No sooner had she said it than Daniel yelled from the living room. "Hope! Come on. You're going to be late for school."

"Okay, okay," Mary said, giving the bow in Hope's hair a last fussing tug. "Don't forget your backpack."

"It's by the door," Hope said.

Mary followed her daughter's exit, unwilling to let go of the both of them at once. But Daniel was at the door with briefcase in hand and Hope was already shouldering her backpack when Mary got there.

"Don't forget I have dance class after school," Hope said.

A wave of panic hit swiftly, leaving Mary floundering for answers to questions she didn't know how to ask.

"Dance class?"

Hope rolled her eyes. "Mommy. I have class *every* Wednesday. Mrs. Barnes will bring me home."

"What time?" Mary asked. "What time will she bring you home?"

Daniel grinned and tweaked Mary's nose. "Five o'clock, honey. Just like always."

"Oh yes…at five. I was thinking of something else. Sorry."

Moments later they were in the car and driving away. Mary held her breath until they were safely out of the driveway, then stepped back inside the house and closed the door. It was just after eight. She started to smile. It was a long time until five o'clock. She would have plenty of time to prowl through the house and familiarize herself with everything in it. The daily paper was lying on the hall table where Daniel had laid it. She picked it up and carried it back into the living room, then tossed it on the coffee table to be read later. Her step was light, but her heart was lighter as she went upstairs because her family was, once again, intact.

Daniel pulled up in front of the school as Hope began scrambling with her backpack.

"Have a good day, honey," he said, and hugged her tight when she leaned over for her goodbye kiss.

"You, too, Daddy. I'll see you this evening, okay?"

"Yep. And don't forget Mrs. Barnes is picking you up after school."

"I know," she said, slamming the door behind her as she hurried up the front walk toward the building.

Daniel watched until he saw her enter the building with several of her friends, then he drove away. His mind was already shifting gears toward the preliminary hearing for one of his clients. He was well prepared and wasn't worried about that outcome, but he was concerned about Mary Faith. Even though she swore she felt fine and had shown

no other symptoms of being ill, he couldn't get over how
startled he'd been when she'd fainted in his arms. Her confusion afterward had cemented his worries even more. He
made a mental note that as soon as he got to the office, he
was going to give their family doctor a call. He wanted to
hear someone else tell him there was nothing for which he
needed to be concerned.

Howard Lee Martin stepped out from beneath the trees
on the south side of the playground, watching as the last of
the children entered the school building to begin morning
classes, then jammed his hands in his pockets and started
walking toward home. His mind was racing, his heart
pounding with anticipation. He'd seen her again. A perfect
little angel. As he walked, he began making a mental list of
all the things he needed to purchase before the adoption. Not
for the first time, he wished he'd gotten a chance to talk to
her. He didn't know what kind of ice cream she liked best
and he needed to know her favorite color. They would play
dress-up. Little angels like her always liked to play dress-
up. And then they would play house. Just the thought made
him smile. His mother had let him make a fort under the
dining room table when he was small, but little girls liked
to play house, not cowboys and Indians.

As he pictured his mother, he grew sad. She'd been gone
almost two years now. He thought of the two little girls
he'd recently adopted and sighed. His children would never
know their grandmother and that was too bad. She'd always
wanted him to marry and settle down.

After she died, he'd tried to make friends, but he didn't
know how. He'd joined a church, but hadn't been able to
bring himself to approach any of the single women who at-
tended. He'd begun hanging out at bowling alleys and coffee shops, watching the interplay between other couples and
trying to figure out how it was done. Not for the first time,

he thought that his mother had demanded too much of his time. He'd never had the chance to socialize with the opposite sex. It was only at his job that he'd come in contact with them, and then he'd been too shy to do more than speak.

Lately, his shyness had given way to frustration, then frustration to anger. It wasn't fair. Everyone had someone but him. That's when he'd decided to make his own family. Lots of single people adopted children. He read about it all the time. But the process hadn't been as simple as he'd believed. He didn't make enough money. He didn't have enough education. The excuses were endless, but they all boiled down to one thing. The authorities were not going to let him adopt. So he'd taken things into his own hands and done what he had to do.

A cat dashed across the street in front of him, just ahead of a small, black dog who was in pursuit. He laughed aloud, wishing the girls had been with him. They would have enjoyed the sight. It was important for children to interact with a parent, and he looked forward to the day when the transition from their old life to the new one was complete. Right now they were shy of him, but he had to believe the day would come when they would welcome him with open arms.

He glanced at his watch, making note of the time and hastening his steps. He had a lot to do before school let out today and he didn't want to be late. It was important to make contact several times before the day of the adoption. Children were taught not to talk to strangers, but after a few innocent meetings, his little angel would no longer view him as such.

Mary was digging through the back of her closet when the phone began to ring. Dropping the shoes she was holding, she backed out of the closet and answered the call with a breathless hello.

"Mary...are you all right? You sound like you're out of breath."

"Daniel... Hi honey! I'm fine...just made a dash for the phone."

There was a note of censure in his voice. "You're supposed to be taking it easy today but something tells me you're not."

"I haven't done one worthwhile thing this morning," she said. "I swear." His soft chuckle tickled her ear.

"Then how about meeting me for lunch?"

"Really? I thought you had court."

"Had it...still having it, but we're not due back for a couple of hours."

"What did you have in mind?" Mary asked.

"We don't have time for what's on my mind, but I'll settle for looking at your pretty face over shrimp scampi."

Mary laughed. "Just tell me where to meet you. We'll worry about the other stuff tonight."

"It's a deal," Daniel said. "You know that little Italian place a couple of blocks down from the courthouse?"

She didn't, but wasn't going to tell him that. "Yes, just give me enough time to call a cab."

"Cab? What's wrong with your car?"

Mary frowned. Another roadblock she hadn't anticipated. She hadn't owned a car since the day she'd seen theirs go up in smoke.

"Uh...I—"

"Don't tell me you've lost your keys again," he teased. "There's an extra set in the top drawer of the dresser. Just drive carefully, okay?"

"Uh...yes...okay."

"I'll get a table. Look for me inside."

"I will."

"Love you, honey."

Mary shivered as his voice softened.

"I love you, too. See you soon," she said, and hung up the phone.

She picked up her purse, then stared at it a moment before moving toward the bed. Impulsively, she turned it upside down and dumped the contents out onto the bed. Even though she saw the ring of keys falling onto the bedspread, it felt strange to accept the fact that they were there. Her hands were shaking as she picked them up. If this was the heaven she'd been given, then she should want for nothing. Okay. So she had a car. So what? She also had a husband and a daughter that she hadn't had two days before. Anxious now to get to Daniel, she stuffed the articles back in her bag and then hurried into the bathroom to put on some makeup and give her hair a quick brushing. A few moments later she was on her way out the front door.

The unattached garage was about twenty-five yards to the right of the house and she headed toward it at a trot. When she walked inside and saw the powder blue Jaguar in the south stall, she couldn't help but stare in disbelief. She'd never heard a preacher talk about a heaven like this, but she wasn't about to question another blessing. She jumped into the driver's seat, started the engine and backed out of the garage. Within seconds, she was out of the driveway and onto the street, heading downtown toward the courthouse. The sun was warm on her face and the wind tunneling through the partially opened window played havoc with the hair that she'd brushed, but she didn't care. How could anything as superficial as windblown hair matter when she had everything her heart desired?

Hope O'Rourke's little backpack was bumping against her shoulders as she marched out of the school toward the bus stops. Only Hope didn't ride a bus. She had to stand in line with the kids who were picked up by their parents and wait for the buses to leave. She craned her neck as she walked, looking for Mrs. Barnes's bright blue van, but she didn't see it. Her steps slowed as she sighed with disappointment. It wasn't the first time Mrs. Barnes had been late to pick her up and she hated having to wait. It always made her a little nervous, afraid that somehow she would be forgotten.

Her teacher was busy sorting through the waiting children, making sure they got on the proper buses, so Hope slipped out of line and dawdled toward one of the benches beneath the big shade trees by the street. She knew she was supposed to wait in line, but today she was tired and hungry and wished it was Mommy who would be picking her up and not Mrs. Barnes.

She tossed her backpack onto the bench and then crawled up beside it as her eyes filled with tears. A big boy walked past her, staring at the look on her face. Embarrassed, she drew her knees up under her chin and hid her face.

"Hey there, are you all right?"

At the touch on her shoulder, Hope flinched, and then looked up. There was a very tall man kneeling on the ground in front of her. Instinctively, she pulled away and looked nervously toward her teacher, Mrs. Kristy. But Mrs. Kristy had not realized that Hope was out of line and was busy with the other students.

"It's okay," the man said. "I just saw you crying and wondered if you were hurt."

"I'm not supposed to talk to strangers," Hope said.

The man smiled and Hope thought he looked like a real clown with his wide, thick lips and the funny little spaces between his teeth. Interested, in spite of her fear, she sat when she should have been moving away.

Howard Lee resisted the urge to laugh. With little girls, it was so easy. It was always so easy. They were born with an innate sense of wanting to please.

"Well, you're right of course. You should never talk to

strangers who might hurt you. But I'm not going to do that, am I?"

Hope shrugged, her gaze still riveted on the way his tongue brushed against the inside of his teeth as he talked.

"You know what?" Howard Lee asked.

Hope shook her head.

"You look like a little girl who's about to have a birthday. Am I right?"

Hope's eyes widened as she nodded. She was inordinately proud of the fact that she would soon be seven and a year older than a lot of the kids in her class.

"I thought so!" Howard Lee said, and clapped his hands together, as if in quick delight. "I'll bet you're having a party, aren't you? Going to invite all your friends and play games and eat cake and ice cream."

Hope's expression fell. "I don't think so," she said.

Howard Lee's mouth turned downward, giving his expression a sudden mournful look. He wanted to touch her, but knew it was far too soon. However, he couldn't resist a quick touch to her hair as he stroked a finger down the length of one curl.

"Why, that's just awful," he said. "A little girl as pretty as you should have a party...lots of parties, in fact."

Instinct kicked in as Hope retreated from the intrusion of his touch. She grabbed her backpack and slid from the bench just as her teacher suddenly realized she was missing.

Lena Kristy saw the familiar blue van pulling up at the curb and looked around for Hope O'Rourke. She frowned when she realized she was no longer in line, but when she turned around to search for her and saw her talking to a stranger, her frustration turned to fear.

"Hope! Hope! Please come here!"

Hope bolted, relieved that the responsibility of conversation had been removed. She saw Mrs. Barnes and headed for the van, but her teacher stopped her before she could get in.

"Who was that man you were talking to?" Lena asked.

Hope shrugged. "I don't know."

"Where did he come from, dear?"

"I was crying. I didn't see."

Lena squatted down beside the little girl and then cupped her chin.

"Why were you crying, dear? Are you ill?"

"No," Hope said.

"Did someone hurt you?"

"No."

"You had to be crying for a reason. Can't you tell me what it was?"

"Mrs. Barnes wasn't here. I don't like it when she's late. It makes me sad."

Lena sighed and gave Hope a quick hug. Anxiety was hard to deal with, especially when you're only six.

"But she's here now, isn't she?" Lena said. "So off you go, and if you see that man again, you run and tell me. It's not okay to talk to him."

Hope nodded.

Lena ushered the child into the van and then turned around, searching the schoolyard for the man she'd seen, but he was no longer in sight. Anxious to report to her principal, she hustled the other children into their parents' cars and then headed for the school building. Two little girls had already gone missing in Savannah and she wasn't taking any chances. While these children were in her care, they were her babies.

"Mommy, it's not okay to talk to strangers, is it?" Hope asked.

The curious inflection in Hope's voice made Mary's skin crawl. She dropped the potato she was peeling into the sink, wiped her hands on a towel and then turned to look at her daughter, who was sitting at the kitchen table. Her head was bent toward her coloring book, the cookie Hope had given her earlier was gone, and her glass of milk was half-empty. It was an innocent scene, but the question Hope asked was not.

"No, it's not okay," Mary said. "Why do you ask?"

Hope shrugged and discarded her red crayon for a blue one.

Mary sat down in the chair across from Hope and for a moment, simply watched the intensity on her daughter's face. As she sat, it occurred to her that fear was not something she would have expected in heaven, and with that came the thought that her theory could be horribly flawed. If so, then she wasn't dead, but if she wasn't dead, then where was she?

It wasn't the first time today that she'd experienced something disturbing, but this was the worst. And while she had no explanation for what was going on in her life, the reality of her "here and now" was too vivid to explain away as a dream.

"Did a stranger talk to you today?"

Without looking up, Hope nodded.

"Where, honey? At dance class?"

"No," Hope said, and abandoned the blue crayon for a yellow one.

Mary sighed. If only she was more confident about this parenting business. She'd only had three months of practice at it before everything had come to an end, and even though she felt a natural and enduring love for this child she was just getting to know, she was uncertain about how to connect.

"Come sit in my lap," Mary asked, and without urging, Hope immediately abandoned her coloring and did as Mary asked.

Mary pulled her close, wrapping her arms around the tiny girl's shoulders and rocking her where they sat.

"Where did you see the stranger?"

"At school." Her features crumpled. "I don't want to go

to dance class with Mrs. Barnes anymore. She's always late. I don't like to be last to go home."

"Okay, sweetie, we'll talk about dance class later. Right now I need you to tell me more about the man. Did he come to your classroom?"

"No. He was by the gate where we go home."

"Where was Mrs. Kristy?"

Hope hesitated, knowing that it was her fault for getting out of line.

"Honey, you can tell me."

Hope sighed. "I got out of line. Mrs. Barnes wasn't there and I sat on the bench."

Mary's heart sank, thinking how swiftly a child could be lost—and in the place where she should have felt safe.

"Did Mrs. Kristy see him?"

"I don't know. I came when she called me, Mommy. Really I did."

"That's good. Now tell me something else. Were you afraid of him?"

Hope shrugged. "I don't know...maybe."

Mary struggled with a sudden fear of her own, knowing that someone they didn't know had violated her daughter's naivety.

"Did he touch you?" Mary asked, and heard the tremble in her own voice.

Hope nodded.

Oh God. Oh God. "Where did he touch you, baby?"

"On my hair. He said I was pretty." At this point, Hope looked up. "Am I, Mommy? Am I pretty?"

Mary made herself smile, but she couldn't talk. Not yet. Not while the taste of bile was so rancid in her mouth.

"He looked like a clown," Hope said.

For a moment, Mary started to relax. A clown. There had been a clown at school—probably in another classroom. It was okay after all.

"Oh…a clown! Did he have a funny costume?"

Hope frowned. "He wasn't a real clown, Mommy. He just looked like one. He had yellow hair and a big mouth with holes between his teeth."

"Holes?"

"Yes, you know…like this."

"Oh! You mean spaces…like his teeth didn't touch each other good."

"Yes. Like that," Hope said.

"What else did he say to you?" Mary asked.

"I don't remember. Mommy, can I go outside and play until Daddy comes home?"

Mary hesitated and then nodded an okay. "But only in the backyard with the fence."

Hope rolled her eyes. "Oh, Mommy. I never play outside my fence. You know that."

Mary made herself laugh, but she felt like crying as Hope bounced off her lap and bolted out the back door. She followed her to the porch, assuring herself that she was right where she'd said she'd be, and then went back inside to finish peeling potatoes.

From the window above the sink, she could see Hope swinging on her swing and sliding down the slide, but it wasn't enough to alleviate the sick feeling in her stomach. And all the while the realization kept growing that she wasn't in heaven after all.

Chapter 6

Daniel's steps were weary as he entered the house, but his spirits lifted as he heard laughter and smelled the welcoming scents of their evening meal. He laid his briefcase on the hall table and then headed for the kitchen. He wanted to shower and change into some comfortable clothes, but he needed to see his girls first.

"I'm home," he yelled, and grinned to himself when he heard his daughter squeal.

"Daddy!" she shrieked, and launched herself toward him, knowing full well he would catch her before she fell.

"Wow," Daniel said, as he hugged her close. "That's quite a welcome. What did I do to deserve that?"

"'Cause you're my Daddy, that's why."

Daniel laughed and pretended to pinch at her nose, then looked over her shoulder toward Mary. She was trying to smile, but he could tell by the look on her face that something was amiss.

"Honey?"

She shook her head and then looked at Hope. He nodded in understanding as Mary spoke.

"Supper is ready, but you have time to change if you want."

He set Hope down and then gave her a playful swat as she dashed toward the kitchen. As soon as Hope was out of hearing, he took Mary in his arms.

"Talk to me."

"Hope said there was a stranger at the schoolyard gates who told her she was pretty. She said he touched her hair."

Daniel's heart stopped, and when it kicked back into rhythm, pounded erratically against his chest.

"God in heaven…where was her teacher?"

"Where she always was, but Hope said she got out of line because she was sad. I don't think Mrs. Kristy knew for a while. Hope also said that Mrs. Barnes wasn't there when school let out. She said she doesn't want to go to dance classes with her anymore because she's always late."

Daniel felt sick to his stomach, absorbing the horror of what he was hearing. At the same time, he thought of the headlines in this morning's paper.

"Two little girls have already been abducted here in the city."

"What?"

Daniel frowned. "Honey…you knew that. We talked about it just last week."

Mary couldn't wrap her thoughts around what she was hearing. The only *last week* she could remember was working as a sales clerk in the dress shop and going home to an empty house.

"Yes, of course," she muttered. "I wasn't thinking."

"Have you talked to Mrs. Kristy?"

Mary flushed. Suddenly she felt as if she'd failed at her duty as a parent.

"No, but Hope only told me about it less than an hour ago. I wanted to talk to you first before I did anything."

"Yes, of course," Daniel said, and then hugged Mary close. "Maybe we're making too much out of nothing, but in this day and age, you can't be too careful."

"That's what I thought," Mary said. "I didn't want to panic and cause Hope to have anxiety. She was already bothered by the fact that in talking to him, she'd disobeyed a very important rule."

"Lord," Daniel muttered, and shoved a hand through his hair. "I'm going to shower and change. Give me five minutes and then I'll be down to supper. We'll call Mrs. Kristy together after Hope goes to bed, okay?"

"Okay," Mary said, and then hugged Daniel tight. "Oh Daniel, when she started talking about that man…" Then she shuddered. "I've never been so scared."

"You did the right thing, honey. Don't worry. Chances are the incident was innocent, but we can never be too careful. She's not even seven years old and still so trusting. Losing her innocence will be inevitable, but not now. Keeping this low-key is the best for her. We don't want to frighten her unnecessarily."

Mary nodded, then watched Daniel bound up the stairs before she went back into the kitchen where Hope was playing. She kept going over and over the sequence of events during the past few hours, certain there was something obvious she was missing, but for the life of her, she couldn't figure out what it was.

She continued to set the table and dish up the food as Hope finished coloring her picture. She was putting ice in their glasses when Hope slapped the coloring book closed and announced.

"Mommy, I'm hungry."

Mary's stomach was in knots as she turned to face her daughter, then she heard Daniel's footsteps as he came hurrying down the stairs.

"Daddy's coming now," Mary said. "Go wash your hands while I put the food on the table, okay?"

"Yea!" Hope cried, and skipped toward the bathroom off the kitchen.

Daniel entered as Hope was leaving. "Yes… Yea! I echo her sentiments," he said. "I'm starving, too."

"After all that shrimp scampi we had at lunch?"

Daniel grinned. "I'm a growing boy."

Mary laughed and handed him a bowl of mashed potatoes.

"Please put these on the table while I get the meatloaf out of the warming oven."

"Man, I love your meatloaf," Daniel said, as he set the potatoes on the table.

"Salad is in the fridge," Mary said. "Would you get it, too?"

Daniel went toward the refrigerator just as Hope came back in the room.

"May I have juice, please?

"And juice for the princess," Daniel said, as he took a pitcher of apple juice from the refrigerator along with the salad.

Hope sat down at the table with all the assurance of a child who knows she is loved.

"Daddy…"

"What honey?"

"I talked to a stranger today."

Daniel glanced at Mary and then sighed. "I know. Mommy told me."

"I'm sorry."

He put the salad and juice on the table and then sat down beside her.

"Want to talk about it?"

She ducked her chin. "I won't do it again."

Daniel laid his hand on her head, thinking as he did, that for such a small child, she had a very huge hold on his heart.

"That's good, honey." He hesitated, then added. "If you ever see the man again, do you know what to do?"

Hope frowned. "Run away?"

"That's right. Run away, then find your teacher and tell her. Can you remember to do that?"

Hope nodded.

Daniel grinned, and tweaked her nose.

"Good girl." Then he winked at Mary as she set a platter of meatloaf on the table. "Let's eat, what do you say?"

"Yes," Hope said. "I say eat, too."

Mary slid into her seat and bowed her head as Daniel started to say grace, but even as her eyes were closing, she was picturing a man with yellow hair, a big mouth and funny teeth touching her daughter and telling her she was pretty. It was all she could do not to throw up.

Lena Kristy was just getting out of the shower when her phone began to ring. She grabbed for a towel, wrapping it around her as she raced for the phone.

"Hello?"

"Mrs. Kristy, it's Daniel O'Rourke. I know this is an imposition to be calling you at this hour, but we've had a little situation at home today that you might be able to help us with."

Lena sat down on the side of the bed. Something told her she knew what he was going to say before it came out of his mouth.

"I had a dentist appointment after school today and I haven't been home very long. I was just getting out of the shower when you called. Actually, you've beat me to the punch, because I intended to call you."

Daniel waved to Mary to pick up the portable phone so that they could both hear at the same time.

"My wife is on the other phone," Daniel said.

"Hello, Mrs. O'Rourke. Is Hope okay?"

"Yes…but why do you ask?"

"I don't know why *you're* calling, but I know why I was going to call you."

"Why is that?" Daniel asked.

"When it was time to go home today, I took the kids out to catch their rides, just like I do every day. They walk in line and know they're not supposed to step away, but Hope did. I don't know how long she'd been out of line when I missed her, but I saw her even as I was turning to look for her. She was sitting on that bench just to the left of the gates. You know the one I mean."

Mary frowned. She could almost picture the school building, but not quite. It was in her memory, but faded, like looking at the world through a thin veil of fog.

"The bench under the trees?" Daniel asked.

"Yes, that's the one," Lena said. "Anyway, when I saw her, she wasn't alone. There was a man talking to her that I didn't know. I immediately called to Hope and she came running as the man walked away. I never did get a good look at his face, but I do know that he had no business on the grounds. He wasn't a substitute teacher because I checked. We only had two today and they were both women. I told the principal immediately and she called the police, but the man was gone. I can't say that he meant her any harm, but he had no business being there."

Daniel sighed and rolled his eyes at Mary. They both knew how hectic it was for teachers after school, trying to get the children in the right cars and on the right buses. He could see how the incident had happened, but it didn't make them feel any better.

"I appreciate the fact that you've already taken steps to increase security at school, especially considering the children who've already gone missing here in Savannah."

Lena sighed. "I'm so sorry. She's my responsibility and I know it, but sometimes there's not enough of me to go around."

"I know the feeling," Mary said.

"Oh," Lena said. "One more thing. Hope cried today after school. The woman who takes her to dance class is often late and it makes Hope very anxious. She worries a lot. I just thought you would want to know."

"Yes, she told me as much," Mary said. "Daniel and I haven't talked about it yet, but as far as I'm concerned, Mrs. Barnes will not be picking Hope up again. In fact, I'm thinking about taking her out of the dance class altogether. She's too young to be doing so much, especially during the school week."

Daniel watched the intensity on Mary's face and marveled at how far she'd come from the shy, inhibited woman she'd once been.

"I agree," Daniel said. "We'll take care of the dance class situation and you make sure that man does not get access to the children again."

"Consider it already done," Lena said. "The principal assured me that there would be uniformed policemen on duty before and after school until the person responsible for the missing children is found."

"That's great," Daniel said. "Thanks again for your help."

"And thank you for your understanding," Lena said.

They hung up, then looked at each other and sighed.

"It isn't easy being a parent, is it?" Mary asked.

Daniel opened his arms. "Come here, baby. I'm thinking I need a hug."

Mary's lower lip quivered as she walked into his arms. "I don't know what I need, but I'm so thankful you're here with me."

"Where else would I be?" Daniel asked.

Mary hid her face against his chest and resisted the urge to roll her eyes. She wanted to tell Daniel how confused she was. She needed to say aloud everything that was happening to her, but if she did, he would probably have her committed.

Howard Lee took the carton of ice cream out of the grocery sack and put it in the freezer. He'd debated for a good thirty minutes before choosing the flavor, but had finally decided on vanilla. You never went wrong with vanilla. Besides, he had several kinds of sprinkles from which his little angel could choose. Tomorrow he would order her a cake. Strawberry cream, he thought. Pink—for little girls.

He put up the other groceries and then moved to the utility room, took the clean sheets out of the dryer and hurried down the hall to the guest room. He was smiling in anticipation as he began to put the new linens on the bed. The sheets were pink with caricatures of Barbie imprinted upon the fabric. Howard Lee prided himself on being the perfect host, and nothing was too good for his little angels. Each one got their own special sheets for the sleepover, just like they got their own presents for the party. He'd had the Little Mermaid for Amy Anne, but she'd done nothing but cry and beg to go home. Unfortunately, he'd had to resort to stern measures to contain her rebellion.

When he'd adopted Justine, the theme in the guest room had been Cinderella. He'd even gotten a small, stuffed mouse for her to sleep with, reminiscent of the ones in the Disney movie. But she'd tried to crawl out the window, so he had to resort to sedatives in her food and move her down below, just as he now did Amy Anne.

But his hopes were high for his new little girl. Maybe she would be the one who would settle right in, and when she did, the others would surely follow.

He hummed beneath his breath as he worked, reveling in the sensuousness of the smooth new sheets and the colorful pillow slips on the pillows. Impulsively, he picked up one of the pillows, lifted it to his face then inhaled. Meadow fresh. His favorite scent.

"Perfect," he said, as he laid it against the headboard, then pulled the eyelet bedspread over the sheets and tucked it in place.

His gaze swept the room as he backed out of the doorway, making sure that everything was perfect for his little angel's arrival. His pulse kicked erratically as he gripped the doorknob and then closed the door. Only a few more days and then she'd be here. For Howard Lee, it would be none too soon.

Daniel sat on the side of the bed, watching Mary sleep. This was the second time he'd been up to check on Hope, making sure she was still safe in her bed. He couldn't get past the gut-wrenching fear of knowing he could not protect her every minute of her day.

Mary moaned, then murmured something beneath her breath that Daniel couldn't hear, but he didn't have to hear the words to know the source of her discomfort. He'd seen the panic on her face. He'd heard her voice tremble and her hands shake. A threat to a child, however impotent, was enough to awaken every violent tendency a parent might have.

He sighed, then stretched out beside Mary and took her in his arms.

"Sssh," he whispered, and spooned her against his body. "It's okay, honey, everything's okay. Just sleep."

Within seconds, he felt her body relaxing, and then heard her breathing even out. Now if he could just follow his own orders, maybe they'd both get some sleep.

Detective Reese Arnaud poured himself a fresh cup of coffee and then headed back to his desk. Last night in Savannah had been a slow night for crime. One hit-and-run without a fatality and a hooker who was claiming rape and assault, along with another crash and grab and two robberies—one at an all-night service station and the other at an ATM.

But he would have willingly worked a night in hell if only they could find the two little girls who'd gone missing last month. Amy Anne Fountain and Justine Marchand were their names—ages six and seven, respectively. Their parents called him every day, and every day he had to tell them that they were still checking out leads. But the truth was, they had no new leads—nothing to lead the police as to where they'd gone or even a hint of who'd taken them.

He took his coffee with him as he headed for the morning meeting where the task force was assembled. Being lead detective on the case made him ultimately responsible for the success or failure of the investigation. It also made him sick to his stomach.

As he walked into the room, his gaze went immediately to the pictures of the two missing victims. The sight of their innocent faces was the stuff of his recent nightmares. What kind of maniac does it take to mess with babies? Tiny little girls whose lives should still be far removed from the ugliness of what the adult world had become. He had nightmares, imagining them crying for their mothers, begging to go home. And that was a best-case scenario. In the real hell that had become his dreams, they were no longer able to cry about anything.

"What do we have?" he asked, "and for God's sake give me some good news."

"Sorry, Arnaud, no can do."

"Then what can you tell me?"

"Well…we're not sure how this connects, or even if it does, but the principal at Robert E. Lee elementary school reported a strange man on the grounds yesterday afternoon."

Arnaud's heart skipped a beat. "Did anybody get a good look at him?"

"Just the kid he was talking to."

"By any chance was it a little girl?"

"Yeah, I think so. Let me check my notes…yeah, here it is. Hope O'Rourke, age six. Her parents are Daniel and Mary O'Rourke."

Arnaud's belly turned. *Ah God...not that Hope.* Pretty, dark-haired, impish little fairy of a female who just happened to be his daughter's best friend.

"God Almighty," Arnaud murmured. Suddenly this was too close to home.

The detective looked up, surprised by Arnaud's reaction. "You know her?"

"She's Molly's best friend. She's spent the night at my house more than once." Then he managed a small smile. "Hell, once she even threw up on my shoe."

"Man...that's cold," the detective said. "What do you want us to do?"

"I'll do the follow-up," Arnaud said. "She knows me, so chances are if there's anything to tell, I'll get more out of her than anyone else. As for the rest of you, I want unmarked cars at every elementary school this afternoon. Tate...you're point man to coordinate with the schools. Make sure the administration knows you're there and why, but keep it low-key. I don't want anyone blowing your covers."

"You got it," Tate said.

Arnaud nodded at the others, glanced one last time at Amy Anne Fountain and Justine Marchand's pictures, then walked out of the room. Whatever it took, he would make sure that Hope O'Rourke's picture did not wind up on there, too.

Daniel's secretary knocked on his door and then stepped inside.

"I know you didn't want to be disturbed, but there's a policeman on the phone who says he needs to talk to you. Line two."

Daniel grabbed the receiver.

"This is Daniel O'Rourke."

"Dan...Reese Arnaud. We need to talk."

Daniel frowned. "What about?"

"We got a report that your daughter was approached yesterday by a stranger on the grounds of her school."

"Since when do homicide detectives investigate those kinds of reports?"

"Since two little girls about her age have gone missing," Arnaud answered.

For a moment, Daniel felt like throwing up, and then he took a deep breath and made himself concentrate.

"Do you think the man Hope saw is the same one who snatched the two girls?"

"I don't know, but at this point, I can't afford to ignore any lead, no matter how small."

Daniel closed his eyes and wearily pinched the bridge of his nose. "What do you want to know?"

"I need to talk to Hope. I want to know what the guy looked like…if she'd ever seen him before. You know… stuff that might give us a lead toward finding the missing children." He paused, then added. "I don't sleep anymore. I find myself getting up at night and going into Molly's room just to make sure she's all right. When they told me about the incident at the school, my first thought was, hell yes…a new lead. And then they told me the child's name and I felt sick to my stomach. Damn it, Daniel, she's Molly's best friend. I've read bedtime stories to her, put Band-Aids on her boo-boos and given up the last of the chocolate chip cookies to her endearing pleas. She's as close to my child as she could be and not be of my blood. I guess what I'm saying is…this hit too close to home."

Daniel stood abruptly and walked to the windows overlooking downtown Savannah, making himself concentrate on the traffic and not the fear in the man's voice, because it made his own far more vivid—and too real. For a while, he'd almost convinced himself that he and Mary had over-reacted last night. But this put a whole new color on the incident. If Reese Arnaud was interested, Hope might really be in danger.

"Just tell me what you want and it's yours," Daniel said.

"I need to talk to Hope, but I don't want to scare her. Do you think it would be all right if I came over after school? I want to bring a sketch artist with me. I know it's a long shot, but it's more than we've had in days."

"Yes, sure. I'll call Mary."

"Good. I'll be there around four, okay?"

"We'll be waiting."

"Don't say anything to Hope about my coming by," Reese added. "She left a jacket at my house the last time she spent the night. I'll just bring it by and then go from there."

"Yes, okay…I see what you mean."

"This may be nothing," Reese said. "You need to know that at the outset. But I've got two sets of grieving parents who want to know where their babies are, and if Hope can help, I can't pass it up."

"I didn't sleep last night, either. I kept going into Hope's room time and again, just to make sure she was safe in bed. I can't imagine the horror of not knowing where she was or what had happened to her. Bring your sketch artist. Stay as long as you need."

Howard Lee stepped out of the shower and reached for a towel to dry himself off. He'd just gotten home from his shift at the hospital and not for the first time, it occurred to him that working the midnight shift was not conducive to parenthood. He didn't like leaving the girls alone after dark, but at the present time he had no choice. And, until they settled down into the adoption a little better, he could hardly send them off to school and trust them to come home.

He finished drying and then reached for his pajamas, anxious to get in bed. Even though the sun was up and the day was promising to be wonderful, he had to get his rest.

He walked out of the bathroom, then paused, staring down at the throw rug beside his bed. He thought of his girls and wondered what they were doing. His eyelids burned from lack of sleep, but his conscience tugged. A parent should spend quality time with the children, no matter what the cost.

With a heartfelt sigh, he kicked the throw rug aside and then unlocked the padlock on the cellar door. The hinges squeaked a bit as he raised it up, and he made a mental note to oil them. He heard a series of scuffling noises and then nothing.

"Girls...do you want Daddy to come down and play for a while?"

There was a long and pregnant moment of utter silence, then what sounded like a muffled sob. He frowned.

"Stop crying, damn it!" he yelled, and slammed the door shut with a bang, then locked it and kicked the throw rug in place.

He yanked back his covers and crawled into bed, too tired to deal with the situation. The sheets were clean and cool, just like his mother had always insisted they should be. It prided him to know that he'd kept the house in the same condition it had always been when his mother had been alive.

Despite the sunlight beaming through the curtains, he closed his eyes and slept.

Justine Marchand had turned seven two months ago, but she was small for her age. She had straight, dark hair, big brown eyes and a slight pout to her rosebud mouth. There were exactly four tiny brown freckles on the bridge of her nose and she liked Mickey Mouse and the PowerPuff girls. When she grew up, she wanted to be a nurse.

And somewhere between the morning she'd left for school and before she'd gone home, she'd been thrust into hell. She didn't understand exactly what was happening, but she wanted to go home.

When the cellar door had opened, she'd grabbed Amy Anne and crawled under the bed. Even though she knew the man would eventually make her come out, it still seemed plausible to resist in every way she dared. She wasn't supposed to talk to strangers, but she was stuck with him, just the same.

However, he hadn't come down as she'd feared, and when he yelled at her and then slammed the door, she went weak with relief. She didn't care how loud he yelled, as long as he stayed away. He smiled too much and was always touching her face and her hair.

As soon as it was quiet, she crawled out from under the bed, pulling Amy Anne with her, then smoothed the hair away from the other girl's face.

"He's gone now," she said, and led Amy Anne to the little table in the middle of the room. "Want to color in the color books or watch TV?"

Amy Anne didn't answer. Justine wasn't even sure she could talk. She hadn't said a word since she'd been here. She didn't even know if the girl belonged to the man, or if she was lost, too.

"We'll color," she said softly, and sat the little girl in a chair. "That way we won't make any noise and wake him up."

She opened a coloring book for herself, then opened one for Amy Anne.

"Here," she said. "You can have the blue crayon and I'll pick red."

She put the crayon in Amy Anne's lifeless hands and waited for her to move. It didn't happen.

"It's okay," she finally said, and patted Amy Anne on the head. "You can watch me, instead."

She picked up the red crayon and then started to cry, softly, so that no one could hear.

"I want to go home, Amy Anne. I don't like it here."

Chapter 7

Mary had started out dusting the bookshelves in the living room, but now the dust cloth and furniture polish was sitting idle on a nearby table and she was cross-legged in the floor with a picture album in her lap. Nothing could have prepared her for what she'd found inside, not even the wildest of dreams.

The first pages were devoted to the first year of her and Daniel's marriage. She remembered those times and the pictures being taken. The pictorial mementos moved from there to Hope's birth, and then the first three months of her life. Most of them consisted of pictures of Daniel holding Hope, or Daniel's parents holding Hope. The images were burned in her mind.

But then she'd turned the next page and faced a truth that was impossible to deny. Page after page, year after year, were pictures of Mary with Hope, and Mary with Daniel, physical proof that she'd been present during all these events. They were nonsensical pictures, the kind that were precious only to the people taking them, ranging in ordinary diversity from braiding Hope's hair to building a sand castle at the beach. Pictures of Christmases past and the first Thanksgiving in their new house, her thirtieth birthday and Daniel giving her the keys to her new car. The more she looked, the more it seemed she remembered. But it made no sense. How could she remember something that hadn't happened?

Then she sighed and rubbed the worry spot between her eyebrows. What on earth was she asking? This had to be more of her increasing insanity. More than once during the past twenty-four hours she'd wondered if she was actually locked up in some hospital somewhere and only living out this fantasy in her mind. It made more sense than anything else she could think of. Then she looked back at the pictures. It just all seemed so real.

Many times over the past six years she'd wished for the ability to turn back time—to relive that moment when Daniel had put Hope in the car and then started to back out of the driveway into the path of that high-speed pursuit. She'd relived that horror over and over every time she'd closed her eyes, but it had always been the same. The fight—Hope crying—Daniel leaving in anger—and her watching them driving away without trying to make him stop.

The flesh suddenly crawled on the back of her neck. It had always been the same.

Until yesterday.

Yesterday in the antique store she'd had the same dream, and it had not changed—until the point where Daniel started to back out of the drive. This time she'd thrown herself on the hood of the car instead of watching him drive away. This time she had screamed for him to stop, then begged him not to leave—and for the first time since the nightmare had begun, he and Hope had lived.

She closed her eyes, remembering the ring that she'd found in that old scrap of lace—and the odd little man who'd looked at her with such sad, sad eyes. The ring had been so small and yet it had slid upon her finger as if it had been made to fit. She took a deep breath, making herself calm and trying to remember what had happened next.

Oh yes—the scent of dust was in the air and another, more subtle scent of faded roses. She'd started to feel faint and reached out to steady herself against a counter.

Mary's heart started to pound. Even now she could feel the heart-stopping panic of knowing something had been set into motion that she could not stop. She vaguely remembered how her head had started to spin, as if everything she was looking at was turning backward.

Backward!

She gasped as a new thought occurred.

Backward?

No. Not that.

It wasn't possible.

There was no such thing as going back in time.

But she couldn't turn loose of the notion. What if that last dream she'd had of their fight had been real? What if she really had been given the opportunity to change their fates? What if she *had* saved their lives and changed the future?

She shoved the picture album back on the shelf and got to her feet, then went to the phone, picked up the receiver and dialed the operator.

"Operator, how may I help you?"

"What's today's date?"

"I'm sorry?" the operator said.

"Please," Mary pleaded. "Just tell me. What's today's date?"

"September 26th."

Mary started to shake. She'd walked into the antique store on October 2nd. She took a deep breath and then asked.

"What's the year?"

"Ma'am, are you ill?"

No, but I may be crazy. "No, just please tell me. What year is this?"

"It's September the 26th, 2002."

Mary replaced the receiver without acknowledgment of

the operator's last answer. What was there to say? *Oh, by the way, I think I've traveled backward in time and don't want to be late for dinner?*

Before she could follow the thought any further, the phone rang. She jerked back in reflex, half expecting to hear the operator's voice telling her to get ready for a permanent trip to the funny farm.

"Hello?"

"Mary, darling, how are you?"

"Phyllis?"

Phyllis O'Rourke laughed. "Yes, it's me. Surely it hasn't been *that* long since we talked."

Only six years...but who's counting. "Sorry, I was sort of preoccupied."

"I certainly know how that is," Phyllis said. "As for the reason I'm calling, it will soon be Hope's birthday. I wanted to know if you'd made any special plans, because if not, Mike and I would love to have all of you over for dinner."

"That sounds wonderful," Mary said. "I'll check with Daniel and get back to you, okay?"

"Great! I wasn't sure if you would be having a party for her or not, and certainly don't want to intrude."

"Grandparents never intrude," Mary said.

"You're a dear," Phyllis said. "I'd love to chat longer but Mike is waiting for me. Let me know about the dinner later. Bye-bye."

"Yes, goodbye," Mary said, and hung up, amazed that the conversation with a woman who had once hated her guts seemed so comfortable and warm.

She started back to the photo albums when the phone suddenly rang again. This time she was a little more composed.

"Hello?"

"Hey, good-looking...it's me."

Relief washed over her in waves and sent her moving backward toward a chair.

"Oh...it's you."

She heard amusement in his voice.

"Who did you think it would be?"

"I just finished talking to your mom. She invited us to dinner for Hope's birthday."

"What did you tell her?"

"That I'd get back to her later after I talked to you."

"Whatever you want is fine with me," Daniel said. "Are you busy?"

"Not really. I was looking at old photo albums when Phyllis called and was still standing by the phone when it rang. It startled me."

He chuckled. "Hey, honey...I don't have long before I have to be in court, but the reason I called is that Reese Arnaud telephoned. He wants to talk to Hope about the man who approached her at school yesterday."

"Reese Arnaud?"

Daniel frowned. These blank spots in Mary's memory were beginning to trouble him.

"Molly's father? Hope's best friend, Molly? He's a detective with the Savannah P.D., remember?"

Mary's stomach knotted. "The police. Oh God...yes... of course, I'd forgotten he was with the police. Oh Daniel, do they think—"

"They don't think anything right now, honey. They're just covering all the bases. With those two little girls still missing, they can't afford to ignore anything, even if it's a long shot, okay?"

"Yes, of course. What do I do?"

"Pick Hope up from school as usual, then go straight home. He's coming over at four on the pretext of bringing back a jacket that she left at their house the last time she spent the night with Molly. He's bringing a sketch artist, too, but let him handle all the explanations. Hope won't think anything of Reese coming there, and he knows how to talk to her without frightening her."

Mary's voice was shaking. She knew it, but she couldn't make it stop.

"Will you be here?"

"You couldn't keep me away."

Mary sighed. "This is awful, isn't it?"

"Yes, but not as awful as what the parents of those two missing children are going through."

"Oh, Daniel…"

"Hang in there, honey. Hope's safe and we're going to make sure she stays that way."

Howard Lee took the two bowls of macaroni and cheese from the microwave and put them on a tray, then added two plastic spoons and two snack-size fruit juices in disposable packs. He stared at the tray for a moment and then moved to the sideboard, took a couple of bananas from a bowl and added them to the tray.

"There now…a perfectly good lunch for growing girls."

He picked up the tray and headed down the hall, then into his own bedroom. Nudging the door closed with the toe of his shoe, he set the tray down on the bed, then shoved aside a small area rug, revealing the metal door on the floor. He lifted it, letting it rest against the side of the bed as he turned for the tray and started down the stairs.

Ignoring the fact that he'd yelled at them earlier, his voice was full of overdone delight.

"Hello, hello, hello," he said, as he began to descend. "I brought you some yummy lunch. Are my two little angels hungry?"

Amy Anne Fountain had once been a happy, smiling little girl, but there was little left of the child that she'd been.

Even though her clothes were spotless and her long brown hair had been brushed and clipped away from her face with a bright red bow, the bruises on her arms and the cut on her lip were impossible to miss. She was sitting on the side of the bed, her stare blank, a spittle of drool barely visible at the edge of her lower lip.

Justine Marchand had been an impish, outgoing child who'd never met a stranger. Then she'd met Howard Lee Martin, and the name "stranger" had taken on a whole different meaning. She'd been putty in his hands from the very first and had never seen the danger coming. He'd used the "puppy on a leash" trick, waited until he'd seen her coming, then dropped the leash, knowing full well that the puppy would bolt. Justine had seen the puppy coming at her, seen the funny man running after the puppy as hard as he could go, and thought she was doing a good deed. Only four blocks from her home she'd gotten down on her knees and caught the puppy in her arms. She was smiling as she'd handed him to the big man, and felt no danger when he'd patted her on the back and thanked her for being so kind.

When he'd offered to let her hold the puppy's leash as they walked toward her home, she'd been distracted by the unexpected treat and had done the unforgivable. She'd walked away with a stranger. She couldn't remember the last time she'd seen her mommy and daddy. She'd quit crying for them at night now and even though Amy Anne didn't talk to her, Justine slept curled around her as if she were a lifeline to sanity.

She heard the door open above them and then the man's voice calling down. She stood abruptly, unwilling to be on the bed. He played games on the bed that she didn't like. Her fingers curled around her friend's wrist as she whispered in desperation.

"Get up, Amy Anne…you have to get up."

But Amy Anne didn't move, and Justine wasn't strong

enough to lift her. Helpless to do anything but take care of herself, she ran to the other side of the room.

Mary had started toward Hope's school almost an hour before school was due to be dismissed. Part of it had been fear that she wouldn't know where to go, but more importantly, she never wanted Hope to be anxious again about being picked up. Even though she hadn't known exactly where to go, she'd driven straight to the school without missing a turn. She was starting to accept the fact that something extraordinary had happened to her life. She parked on the street and then leaned back against the seat, willing her pounding heart to ease.

As she waited, she glanced up in the rearview mirror and saw a tall, blond-haired man dressed in jogging clothes coming down the sidewalk. He was walking casually, once stopping to tie his shoe. When he straightened up, he glanced around as if looking to see if he'd been observed.

Mary's fingers curled around the steering wheel. He had blond hair. What if it was the man who'd talked to Hope? She reached for her purse and took out her phone. If he would only come a little closer, she would be able to see his face better.

As she waited, her finger poised to call 9-1-1, a yellow school bus came up behind her, passed where she was waiting, and pulled into line at the curb. At that point, she could no longer see the jogger. Seconds later, a second bus pulled to the curb, then a third and a fourth until the curb was lined with buses waiting to load and her view of the sidewalk was completely blocked.

A couple of drivers got out. One of them lit up a cigarette and started to smoke while another circled his bus, kicking at the tires and checking the back door to make sure it was securely fastened.

Mary got out of her car and moved toward the sidewalk

in front of the school, still looking for the man in the jogging suit, but he was nowhere in sight. Then she noticed a uniformed policeman just inside the front gate and began to relax.

At that moment, she heard a loud, strident bell from within the building behind her. Seconds later, the front doors opened and children came spilling out of the schoolhouse and down the steps. Frustration set in as the teachers and the children came toward her. She tried not to panic, but she had absolutely no idea what her own daughter's teacher looked like.

"Hi, Mrs. O'Rourke! Are you looking for Hope?"

Mary turned around, then looked down. A small, blond-haired girl with chubby cheeks was looking up at her, smiling in obvious recognition.

"Yes, I am," she said. "Who are you?"

The little girl laughed out loud, as if Mary had just told her a funny joke.

"It's me, Molly."

Molly. Hope's best friend. "Why, so it is," Mary said, and pretended to rub sleep from her eyes.

Molly laughed again and then pointed behind her.

"There they come now. The last rows had to wait in the hall because Frances Sheffield threw up."

"Oh, my," Mary said.

"Mommy! Mommy!"

Mary turned, saw Hope waving at her from the front of the line, and breathed a huge sigh of relief.

"Hi, honey," she called.

"Mary...good afternoon."

Mary took a calculated guess at the identity of the woman and jumped into the conversation with both feet.

"Hello, Mrs. Kristy. I hear someone had a little accident in the hall."

Lena Kristy rolled her eyes. "Five more seconds and we would have been out of the building, too."

Mary smiled sympathetically as Hope slipped her hand in her mother's palm.

"Mommy, can we go home now?"

Mary looked down at her daughter, her heart filling with a love she would have been hard-pressed to describe.

"Yes, darling…we can go home." She glanced at Mrs. Kristy. "Okay?"

"Very okay," Mrs. Kristy said, then she began loading her children, making sure they got on the proper buses while the other parents who picked up their children still waited in their cars.

Hope was talking nonstop, skipping as she walked, secure that all was right with her world. Mary listened absently, answering only when necessary as they moved toward the car. She kept looking at everyone they passed, as well as the people who waited in cars. Some waved at her. She waved back, assuming she should know who they were.

"Mommy, I'm hungry. Can we stop on the way home for a Slushee?"

Mary thought of the detective who was due soon at their house. "Not today, Hope. We need to hurry home."

"Why?"

She hesitated. Daniel had told her not to let Hope know Detective Arnaud was coming to talk to her.

"Because…because I think Daddy is coming home early and we don't want to miss him."

"Yea!" Hope cried. "Maybe he'll play ball with me."

Mary smiled. "Maybe…but we'll have to wait and see, okay?"

"Okay."

Howard Lee glared at the presence of the policeman while watching the buses loading from across the street.

When the cop looked his way, he picked up the clippers that were lying by the hedge where he was standing and began clipping at the bushes as if he lived there. He'd seen the woman get out of the car and thought nothing of it. There were hundreds of children in that school. What were the odds that she would be there for his angel?

He cut at the shrubbery in short, angry jerks, telling himself it didn't matter—that he still had plenty of time to make the plan work.

He watched the buses pull away and then stepped back into the shade of a magnolia tree as the first of the cars began to depart. He saw her then, in her pretty blue car, all smiling and happy, and his anger spiked. It wasn't fair. This was his little girl. He'd picked her out special. That woman couldn't possibly know how to make a little girl happy. Not like he did. Amy Anne and Justine needed that new sister and he wasn't going to disappoint them. He threw the clippers down with a curse and then started jogging toward home.

Reese Arnaud pulled up in front of the O'Rourke house and then reached over in the back seat and got the little pink jacket that Hope had left at his house. He eyed the sketch artist, giving him one last reminder.

"Okay, Kelly, remember we take this slow. If we frighten her, it's over."

"Yes, sir," the officer said, and gathered up his briefcase as he got out of the car.

Reese's focus was on high as he rang the doorbell. *Please God, let this be the break we've been waiting for.*

Moments later, the door opened and Mary let them inside.

Reese hugged her briefly, wanting to allay the fear he saw on her face.

"Hello, Mary. Sorry that this is happening."

"No more than we are," she said. "Hope is in her room. I'll call her."

"We need to make this real informal. How about we set up in the kitchen? Maybe with cookies and milk?"

Mary smiled. "It will be her second round. Something tells me she won't object."

Reese chuckled. "Yeah, she's hell on chocolate chip cookies, isn't she?"

Mary nodded, but her thoughts were somewhere else. *Chocolate chip cookies were her favorites? Another thing I hadn't known.* "Please see yourselves to the kitchen. We'll be right there."

As she started up the stairs, it occurred to her that Reese Arnaud probably knew more about her daughter's likes and dislikes than she did. The thought was not only daunting but made her feel lacking as the mother she wanted to be. She headed down the hall and then pushed the door open to Hope's room.

"Hi, Mommy! Is Daddy home yet?"

"No, but you have a visitor."

"Who? Is it Molly?"

"Close, but not Molly."

Abandoning the puzzle she'd been working, Hope jumped up from her little chair and ran out of her room and down the hall.

"Don't run down the stairs," Mary cautioned, then groaned beneath her breath as Hope bounded down the stairs anyway.

Mary hurried down behind her and followed Hope into the kitchen, just in time to hear her cry, "Uncle Reese…it's you! Did you bring Molly to play with me?"

Reese Arnaud scooped the little girl up into his arms and gave her a quick hug.

"No, but I brought your pink jacket."

"Oh, goody. Is that where it was?"

He grinned. "Yep. I wanted to wear it, but pink's not my color."

Hope giggled. "Uncle Reese, you're so silly. You can't wear my jacket. You're too big."

"Maybe you're right," he said, then pointed to the officer he'd brought with him. "This is my friend, Kelly. We're having cookies and milk. Want to have some with us?"

Hope looked to Mary for permission. When Mary nodded, she wiggled out of Reese's arms and headed for the fridge.

"I'll get my own milk," she said, and dragged a nearly full gallon of milk from the shelf.

"Maybe I'd better help," Mary said, and grabbed the gallon carton from Hope's hands before the milk hit the floor. "Why don't you sit down by Uncle Reese while I get your snack?"

Before Hope could settle, they heard the front door open.

"Daddy's home!" Hope cried. "Daddy! We're in here!" she yelled, and then snagged a cookie from the plate before anyone changed their minds about letting her have a second snack.

Mary nodded at the two officers then went to meet Daniel.

"Sorry I'm late. Got a late phone call I couldn't ignore. Have they started yet?" Daniel asked.

"No, they just got here."

"Good. Give me a second and I'll join you."

He set his briefcase on the floor beside the hall table and then took off his suit coat and hung it on the newel post as they passed the staircase.

As they entered the kitchen, Daniel's gaze met and then slid past Reese Arnaud to the little girl sitting across the table from him.

"Hey, punkin…did you save me any cookies?"

Hope giggled and took another big bite. "Nope."

"You little pig…then I'm going to eat yours," Daniel

teased, and grabbed at his daughter's wrist, pretending to eat her cookie.

Reese's nerves were on edge as he waited for the hilarity to cease. He couldn't help thinking about the two missing children—wondering if they were even alive—knowing if they were, they might never laugh again.

Finally, the silliness stopped as Daniel sat at the table and then took Hope on his lap. At his nod, the sketch artist took a pad and charcoal pencil from his briefcase and started to draw. Immediately, Hope's interest shifted.

"What are you doing?" she asked.

Reese leaned forward, his gaze fixed on Hope's face.

"He's going to draw me a picture."

"What kind of a picture?" Hope asked.

"Oh, I don't know, do you have a suggestion?"

Hope grinned. "A horse! Draw a picture of a horse!"

Mary slid into the seat beside Daniel and Hope. She didn't touch them, but she needed to be close. What happened during the next few minutes might be vital to finding the missing children as well as keeping her own daughter safe.

"How about a clown?" Mary asked. "Ask him if he knows how to draw a clown."

Reese already knew that Hope had referred to the stranger at school as looking like a clown. He nodded his approval at Mary for introducing the subject for him.

"That sounds like a good idea," Reese said.

Hope frowned. "I don't think I like clowns."

"Why not?" Reese asked.

Hope leaned back against Daniel's chest, taking comfort in his presence.

"It's okay, honey," Daniel said. "You can tell Uncle Reese."

"I did something bad," she said, and then looked away.

"No, it wasn't bad," Daniel said. "But it was wrong, wasn't it?"

She nodded.

"So, tell me what happened, honey."

"I talked to a stranger at school." Then she added. "I'm not supposed to talk to strangers."

"That's right, children don't talk to strangers, but the stranger did something bad, too, didn't he?"

Hope's eyes widened. It was the first time she'd thought about what had happened from another standpoint.

"What did he do?" she asked.

"He talked to you when your mommy and daddy weren't there. He knew better, but he did it anyway. I need to find that man and tell him not to do that again. Do you think that you could help me?"

"I don't know where he lives," Hope said.

"But you know what he looks like, don't you, honey?"

Hope thought about it a moment, then looked at Daniel and Mary.

"It's okay, honey. Mommy and Daddy want you to help Uncle Reese," Mary said. "Do you think you can?"

"Yes, I can do that."

"Great," Reese said, and gave her nose a tweak. "So come sit in my lap and you can watch Kelly drawing, okay?"

"Yes," Hope said, and slid out of Daniel's lap.

"So, this is how we do it," Reese said, as he settled the little girl in his lap. "I'll ask you questions about what he looked like and Kelly will draw what we tell him to draw."

"Was his face round like a balloon, or more square, like a box?"

"Round," Hope answered immediately. "Just like his eyes. They were big and round, too."

Reese's pulse accelerated. Maybe this was going to work after all.

Chapter 8

Howard Lee took a chunk of raw hamburger from the bowl on the counter, made a third hamburger patty and then put it in the hot skillet beside the other two he already had cooking. He turned down the heat, blithely unaware that his premature meeting with Hope O'Rourke had put himself in danger. A few minutes later he took the meat from the pan and put them on a platter to cool while he began to fix the buns.

Amy Anne liked ketchup on her hamburger. Ketchup and nothing else. Justine like mustard and pickles and wanted her hamburger cut into quarters. He put the burgers onto the plates and then added a handful of chips for each girl.

He hummed as he worked, confident that his growing family was intact. Once the plates were to his liking, he moved to the cabinet, took out a bottle of over-the-counter sleeping medicine and measured a small dose into two cups, then filled the cups with milk, adding a dollop of chocolate syrup to make sure the taste of the medicine was masked. He'd never intended to use this method of control, but after the first night with Amy Anne in the guest room, he'd been forced to resort to other measures.

A few minutes later he started down into the cellar. As

he did, he heard a scurrying of feet and smiled to himself, knowing that his girls were aware of his imminent arrival.

"Daddy's here," he called, then frowned when there was no welcoming response.

It aggravated him that after all he'd given them and done for them, they still withheld their affections. Even though their room was technically a cellar, he had not spared expenses in outfitting it. Besides the large room that served as living room and bedroom, he'd gone to a lot of trouble to install their own bathroom with tub and shower.

There was a television, a VCR and more than a dozen children's videos for them to watch. There were two white twin-size brass beds against one wall and a wooden table and chairs near the center of the room, piled high with coloring books, crayons and puzzles. As he came down the steps, he noticed that none of the toys had been moved, although the television was on.

Refusing to admit that his plan to create his own family was less successful than he had imagined, he set the tray down on the table and then fixed a place setting at each chair, carefully laying out their plate of food, a napkin, a fork and their cups of chocolate milk.

"Look what Daddy's made for you tonight."

"My daddy doesn't know how to cook," Justine murmured, and slipped into one of the chairs.

Howard Lee frowned. "I'm your Daddy now," he said sharply.

Justine's lower lip trembled and her eyes welled with tears, but she'd learned early on that arguing with the man just made things worse. Without saying anything more, she began nibbling on a potato chip as the man took Amy Anne in his lap and started to feed her.

As usual, ever since she'd been with the man, Amy Anne only sat and stared.

"Eat your hamburger," Howard Lee said.

Justine grabbed one of the pieces and took a big bite, not because she was particularly hungry, but because she didn't want to make the man angry.

"Is it good?" Howard Lee asked.

She nodded.

"Drink all your milk, too."

She eyed the cup of chocolate milk, wishing she had the nerve to tell him she didn't like chocolate in her milk, then thought better of it.

"When can we go outside and play?" Justine asked.

Howard Lee's frown deepened. The dilemma of keeping his family intact was warring with the knowledge that growing children needed fresh air and sunshine.

"After we move. When we get to our new house, then you can go outside, all right?"

The food suddenly knotted in Justine's stomach. She didn't want to go anywhere with the man but back to her real home. She thought of Charlie, her puppy, and her mother and daddy. She wondered if they cried for her like she cried for them.

"I want my mother," Justine muttered, then took another bite.

Ignoring her discontent, Howard Lee shifted Amy Anne to a more comfortable position, then picked up the hamburger and offered her a bite. At his bidding, Amy opened her mouth, accepting the food without acknowledging the giver.

"See, Amy Anne, just like you like it," Howard Lee said. "Is it good?"

Even if she'd been capable of answering, she would have been hard-pressed to tell Howard Lee what he wanted to hear. There was no longer such a thing as "good" in Amy Anne's world.

Hiding his frustration, he dabbed at a dribble of ketchup hanging at the corner of her mouth and then offered her a drink of milk. She drank without purpose, neither acknowledging hunger or thirst, but simply acquiescing to his demands. It wasn't what he wanted, but her withdrawal had left him with no leverage.

"When you finish your food, we need to take our baths and get ready for bed," Howard Lee said.

Justine looked down at her half-eaten burger and wanted to cry. She wanted to play in her yard and sleep in her own little bed. At home, she always slept with her dolly, Freckles. The man had given her a different dolly to sleep with, but it wasn't the same.

"Drink your milk," Howard Lee said.

Afraid of what he might do if she chose to disobey him, she emptied the glass. Within minutes, both she and Amy Anne were asleep where they sat.

Howard Lee smiled to himself in satisfaction as he began to take off their clothes. It was always easier to bathe them and put on their nightclothes when they were quiet and compliant. He set Amy Anne aside, went into the small bathroom and ran some water in the tub. Then he turned around, looking from one little girl to the other and decided.

"Justine, tonight you can be first."

It was a blessing for the child that the sedation he'd given her had already taken effect. She never knew when he took off her clothes, or carried her into the bathroom and lowered her in the tub. She did not have to suffer the indignity of a stranger's hands upon her body or wonder about the look in his eyes.

Reese Arnaud stared down at the face on the sketch pad, wondering how accurate a child's description was going to be in aiding their investigation. In a way, the image was almost comical. The man Hope described had a wide mouth and thick lips, with short, blond bangs cut straight across his forehead. His big, round eyes were set in an even rounder face. And his teeth. Hope had been adamant about his teeth. The spaces between the teeth were definitely unique. No wonder she'd thought he was a clown.

It dawned on Reese as he fixed the image in his mind that, if the man was the one they were looking for, he might very well be using the oddity of his features to his advantage. Most children loved clowns. What better way to approach a child than with humor?

"So, Hope, what do you think?"

"It's the man, Uncle Reese. It's the man who touched my hair and told me I was pretty."

The connotation behind the words make Reese sick, but he hid his feelings as he leaned forward and gave her a big hug.

"Thank you so much, honey. You've been a big help."

"You're welcome," she said, and then looked up at Mary. "Mommy, may I go outside and play on my swing until supper?"

"Yes."

With the innocence of youth, and unaware of the dangers she had skirted, Hope was out the back door, leaving the adults speechless.

"Just like that," Daniel said.

Mary leaned her head against Daniel's shoulder. "She's little, and thank God, was unaffected by the incident."

Daniel looked at Reese. "What are the odds that the man Hope saw is the man you're looking for?"

Reese shrugged. "Probably far less than we'd like, but we can't afford to ignore anything."

"If there's something else we can do, don't hesitate to ask."

"Will do," Reese said. "Kelly, pack it up. I want to get back to the department and get this out to the officers."

"Are you going to go public with the picture?" Mary asked.

"We can't…at least not yet. If he's who we're looking for, we don't want to give him a chance to run."

"Yes, of course. I wasn't thinking. I just want this man found."

"Thanks to your daughter, it might happen."

Mary walked the two officers to the door and then stopped Reese just before he exited.

"Will you let us know what happens?"

"You know we will."

Mary stood and watched until they drove away. As she started back in the house, a car backfired at the corner of the block. She jumped and spun, her eyes wide and startled. Only after she realized what she'd heard, did she start to relax. She stepped inside, scanning the area with a nervous glance as if she half-expected to find danger lurking nearby, then she shut the door and went back into the kitchen.

Daniel was standing at the window, watching Hope play. She put her arms around his waist and laid her head in the middle of his back. As they stood together in silence, she felt a shudder run through him.

"Daniel?"

"What?"

"What are you thinking?"

"How do we keep her safe?" Then he turned around and took Mary in his arms. "I'm not referring to just this incident. How do we ever let her out of our sight again?"

Mary knew how he felt, but she'd learned the hard way that living in fear was not really living at all.

"We love her with all our hearts, teach her everything we know to help her make the right choices, and after that, Daniel, it's all up to God."

"God? Where was he when those two little girls were taken? Why are men like that allowed to live? Tell me that."

Mary had lived with negative thinking for six years and it had nearly killed her.

"God doesn't do that stuff, Daniel, but he's there to help us through it when it happens."

Daniel sighed. "I know. I didn't mean what I said, it's just that this is scary as hell."

"I know, but for Hope's sake, we've got to keep everything as ordinary as possible."

"Yes, I know you're right, but it's not going to be easy."

Mary slid her arms around his neck and then kissed the small indentation on his chin.

"Who said being a parent was going to be easy?"

Daniel took one look at the expression on Mary's face and groaned beneath his breath.

"Are you thinking what I think you're thinking?"

"Probably, but it's going to have to wait."

"This doesn't have to wait," Daniel said, and slanted his mouth across Mary's lips.

It was just after midnight when Mary woke and found herself alone. She lay there for a moment, listening to the sounds within the house. Somewhere a faucet was dripping. She could hear the occasional plink as the water hit something metal. Outside, a wind had come up, causing one of the limbs of the live oak to rub against the window nearest the bed. The intermittent scratch of wood against glass set her nerves on edge. Still wondering where Daniel had gone, she got out of bed and went across the hall to check on Hope.

The room was dark, lit only by the Little Mermaid nightlight plugged in near her bed. God...six years of her daughter's life that she could barely remember. She was past wondering how this had happened. That she had them back in her life was all that she would let matter.

A gust of wind rattled the windows across the hall. She looked up just as a streak of lightning slashed through the darkness. One second it was there, brilliant and dangerous in all its fury, and then it was gone. She shivered as she reached for the curtains, pulling them shut and hoping that the approaching storm wouldn't disturb Hope's sleep. Another gust of wind slammed against the house, followed by a second clap of thunder. Hope seemed undisturbed by the noise. Satisfied that her daughter was well, she pulled the covers back over her shoulders and then went in search of Daniel.

The lower level of the house was in shadows, but she thought she felt a draft on her bare feet as she moved through the rooms. Surely a door had been opened, but where? More to the point, she should be asking herself why?

"Daniel?"

She held her breath, waiting for an answer that didn't come. She continued through the house, her anxiety growing as she looked in every room. She hurried into the dining room and tested the French doors on the off chance that he'd gone out the back, but they were still locked.

Anxiety changed to panic as she paused in the living room, trying to focus. What was she missing? He couldn't just disappear.

While she was debating about where to look next, she felt cold air on her feet again and realized the front door was ajar.

Thunder rumbled. As she moved toward the window, another slash of lightning seared the air, momentarily lighting the dark. In that brief moment, she saw someone standing beneath the portico. Another flash of lightning came and went, and in that moment she recognized the set of Daniel's shoulders. Almost weak with relief, she dashed outside and into his arms.

He'd been out here for what seemed like hours, still troubled that his daughter's safety had been breeched and that she was now involved in a police investigation. Mary had cried herself to sleep in his arms and it had been all he could do not to cry with her. His heart ached, he felt sick to his stomach and he was afraid to close his eyes. He was not a violent man, but he didn't want to think about what he'd do if he came face-to-face with the man who'd messed with his child.

The approaching storm mirrored his angry emotions. Turning his face to the wind, he lifted his chin. The force of it almost took his breath away. The first droplets of rain were just starting to fall when he heard the door open behind him. He turned just as Mary burst from the house.

The storm was upon them now, and even though he had been somewhat sheltered by the portico, the blowing wind and rain immediately plastered their clothes to their bodies as she threw herself into his arms.

"Mary, darling…what's wrong?"

"I thought you were gone."

He turned her in his arms, using his body to shelter her from the storm, and ran with her toward the house. Once inside, he shut and locked the door behind them. Almost immediately, she started to shake.

"Sweetheart…talk to me…tell me what's wrong."

"I woke up and couldn't find you. I thought it was over. Just like before."

Daniel frowned. She wasn't making any sense.

"Over? You thought what was over? And what do you mean…like before?"

"Nothing. Never mind. Just love me, Daniel. Don't let me go."

"Come here to me, baby…never doubt me, Mary Faith. Never."

Daniel picked her up and carried her up the stairs. By the time he got to their bedroom, she was shivering from the cold, her nightgown wet and clinging to her body. He set her on her feet and then shut the door behind them. When the tumblers turned in the lock, he took the hem of Mary's gown and lifted it over her head.

She sighed, shuddering slightly from the chill, as well as

from want. Her breasts felt heavy, throbbing with a longing echoed low in her belly.

"Daniel…"

"I know, baby…I know."

Rain splattered against the window as Daniel laid her on the bed. When he crawled in beside her, she lifted her arms and pulled him down to her side.

"I love you, Daniel. You will never know how much."

"I love you, too, baby."

"Show me."

Daniel brushed a kiss across her lips and then did as she asked.

Mary watched Daniel's head dipping toward her, saw his lips parting slightly, smelled the rain on their bodies, then closed her eyes and waited to be swept away by passion.

It didn't take long.

Without foreplay. Without warning. Daniel was on top of her and then in her. Mary parted her legs and arched to meet him, and when he started to move, she met him stroke for stroke.

Outside, the storm was passing, but inside, it had just begun. Daniel had long since lost focus on anything but the feel of being inside his Mary Faith. Her sweet heat wrapped around him, pulling at every nerve ending on his body, making him crazy with the need to let go. Harder and harder, faster and faster; the mating had gone beyond passion to madness.

Mary clung to his shoulders with a feral intensity, focusing on the building heat between her legs. Her heartbeat pounded against her eardrums, deafening her to everything but the uneven sounds of her own breaths.

In their need to reaffirm their faith in each other, they had taken their fear and desperation and turned it into passion. Using the mind-blowing pleasure of sexual release for an antidote, they had created an emotional fire, and they were burning right down to the bone.

One second Mary was with Daniel stroke for stroke and the next she began to shatter. The rush from the climax all but pulled her off the bed. With an inarticulate cry, she wrapped her legs around Daniel's waist and held him deep inside her. In that instant, his own control finally snapped. A guttural groan ripped up his throat as he spilled himself into her. Still shaking from the adrenaline rush, he collapsed.

"Oh, Daniel…"

"Oh, yeah," he said softly, then pulled her head on his chest and just held her, using her for the anchor that would keep him from complete disintegration.

"Mary…my Mary."

Shuddering slightly as the last convulsions of her climax rippled through her body, Mary lay without moving, savoring Daniel's warmth and strength, as well as the pleasure that only he could give her.

"Go to sleep, darling," Mary whispered.

Daniel was uneasy about letting down his guard, but his trust in Mary Faith was complete, and so he tunneled his hands through her hair and closed his eyes. A short time later he had fallen asleep, his breathing in perfect rhythm to hers.

Howard Lee clocked in at Savannah Memorial Hospital and then proceeded to the basement where the employees' lounge was located. He put his lunch in the refrigerator, along with a sixteen-ounce bottle of pop, then took off his jacket, shaking off the raindrops before hanging it inside his locker. He took out a pair of coveralls and pulled them over his street clothes, then exited the lounge and headed toward the storage room. A few minutes later he had filled his cleaning cart and was ready to begin his shift on the third-floor pediatric ward. He had always planned on furthering his education, but taking care of his mother in her waning years had ended most of that. And he'd never been able to channel his loneliness afterward into anything substantial. Now, since he'd embarked upon the quest to create his own family, his lifestyle precluded any long-term commitment to getting a degree. Besides, Howard Lee was of the belief that manual labor was good for the body. His father had been a drywall contractor and he'd grown up watching men make a living by manual skill, as well as physical strength. He did not consider it beneath him to clean floors and toilets, and besides, the job was perfect—low-key and virtually anonymous. He was counting on the fact that the people who push the brooms were all but invisible, and when it was time to move on, he would not be missed.

He moved from room to room on the floor, doing what he'd been hired to do without communicating with anyone else. Only now and then did a nurse address him, and when they did, it was impersonal.

Yesterday he'd overheard two nurses talking and only after he'd listened for a moment, realized they'd been talking about him. They thought he was slow-witted. Retarded, his mother used to say. But he wasn't. He knew because people who were slow-witted couldn't take care of themselves, and he'd been taking care of himself and his mother almost all his life. He started to tell them they were wrong—that he not only took care of himself and his two daughters—but he also drove a car. Then he discarded the notion. He didn't care what they thought.

He picked up a handful of new trash bags and looped them on his belt, then moved into the next room. Only a few more hours, and he could go home to his girls.

Chapter 9

It had been a long night and it was just after 7:00 a.m. when Howard Lee got home. He was tired and in desperate need of sleep, but first, he had to feed his daughters. He reminded himself it was a sacrifice that every good parent must make—tending to their children's needs before tending to their own. In lieu of the hot food he normally served, he filled two bowls with cereal, got cups and spoons from the cabinets, plucked a couple of bananas from a bowl on the sideboard and set it all on a tray, then headed for his room. Kicking aside the throw rug, he set the tray on his bed, lifted the cellar door and called down to the girls.

"Good morning, my darlings…Daddy's home."

He thought nothing of the fact that they didn't answer, but when he got to the bottom of the stairs and realized they were still in bed, he frowned.

"Girls…breakfast. I brought your favorite Crunchy Crispies."

One of them moaned as he set the tray on the table and turned toward the twin beds. He lifted the covers and started to shake them awake.

"Girls…wake up. Breakfast is ready."

Justine whimpered but didn't open her eyes. Amy Anne

rolled limply beneath his touch. He frowned. Something wasn't right. They'd never behaved this way before. Then he noticed the bright red flush on their cheeks and laid the back of his hand against Justine's forehead. It was hot to the touch. His heart skipped a beat as he did the same to Amy Anne. She was even hotter. He panicked.

Oh Lord. Oh no.

This hadn't been part of the plan. His babies were sick and taking them to a doctor was out of the question. The authorities would find out that the adoptions weren't final and then they would take them away from him. But what could he do?

Mary woke slowly, coming from a deep, dreamless sleep to total consciousness in tiny increments, remembering the panic of thinking Daniel had disappeared, then finding him standing out in the storm, like a soldier on sentry. She shivered, reliving the abandonment of their lovemaking and remembering that she had barely existed when she'd lost him before. She could hear the shower running in their bathroom and closed her eyes, picturing his big, beautiful body all steamy and wet. Before she could follow up on the thought of joining him, she heard the door to their bedroom open. She rolled over and smiled as Hope peeked inside. Seeing Daniel in the child she'd given birth to made the love she felt for her even more intense.

"Hey, little girl...you're awake awfully early."

"Mommy, can we have waffles?"

Mary grinned. "*May* we have waffles."

Hope's little brows knitted in confusion. "That's what I asked you. I thought you would know."

Mary laughed, and pulled back the covers. "Want to get in bed with me for a while?"

"Am I getting waffles?"

"You bet," Mary said.

"With peanut butter and jelly instead of syrup?"

"If you can eat them like that, I can cook them," Mary promised.

"Goody," Hope said, and crawled in bed with Mary, dragging her one-eared bunny as she went.

"Why don't kids ever sleep late on Saturdays?" Mary muttered, more to herself than to Hope, as she scooted her close to her side.

Hope looked at her mother as if she'd suddenly lost her mind for asking such a dumb question.

"Because we'd miss the best cartoons," she said, and pointed toward the television mounted on the wall. "Can I watch cartoons until Daddy is through taking his bath?"

"If you'll say *may,* and not *can.*"

Hope grinned. "May."

"May what?" Mary asked.

"I don't know," Hope said, then she suddenly smiled. "Oh! I know! May I watch cartoons and may I have waffles! Right, Mommy?"

Mary wrapped her arms around her daughter as she laughed aloud.

"Yes, that's right, sweet pea." She reached for the remote and turned on the TV, then searched the channels until she found the Disney channel. "Okay. Two cartoons, then down to breakfast, okay?"

Hope nodded, her focus already shifting to the cartoon characters appearing on the screen.

"Hey," Daniel said, as he exited the bathroom in a pair of dilapidated gray sweatpants. "How did I get so lucky as to find my two favorite girls in my bed?"

Before Hope could answer, he pounced, sending her into fits of shrieks and squeals.

Mary escaped, grabbing clothes as she headed for the bathroom. She washed her face and brushed her teeth, dressing quickly before pulling her hair up into a ponytail, shift-

ing her focus from wife to mother with ease, as if she'd done
so many times before.

She paused in front of the mirror, giving herself a quick
glance before turning away. Her hand was on the doorknob
when something made her hesitate. She stood there a moment, staring down at her fingers, absently noting that she'd
broken a nail, and then closed her eyes and took a slow deep
breath. There was no earthly way she could explain what
she suddenly felt or how she knew it—but she knew it just
the same. She turned around and faced herself in the mirror, curious to know if she looked any different.

But her appearance was still the same—hair the color of
dark caramel that barely brushed her shoulders, bluish-green
eyes in a too-slender face, and lips slightly bruised from the
passion of last night's lovemaking. And still a little too thin.

But she knew that would change.

She reached toward the mirror, laying the flat of her hand
against the glass, then against her belly. Last night had been
magic. She and Daniel had made love—and also a baby.

She shivered suddenly, uncomfortable with the strong
feeling of precognition. Even though another child with
Daniel would be a true blessing, there was too much going
on now to let herself lose focus. Hope's safety had to come
first.

A short while later, the first waffle was baking and the
sounds of Hope's laughter and Daniel's commentary on the
cartoons kept drifting down the stairs. Mary smiled to herself as she got out some plates and began setting the table.
As she did, she went over the things that she needed to do.
There was an accumulation of Daniel's suits that needed to
go to the cleaners, a grocery list that would take at least two
hours to complete, and she'd never been happier. All she had
to do was think back to the emptiness of her life before to
put things in perspective.

"Mommy...is my waffle done yet?"

"Almost," Mary said, as Hope slipped into her seat at the table. "Where's Daddy?"

"Right behind her," Daniel said, as he came in the kitchen and swooped Mary off her feet, then kissed her soundly in front of Hope.

Hope giggled. "Daddy's funny."

"Daddy makes Mommy's toes curl," Mary whispered, careful that only Daniel could hear.

Daniel grinned. "Given another chance…I can do better than that."

"Be still my heart," Mary said, and wiggled her eyebrows.

"Mommy…my waffle!"

Mary spun out of Daniel's arms and headed for the waffle iron.

"One waffle, coming up!"

"With peanut butter and starberry jelly?"

"Of course," Mary said. "Is there any other way?"

"One can only hope," Daniel muttered, and poured himself a cup of coffee before taking his seat.

Mary took the waffle out of the waffle iron and put in on a plate, then began fixing it as Hope had ordered. It wasn't until she was carrying it to the table that she realized her memories were changing. It seemed she'd done this countless times before.

"Yum, Mommy. You always make the best breakfasts," Hope said, and then took her first bite.

"Always?" Mary asked.

"As long as I can remember," Hope mumbled.

As long as she can remember. Mary turned away quickly and began pouring batter into the waffle iron to make another waffle, unwilling for anyone to see that her eyes were filling with tears.

"What's on the agenda, today, honey?" Daniel asked.

"For starters, clothes to the cleaners and groceries."

"Hope and I can take the clothes to the cleaners and pick up some fertilizer for the lawn at the garden center. You make the grocery run and we should all be back home together about the same time. How's that for organization?"

Mary took a deep breath and made herself smile. "It's perfect. Thank you."

Daniel winked at his daughter. "It's our pleasure, isn't it Hope?"

"Yes, we'll help you, Mommy. We're your good helpers, aren't we?"

"You sure are," Mary said. "I don't know what I would do without you…either of you."

She poured a glass of juice for Hope and took it to the table, lingering long enough to smooth her hand down the back of the little girl's hair. Her hands were shaking as she went back to retrieve the next waffle, because she *did* know what it was like to be without them. It's just that they would never understand.

Howard Lee slipped into the lower level of the hospital where he worked and made a beeline for his locker. It was his day off, but no one would know the difference. His job schedule was the last thing of concern in a place where, daily, people fought for their lives. Once in his hospital coveralls with the ID badge clipped to his pocket, he was all but invisible to the staff. He dressed quickly, grabbing a mop bucket and a mop to use as cover in case he was questioned, then headed for the pediatric ward. The main pharmacy for the hospital was on a different floor, but each floor stored a small supply of certain drugs, and he knew where they were kept. All he had to do was create a diversion, take what he needed and no one would be the wiser. He'd heard the staff commenting about a strain of flu going around and decided that was what had made his girls sick. He also remembered enough from his own childhood illnesses to guess what medicines a doctor might prescribe.

Moments later, he exited the elevator on the third floor, pausing a moment to locate the staff on duty, then waited until the hall was empty. Without hesitation, he pulled the fire alarm and then slipped into a laundry closet, well aware that an evacuation would immediately begin. In the confusion, he could get what he needed and be gone before anyone knew what he'd taken. Oh sure, they would eventually miss the drugs, but since he'd clocked out at seven this morning, he would be beyond suspicion.

The sounds of running footsteps sounded in the hallway as nurses began calling out to each other, readying to evacuate their floor. As soon as the footsteps moved away, Howard Lee stuffed his employee ID into his pocket and slipped out of the closet. Two nurses ran past him as he ran toward the drug room behind the nurses' station, but just as he predicted, they paid him no mind. He had to restrain himself from smiling as he slipped behind the desk and then into the room behind.

With little effort, he picked the lock on the drug cabinet, opened the doors, and reached for a bottle of penicillin, when he suddenly remembered the Medic Alert bracelet that Amy Anne wore. She was allergic to penicillin. His mother had been allergic to penicillin. He would have to take a substitute for her. After a quick scan of the shelves, he took two different antibiotics, slipped the vials inside his pocket and relocked the cabinets. On the way out of the room, he grabbed a handful of disposable syringes and headed for the stairwell at the far end of the hallway.

Within minutes, his coveralls were back in his locker and he was leaving through the employees' lounge just as the first of the fire trucks arrived. Fifteen minutes later, he pulled into the driveway of his home, parked in the garage, then dashed into the house. He hurried through the rooms, then down the stairs into the cellar.

Panicked that the girls didn't appear to have moved, he took the antibiotics and two syringes from his pocket, then hurried to their bedside, his heart pounding with fear. At that moment, he realized he hadn't considered the dosages. What if he gave them too much and they died?

Groaning, he dropped onto the mattress at the foot of Amy Anne's bed, his legs too weak to stand. Their breathing was shallow, their faces flushed. He kept thinking that if he did nothing, they would only get worse. They might even die. He was still trying to decide what to do when Justine rolled over on her back and started to cry.

"My head's hot. I want my Mommy. Please, I want my Mommy."

That did it.

Howard Lee set his jaw and took out the first syringe, shook the vial of penicillin because it seemed like a prudent thing to do, and then drew the syringe half-full. He started to pull back the covers and then remembered the area where he administered the shots needed to be disinfected. He grabbed some cotton swabs and a bottle of alcohol from the bathroom then hurried back to the girls. Gritting his teeth, he reached for Justine.

He'd never given anyone a shot before and started to plunge the needle into her tiny arm when he realized he was doing it all wrong. Children's arms were too small. There wasn't enough muscle. It had to go in a hip.

He set the syringe down on the bedside table and pulled down her covers. She whimpered in protest and pushed at his hands as he tugged at the hem of her gown.

"No, no," Howard Lee said. "Daddy is sorry, but he has to do this."

He rubbed the alcohol swab on her backside, took a deep

breath and plunged the needle into her flesh, praying that he was doing this right.

The little girl wailed as the antibiotic went in—a high-pitched, feverish squeal that tore at his conscience. He told himself her shriek was from the shock of the needle prick and not an overdose of medicine, but he couldn't be sure until some time had passed.

Still shaking, he withdrew the used syringe and laid it aside, got out a fresh one, drew a dose from the other vial for Amy Anne and gave her an injection, too. The fact that she didn't even acknowledge the pain, was, to Howard Lee, even more frightening.

Once the medicine had been given, he got a washcloth and a basin of cool water and proceeded to bathe their arms and faces. Afterward, he put them in fresh nightgowns and then sat beside their beds, watching until they fell back asleep.

Convinced that he'd done all he knew to do, he gathered up the uneaten food and medicine and went upstairs. As always, he closed the cellar door and locked it behind him, but for the first time since he'd "adopted" the girls, he felt guilt.

He'd gone to great lengths to make sure that their room had been well-lit and ventilated, and that they had plenty of toys and games to entertain them, but it was still a cellar all the same. And, no matter how many ways he tried to justify it, there was nothing healthy about raising children below ground. In his single-minded intent to acquire a family, he'd thought more of himself than the children. He should have provided different accommodations—certainly safer ones. But that was hindsight. He had to deal with the ramifications of what he'd done and then make it better.

He put the antibiotics into the refrigerator then dumped the uneaten food into the garbage disposal. Although his body was crying out for sleep, there were too many things to be done before he could let himself rest, the first of which was to buy food that would be more enticing for sick children.

He popped a couple of No-Sleeps into his mouth and washed them down with a glass of milk, then started to make a grocery list. The first item he wrote down was soup. As a child, it was what his mother had fed him, and his mother had always done what was right.

He finished the list, then went to check on the girls one last time before leaving the house. They seemed to be resting a little easier. Satisfied that he had done the right thing, he hurried back up the stairs and out the door to the supermarket.

Reese Arnaud sat at his desk, staring at the sketch of the blond-headed man with funny teeth. It had gone out last night with the late shift of officers and even though he'd known it would be a long shot, he'd hoped for some news this morning when he'd come to work.

But when he'd reached his desk and found nothing but a handful of phone messages regarding other cases, his hopes had been dashed. Disappointed, he reached for his coffee cup. Phone time was prime time for sneaking that extra jolt of caffeine, and something told him he was going to need it today.

A short while later, he had returned all the calls and was finishing up some paperwork when his gaze fell on the sketch once again. He picked it up, then cursed softly beneath his breath. The more he looked at it, the more he realized what a stretch this was going to be. Just because some man got too friendly with one little girl on public school grounds did not mean he was the person responsible for the disappearance of two others. The world was full of perverts.

Assuming that this one was the one they were looking for was too much to expect.

A muscle jerked at the side of his jaw and he could feel another pulling at the corner of his eyelid. They needed a break in this case—and soon. He had to find those missing girls. Maybe then he would be able to sleep.

Mary stood at the door waving goodbye to Daniel and Hope, then hurried back into the house to get her purse. Daniel had promised Hope a trip to the park this afternoon and Mary wanted to go, too. Being given a second chance had made her all too aware of how precious life was and how swiftly it could be taken away.

As she swung her purse over her shoulder, something bumped against her side. Frowning, she thrust her hand into the bag. Moments later, her fingers curled around her cell phone. Her purse was already heavy and she started to leave it behind, then at the last second, changed her mind. With one last glance around the room, she hurried out the door, taking care to lock it behind her. A short while later she was pulling into the supermarket parking lot with nothing more serious on her mind than what kind of breakfast cereal to buy.

Howard Lee was standing in the soup aisle, debating with himself as to whether it would be more judicious to purchase dehydrated soup that came prepacked in envelopes or the canned kinds that only needed to be heated. He wished his mother was still alive. She would know which kinds of soups sick children preferred.

A woman with two toddlers at her heels turned down the aisle in which he was standing. He watched her coming and considered asking her for advice, but her children were raising such a fuss he decided against it. He winced at the shrillness in her voice as she yelled at one of the kids to shut up. It was a good thing he'd decided against talking to her. She wouldn't have anything positive to say.

Frustrated, he picked up a can of chicken noodle soup and began reading the instructions. Heat and eat seemed simple enough. Maybe that would work. He tossed a half-dozen cans in his shopping cart and then moved slowly down the aisles, adding a box of crackers, a couple of jars of flavored applesauce and a small bag of vanilla wafers.

He was on his way to the checkout counter when he remembered he was almost out of milk and juice. Wheeling the cart in a quick one-eighty, he found himself face-to-face with a pretty dark-haired woman who was just turning down the aisle. Their carts bumped slightly and then each of them swerved in an opposite direction.

"Oh! Excuse me!" Howard Lee said, and then smiled bashfully. "These things need horns and sirens on them, don't they?"

Mary started to apologize for her own inattention to what she'd been doing and then she focused on his smile. She knew he was waiting for a response from her, but she couldn't speak for staring at the spaces between his teeth.

"Ma'am...are you all right?" Howard Lee asked, thinking he must have bumped her harder than he'd first believed.

Mary blinked. "Uh...yes...I'm fine." She took a deep breath, trying to calm a racing heart as her gaze slid to his face. A tall skinny man with yellow hair, round eyes and funny teeth. A clown face. Just like Hope had described.

Howard Lee frowned. What was wrong with this woman? Then he looked at her again, thinking she looked vaguely familiar, but he couldn't place where he'd seen her. Shrugging it off, he gripped the shopping cart.

"I'll just be going then," he said. "I need to get home to my girls. They're not feeling too well."

He steered his cart around Mary and moved toward the far end of the store where the refrigerated section was located.

* * *

Mary's heart was pounding erratically as she thrust her hand in her purse, searching for the cell phone. She pulled it out with a jerk, then punched in the numbers to Daniel's office with trembling fingers. Twice she messed up and had to start all over. By the time she got the right numbers entered, she was shaking all over.

She closed her eyes as she counted the rings, praying that he would answer.

Howard Lee had the milk in his cart and was reaching for the orange juice when he remembered where he'd seen the woman—at the school—picking up the little girl he was going to adopt. But she hadn't seen him, so it didn't make sense why she would have been staring at him in that way.

He put the orange juice in his cart and then started toward the checkout stand, when he caught sight of her again. She was still in the same aisle, and using her cell phone. That, in itself, didn't set off any alarms until she looked up and saw him watching her. The fear on her face was shocking. In that moment, he knew it was over. He didn't know how it had happened, but he knew that she knew.

The phone was still ringing and Mary was trying to figure out where Daniel had gone and why he didn't answer when she looked up and saw the clown man watching her from the end of the aisle.

"Oh God, oh God," she muttered, debating with herself as to what to do. Then it hit her. Reese. She should be calling Reese Arnaud, not Daniel. She disconnected her call and quickly punched in 9-1-1.

"Savannah P.D., what is your emergency?"

"This is Mary O'Rourke. I'm in Vinter's supermarket and I need you to tell Detective Reese Arnaud that the man he's looking for is here."

"Ma'am…are you in danger?"

"No, I don't think so," Mary mumbled, and then glanced over her shoulder. The man had disappeared. "Oh no," she muttered.

"Ma'am?"

"He's gone," Mary cried. She abandoned her cart in the middle of the aisle and started running toward the front of the store. If he got out of the store before the police arrived, there would be no way of telling which direction he'd gone.

"Who's gone, ma'am?"

"The man! The man!" Mary muttered, resisting the urge to scream. "Just tell Reese Arnaud! Please! He'll know who I mean."

"Yes, ma'am, your message is being relayed at this moment, but I need you to stay on the line."

"Yes, yes, I'm still here," Mary said, puffing slightly as she bolted through the checkout line and out the front door, the phone still pressed to her ear.

She paused in front of the store, searching the parking lot with a frantic gaze, unaware that Howard Lee was watching her from behind the corner of his van.

He'd tossed the groceries into his vehicle and was debating with himself about driving away when he'd seen the woman come running out of the store with the phone still in her hand. At that point, he'd known his suspicions were correct. His first urge was to escape, but he couldn't risk leaving her there. The way she kept looking around the parking lot made him think she was waiting for the police, and that left him no choice.

He jumped in his van and quickly backed out of the parking space, then circled the lot and headed for the front of the store. The woman was still there, the phone clutched to her ear. Knowing the tinted windows in the van would conceal his identity right up to the moment he opened the door, he drove straight for her.

* * *

Mary was frantic, certain that she'd lost sight of him for good.

"Please," she begged of the dispatcher. "Did you tell Detective Arnaud? If they don't hurry, it's going to be too late."

"Yes, ma'am, he got the message," the dispatcher said. "The police are on the way. Just stay where you are until they arrive, okay?"

Frustrated, Mary moved a little farther away from the front of the store, still searching for sight of a tall blond man between the parked cars. A white van was coming toward her, then slowing down in front of the loading zone, and she took a couple of steps backward to get out of the way. The van stopped in front of her. She heard the driver's side door open, then heard the footsteps of the driver circling the van.

Before she could react, she was face-to-face with the man she'd been seeking. She threw up her hands and started to run, when he grabbed her by the arm.

"No!" She screamed. "Help! Somebody help me!"

She clawed at his arm, trying to pull herself free. One moment she was screaming bloody murder and then everything went black as he hit her with his fist. She hit the pavement with her elbow, then her chin, but never felt the pain. Seconds later, he dragged her off the street, flung her into the van and sped away.

Her phone was on the pavement beside her purse as the clerk who'd witnessed the event came running out of the store. She picked up the phone as the 9-1-1 dispatcher kept asking if something was wrong.

"Yes!" the clerk cried. "The woman you were talking to has just been abducted by a man in a white van. Please hurry. They're getting away."

Chapter 10

Daniel pulled up in front of the house and parked in the shade of the portico, then glanced in the back seat. Hope was still asleep. Opening the door quietly, he unlocked the house and then went back to the car to carry her inside. She roused briefly.

"Daddy, are we home?"

"Yes, honey, we're home."

"I want bunny," she muttered, without opening her eyes.

"He can take a nap with you, okay?"

She nodded once without bothering to answer.

He smiled as he carried her up the stairs, then down the hall to her room. He pushed the door inward with the toe of his shoe and then laid her on her bed, tucking the one-eared bunny beneath her arm and a blanket over her legs.

She fidgeted briefly, then settled.

Daniel watched until he was sure she was still sound asleep, then hurried back down the stairs to unload the car. He was just coming out of the house as Reese Arnaud pulled in behind him. He waved and smiled as he opened the trunk of the car, but Reese didn't smile back. A warning bell went off in the back of Daniel's mind, but it wasn't enough to prepare him for the news Arnaud brought.

"What's wrong?"

Reese sighed. It was days like these that made him wish he'd become a priest like his mother had wanted, instead of following his father's footsteps into law enforcement.

"It's Mary," Reese said. "She's been abducted."

Shock, coupled with a mind-blowing pain, ricocheted through Daniel's mind. He took an unsteady step backward and pointed at Reese.

"No, you're wrong. She's just gone to the supermarket. She'll be right back. Come in and I'll make us some coffee until—"

Reese grabbed Daniel, almost shaking him to make him listen.

"She was on the phone to 9-1-1 when it happened. She said she saw the man we're looking for in the market. I don't know exactly what happened, but he must have overheard her in some way and panicked."

Daniel moaned, then staggered backward against his car.

"No…God, no…not Mary. You've got to be mistaken."

"It's not a mistake," Reese said. "I wish to God it was, but we had an eyewitness. A clerk saw it happening. By the time she got outside, they were gone. We know it was a white van. We've got the first three letters on the license plate and a description on the man that fits the one Hope gave us."

"Why in hell is this happening?"

"If I had to guess, I'd say this is the man who snatched the two little girls."

"But why take Mary?"

"Who knows? But something put him on the alert and he took her, maybe believing she was the only person who could identify him."

Daniel paled. "If that's what he thinks, he'll kill her."

Reese's gut knotted. "I don't know what he's thinking. But he doesn't know about the sketch."

Daniel grabbed Reese's arm. "You've got to release it

now! If the media gets hold of it, he'll realize she's not the only witness. Then he won't think he has to kill her."

"Already got it covered," Reese said. "It went out about a half hour ago, the moment we learned about Mary. We won't take chances with her life, even if it means the man might run."

Daniel's vision blurred. "This can't be happening."

"I'm sorry…so sorry," Reese said.

Daniel stood for a moment, his head down. Reese thought he was crying, then Daniel looked up.

"If he hurts her, I'll kill him."

Reese empathized with Daniel, but as a cop, he had to persuade him otherwise.

"You can't think like that. You have a daughter to raise."

Daniel poked a finger in Reese's chest, his voice so low that Reese had to lean forward to hear.

"You heard me. If he so much as makes her cry, he'll pray to die before I'm through." Then he turned away and strode toward the house.

"Where are you going?"

"To call my parents to come get Hope, then I'm going to look for my wife."

"Damn it, O'Rourke, you're a lawyer. You know better than this. You've got to leave this to the police."

"Then you better find him before I do," Daniel said, and slammed the door in Reese's face.

Mary woke up in a strange bed and in pain. Her face throbbed where the man had hit her with his fist and her right shoulder and hip were stiff and aching. As she rolled from the bed to her feet, sheer terror hit her like a fist to the gut. The man was here—staring at her from across the room. She didn't know how long he'd been there, or what he'd done to her while she'd been unconscious, but the look in his eyes made her want to throw up.

"Who are you?"

"My name is Howard Lee Martin."

"Okay, Howard Lee…I need to know why you are doing this."

He smiled. It made Mary's skin crawl.

"It's all going to work out for the best, you know."

Mary shuddered. The calm, conversational tone of his voice seemed obscene in the face of what he'd just done.

"What's best is that you let me go home to my family."

His smile turned downward. "This is your family. You are home now. You'll soon get used to it. I have a good job and I can take good care of all of us."

Mary stifled her shock. It wasn't enough that the man was a criminal, but he had to be crazy, as well. She wanted to cry—to wail aloud at the injustice of being snatched from a family she'd just regained, but something told her that Howard Lee wouldn't deal well with panic.

"Look, Mr. Martin, I—"

"Not Mr. Martin. Call me Howard Lee and you're going to be Sophie. It was my mother's name. I loved my mother deeply. She would be proud to know you had the same name."

Mary shivered. "My name is Mary, not Sophie. I can't be a mother to your children because I'm already someone else's mother. I have a daughter, Howard Lee. She'll be worried about me."

"I have two daughters and they need a mother, too." Then he pointed over Mary's shoulder. "They haven't been feeling well. See for yourself. They need you far more than your child does. Their medicine is on the table. I've already given them injections for today, but they need to be bathed and fed. I'll leave you to it."

Mary gasped, then turned. For the first time since she'd awakened, she saw another small bed pushed up against the wall. A loud clunk startled her and she spun back around to find the man had disappeared and the door he'd come through was closed. She ran up the steps, screaming for him to come back and let her out, but the door was heavy and obviously locked from above. No matter how hard she pushed, it wouldn't give. Daniel and Hope were bound to be home from their errands by now. When she didn't come home they would be frantic.

She ran her fingers along the edges, trying to find a weakness in the door, to find a way to set herself free, but the man had been too thorough. She felt nothing but cold, smooth steel.

"No," she muttered, then pounded on the door. "No, no, you can't do this! Let me out! Let me out! Somebody help!"

"No one ever comes but him."

At the sound of the voice, Mary spun. The little girl looking up at her from the foot of the stairs resembled Hope so much that it gave her chills. Thinking how close Hope had come to falling into this awful man's grasp, she took a deep breath and then went back down the steps. If this had to happen, thank God it happened to her and not her baby. She dropped to her knees and then lifted a wayward strand of hair from the little girl's eyes.

"Honey…is he your father?"

The little girl frowned. "No. My daddy's nice."

Oh God…oh God. "Do you know long have you been here?"

"I don't know. Lots of nights, I guess."

Mary shuddered, trying to imagine what those nights had been like.

"What's your name?"

"Justine." She pointed toward the bed. "She's Amy Anne, but she doesn't talk."

Mary stifled a gasp. The two missing girls! My God! They were alive after all. She touched a hand to Justine's forehead. It was hot and dry.

"He said you were sick."

She nodded, then her lower lip quivered and she started to cry.

"I want my Mommy."

"I know, baby," Mary said softly, then picked her up and carried her back to the bed.

She lay Justine down, then smoothed the dark tangles away from her feverish face before turning to the other little girl. She lay on the side of the bed next to the wall, her gaze focused on a spot on the ceiling above her head. When Mary touched her face to test for fever, she didn't even blink.

"Amy Anne…is that your name?"

"She won't talk to you. She doesn't talk to anyone," Justine said, and then coughed.

The cough was more like a rattle deep in the little girl's chest. There was a box of tissues, as well as some cough drops and cough syrup on the table beside the bed. Mary reached for the bottle.

"How about we take a little cough medicine?" Mary asked. "It's grape flavored. Do you like grape?"

Justine nodded, then sat up in bed as Mary poured a measure of the medicine into a small plastic cup.

Justine drank it without comment and Mary wondered what else she had endured without complaint.

"Amy Anne has a cough, too." Justine said.

"Then we'll give her some, too," Mary said. "Okay?"

The child nodded, watching intently as Mary slipped an arm beneath the girl's shoulders and lifted her up.

"Swallow it, honey," Mary urged.

Amy Anne opened her mouth and swallowed. When Mary slid her arm out from under her shoulders, she looked so tiny and lost against the bedclothes that it broke Mary's heart.

"Come here, babies…it's going to be okay," Mary said, and then crawled into the bed, took both children into her arms and pulled them close. "I'm here. I won't let him hurt you anymore."

"I want to go home," Justine whispered.

"So do I, sweet baby," Mary said. "So do I."

Mike and Phyllis O'Rourke were doing their best to hide the horror of Mary's abduction from their granddaughter. At Daniel's bidding, they were taking her home to spend the weekend, and Hope was so excited she hadn't realized Mary was not back from the supermarket. It wasn't until she was packed and ready to leave that she mentioned her mother.

"Daddy, I didn't get to tell Mommy goodbye."

Daniel was struggling with tears as he picked Hope up and held her to his chest.

"I'll tell her for you, okay?" he said, as he kissed her cheek.

Hope smiled. "Okay. And give her this, too." She blew a kiss in her own hand and then handed it to Daniel as if it was real.

Daniel pretended to take it and put it in his pocket, then hugged her again before setting her down.

"Mommy's going to love that," he said. "I'll be sure she gets it." He looked at his parents, who were struggling to keep smiles on their own faces, too. "I'll call," he promised.

Mike nodded, while Phyllis didn't trust herself to speak. Instead, she picked up Hope's overnight bag, then took Hope by the hand.

"We'll be in the car," she said.

Mike stayed behind, not knowing what to say, but aware that his son was at a breaking point.

"Daniel...I'm so sorry. I don't know what to say to make this better."

"There's nothing to say."

"Please don't do anything rash. Let the police do their job."

A muscle jerked in Daniel's jaw. "What if this had happened to Mom?"

Mike sighed. "Just remember you've still got a daughter to raise."

"She deserves both parents, Dad, not just me."

"Just be careful," Mike cautioned.

"There's no time for caution. I've got to find her, or life won't be worth living."

"Not even for Hope?"

"No Dad…because of Hope. She needs Mary as much or more than I do. I don't know how long this is going to take, but I thank you and Mom for taking care of her."

Tears welled in Mike's eyes. "No thanks are necessary. Just stay in touch."

Daniel walked his father to the door, then stood on the doorstep and waved until they were gone. The moment he was alone, he went back in the house and headed for his office. He couldn't let himself think about what Mary was going through or he'd lose it completely, but waiting helplessly while someone else went to rescue his reason for living made no sense. Arnaud said the man who took her was the same man that Hope had seen. That couldn't be good. He had to know he'd been made. It also meant that Mary's life was, more than likely, hanging on a very thin thread. He took a deep breath and then swiped his hands across his face.

"Ah God…please…don't take her away from me."

Before he could think past the prayer, the phone rang. He grabbed it immediately, needing it to be Mary.

"Hello."

"Mr. Daniel O'Rourke?"

His heart started to hammer. "Yes, this is Daniel O'Rourke."

"Mr. O'Rourke, how much do you pay for your long distance service?"

Daniel stared at the phone in disbelief and then slammed the receiver down on the cradle. Seconds later, he picked up the paperweight and flung it angrily toward the fireplace.

It hit the brick firewall with a vicious thud then shattered in a dozen pieces.

"Damn, damn, damn it all to hell!"

He'd talked big to Reese Arnaud, but the truth was he didn't have the first idea of how to start looking for Mary Faith.

He slumped against the desk, his gaze wandering aimlessly about the room as he waited for a miracle. He sat that way for several minutes, unmoving—mind blank to everything but the panic threatening to overwhelm him.

It was a bit before he began to realize that he was staring at a small framed picture hanging on the wall. When he finally focused on what he'd been looking at, he reached for the phone. It would take more than a miracle to find Mary Faith. He needed help, and from someone who had no qualms about bending the law.

Bobby Joe Killian tossed his gun and holster on his desk, then sat down in his chair and kicked back with a weary groan. His head hurt, and he would give half a month's wages for a thick steak and a good massage.

The sign on the door to his office read Killian Investigations, but he considered it more than slightly deceiving. The last three cases he'd been on had been more like hunts. Hunting for cheating wives and men who'd jumped bail. The money was good—damned good—but the lifestyle was getting harder and harder to keep up with.

He glanced at his watch and then picked up the phone. It said something for his personal life that the first number on his automatic dial was his bookie.

"Harrison, this is Bobby Joe. Give me five hundred on Merlin's Pride in the fifth."

"Damn it, Bobby Joe. You still owe me for the last race you bet on. What makes you think I'm stupid enough to do this again?"

Bobby Joe grinned as he pivoted his chair toward the windows. The view from his third-floor office was not exactly on the tourist route, but it suited his purposes. Being low-profile was invaluable. The less his face was known, the better he was able to do his job. He thrust his fingers through his dark, too-long hair, absently combing it away from his face, then reached for a couple of peanuts from a dish on his desk and began shelling them onto the floor as he continued to talk.

"Now Harrison, you know damn good and well you still owe me for that last bail-jumper I found for you. The way I see it, I've still got a good fifteen hundred dollars in credit and I'm spending a nickel of it today."

A string of muffled curses rolled through the line and into Bobby Joe's ears. He grinned to himself and popped the peanuts into his mouth as the bookie continued to vent.

"Hey, Harrison…you about finished?"

"Does it really matter?" the bookie muttered.

"Sure it does," Bobby Joe said. "You know I care what you think."

"Bull."

"So…are we still on the same page?"

"Oh, hell yes, I've got the whole book in my lap. Is that what you wanted to hear?"

"It'll do," Bobby Joe said, and then cut the man short when his phone started beeping in his ear. "Got another call. Make my bet."

He hit the flash button and then answered again.

"Killian Investigations."

"Bobby Joe, I need your help."

Bobby Joe's feet hit the floor, inadvertently crushing peanut hulls beneath his boots.

"Daniel?"

"Yeah, it's me."

"What's wrong?"

"Mary's been abducted."

"Abducted? My God!"

"Help me," Daniel said.

"Are you home?"

"Yes."

"I'm on my way."

Howard Lee snored in his sleep. The sound roused him just enough that he rolled from his back to his side. A few seconds later, his arm slid off the bed, his fingers dangling toward the floor only inches from the cellar door. He shifted slightly then settled, confident that his family was close by. His alarm was set for 4:00 p.m. It would give him plenty of time to get some rest before preparing his family's supper. His girls would be fine now that he'd brought the woman. Little Justine had been right. Sick children need a mother. He sighed, then licked his lips before falling back into a deep, dreamless sleep.

Mary was afraid to close her eyes. Just the thought of that man coming back and finding her sleeping and vulnerable made her sick to her stomach. Both little girls still lay in her arms, although the fever she'd felt on their bodies earlier seemed to be subsiding.

Even in her sleep, Justine clung to Mary in quiet desperation, her fingers wrapped in the fabric of her clothes. The other child, the one Justine called Amy Anne, was too still. Mary could only imagine the horror that she had gone through, being the first child taken—being put into this place all alone—having to suffer through whatever hell the man had put her through. She wondered how long she had endured before she'd slipped this far away. A child who couldn't cry was a child too close to death.

Mary pulled her closer, holding her gently against her breast. She needed to do something to try and bring Amy

Anne back from the mental precipice on which she was hovering, but wasn't certain what would be safe. The last thing she wanted to do was drive her even farther away from reality, so she started to talk, unwilling to give Amy Anne permission to slip any farther away.

"Amy Anne, my name is Mary. I know you're afraid. We're all afraid, but we're going to be all right. People are looking for us. Did you know that? Oh, yes, it's true. And you know what else? I have a little girl who's just about your age. Her name is Hope. When we get out of here and go home, maybe you and Justine can come to my house and play with her. She would like that, and so would I."

Mary swallowed, fighting back tears. *Daniel...I need you. Please find me.*

Justine shifted on the bed beside her and then opened her eyes. Mary looked down at her and smiled.

"You're still here," the little girl said.

Mary nodded.

Justine sighed. "I thought I'd dreamed you."

"No, baby. It's not a dream." *It's a nightmare.* "I'm right beside you."

Justine sniffed and looked at Amy Anne. "Is she going to talk to us?"

Mary's gaze shifted back to the child in her arms. Her face was pale and immobile, as was her body. If she hadn't felt her warmth, she would have thought she was dead.

"I don't know. I hope so. Did she ever talk to you?"

"No."

"Not even when you were first here?"

"Nope. Not even when I used to cry."

"You don't cry anymore?"

Justine shrugged. "Sometimes...but not so he can see me. It makes him mad when I cry."

Mary shivered. This was hell and he was the devil.

"Does he hurt you?"

"No."

Mary hesitated, almost afraid to ask anything more, but she needed to know what was in store. She had to be prepared for the worst, should it come.

"Does he do other things to you, honey? Does he touch you in places he shouldn't?"

Justine frowned. "He brings us food and brushes our hair. We always fall asleep after supper."

"You mean, after you've bathed and put on your nightgowns?"

Justine shook her head. "Oh no. I don't remember taking baths except I know I'm always clean because I smell good. And I don't put on my own nightgown. The man does it, I guess. I don't remember."

Mary's flesh crawled. *Dear God, he must be doping their food. God only knows what happens after that.*

Chapter 11

Bobby Joe Killian came to a sliding halt in Daniel's driveway. Seconds later, the police cruiser that had been in pursuit pulled in behind him. He got out holding his ID and walked toward the patrolman who was emerging from the car with his gun in his hand.

"Hey, Doolan, is that you?" Bobby Joe asked.

Officer Henry Doolan recognized the drawl behind the too-long hair, then rolled his eyes and holstered his gun.

"Thunderation, Killian, a man driving like a bat out of hell...I should have known it was you." Then he gestured toward the low-slung sports car Bobby Joe was driving. "When did you get that?"

"Last month. Won it in a poker game."

"You ran a stop sign," Doolan growled.

Bobby Joe gestured toward the house. "Sorry. I was in a hurry. Official business."

Doolan snorted. "Oh yeah, right. You expect me to believe that?"

"It's true," Bobby Joe said. "Daniel O'Rourke lives here. His wife has been abducted."

Doolan's smirk disappeared. "The woman from Vinter's supermarket?"

"I don't know where it happened. All I know is a friend called for help and I came. You gonna give me a ticket or what? I've got a good woman to go find."

Doolan cursed beneath his breath and then pointed a finger in Bobby Joe's face.

"You lucked out this time, Killian. Under the circumstances, I'll let this slide. But next time, pay the hell attention, will you?"

"You got it, Doolan, and thanks," Bobby Joe said, and headed for the front door.

Before he could knock, Daniel jerked it open, then saw the police car pulling away.

"I'm not going to ask what that was about," Daniel said.

"It was nothing," Bobby Joe said. "Tell me about Mary."

Daniel's expression never changed, although Bobby Joe could tell he was in shock.

"She's gone."

Bobby Joe pushed his way past Daniel and walked into the house.

"We'll get her back, buddy. Now tell me everything you know."

Howard Lee woke up slowly, trying to remember what was different in his home and then he smiled as he stretched and kicked back the covers. He'd brought a mother home for the girls. He hadn't planned on doing it so suddenly, but considering what had transpired, he'd had no choice.

Reluctantly, he made himself get up. Swinging his legs over the side of the bed, he felt the cool metal of the cellar door beneath his feet, thought of her—his very own Sophie, and smiled.

Mary was sitting cross-legged on the bed with Amy Anne in her lap and Justine scrunched up beside her. A couple of hours ago Justine had awakened and headed straight for the

television. Mary knew this must be part of her normal routine and marveled at the resiliency of youth. Personally, she
would like to give in to her fear and frustration and scream
bloody murder. Before she could follow the thought, she
heard something squeak, then a solid thump followed. She
bolted from the bed and started toward the stairs when suddenly Howard Lee was there, coming down the steps carrying a tray full of food. She stopped in midstep and then
began backing up.

"Sophie…darling!" Howard Lee said. "What a warm
welcome! I couldn't ask for anything more."

Ignoring the fact that he was calling her by another name,
Mary pleaded with him.

"Mr.…please, let us go."

"Howard Lee. You must call me Howard Lee."

The smile on his face was too broad. The look in his eyes
too full of an expectation she could never fulfill.

"The girls are sick. Please let me take them to a doctor."

He put the tray down on the table and then began to set
the places, just as he did at every meal. Ignoring her request, he looked at the girls and gestured toward the food.

"Sit down," he said shortly.

Justine quickly did as he asked, but Mary stayed where
she was.

Howard Lee looked at the girls and then frowned at Mary.

"Sophie! They're still in their nightgowns. As their
mother, I expected you to at least brush their hair and help
them dress. I can't do everything by myself forever. I have
a job, you know."

Great…he's not just a pervert…he's crazy, too.

Even though she was afraid, she held her ground.

"They've been in bed all day and are more comfortable
in their gowns."

Howard Lee's frown deepened. "I don't want them to
appear slovenly."

"Then get them out of this cellar and into the sunshine," Mary snapped.

Howard Lee spun angrily. Suddenly the spoon in his hand took on an ominous appearance.

"You don't talk to me like that," he snapped. "A wife is supposed to honor her husband."

"I do honor my husband," Mary said. "His name is Daniel."

Howard Lee hit her with the flat of his hand. The sound echoed in the sudden silence of the room.

Mary groaned. It was the same place he'd hit her before and the ache went all the way to the back of her teeth. He hovered over her as he glared, but she wouldn't let him see her fear.

"So you're into hitting women as well as stealing other people's children. I wonder what other ugly little secrets you're hiding."

Rage rolled through Howard Lee like tide on the shore, ebbing and flowing in sudden surges. She was talking back to him. How dare she talk back? Didn't she know what a terrible example she was setting for the girls?

"You don't talk to me like that in front of our girls."

Mary doubled up her fists and laughed. It was an ugly, choking sound that was too close to a sob, but she couldn't take it back. It was too late and her rage was too swift.

"Those aren't our girls. They belong to four other people who are desperate to get them back. I don't know why you're doing this but I can tell you it's never going to work."

Howard Lee grabbed her arm and yanked her hard against his chest.

"It's already working," he said. "They're my girls. Do you hear me? I adopted them. The papers will be coming through any day now and then you'll see."

There was coffee on his breath and a fleck of spittle at the corner of his mouth and Mary felt like throwing up.

"What about me?" she asked. "There aren't any papers, real or imagined, that are going to make kidnapping me okay. The police might stop looking for us, but my husband never will."

"Don't threaten me," Howard Lee growled. "I can make you disappear."

Mary's heart sank. It was nothing more than what she'd feared all along, but she'd be damned if she'd let him know it mattered.

"It won't matter how many times you kill me, Howard Lee. He knows what you look like. The police know what you look like, too. You can't hide forever."

Howard Lee paled.

"You're lying."

Mary shrugged. "Believe what you want."

Howard Lee shoved the rest of the food from the tray and stomped up the stairs, dropping the door shut with a resounding thud. Mary flinched at the sound, but by God, she'd stood her ground.

"You made him mad," Justine said.

Mary turned and looked down at the little girl, then grinned.

"I did, didn't I?"

Justine hesitated just a moment and then slipped her hand in Mary's hand and smiled.

Mary winked at her. "I told you it was going to be okay, didn't I?"

Justine pointed at Amy Anne.

"You have to hold her on your lap to help her eat."

Mary nodded. "Okay. Thank you, Justine."

"You're welcome."

Mary went to the bed and picked up the little girl, then sat down at the table with Amy Anne in her lap.

"Hey, kiddo. How about some supper? Looks like we've got chicken noodle soup and cheese sandwiches. Do you like chicken noodle soup? I do. Ooh, and I see chocolate chip cookies for dessert. How about a cookie, Amy Anne?"

She put the cookie in Amy Anne's fingers, then scooped up a spoonful of soup and held it to the little girl's mouth. Amy Anne's lips opened like a baby bird and Mary slipped the soup inside.

Justine looked at the cookie Amy Anne was holding.

"We're not supposed to eat dessert first," she said.

"I know," Mary said. "But this place is different, isn't it? The man broke the rules first, so we can too."

Justine thought about it a moment and then giggled.

Mary wanted to cry. It was the first time she'd seen her really smile.

"Is your soup too hot?"

"Nope. It's just right," Justine said.

"Then eat it up before it gets cold, okay?"

"Okay."

Mary took a bite of her own cheese sandwich and then spooned another bite of soup into Amy Anne's mouth. She was reaching for her juice when she remembered that Howard Lee was doping them with sedatives. She set Amy Anne aside and then picked up the glasses and took them to the bathroom, poured out the juice, and filled the glasses with water. As she walked back to the table, she saw Amy Anne lift the cookie to her mouth and take a bite.

Justine gasped. "Look, Mary! Look at Amy Anne! She's feeding herself."

"Is that good?"

"I think so," Justine said. "I've never seen her do it before."

Mary set the water glasses down and gave Amy Anne a quick hug.

"I'll bet she can do lots of things, can't you honey?"

Mary felt the momentary weight of the little girl's body

against her, as if she'd leaned into the hug, and then the moment was gone.

"You're going to be just fine, little girl," Mary said softly, and pressed a kiss against her cheek. "Now let's eat our supper. Afterward we can play some games or maybe work some puzzles. Do you like to play puzzles?"

Amy Anne didn't answer, but it didn't matter. She was eating on her own.

Daniel stood on the sidewalk in front of Vinter's supermarket, staring down at the pavement where several small specks of blood had been circled with chalk. The area had been roped off with yellow crime scene tape and all of the videotapes from the supermarket's security cameras had been confiscated by the police. While Bobby Joe didn't have access to the tapes, he was working his magic on the clerk who'd witnessed the abduction. Between the flashing smile and his dark, bad-boy looks, Bobby Joe Killian could get just about anything he wanted.

And according to the clerk, this was where Mary had been taken. The man had hit her with his fist and shoved her into a late-model white van. They had the first three letters of the license tag and a description of the man that fit the one Hope had given them, but no idea of where to look first.

Daniel spun away from the blood-spattered sidewalk and looked back into the store where Bobby Joe had gone. He could see him through the window, still talking to the clerk. Daniel doubled up his fists and strode toward the car. He'd never felt this helpless or this afraid. He couldn't let himself think of what Mary must be enduring, or if she was even alive. He sat down inside Bobby Joe's sports car and waited for him to return.

Less than five minutes later, Bobby Joe came out of the store on the run. When he slid behind the wheel, he was grinning.

"Tell me something to make me smile, too," Daniel said.

Bobby Joe started the car and put it in gear, peeling out of the parking lot.

"Do we know where we're going?"

Bobby Joe looked at Daniel and then grinned.

"Hell yes. We're going to find Mary Faith."

Daniel wished he felt as optimistic as Bobby Joe acted.

"What did the clerk tell you that she didn't tell the police?"

Bobby Joe looked at him and then grinned.

"She said the guy is a regular, that he shops in there at least once a week, and for the past few weeks has been buying the same kind of stuff that parents with small kids usually buy."

"How does that help us?"

"If he's recently started buying food geared toward kids, then we can assume he's got some kids to feed. And...if he shops in there on a regular basis, then he must live in the area. I've got a friend in the department of motor vehicles running down the license numbers. Once we get a printout, we can compare it to the addresses in the area. It's all a matter of elimination."

"How long will that take?" Daniel asked.

"I don't know...maybe first thing tomorrow."

Daniel groaned and hit the dashboard with the flat of his hand. "Damn...damn...damn."

"What?" Bobby Joe asked.

"All night...in that man's grasp? I can't let that happen."

Bobby Joe shook his head. "I know, Daniel. I wish to hell I had a better answer."

"It's not knowing that makes it so bad."

"Knowing what?"

Daniel didn't answer and Bobby Joe knew he was hurting bad.

"Talk to me, friend."

Daniel shuddered and had to swallow twice before he could spit out the words.

"What he's doing to her. I don't know what he's doing to her. I imagine the worst. Every minute I breathe without knowing where she is is like a knife in my heart."

Bobby Joe sighed. "We'll find her, Daniel."

"We have to."

"Yeah, I know."

But he didn't. He had no ties to anyone in the way that Daniel and Mary felt about each other, and it was just the way he liked it. If he screwed up, he didn't have to answer to anyone but himself.

Howard Lee drove into the hospital parking lot and parked in his usual space. He reached across the seat and got his lunch bucket from the passenger seat, then grabbed his cap as he got out of the van, taking care to lock it before heading for the employee entrance of Savannah Memorial. The shift change was already in progress as he reached his locker.

"Hey, Martin...how's it going?"

Howard Lee nodded and waved as he got his coveralls off the shelf. He wanted to share the news of his new family with the man, but couldn't take the chance. Not here. Not now. Maybe when they moved it would be better. And he'd been thinking about the move all evening. Even though his Sophie was still in a stage of revolt, it would pass, just like it did with his girls. Of course Amy Anne had gone a little too far the other way, but she would come back when she was ready.

He put on his coveralls, then began to fill his cart with cleaning supplies, making sure he had everything he would need to work his shift before heading for the employee elevator. A couple of women waved at him—one even stopped and spoke a few words. Her name was Mavis. He liked to be part of the machine that ran the hospital even though his education was barely enough to qualify him for cleaning toilets.

The elevator finally arrived and he pushed his cart forward. Mavis followed with her own cart as she continued to talk.

"Did you hear about the break-in on Pediatrics?"

Howard Lee's heartbeat broke rhythm, but only for a moment. There was no way they would know it was him.

"No, I didn't. When did it happen?"

"Earlier this morning, a little before nine."

"Oh…well, I clocked out at seven. I guess that's why I hadn't heard."

"Yeah, me too, but my sister is a nurse on four. She called and told me! Can you believe it?"

Howard Lee shook his head. He didn't really want to get into a conversation about the crime, especially since he was the one who'd committed it.

"Well, here's my floor."

"See you later," she said, and smiled a goodbye as Howard Lee pushed his cart off the elevator onto the Pediatric ward, then headed for the first room on the right.

It was a simple job—one he could perform without thought, leaving his mind free to entertain scenarios of him and his new family—picturing the evening meals together around the table. And the holidays. He couldn't wait for the holidays. Maybe he'd dress up like Santa Claus. The girls would love it, he was sure.

He reached room 301 and pushed the cart up against the wall, grabbed a handful of trash bags as he entered.

The door was open. The two-bed room had only one occupant—a young boy with no hair. Howard Lee knew he was a cancer patient. He also knew the boy was dying. He headed for the bathrooms without looking at the boy, nodding only briefly to the sad-eyed parent sitting quietly at the bedside. He changed out the trash cans, refilled the paper towel holders and made sure there was sufficient antibacterial soap in the dispenser. Then he went to his cart, got the big dust mop from the rack and ran it over the cold, white-tiled floor, making sure to keep his head down and his thoughts to himself. The moment he was through, he was on to the next, taking comfort in the mindless routine of the job.

It wasn't until he neared the nurses' station that his equilibrium shifted. They were talking about the theft. He smiled as he worked, silently congratulating himself on his prowess when one of the nurses saw him and called out.

"Mr. Martin…we're out of paper cups in the break room. Could you bring up a carton?"

"Yes, certainly," he said.

The nurse smiled her thanks and went back to her paperwork. Moments later, the desk phone rang. Howard Lee was still nearby when he heard her answer.

"Pediatrics. Nurse Hanson. Yes sir…send him up, we'll be waiting."

She hung up, then called to a nurse who was coming out of a nearby room.

"Security's coming up to pull the tapes," she said. "I've got to go down to 356. Will you wait and escort them into the drug room?"

"Sure," the nurse said, and moved behind the desk.

Howard Lee straightened abruptly and turned toward the nurses' station then to the room beyond. Tapes? What tapes?

He searched the hallways with a frantic gaze, looking for signs of security cameras, but saw nothing that would put him on alert. He'd been so sure of the territory in which he worked he hadn't thought past the need to get medicine for the girls. But in doing so, he'd moved beyond his safety zone into a place he'd never been, and so might have signed his own arrest warrant.

He grabbed his cart, all but running as he started pushing it toward the employee elevator. Sweat was running down his back and his stomach was rolling in panic as he waited impatiently for the car to arrive. Behind him, he heard the ding as the public elevator stopped on third, heard the near-silent swish as the doors slid inward. He wouldn't turn. He couldn't look. He just held his breath and prayed.

Moments later the employee elevator arrived. The moment the doors opened, he was shoving the cart inside. He fought nausea all the way down to the basement, and the moment the car stopped he was out and running. He shoved his cart into an alcove, stripped off his coveralls and bolted for the exit.

"Hey, Martin…where are you going?" someone yelled.

Howard Lee never answered and didn't look back. He was all the way to the van before he realized he'd left his lunch box in the fridge. He hesitated, wondering if he should go back and retrieve it and then decided against it. There was nothing in it to incriminate him, although he wondered why he cared. He'd already taken care of that by stealing drugs in full view of his employer's security cameras.

His hands were shaking as he unlocked the van and jumped inside.

"Oh God…oh God…oh God."

He jammed the key in the ignition and started the engine, then paused for a moment with his head on the steering wheel. What was he going to do? Yes, he'd planned on moving, but not now. Not without proper planning.

There was a sudden and sharp rap on the window. He jerked. A security guard was standing beside his van. *God!*

"Hey, buddy…are you okay?"

Certain he was about to be arrested, Howard Lee gunned the engine and peeled out of the parking lot, barely missing the toes of the stunned security guard. He needed to get home. All he had to do was get home, then he would be safe. Safe with his girls…and his bride.

Chapter 12

Mary tiptoed out of the bathroom, her skin still damp from the shower. She didn't know what time it was because her watch had been broken when she'd been tossed into the van, but she kept feeling an overwhelming need to wash. It had something to do with being abducted—the mental trauma that rape victims go through in a constant need to wash their abductor's touch from their bodies.

At the thought of rape, she shuddered. She couldn't let herself go there. Whatever else she might still endure was up to God, Daniel and the police. All she could hope was that whatever Howard Lee did to her, he didn't do it in front of the girls.

She tugged at her rumpled clothes, wishing for something clean to put on, then noticed the two little girls had finally gone to sleep. Since her arrival, she'd put them both in one bed, leaving the other bed for herself. Although she was sick at heart about being abducted, and could only imagine the hell that Daniel and Hope must be going through, she didn't regret being here. Now that she'd seen Justine and Amy Anne, she couldn't bear to think of them alone with this man or what he'd made them endure.

She moved to their bedside. Amy Anne might not have

much to say when she was awake, but there was obviously a part of her that was still fighting. Her covers were a mess—wadded at the foot of the bed and in a tangle beneath her feet. Justine slept with her face toward the wall with Amy Anne curled up behind her. Mary couldn't help but think that putting the girls in bed together had been inspired. Before, Amy Anne had refused to instigate any form of communication. Now, she slept with her arm slung around Justine and her nose buried in the middle of her back.

Mary could only imagine the fear their parents must be going through and wished they knew the girls were alive and no longer alone. Exhaustion hit as she bent down to untangle the covers. Her hands were trembling as she straightened the sheets and pulled them back over the girls. It made her think of her nightly ritual with Hope. Instead of going straight to bed, she turned back to the girls.

"Good night, sweet babies," she said softly, kissed them each on the cheek.

She would like nothing better than to strip down to bare skin and crawl between the sheets, but there was no way she would risk being found naked by Howard Lee. He had decided she was going to be the girls' mother. The last thing she needed was for him to decide she would also be his wife.

She started to lay down, then glanced toward the stairwell and frowned. She was so exhausted, but was afraid to close her eyes. What if he came down here while she was sleeping and took one of the girls?

She looked back toward the beds, studying the layout of the room, and then grabbed the foot of her bed and pulled, angling it until it was abutted firmly against the other bed with no space between. Now if Howard Lee tried to get to the girls, he would have to go over her to do it.

Her shoulders slumped as she sat down and kicked off her shoes. Last night she'd slept in Daniel's arms. Who could have known that tonight she would sleep in hell?

Finally, she stretched out. Wincing from sore muscles, she pulled the covers up over her legs and then scooted backward until she could feel the warmth of the girls' bodies against her back.

The shadows from the nightlights cast strange shapes against the walls. She watched, half-expecting them to come to life and decimate what was left of her sanity, but they remained in place. Finally she was satisfied that, for the moment, they were alone and safe. At that point, she began to relax. Just before she drifted off to sleep, something occurred to her that she'd never thought of before.

Maybe there had been more than one reason why she'd been sent back in time. Maybe it wasn't all about being given a second chance with Daniel and Hope. She distinctly remembered that day—the day everything had changed. She'd been standing at the stop light, half-listening to the conversation that the two women had been having about the three missing children. Right after that, she'd found the antique shop and gone inside.

Mary had finally accepted the unbelievable fact that she'd gone back in time and changed the outcome of her own fate, as well as Daniel and Hope's. But in coming back, she'd also changed the fate of these children, as well. Unless Howard Lee had a third child stashed in another location, she'd changed his future, too, because he'd taken her, and not another little girl. And because Hope hadn't died when she was a child, she'd lived to give the police a description of the man responsible for the abductions.

Once, Mary might have thought these notions far-fetched, but not now. Satisfied that she was in the right place whether she liked it or not, she snuggled a little farther beneath her covers and closed her eyes, unaware that their fragile world was about to shatter.

It had started to rain—a soft, gentle shower that fell on the pavement and turned the puddles into psychedelic mir-

rors for the illumination from the streetlights above. Howard Lee drove with a patent disregard for rules, running
through yellow lights, taking corners on two wheels, and
sending up the occasional spray of water from beneath the
van's tires. His thoughts were scattered, his equilibrium
shot. Had his mother still been alive, she would have predicted that he'd react in such a manner. Howard Lee had
never taken surprises well.

When he was about ten blocks from home, he saw the
lights of an all-night ATM. Impulsively, he exited the street
and turned toward the drive-thru, coming to a halt in front
of the machine. Twice, he tried to get his wallet out of his
pocket and both times it slipped out of his grasp. He took a
deep breath, wiped the sweat from the palms of his hands
onto his pants legs, and then reached for the wallet again.
Finally, he got the ATM card and thrust it into the slot, entered his PIN number and took five hundred dollars out of
his account. Once he had the cash in hand, he tried to repeat the process but was denied. Cursing the safeguard his
bank had put on his own account, he pocketed the money
and drove back onto the streets, heading for home.

Minutes later, he pulled into his driveway, hit the garage
door opener, and drove inside. Only after the door was down
and the engine off, did he take a deep breath. His heart was
still hammering, but he was beginning to regain focus.

He was home. The familiarity of his surroundings calmed
his panic. He took another deep breath and got out of the
van. The sounds of his footsteps echoed loudly within the
roomy old garage and he caught himself tiptoeing into the
house, then cursed his foolishness. There was nothing to
be afraid of here. This was his territory. Here was where
he made the rules.

He moved into the kitchen, quickly locking the door behind him, and then headed for the living room, gave the
front door a quick tug to make sure it was locked, too, then
paused.

This wasn't the way he'd planned their future, but plans were made to be changed. He patted his pocket, taking some assurance from the fat wad of bills he'd just withdrawn from the bank, and headed for the bedroom. As he started down the hall, he paused at the door to the guest bedroom, remembering all the preparations he'd made for the arrival of his new daughter, and frowned. After a moment, he sighed, reminding himself that the plan had already changed and the world hadn't come to an end. In fact, things were already better now that his girls had a mother to look after them when he was at work.

Then his frown deepened. Besides getting out of town, he was going to have to find a new job and possibly a new identity. This was a setback he hadn't planned on, but he would find a way to make it work. He had to.

He shrugged off his jacket and dropped it on the back of a chair as he moved across the hall into his bedroom. There were things to be done and not a lot of time to do them. He kicked away the throw rug over the cellar door and then took a key out of his pocket and unlocked the padlock. Halfway down the stairs, he knew something was different. By the time he reached the bottom, he was frowning.

Mary was on her feet, standing between him and the bed where the girls were sleeping.

"Sophie...why aren't you asleep?"

"Stop calling me that," she said sharply. "As for not being asleep, I'm guessing you're curious as to why I'm not doped out of my mind, right?"

His frown deepened. How could she know this so quickly? What kind of a woman had he brought into his home?

"What are you?" he asked.

Mary took a step forward. "The biggest mistake you ever made."

For the second time tonight his fear spiked.

"Don't threaten me," he said, and pointed a finger toward her. "I'm the one in charge." Then he glanced toward the girls, who were obviously no longer asleep, either. "So you choose to sleep on your terms? Fine. But you will live on mine, so I suggest you put our girls back to bed and get some rest. Tomorrow is going to be a very busy day."

"Why? What's so special about tomorrow?" Mary asked.

Howard Lee smiled. "Why…we're moving, that's what. I think it's time for a change of scenery, don't you? After all, you said it yourself. The girls need a more comfortable and healthy environment. I intend to see that they get what they need."

He pivoted quickly and took the stairs up two at a time. The cellar door was down and locked before Mary could react. She felt as helpless now as she had when he'd thrown her in the van. Filled with despair, she dropped down on the bed and covered her face with her hands.

No…oh no…if he takes us away, Daniel might never find us. Please Lord…help me stop him before it's too late.

"Don't cry, Mary."

Mary looked up just as Justine crawled into her lap. She wrapped her arms around the little girl. Once again, she was struck by how strong the spirit could be in such a tiny child.

"I'm not crying, honey. I'm just tired. How about you?"

Justine nodded, then pointed to Amy Anne. "She's sleepy, too, aren't you, Amy Anne?"

Mary turned around. Amy Anne was sitting cross-legged in the bed, picking at a raveling thread on the blanket. She held her breath, hoping that Amy Anne would talk. She didn't get the words, but she did get a brief moment of eye contact before Amy Anne nodded.

"Okay…" she said. "Then let's get some sleep, what do you say?"

"Is the man going to come back?" Justine asked.

"I don't think so. At least not again tonight. But you

don't worry. I'm here and I won't let anything happen to you again."

She gave each little girl a hug and then started tucking them back beneath the covers before stretching out in front of them, using her body as a shield between them and Howard Lee.

She was almost asleep when she felt the brush of a small hand against her arm. Tears welled behind her eyelids as she felt the hesitancy of the touch. Justine was too far away to reach her like this. It had to be Amy Anne. Without speaking, she reached for the tiny fingers and then covered them with her own. There was a moment when she thought she felt hesitance, then quietly, without disturbing the covers, Mary felt the child scooting just a tiny bit closer.

For now, it was enough.

It was raining. Daniel stood at the living room window, watching it fall and praying with every breath in his body that Mary was still alive. There was a growing ache in his gut and what felt like a permanent knot at the back of his throat. He kept alternating with the need to break something or break down and cry. Bobby Joe had gone home hours earlier with a promise to pick him up first thing in the morning, and now he was left alone with the horror of his reality.

He glanced at his watch. It was ten minutes after two in the morning. He needed to sleep, but resting while Mary was missing seemed somehow disloyal. However, tomorrow would be hell if he didn't. Reluctantly, he went upstairs to their room and laid down on the bed without undressing. Within minutes, he'd succumbed to exhaustion.

"Daniel...come and get me."
"Mary? Mary? Is that you?"
Daniel turned toward the sound of her voice, trying desperately to fight his way out of the dream.

"We're alive, Daniel. We're all alive."

"Who's we?"

"Me and Justine and Amy Anne, but we're running out of time. Please, Danny...come and get us before Howard Lee takes us away. We want to go home."

Daniel woke with a gasp and sat straight up in bed.

"Mary?"

He'd said her name out of reflex, although he hadn't expected an answer. He knew he'd been dreaming, but it wasn't like any dream he'd ever had. It seemed as if he'd heard her as clearly as if she'd been lying right beside him. As for the mention of the two little girls, that was weird. What had she called them? Oh yeah...Justine and Amy Anne. And Howard Lee? Who the hell was Howard Lee?

Dismissing it as nothing more than part of the nightmare in which they were caught, he still made a mental note of the names. He would call Reese Arnaud tomorrow and see if any progress had been made. Chances are he'd heard the girls' names on the news and then forgotten them until his subconscious had drawn them up into his dream. As for a man named Howard Lee, he couldn't believe it meant anything. As much as he wanted to think he and Mary were soul mates, he didn't believe in psychic communication.

Too awake now to go back to sleep, he got out of bed and walked to the window. It was still raining. The wet streets had taken on a look of obsidian—their dark, mirrored surfaces a reflection of his soul.

Time passed slowly, and still he couldn't get the sound of Mary's voice out of his mind. It had been so vivid, and the dream so specific. If only he dared believe. He swiped a hand over his face and then turned away from the windows, and as he did, his gaze fell on the bed. It was so damned big—and too empty without her.

Without warning, he started to cry. *Please God, don't let me spend the rest of my life without her in it.*

* * *

Reese Arnaud was at his desk by 5:00 a.m., poring over the computer printout that had come from the Department of Motor Vehicles. He couldn't believe how many people in the city of Savannah owned white vans. He'd quit counting at four hundred and thirty-seven. What was frightening was the thought that the man they were looking for might not even be a resident of Georgia. If that was the case, then the names on this list could be moot.

He poured himself a third cup of coffee as he downed the last bite of his sausage biscuit, then flopped back in his chair. Someone told him yesterday that Bobby Joe Killian was asking questions at the supermarket where Mary O'Rourke had been abducted and that Daniel was with him. It didn't make his job any easier to know that the man he called his friend didn't trust him to bring his wife home. That he had turned to a P.I. with a less than perfect reputation made it worse. Then he frowned. That wasn't entirely the truth. Truth was, Reese couldn't blame him. The little girls had been missing for more than six weeks, and they hadn't had a solid lead until the sketch. If it was his wife, he wouldn't want to wait in the wings, either. He'd be turning over every known perp on the streets and yanking until one of them squealed.

Heartsick and exhausted, he took a long drink of the coffee and then went back to the list, marking off all the names of owners with vans that were more than ten years old.

A short while later, his phone rang. He picked it up without thought, his focus still on the pages.

"Savannah P.D."

"Arnaud…this is Williams in Vice. Got a little piece of video with a person on it you might want to see."

"Unless she's six feet tall and naked, I don't think so," Reese muttered.

The detective chuckled, then dropped another line that got Reese's attention.

"It's not a she, it's a he, and he's stealing medicine from the third floor of Savannah Memorial."

"What's that got to do with me?" Reese asked.

"Well, one of the guys here in Vice thought the perp looked a little like that man in the sketch you've been circulating."

Reese stood abruptly. "I'm on my way."

A short while later Reese was sitting alongside Detective Williams, as well as two other detectives, viewing the tape.

"What do you think?" Williamson asked.

Reese leaned forward, resting his elbows on his knees. Holding the remote, he hit Rewind, then Play. It was the fourth time he'd viewed the piece of tape and still he couldn't be sure.

"I don't know," Reese said. "The tape quality is poor. The images are grainy. It's a tall, blond man, but we don't have a real clear view of his face."

"Yeah, I know," Williams said. "But you don't see a crazy haircut like that every day."

Reese nodded, eyeing the man's bone-straight hair. Williams was right about that. It looked like someone had turned a bowl upside down on his head and trimmed off everything that stuck out from under it.

"I'd feel better about it if he'd smiled for the camera," Reese muttered.

Williams frowned. "What?"

"Oh, nothing," Reese said. "It's just that he's supposed to have this goofy set of teeth. Distinctive enough to set him aside from the crowd, you know?"

"Yeah, okay. So what do you want to do about this?" Williams asked.

Reese frowned. "What does the hospital have to say about the tape? Anyone there identified the man?"

"They've shown it to the nurses on the third floor, but identification is a bust. Supposedly he looks like someone named Barry, who's an ex-husband of one RN. Also, someone else said he looks like their brother, but that's a dead-end too because the brother is in the Navy and stationed in the Black Sea. Another said he looked a little like one of the janitors, but that man wasn't even on duty when the robbery went down."

Reese thought of the janitor angle. It made sense.

"It has to be someone who knew the layout of the floor," Reese said.

"Why do you say that?"

"Because my daughter, Molly, had her tonsils out there two years ago. They only have minimal medications on site. The main pharmacy for the hospital is on the first floor."

Williams glared at the two detectives nearby. "Why does he know that and we don't?"

They shrugged and grinned.

"What did he steal?" Reese asked.

Williams looked at his notes. "Some antibiotics. No hard drugs like you would expect."

"What kind of antibiotics?" Reese asked.

"Ummm…ampicillin and something I can't pronounce that the doctor said is used for people who are allergic to penicillin. Also, some hypodermic syringes."

"Oh damn," Reese said, and got up from the chair.

"What?" Williams asked.

"One of the little girls who's missing…she's allergic to penicillin. Her mother says she was wearing a Medic Alert bracelet."

"Oh man…if this is the guy who took them and he's stealing medicine, then that means the girls are sick."

Reese grinned. "No…it means that the girls are alive."

"Oh yeah…right!" Williams said. "So what are you going to do?"

"Before we jump to too many conclusions, I need a list of employees at the hospital and I want the clerk at the supermarket to look at this tape. If she thinks it's the man who snatched Mary O'Rourke, then at least we'll know we're looking for the same perp for all three abductions."

Bobby Joe Killian swerved off the street and into the drive in front of Daniel's house. He stomped the brakes, leaving a streak of black rubber on the pavement as he killed the engine.

Daniel was coming out of the house before Bobby Joe could get out of the car.

"Hurry," Bobby Joe said.

"Why?" Daniel asked, as he slid into the seat.

"You know that pretty little clerk at the supermarket?"

"The one who witnessed Mary's abduction?"

"Yep."

"What about her?" Daniel asked.

"She's going on her way to the police station to look at a tape."

"A tape of what?"

"Not sure," Bobby Joe said, as he peeled out of the driveway and back onto the street.

"How do you know this?" Daniel asked.

Bobby Joe grinned. "We were still in her bed when she got the call."

"You slept with her?"

Bobby Joe shrugged. "Yeah, why not? She's pretty, she's single and she asked."

"Isn't that some kind of conflict of interest?" Daniel asked.

"Not for me," Bobby Joe said.

"Yeah, right. What was I thinking?"

Chapter 13

Reese was still in Detective Williams's office, waiting for the supermarket clerk to arrive when Bobby Joe and Daniel showed up. His first instinct was to give Daniel a hard time for getting mixed up with Killian, and then he looked at his face. The man looked haunted. It was enough to temper his greeting.

"You guys lost?" he asked.

"I want to see the security tape from the hospital robbery," Daniel said.

Reese didn't bother to hide his surprise. "How the hell did you find out about that?"

"A little birdie named Carol told me," Bobby Joe said.

Detective Williams eyebrows shot up toward his hairline. "You know Carol Shane?"

"Intimately."

"Well hell, Killian, is there no woman safe from you in the city of Savannah?"

Bobby Joe grinned. "I have yet to hear a complaint."

Ignoring the byplay between Williams and Killian, Reese turned to Daniel.

"Look, friend, I understand where you're coming from, but trust me, it won't make you feel a damn bit better to see it. We're not even sure the man we've got on film is the same one who took Mary."

Before Daniel could answer, another detective yelled from across the room.

"Hey, Williams. There's a woman here named Carol Shane who says you're expecting her."

They all turned to look at the young blonde who was waiting in the doorway. Williams got up to go meet her, but Bobby Joe beat him to it. In seconds, he was at the door and kissing the woman on the cheek.

Williams snorted beneath his breath. "He's a real piece of work, isn't he?"

"He's a friend," Daniel said. "He came when I called."

Williams looked taken aback. "I didn't mean anything by it. It's just—"

"Never mind," Daniel said. "It doesn't matter. Nothing matters but getting Mary back."

"And those two little girls," Reese added.

"If they're still alive," a detective remarked.

Daniel shoved his hands in his pockets and then looked at the floor. When he spoke it was so low, Reese had to lean forward to hear him.

"According to Mary, they're still alive," Daniel muttered.

Reese jerked as if he'd been hit.

"What the hell do you mean? Have you talked to her? Did you get a ransom call?"

"No, no, nothing like that," Daniel said. "I shouldn't have said anything. Forget it."

"Damn it, Daniel, talk to me."

"Look, I dreamed it, okay?"

"What do you mean, you dreamed it?"

"Last night...I saw Mary. She was telling me she was okay and that the girls were alive. She said Justine and Amy Anne. Are those their names?"

Reese paled. "Yeah. But you could have heard that on the news and forgotten it until last night in your sleep."

Daniel nodded. "I know. It was just so real."

Williams yelled at Bobby Joe. "Hey, Killian. Save the Romeo stuff for later and escort Ms. Shane to the front-row seat we've saved for her."

Bobby Joe cupped a hand underneath the woman's elbow and walked her across the room. "Detectives...this is Carol Shane. Be nice. She's nervous, okay?"

Williams glared at Bobby Joe and then helped the woman to a chair in front of the TV and VCR.

"Ms. Shane, we appreciate you coming in like this. There's no reason to be afraid, and the tape we want you to see is very brief. There's nothing violent on it. Just a man going in and then leaving a room. What I want you to do is look at his face and tell us if he's the same man who abducted Mary O'Rourke yesterday."

She glanced nervously at each of the men and then nodded before fixing her gaze on the blank television screen. Williams hit the remote and immediately, the screen was filled with images from the robbery.

Daniel tensed as Carol Shane leaned forward, and like before, they replayed the same bit of footage several times before they asked for her answer.

"Well, Ms. Shane, what do you think?" Reese asked.

Carol looked up. "I can't be sure, but it certainly looked like him. Not many people wear their hair like that, and although there wasn't a real good shot of his face, I'd say it was him."

"Are you sure?" Williams asked. "Remember, you only got a brief look at him yesterday at the supermarket."

Bobby Joe stepped forward and laid a hand on Carol's back.

"Oh no, that's not exactly true, is it, honey?"

"What do you mean?" Reese asked.

Carol was fidgeting with the hem of her T-shirt as she looked up at the men ringed around her.

"Well, it's like I told Bobby Joe last night...the man who took that woman...uh...he's a regular in the store."

Reese cursed beneath his breath. "Why don't we know this?"

Carol Shane looked like she was going to cry.

"I told the first officer on the scene that I'd seen him before, but that I didn't know his name."

"Tell him what else you told me, honey," Bobby Joe urged. "You know...about what he's been buying."

"Oh! That!" Carol said. "I've been working at Vinter's for almost a year and I've seen him off and on from the start. Only he used to buy stuff like a single man buys. You know...frozen dinners, Hamburger Helper, stuff like that. Only lately he's started buying stuff like people buy when they have kids."

"Like what?" Reese asked.

"Like fun cereal with marshmallows in it and different juices and lots of milk. Oh...and frozen chicken nuggets, wieners, little individual kid snacks."

"Did he ever say anything to you?"

Carol shook her head. "No. He doesn't even look at me. Just looks down, digs the money out of his wallet and leaves."

"Can you remember him ever paying by check?"

"Not to me."

"How can you be sure?" Daniel asked.

"Because I know a lot of my regulars and he's the only one I used to see fairly often that I didn't know by name."

Reese stood, and then helped Carol Shane to her feet.

"Okay, Ms. Shane. Thank you so much for coming in. If you remember anything else, please give me a call." He handed her his card and then nodded at Bobby Joe.

Bobby Joe winked at Daniel. "Be right back," he said, and walked her out of the office.

Daniel turned to Reese. "So what do you think?"

"I think we're probably looking at the same man."

"And…"

Reese frowned. "Without a name, we're right back where we were this morning. We're looking for a man who drives a white van. The fact that he's buying kid food at a supermarket and stealing antibiotics that one would ordinarily administer to children only tells me that the girls are probably alive. The fact that he's stealing medicine isn't a good sign that the girls are well, but at least they're still breathing. That's more than we knew two days ago."

Daniel shoved a hand through his hair in frustration.

"How many names on the DMV list?"

"You don't want to know," Reese muttered.

"Actually, yes I do," Daniel said. "I'm dying here."

Reese put a hand on his friend's shoulder, wishing there was something he could say that would help, but there was not.

Then Daniel looked up, unashamed of the tears blurring his vision.

"Find her, Reese. Please."

"I'm doing my best, Daniel."

Daniel's mouth twisted into something between a grimace and a smile.

"Last night…in my dream…"

"Yeah, what about it?" Reese asked.

"Mary called the man Howard Lee."

Reese's eyes widened. "Hell. You dreamed that, too?"

Daniel shrugged. "I didn't dream it. It's what she said. Howard Lee."

"Yeah, right," Reese said, then he added. "There's one other thing Carol Shane said that should help us eliminate some more names on the DMV list."

"What's that?" Daniel asked.

"If he shops in that supermarket regularly, then he must live in the general area. We'll keep that in mind when we're going through the list."

Bobby Joe Killian walked into the room. Daniel knew about his bad-boy image, but he didn't care. He was also relentless.

"Let us help," Daniel begged.

Reese frowned. "No. Absolutely not. This is a police matter."

"Fine," Daniel said. "Just know that we're going to be looking anyway, whether you like it or not."

"Damn it, Daniel, you're making my job harder."

"Then don't shut me out," Daniel said. "Bobby Joe is a licensed private investigator. He's already got the same list from the DMV that you have. We can either work together and maybe find Mary and those girls before it's too late, or you can keep stalling me and make everything take twice as long."

"He's right, you know," Bobby Joe said.

Reese turned. "You're back already? Surely you weren't gone long enough to get her phone number and address?"

"Already been there, done that," he said. "So are you going to let us help or do we go maverick on you?"

"I should lock you both up," Reese said.

"No, let's find the bastard and lock him up, instead," Bobby Joe said.

Reese threw his hands up in disgust.

"Okay, fine," Reese said. "We'll divide up the list. If you find someone suspicious, you call it in. You don't play cowboy and go after him on your own."

Daniel shook his head. "No deal. If we find him, we'll call it in, but if he has Mary, he's mine."

Howard Lee's phone began to ring just as he was putting bacon in the frying pan. He looked at the caller ID as he wiped his hands and then frowned. Savannah Memorial. Someone from work was calling him. This wasn't good. Not once in his entire time with the hospital had anyone ever called before.

He let the phone ring as he went back to breakfast. Time was precious. If he did what instinct told him to do, he'd already be gone. But the girls had been sick and he'd been afraid to yank them out of their beds without rest and food.

He turned the fire down under the skillet and then took some eggs from the fridge and began breaking them into a bowl. Normally, he would have served the girls cereal, but there was no telling how long it would be before he could take a chance and stop to feed them. They needed a good, solid meal before the journey began.

As he popped bread into the toaster, he thought of Sophie and frowned. If she'd been a good wife, she would be the one making breakfast. But he couldn't trust her. Instead, he had to keep her shut up with the girls.

He turned the bacon and then took glasses from the cabinet and filled them with milk. He started to put sedatives in the milk so that the girls would be complacent on the trip, and then realized that Sophie probably wouldn't let them drink it. She'd obviously tossed their drinks the night before. He discarded the thought, reminding himself that he could easily give it to them later in a soft drink before they left.

As for Sophie, he didn't know exactly what he was going to do with her, but he damned sure wasn't taking her along.

A short while later he started down the stairs with their food on a tray, taking care not to spill as he maneuvered the narrow opening. As he got to the bottom step, he saw the beds were empty. He started to frown and then noticed the bathroom door was shut.

"Breakfast," he called out.

The bathroom door opened almost instantly and Mary looked out.

"We'll be there in a minute."

He set the food down on the table and then started toward the bathroom.

"Is there a problem?" he asked.

"No. The girls are getting out of the tub. They're just not dressed yet."

"I can help," he said, and started to push the door wider when Mary put a hand in the middle of his chest and pushed him backward.

"You don't touch these girls again," she said. "God only knows what you've already done to them."

Howard Lee paled. The idea that he would be improper with his daughters was appalling.

"I've done nothing wrong!" he cried, and then yanked Mary out of the doorway, shaking her roughly as he shouted in her face. "You're evil for even thinking such a thing."

Mary flinched. His features had twisted into an angry grimace and the grip he had on her arms was beginning to hurt, but couldn't let him see her fear. She tore out of his grasp and then put herself between him and bathroom, where the girls were still dressing.

"You're the one who's evil," she snapped. "How can you stand there and tell me you've done nothing wrong? You stole these children! You locked them up in this…this…dungeon, and then you drugged them senseless. My God! Have you no shame? Have you no conscience? Don't you care that they weep for their parents? They're not your daughters, they're your captives…just like I am."

Howard Lee was livid. He didn't want to hear this. He wouldn't listen to the lies anymore.

"You're wrong!" he shouted. "They're mine. But you can quit worrying about yourself. I don't want you around them anymore. We're leaving…but you're not. Do you hear me, woman?" Then he pointed to the table. "Get the children out here and make sure they eat a proper meal. And please see that they drink their milk. I did not put any medicine in it, although when I come back, I will have to administer another shot of antibiotic to each of them."

"I don't want no shot."

They both turned. Justine was standing in the doorway, holding Amy Anne's hand. "Neither does Amy Anne."

Howard Lee's mood darkened even more. He did not like dissension.

"Shut up! All of you!" he yelled. "I've got things to do and clothes to pack. Sit down and eat your food. I'll be back in a while to help you pack your things. Then we're going on a trip."

"I don't want to go on a trip, either," Justine said. "I want to stay with Mary."

Mary moved to the children and then pulled them close. It angered Howard Lee to see how they clung to her.

"Do as I say!" he ordered, and then stalked back up the stairs, slamming the door shut with a ferocious thud.

"He's good and mad," Justine said.

Mary shuddered. "Yes, he is," she said, and then made herself smile. "Come on girls, lets eat some breakfast. We've got to keep our strength up. And while we eat, we need to make a plan. Okay?"

They nodded and then followed her to the table. It did Mary good to see both girls tuck into the food. While she wasn't so sure about their future, hers looked even worse. If he didn't plan to take her with him, then what? Would he just leave her locked up in here, or would he kill her?

She took a bite of the toast and then helped the girls spread jelly on theirs. Justine dug into the food with the exuberance of youth, confident that with Mary as their ally, she would make everything all right. Amy Anne was more hesitant, but with Mary's help, ate her food, too. Mary was glad that they believed in her. It would make things easier, but she wished she had as much confidence in herself. Dear God, she wanted to go home.

* * *

Daniel stood against the car with his arms crossed, waiting for Bobby Joe to finish talking to the woman across the street. She was the eighth person on the list that they'd talked to since they'd left the precinct and so far, no luck. He took his cell phone out of his pocket and called his parents. He needed to hear Hope's voice and to reassure her that everything was all right. So far, she had no idea her mother was missing and he wanted to keep it that way. A few seconds later, his mother answered.

"Mom, it's me. How's Hope?"

"She's fine. She's having a ball and knows nothing about what's going on."

Daniel looked down at the toe of his boot, concentrating on the scuff marks to keep from losing his mind.

"Good. Is she with Dad?"

"Yes, they went to the park."

Unconsciously, his shoulders slumped. He'd wanted to talk to her, but it was probably better that he didn't. It was getting harder and harder to hide his emotions.

"Okay…good."

"Do you have any news?" Phyllis asked.

"Well, we know that the same guy who snatched Mary is probably the man who took the two little girls who are missing."

"My God!" Phyllis gasped. "Are they…do you know if—"

"We're pretty sure they're alive because he was caught on tape stealing some antibiotics from the hospital. The doctors said it was stuff normally given to children. One of the medicines he stole is a substitute for people who are allergic to penicillin and one of the little girls who is missing is allergic to it. A lot of this is circumstantial guesswork, but it's pretty close to the mark."

"I'm so sorry," Phyllis said.

"So am I, Mom. So am I." Then his voice shook. "I can't do this without her."

"Do what?" Phyllis asked.

"Live." He choked back a sob. "I can't even imagine my life without her."

"Then don't," Phyllis said shortly. "Think positive, darling."

"Yeah...well...tell Hope I called, okay? And I don't know how long this is going to take so—"

"Don't worry about it. If you haven't found her by Monday, we'll see that Hope gets to school."

"Monday is October the 2nd...Hope's birthday."

"Oh, we know. She's already reminded us a dozen times. Had Mary planned a party?"

Daniel frowned, remembering how pale Mary had gotten in the antique shop before she'd passed out, and how confused she'd been for a while afterward.

"No, not really. She hadn't been feeling too well the past few days."

"Don't worry," she said. "We'll make a big deal out of the day for her, although you know if Mary is still gone then, you're going to have to tell her something. She'll expect her mother to be present on her birthday."

Hell. "What if she's not?"

"One thing at a time, dear. For now, she's fine. Who knows? Maybe you'll get a break in the case."

"From your lips to God's ears," Daniel muttered.

"Goodbye, honey. If you need anything, just let us know."

"Yeah, all right, Mom. And thanks."

"No thanks are necessary."

He disconnected and dropped the cell phone back in his pocket as Bobby Joe came running to the car.

"Any luck?" Daniel asked.

"Nope. Who's next on the list?"

"I don't know. I'll look as you drive."

They got inside the car. Bobby Joe started the engine as Daniel took the list from the dashboard. He marked off the name from the address they'd just left and then ran his finger down the paper to the next one.

"Uh…a Delmar Watts on—"

But Daniel didn't finish what he'd been going to say.

"What's wrong?" Bobby Joe asked.

"This," Daniel said, pointing to a name farther down on the page.

"What about it?"

"Howard Lee Martin. It says Howard Lee Martin, 1449 Raleigh Avenue."

"So? Do you know him?"

Daniel shivered suddenly, as if a ghost had just walked past his ear.

"No."

"Then what's the big deal?"

Daniel looked up, his face devoid of all expression.

"Last night in my dream, Mary called the man Howard Lee."

Bobby Joe pulled to the curb and then turned and looked at Daniel.

"Well hell," he said softly.

"Exactly."

Bobby Joe frowned. "Do you believe in precognition?"

Daniel shook his head. "No, but I believe in Mary Faith."

"That's good enough for me," Bobby Joe said. "What street did you say he lived on?"

"Raleigh. 1449 Raleigh."

"Hand me the city map."

Daniel did as he was asked, watching anxiously as Bobby Joe scanned the map. The longer he sat, the more certain he felt that this meant something.

"Hurry," he said.

Bobby Joe looked up.

"Is there something you're not telling me?" he asked.

"Just hurry."

Bobby Joe slammed the car in gear and peeled away from the curb, leaving a short streak of black rubber on the pavement behind him.

Daniel braced himself and hung on.

Reese Arnaud pulled the last sheet from the fax machine and dropped it on the desk next to the list from the DMV. It was a complete listing of every employee from Savannah Memorial. Now he had to see if any of the names cross-matched with the names from the DMV. He sat down with a thump, shifted the lists so that they were side by side, then started reading.

He was halfway through the list from Savannah General when one of the names jumped out at him. He frowned, trying to remember why the name Howard Lee Martin would mean anything, and then it hit him. Daniel's dream! He said Mary had told him the man name's was Howard Lee.

He shivered suddenly, and then dug through the DMV list, telling himself the name wouldn't—no, couldn't—be there, too. But it was. Howard Lee Martin. 1449 Raleigh Avenue.

Reese reached for a city map, looking to see where Raleigh Street was in conjunction with Vinter's supermarket.

"Son of a bitch," he said softly, and then stood.

"Patrick...come with me," he yelled.

"Where are we going?" the detective asked, as he got up from his desk.

"I'm not sure," Reese muttered. "But I'm desperate enough to give this a try."

Chapter 14

All during breakfast, Mary was encouraged by Amy Anne's behavior. Twice during the meal she'd caught the little girl watching her when she thought she wasn't looking. While she was encouraged by Amy Anne's improvement, Mary wasn't sure if she was strong enough to go through with her plan.

After Howard Lee's threat, Mary had been given no choice. She had to make a move before Howard Lee separated her from the girls. If he got away from Savannah, they would be lost for good.

What she'd planned would be dangerous for her and would hinge upon Howard Lee keeping the cellar door open when he came down to get the girls. He'd never closed it before and the plan would work only if he kept to the routine.

And she'd talked to the girls. Justine knew what to do and was excited to the point of hysteria, but Amy Anne had only listened. Mary wasn't certain if she even understood what was expected, but she had to be sure.

Taking both girls by the hand, she sat down on the bed and scooted them up on her lap.

"Justine, can you be a brave girl for me?"

"Oh, yes!" she said, her eyes sparkling with anticipation.

"When Howard Lee comes back, do you remember what to do?"

"We hide by the wall and don't make any sounds, and when he comes down, you yell for us to run and we go up the steps and out of the house."

"And what else?" Mary asked.

"We yell for help and we don't stop running or yelling until someone calls the police."

"Right," Mary said.

Justine wiggled with excitement, picking nervously at the buttons on Mary's shirt as she thought about getting home. Then a thought occurred and she started to frown.

"But what if he follows us? He's got very long legs. He'll catch us and then he'll be mad."

Mary hugged them close, making herself smile.

"No, no, remember what I said. He can't follow you because I'm going to grab him by the legs. I'll hold on very, very tight. He won't be able to move and you can get far, far away."

"Oh yes! I remember!" Justine said.

"Good," Mary said, then she looked at Amy Anne. She was so small and so quiet—a tiny doll with big blue eyes on the constant verge of tears. "Honey, do you understand what you need to do, too?"

Amy Anne was looking down at her shoes, not talking, not moving. Mary put a finger under Amy Anne's chin and tilted her face until they were face to face.

"Amy Anne…do you want to go home?"

Tears welled in the her eyes as she stared at Mary's face. Finally, she nodded.

Mary cupped her face with both hands. "When I tell you to run, will you run with Justine? Will you run as fast as you can and never look back?"

Amy Anne nodded.

"Good girl. Okay, you girls go sit where I showed you to

sit. I'm going to fix the beds so it looks like you are in them asleep. That way Howard Lee will see the lumps and think it's you. I'll make sure he comes toward me. As soon as he's far enough in the room, I'll shout for you to run. When I do, Justine, you grab Amy Anne by the hand and you girls run up the stairs and out of the house as fast as you can."

Justine quivered, she was so excited. "I will be home to-night, won't I, Mary?"

Mary hugged them tightly. "Yes, baby…you and Amy Anne will be in your very own homes tonight. You'll be with your mommies and daddies and this man won't ever hurt you again."

"And you, too," Justine said.

Mary's heart twisted. Her fate wasn't nearly as certain, but she wasn't going to tell the girls.

"Yes, darling, me, too."

"And we will come and play with Hope."

At the thought of her own little girl, her determination not to cry in front of them nearly splintered. Her voice was shaking as she gave them a last quick hug.

"Yes, baby…you'll both come and play with Hope. Now go get in your places and remember, when you hear him opening the cellar door, don't talk…don't move."

"Okay," Justine said, and took Amy Anne by the hand and led her toward the stairs.

Mary jumped up quickly and began padding the beds, making it appear as if the girls were under the covers asleep. Then she poured a glass of water in the middle of the floor a good distance away from the stairs, positioned herself to look as if she'd slipped in the water and fallen, then waited for Howard Lee.

Howard Lee tossed the last of his shirts into his suitcase, emptied the drawer containing his underwear and socks on top of them, and closed the lid. The rest of his clothes that were on hangers had been loaded in the van next to the pallets he'd made for the girls. He'd packed an ice chest with food and drink and packed his camping port-a-potty into the back of the van. Now all he needed was the girls and their clothes and he was ready to go. He glanced at his watch. It was just after 2:00 p.m. If he hurried, he'd be on the road and out of the city long before rush hour hit.

He reached into his pocket to get the key to unlock the cellar door, and then stopped and looked around for the rope. He didn't want Sophie. No, that was wrong. He had to stop thinking of her as that. Her name was Mary, and he couldn't afford to let her go.

The rope was on the floor near the door, right beside his hunting knife. He picked up the rope, stood for a moment looking down at the knife, then bent down and dropped it in his pocket.

His expression was grim as he unlocked the padlock on the cellar. All the way down the stairs he kept telling himself he could do this—that what he was planning wasn't a crime. A real father would do anything—even murder—to protect his family.

Then he saw her in the small pool of water—lying crumpled and still upon the floor. Her eyes were closed, her lips slightly parted, as if she'd been in the act of crying out when she'd slipped. He dropped the rope at his feet and ran toward her.

The empty glass was near her hand, the water still puddled beneath her body. He could only guess at what must have happened. He looked toward the beds and saw that the girls had gone back to sleep, which was good. It would make them easier to move to the van. But first, he needed to make sure Mary would not hinder his plans.

He bent down, reaching for her shoulders to drag her out of the way, when she suddenly came alive. Before he knew it, she had grabbed him by the ankles and yanked. He went down like a felled ox, thumping his head on the floor and momentarily knocking the wind from his body.

Mary crawled the length of his body, wrapped her arms around the upper part of his thighs, locked her legs below his knees, then held on. She held on for her life—and for Justine and Amy Anne.

"Run!" she screamed. "Run as fast as you can and don't look back!"

Both little girls bolted up from where they'd been crouching and ran up the steps, already screaming for help, just as Mary had told them.

A low groan came up and then out of Howard Lee's lips as he slowly came to. Almost immediately, he realized what she'd done and grabbed Mary by the hair, yanking viciously as he struggled to get free.

"You bitch! You bitch! You're ruining everything. Let me go!"

Mary ducked her head, shielding her face from his blows and tightened her grip.

Howard Lee struggled to sit up, but couldn't shake Mary's grasp. Then he heard the sound of little girls screaming and realized they were gone. Rage swamped him.

"What have you done? What have you done?" he screamed, then doubled up his fists and began raining blow after blow upon her shoulders and the back of her head as they rolled from side to side on the wet floor.

Mary cried out in pain, adding her own screams for help and prayed for a miracle.

"How far away from Raleigh Avenue?" Daniel asked.

"About three blocks. The house should be in the middle of the block on the left," Bobby Joe said, downshifted to pass a biker, then shifted back into high gear as soon as they were past him. "Think we should call Arnaud?"

"And tell him what? That we're looking for the man from a dream?"

"Yeah, right," Bobby Joe said and then suddenly braked when two little girls darted out from between some shrubbery and ran into the street.

"Son of a—"

He swerved sideways, bringing the car to a sliding halt only inches from the little girls' feet. Immediately, he and Daniel were out and running.

"Help! Help!" they screamed.

"It's okay, it's okay," Daniel said, and went down on his knees, gathering both girls in his arms. "You're all right. The car didn't hit you." Then he looked up and around, expecting to see a parent somewhere nearby.

"Where are your parents?" he asked.

"We don't know. The man took us. He wouldn't let us go home. Mary grabbed him and told us to run. She said to yell for help, so we ran and ran. You have to call the police before the man finds us again."

Daniel's heart skipped a beat as he took her by the arms and held her still.

"Who's Mary? Please, baby…who's Mary?" he asked.

Justine shivered. "The man brought her. She slept with us and she yelled at the man. She made him mad."

Daniel started to shake. "Honey…what's your name?"

"Justine." Then she tugged on the other girl's hand. "This is Amy Anne. Mary said we could go home."

"Sweet God," Daniel said, and then picked them up in his arms and ran toward the car, yelling at Bobby Joe as he went. "Call 9-1-1. Tell them we found the missing girls and tell them to contact Arnaud."

Bobby Joe yanked his phone from his pocket as Daniel slid into the seat, still holding both girls in his arms.

"Honey, are you okay? Did the man hurt you? Is Mary okay?"

"Do you know our Mary?" Justine asked.

It was all Daniel could do to answer without coming undone.

"Yes, honey, I know Mary. She's my Mary, too."

Justine smiled. "She wants to go home."

"Where is she, honey? Did the man keep you in his house?"

"Not exactly," Justine said.

"Then where. You have to tell me, honey, so I can go find her."

"Kind of like a basement, only nicer than the one at my house."

"Okay. That's a good girl. Mary will be proud of you."

Bobby Joe jumped into the car.

"The dispatcher patched me through to Arnaud. He's already on the way, and there was a cruiser only a couple of blocks from here. They'll be here any minute."

Daniel could hear the sounds of an approaching siren, but Mary had obviously put herself between the children and danger to make sure they escaped. He owed it to her to make sure they were safe.

"You stay with the girls," he said. "I'm going after Mary."

Bobby Joe frowned. "No way, man. Don't leave me alone with two kids."

Daniel set both the little girls in the seat beside Bobby Joe.

"They won't hurt you," he said. "Consider them little women in waiting, use your considerable charm on them until the police get here and you'll be fine."

"Damn it, Daniel, don't—"

Daniel was out of the car and running before Bobby Joe could finish. The last thing he heard was one of them telling Bobby Joe that he shouldn't say bad words. If he hadn't been so scared, he would have laughed.

Howard Lee couldn't believe what was happening. He'd beaten this woman almost senseless and she still wouldn't let go. With unfettered rage, he thrust his hands into her hair and pulled, yanking her head backward and baring the tender underside of her throat. At that moment, he remembered his knife.

"I'll show you," he shrieked. "You'll be sorry you came between me and my girls."

He turned loose of her hair and began trying to get his hands in his pockets, while Mary struggled to stay conscious.

Every bone in her body throbbed from the beating she was taking and her vision kept going in and out of focus. She was so tired and too weak to hold on much longer, but letting go meant certain death. She heard him muttering and cursing and closed her ears to the sounds. She couldn't think about what he was doing to her. All she could do was hold on.

Daniel ran, his long legs marking off the distance between him and Mary Faith. He took shortcuts through lush, green lawns and down the alleys between houses, startling one lady who was in her backyard watering flowers and causing dogs in neighboring yards to start barking. The woman jumped back in fright, thinking she was about to be attacked. When Daniel ran past her instead, she dashed into her house and locked the door.

Daniel ran with Mary's name in his heart, remembering what Justine had said, that Mary grabbed the man by the legs and then told them to run. God. He'd never known she had that kind of strength. He needed to find her. He needed to find her alive—so that he could tell her how proud he was to call her his wife. He lengthened his stride, and moments later come out of an alley from between two houses to find himself in the middle of Raleigh Avenue. He paused briefly, his heart pounding and gasping for breath, uncertain of which way to go. The houses in front of him had no house numbers and the one behind him was missing two and the others were so faded he couldn't read them.

He turned in place, trying to find a numbered house

on which to fix his location, and as he did, saw an elderly man coming toward him on the sidewalk with a small dog on a leash.

"Which way to 1449 Raleigh?" he yelled.

The man pointed over his shoulder.

Daniel bolted past him, praying for strength as he ran.

Halfway down the block, he began hearing the faint, but persistent, shriek of sirens. Although help was on the way, it didn't slow his steps. Moments later, he saw the numbers he'd been looking for, then the front door standing ajar at the house. He remembered the panicked looks on those little girls' faces, imagining their terror as they made their escape. In two long steps, he cleared the curb and was running through the yard.

Even before he was inside, he heard them fighting. Male rage mingling with a woman's weak, high-pitched shrieks sent a rush of adrenaline through his body. He hit the porch on the run, shouting Mary's name as he went.

Howard Lee's shirt was stuck to his body. His straight, Dutch-boy haircut was wet with sweat as he struggled to get the hunting knife out of his pocket.

"Move, bitch, move," he screamed, and whacked at Mary's shoulder with his fist. He felt her flinch, but she wouldn't let go and he couldn't get his hand in his pocket.

Mary continued to fight, screaming when she could gather the breath. A few seconds ago she'd thought she'd heard Daniel's voice and knew that was impossible. Daniel didn't know where she was. Maybe she was dying.

Suddenly, Howard Lee bucked and she went flying across the floor before hitting the wall in a sliding thump. Instantly, she rolled to her hands and knees as Howard Lee was pulling the knife from his pocket. She struggled to her feet and looked around for a weapon, but there was nothing. When he started toward her, she began backing up, using her hands for a shield as Howard Lee slide the blade from its sheath.

The sight of the weapon splintered her courage.

"Oh God…no, please no," Mary begged, and reached behind her, her fingernails raking the concrete surface of the walls as she faced her mortality.

"You destroyed my family!" Howard Lee shrieked.

Mary couldn't believe what she was hearing. He was going to kill her and then blame her for her own death? Not while she had breath in her body. She yanked the spread from one of the beds and wrapped it around her arm as he came at her.

"You're crazy! You don't have daughters. You stole someone else's. I'm not your wife! I belong to—"

"Mary! Mary!"

Mary gasped. That was Daniel! She hadn't imagined it before. She could hear him calling her name.

"Here!" she screamed. "I'm down here!"

Before Howard Lee could turn around, Daniel hit him from behind in a tackle worthy of the NFL. Howard Lee grunted. The knife went flying out of his hands. Once again, he went down, this time reaching outward and bracing himself for the fall. As he hit, his neck popped and he bit his own tongue. The coppery taste of blood spurted inside his mouth as he struggled to right himself beneath the weight of the man's body, but it was no use. Instead, he covered his head with his hands and started begging for mercy.

Reese Arnaud and Bobby Joe Killian came to a sliding halt in front of the house on Raleigh Street at almost the same time. They both came out of their cars, armed and running.

"Look for a basement," Bobby Joe yelled, as he vaulted onto the porch. "The kid said he kept them in a basement."

They entered the living room, one only a half step behind

the other and then followed the sounds of the high-pitched screams into the bedroom, then down the cellar steps.

Reese was the first to reach bottom.

"Get Mary out of here," he yelled, and stepped aside as Bobby Joe dashed past. Then he holstered his gun and moved toward Daniel. He needed to pull him off the man before he killed him.

"Daniel! Daniel…let him go!"

But Daniel didn't relent, which left Reese with the job of making it happen. He wrapped his arms around Daniel's upper body and pulled, wrenching the beaten and bloody man out of Daniel's grasp and leaving him limp and moaning on the floor.

Daniel spun, his fists still doubled, at the ready to throw another punch when he realized it was Reese.

"Son of a bitch," he muttered, and then took a deep, shuddering breath.

"Leave enough for me to arrest, and go tend to your wife."

Mary! Daniel spun, his gaze wide and frantic. Then he saw her slumped over on the bed. Bobby Joe stood between them, his gun still drawn. Daniel's legs were shaking as he took the first step. Was she all right? Had he come too late?

"Ah God…Mary."

She staggered to her feet and into his arms.

The moment Daniel's arms went around her, Mary started to cry—huge, choking sobs that ripped up her throat and burned the back of her nostrils. She threw her arms around his neck and pressed herself fast to his strength, praying that this wasn't another horrible dream and that he was really, truly here.

"The girls…the girls…did you find them? Are they okay?"

"Yes, baby…the girls are fine. We found them a few minutes ago."

"Thank God," Mary muttered, then felt the world going black.

Daniel caught her as she fainted, then swept her up in his arms. He looked down at Howard Lee, his rage still intact.

"Consider yourself lucky, you miserable son of a bitch. I would have killed you for what you did."

With Reese Arnaud already in the act of handcuffing the man, he sidestepped what was left of Howard Lee and carried Mary up and out of the basement, knowing Bobby Joe was right behind him. Sunlight hit him full in the face as he walked out of the house. He looked down at Mary, wincing at the array of bruising that he could see, and started to cry.

"There's an ambulance on the way," Bobby Joe said.

"I won't let her go."

Bobby Joe put a hand on Daniel's shoulder.

"That's all right, buddy. You don't have to. You'll be with her all the way."

Mary woke up in the ambulance and began to struggle.

"Let me go. Let me go," she mumbled. "Got to find the girls."

Daniel leaned over and cupped her face. "Mary…honey… the girls are fine. You're on your way to the hospital and I'll be with you every step of the way."

"Can't close my eyes…don't close my eyes. He'll take them away."

"He can't touch you, baby. He'll never bother anyone again."

"Don't drink the juice. It will put you to sleep."

"God Almighty," Daniel said, and laid his face against her shoulder.

The paramedic put his hand on Daniel's shoulder.

"Hey, mister, she's going to be okay."

Daniel nodded through tears. "Yes, I know, but I'm not so sure about myself."

Chapter 15

Mary woke up once in the night, panicked at the unfamiliar surroundings, then she saw Daniel slumped over in a chair beside her bed.

Is this real or am I dreaming?

"Daniel?"

He jerked. Seconds later he was on his feet and at her side.

"Baby...what's wrong? Are you in pain? Do you want me to get the nurse?"

"No. I just needed to touch you...to know if you were real."

Daniel took her hand and lifted it to his lips, pressing a kiss in the palm of her hand.

"I'm real, baby...and so are you." He drew a deep, shuddering breath. "God, Mary...I've never been so scared."

"Me, too."

Gently, he lifted the wayward strands of hair from her forehead, then bent down and kissed her.

"The girls...they told us what you did. I am so proud of you."

"Are they all right?"

"Yes...oh, and Reese said that Justine wanted you to know that Amy Anne talked. Is that important?"

Mary closed her eyes briefly, picturing the silent child with horror-filled eyes.

"Very important. She was the first one he took. She was alone with that...that man...for almost a month before he took Justine. By that time she wouldn't make eye contact or react in any manner to what was happening. All the time I was with them I kept thinking...what if this had happened to Hope?"

"You saved their lives, honey. You're a real heroine, did you know that?"

"Does the media know about me?"

"No. At my request, Reese kept it quiet...mostly because of Hope."

Mary sighed. "Thank God. Could we please keep it that way?"

"You can have anything you want," Daniel said.

She tried to smile and then winced from the pain in her jaw. "What I want is to turn over, but I think I'm going to need some help."

"Sure, honey," Daniel said, and slid his hands beneath her shoulders. Just as he started to lift, she cried out in pain. He withdrew immediately, uncertain as to how he had hurt her.

"Mary...darling, I'm so sorry. What did I do?"

She grabbed his hand. "No, Danny...I'm the one who's sorry. I didn't mean to frighten you. It's just that my back and shoulders are so sore."

"Your back? What did he do?"

"I had to stop him from running after the girls, so I grabbed his legs. The only way I could keep him from kicking me loose was to wrap myself around the lower half of his body. I had control of his mobility, but not his fists."

"He beat you?"

The tone in Daniel's voice was chilling. Mary knew he was struggling with a terrible rage. She tried to make light of it by teasing.

"I stuck to him like a tick. You should have heard him screaming at me to let go."

"The bastard," Daniel muttered. "Let me see."

He turned on the light and then opened the back of her gown. Her skin was a mass of bruises, ranging in color from faint blue to a deep, dark purple. Some of them bore deep scratches, as if he tried to claw himself free. The shock of what Mary had endured made him sick. He stroked her arm, then her face, then lowered his head until their foreheads were touching.

"Oh sweet heaven...oh baby...I didn't know. I didn't know."

"Daniel...don't. They will heal and I still want to turn to my side."

Still Daniel hesitated. Mary sighed. The shock on his face was impossible to miss.

"Please," she begged, and then gritted her teeth when Daniel slid his hands back beneath her body and began to help her turn.

Groaning softly from the relief, she settled into a new position.

"Thank you, darling. That's much better."

Daniel stared at her without moving.

"How is Hope? Is she with Mike and Phyllis?"

"Yes, and she's fine. She doesn't even know you were gone."

Mary sighed. "What's the date today?"

"The 2nd of October."

"Oh no...it's her birthday. What's she going to think?"

"She doesn't know what day it is. Mom and Dad made sure of that. We'll celebrate her birthday when we're all home together."

"That's good."

There was a brief and uncomfortable moment of silence.

Neither Mary nor Daniel could think of a safe topic of conversation.

"Do you need anything for pain?" Daniel finally asked.

"No," Mary said, and then to her horror, felt tears rolling down her face.

For Daniel, it was the proverbial last straw. Rage spilled out of him in violent waves, making his body tremble.

"I should have killed the son of a bitch."

"Just hold me," Mary begged.

He lowered the bed rail and crawled in beside her. Sliding his arm beneath her neck, he pillowed her head on his chest and held her while she cried. He wanted to tell her that whatever that man had done to her would never destroy what was between them. He wanted to say it—but he was afraid to bring it up and so he held her and thanked God that she was still alive.

Several minutes passed, then several more, and Daniel was certain that Mary had fallen asleep. He figured he would catch hell from the first nurse to come in and find him in bed with her, but he didn't really care. He closed his eyes, trying to make himself relax. One moment led to another and then another, and just when he was on the verge of going under, he heard Mary's voice. The words were slurred, as if she were talking in her sleep, but they were a gift, just the same.

"He didn't rape me."

Ah God...thank you for sparing her that. "It's okay, baby...go back to sleep," he said softly.

Mary sighed. Her breathing slowed and he felt her muscles relax.

"Daniel..."

"What, honey?"

"The baby is okay."

He smiled to himself. She was so sleepy she was barely making sense.

"Yes, honey…Hope is okay."

She sighed. "Not Hope. The baby." Then she reached for his hand and laid it on her stomach. "Our baby," she mumbled, and fell back to sleep.

Daniel went from shock to elation. He splayed his fingers across her belly and realized that she hadn't just been fighting for Justine and Amy Anne's lives, but for the life of her unborn child. He laid his face against the back of her neck, unashamed of the tears that he shed.

"Thank you, Mary Faith," he said softly.

And then it was morning.

Mary was going to be dismissed, but she had adamantly refused to wear her dirty clothes ever again, and at her insistence, Daniel had gone home to get her some clean clothes.

She had showered earlier, and was sitting on the side of the bed in her gown and robe, waiting for Daniel to come back when she heard a knock at the door.

"Come in," she called.

The door swung slowly inward, and then Mary started to smile. She didn't recognize the four adults, but she knew the two little girls with them. She slid off the bed and then opened her arms.

"My heroes," she cried, and gathered them close to her breast. "Did you girls know that you saved me?"

Justine nodded importantly, while Amy Anne ducked her head and then buried her face in the curve of Mary's neck. Mary looked up then, remembering the adults who'd come with them.

"Where are my manners?" she said. "Please sit down."

"Not until you get back in bed," one of the women said.

Justine took Mary by the hand. "We'll help you, won't we, Amy Anne?"

Amy Anne nodded, then looked nervously toward her parents.

"The girls can sit with me," Mary said, as she got back in bed, and helped both of them up in her lap.

Justine giggled as they snuggled close. "This is the way we slept in the room, isn't it, Mary?"

Mary's eyes filled with tears. "Yes, it sure is."

The parents gathered around her bed, all talking at once. Finally, it was Amy Anne's father, Michael Fountain, who spoke for them all.

"We don't know how to thank you," he said, his voice breaking with emotion. "Justine told us what you did. You saved their lives, and we will be forever in your debt."

"No," Mary said. "You don't owe me anything." She thought back to the day she'd walked into that antique shop. "I didn't used to believe this, but I do now. I think everything happens for a reason. Even the bad stuff. We don't always understand why, but, eventually, it finally becomes clear. I was in that place because it was meant to be. I had to be there because of them, so don't thank me, thank God. He's the One who made it possible."

Then she hugged both the girls and tickled Amy Anne's ear.

"Do you remember what we promised we would do when we got to go home?"

To Mary's surprise, it was Amy Anne who answered.

"Play with Hope."

Mary laughed with delight, then began to explain to the parents.

"Hope is my little girl. Yesterday was her seventh birthday, but the party has been a little delayed. I kept telling the girls that they would soon see you again, and that when you said it was okay, that they could come and play with Hope."

"It's a promise," they echoed, then added, "And it's also time for us to go. You need to rest, but the girls were adamant about coming to visit. I think they needed to see for themselves that you were all right."

Mary hugged them close. "I am very okay, aren't I?"

Justine's mother handed Mary a card.

"Just a little something from all of us for what you did. Our phone numbers and addresses are enclosed. Please stay in touch."

"Thank you," Mary said, and kissed both of the girls goodbye. As she did, it made her think of Hope and how badly she needed to hold her own child again.

They left as quietly as they'd come. Mary waved until the door went shut, then she turned the card over, smiling to herself at the awkward writing of her name. Something told her that Justine and Amy Anne had done it themselves.

She slid a fingernail beneath the flap and popped it open, then pulled out the card. As she read the verses, the hair on the back of her neck began to crawl.

A promise made is a thing to behold
A promise kept is worth more than gold.
So I promise you forever a love strong and true
Because you kept your promise when I needed you.

Justine and Amy Anne had signed it, one in green pencil, one with a pink marker. But it was the verse that gave her a chill. She closed her eyes, picturing the antique store and the sign, Time After Time. She saw herself going inside, then moving down the narrow, dusty aisles to the back of the store—finding the jewelry case and then that ring. That marvelous ring that had let her change the future and her fate.

There had been an engraving inside.

I promise you forever.

Forever was a long, long time with Daniel at her side.

She leaned back against the pillows as the last of her uncertainty ebbed. As she waited for him to come back, she felt a tiny flutter beneath her heartbeat. A sigh of contentment slid through her, filling her with such a sense of peace.

Yes, baby...I know you're still there.

Then she laid her hand on the flat of her stomach, as if in comfort to the tiny spark of new life that still burned.

The girls weren't the only ones who were depending on me, were they, sweet thing?

She closed her eyes, letting the silence envelope her. A few minutes later, she heard the familiar tread of Daniel's footsteps and sat up on the side of the bed, awaiting him with a smile.

Epilogue

The staircase at the O'Rourke house was entwined with fresh pine boughs and holly, and in the living room the lights twinkled brightly on the six-foot Norfolk pine that Daniel, Mary and Hope had decorated last night. The scents of fresh greenery mingled with a simmering potpourri of sweet spices that Mary had going on the sideboard. She sat cross-legged in the floor in front of the tree, staring up at the lights, wanting to be close to the joy. Then her gaze slid to a very obviously handmade elf hanging from the lower branches.

Last night she'd watched Hope pull it from the box of decorations and listened to her chatter as she reminisced about making it at school the year before. It had been made from a juice carton and a dozen or so multicolored pompons. It looked more like an explosion of fuzzy M&M's, than one of Santa's elves. The odd thing was, Mary thought she could remember watching Hope hang it proudly on the tree, when she knew in her heart she'd been very alone last year. The transition between her life before the antique shop and her life after was something she would never be able to share, but however it happened, she was forever thankful.

Her wounds from the abduction had long since healed, although there were still nights when she woke up in a sweaty panic, thinking she was still fighting Howard Lee Martin for her life.

Both Justine and Amy Anne were still in therapy but had become fast friends with Hope. With the naïveté of the child that she was, Hope had blithely accepted them as Mommy's friends who had now becomes hers, as well.

Howard Lee Martin had never gone to trial, but Daniel had assured Mary that the institution for the criminally insane where he had been committed was a far worse sentence than anything else he could have ever received. He would never see the light of day as a free man again, and for Mary and the little girls' families, it would have to suffice.

Her life was peaceful and filled with joy on a daily basis. She went to bed each night with a prayer of thanksgiving on her lips and woke up each morning, grateful for what she had. By this time next year, there would also be an addition to their family and for that Mary was ecstatic. She'd missed all those early memories with Hope, but she wasn't going to miss them again.

She glanced at the clock. It wasn't quite ten. She still had time to run a quick errand before she met Daniel for lunch and she didn't want to be late. Even though she was moving on with her new life, there was a part of her old one she needed to put to rest. She got to her feet, grabbed her coat and her purse as she headed out the door.

The December wind was chilly, even for Savannah, and Mary was glad that she'd worn her long coat. She had been walking for blocks, trying to retrace the steps that she'd taken on the day her life had changed. Yesterday she'd taken a chance and called the dress shop where she once had worked, only no one there even knew her name. She accepted it as part of the confirmation for which she was searching, but she still wanted to see the old man.

She'd found the Mimosa easily, the restaurant where she'd

been supposed to meet her friend. From there, she'd walked up and down the renovated area of the old town, admiring the Christmas decorations in the windows while trying to find the antique store. But each time she turned down a new block, she came up empty. Frustrated, she thought about calling Daniel for directions, then discarded the notion. It would do nothing but worry him if he thought she was still locked in the past.

She glanced at her watch and then sighed. If she didn't start back to the parking garage where she'd left her car, she would be late meeting Daniel for lunch.

She started to turn away when she noticed the window display in the jewelry store next door. Something about it rang a bell. She moved closer to look inside and realized she'd been here before.

She turned abruptly, expecting to see the antique store directly across the street, but there was nothing but an empty lot. She frowned, thinking maybe she was confused about the area, then saw the knitting shop that had been on the east side of Time After Time. It was still there, as was the small coffee shop on the west, only there was nothing in between the two small businesses but dirt lot and space. Curious as to what had happened in the months since she'd been here, she hurried across the street to inquire.

The knitting shop was small; overflowing with a bounty of yarns—opulent mohair, baby-soft cottons, as well as the sturdy, multi-hued wools. But Mary's interest was not on the well-stocked store. She wanted to know what had happened to the shop that had been next door.

"Good morning," the clerk said, as Mary walked up to the counter. "May I help you find some yarns?"

"Actually, I need some information about the store that was next door."

"You mean the coffee shop?"

"No, the antique store."

The clerk frowned. "I'm sorry, ma'am, but there's no antique store in the area."

Mary looked at the woman as if she'd suddenly lost her mind.

"It was here in September and so was I. How long have you worked here?"

"Ever since my mother retired, which is almost ten years now."

Mary's palms started to sweat. This wasn't making sense.

"I don't understand. I was in the store only a couple of months ago. I talked to the old man behind the counter. There was dust all over the stock, but I was there."

"You must have the wrong street," the clerk said. "A lot of these blocks look alike, especially in the older part of the city."

"No. It was here," Mary said. "I distinctly remember standing across the street and seeing the reflection in that window." She pointed at the jewelry store across the street.

"I don't know what to tell you," the clerk said.

Before Mary could answer, the door to the back of the shop opened and a small, gray-haired woman came in.

"That's my mother. She's lived here all her life. Maybe she can help."

Mary nodded, although she couldn't imagine what the old woman might say that would eliminate this confusion.

"Mother, this lady is looking for an antique store. She thought—"

Mary interrupted. "It was on the lot between this store and the coffee shop. I was in there in September."

The old woman frowned. "No, honey…you must be mistaken. There hasn't been anything on that lot since the late twenties."

"But I was there," Mary said. "The store was called Time After Time and was full of dusty antiques."

"Not next door, you weren't," she said. "When I was a young girl, a man named Saul Blumenthal had a second-hand furniture store next door. He lived above it with his wife and baby boy. The store caught fire one night when Saul was at a meeting. By the time he got back, his business was gone and his family with it. It was the tragedy of our times."

"No," Mary muttered, remembering the sad eyes in the old man's face. "That's not possible."

The old woman shrugged. "Well…it happened just the same."

"What happened to Saul Blumenthal?" Mary asked.

"Oh, that was the saddest part. A couple of days later, he hanged himself from what was left of the structure. I think they shipped the bodies back East to be buried."

Mary took a deep breath and then walked out of the store. She paused on the sidewalk and then looked back at the lot, trying to make sense of what she'd just heard.

She hadn't dreamed it, because Daniel had mentioned the store more than once since she'd come home, commenting on the fact that when she'd passed out in the antique store it must have been because she'd been pregnant. Only she knew that hadn't been so.

As she stared at the small patch of dirt, she felt something against her face, like the breath of someone who'd passed too close to where she was standing.

But there was no one there.

Goose bumps rose on her arms as she shivered. She had no explanation for what had happened, but the longer she stood there, the more confused she became. There were all kinds of fancy words that some might apply to her story, should they have chosen to believe it.

Time travel.

Time warp.

By whatever name, it was still a mystery. Whether it came from God's hand or an old man's wandering soul seeking forgiveness for what he had done by giving others a second chance, she knew what had happened. She didn't understand it. But she knew it was true.

She glanced at the empty lot one last time and then turned away, suddenly needing to be as far away from this place as she could get.

By the time she got to the parking garage, she was almost running. She slid behind the wheel and then took a deep breath. As she glanced at herself in the rearview mirror, she suddenly wondered why she'd been in such a hurry. She started the car and carefully backed out of the parking space. She still had a good half hour before it was time to meet Daniel. Taking a deep breath, she brushed the hair away from her face and accelerated carefully through the maze of ramps.

By the time she pulled out onto the street and headed downtown, the memories of her years without Daniel and Hope were swiftly fading and her mind was filling with all the things she needed to do before Hope's Christmas party at school.

She stopped at a red light and glanced at her watch. Someone honked loudly as they sped through the intersection. Startled by the sound, she looked up, and as she did, realized she didn't know where she was. Frowning, she glanced up at a street sign, trying to figure out why she was here and then shrugged. She must have taken a wrong turn on her way to meet Daniel for lunch.

The light changed and she drove through the intersection with a smile on her face. The further she drove, the fainter the past became. A few minutes later, she pulled up outside Daniel's office. When she saw him coming toward her with a smile on his face, what had been was no more. There was nothing left of who she'd been.

All she knew was right now, she was the luckiest woman on God's earth.

* * * * *

SHADES OF
A DESPERADO

To the people who have the faith to trust in something other than what they see before their eyes, God will bless you.

To those who act on instinct, rather than rules, God watches over you.

To those who trust with their hearts and not their heads, I thank God.

To those who live today with memories of a past that won't let go, have faith in God.

To Leslie Wainger, who shared a dream, may God be with you always.

Prologue

1877
The Black Hills of the Dakota Territory

The gun in Dakota's hands felt warm and familiar to him, but the look in his eyes was as harsh and bitter as the Dakota lands for which he'd been named. Across the room, he watched Mercy Hollister from the tiny cabin's only bed like a hawk with its prey; the knot in his gut tightening with every breath that he took.

Damn her beautiful, lying face.

Twice his forefinger brushed the pistol's hair trigger as he contemplated the hole the bullet would make in her soft white body, and each time, the knot in his belly gave a lurch, reminding him that he'd been a fool to trust, and an even bigger fool to love.

Angry with himself and the futility of it all, he brushed a hand across his face, as if wiping away what was left of a bad dream, yet when he looked up, the reality of the situation remained. He was running from the law with the woman he now believed had betrayed him…and he still loved her.

He raised himself from a reclining position long enough to glance out the small, dusty windowpane. The plume of

dust he'd seen earlier down on the flats was just that little
bit closer, evidence that Sheriff Ab Schuler and his posse
had found them after all.

He dropped back against the wall, only half-aware of
the soft, aimless tune Mercy was humming as she stripped
down to wash her trail-weary body. As his gaze swept her
nudity, he hated himself for the weakness of still wanting
a woman who'd turned him in for the money, and he was
certain Mercy had done just that.

If she wasn't the one who'd told where they were going,
how else had they been found? He'd been using this hideout
for more than three years, and to date, no lawman had even
gotten close to finding it. But, Dakota reminded himself,
he'd never been fool enough before to tell a woman anything but a lie. That was before Mercy—before he'd let her
into his heart and into his life. Now Ab Schuler was riding
Dakota's trail like it was a marked map.

He knew the price on his head was enough to make brother
turn against brother. Why had he let himself believe a harlot
would be different? Why had he let himself fall in love with a
woman whose last lover before him had been the very sheriff
who was dogging their trail? Just because she cried out with
joy when they made love, just because she swore she loved
him more than life itself, that didn't make it so.

The gun felt heavy in his hands, almost as heavy as the
weight in his heart. With a slow, angry sigh, he laid it on his
belly, letting it balance on the flat, bare plane as he put his
hands behind his head and leaned against the wall. Using
his fists for a pillow, he angled his long legs off one side of
the narrow bunk, watching her as she washed and wondering if he had the guts to kill her.

Unaware of the drama being played out in Dakota's mind,
Mercy dipped a rag in a basin of tepid water, ignoring the
sediment in the bottom of the pan. Riding the trail with an
outlaw had been harder than she'd imagined, but she had

no regrets. Ever since she and Dakota left Trinity three days ago, she'd been eating dirt, as well as wearing it. Washing it off her body felt like heaven.

And, for the first time in as long as she could remember, she was happy—truly happy. It had taken guts for her to leave the security of a roof over her head, a warm, dry bed and daily food on the table, even if she'd had to earn it by lying down for every sorry-ass man who passed through town.

Loving an outlaw hadn't been in Mercy's plans, but Dakota had been a hard man to resist. His black hair was only a few shades darker than his gaze, yet when he smiled at her, she saw the man he could have been…and in his eyes, she was the woman she should have been. She saw something in Dakota's face that she'd never seen before in another living soul. Trust. He not only loved her, he trusted her. She didn't know where this crazy life she'd chosen was going to lead, but as long as she was by Dakota's side, she would be happy.

She dipped the rag in the basin again, swishing it around and then wringing it out before lifting the weight of her long, dark hair to wash the back of her neck. Even though the water was less than clear, she couldn't remember ever being as glad to feel clean as she did right now.

The bunk creaked behind her, and she smiled. She could feel Dakota's gaze on her bare body. The cabin he'd brought her to was little more than a roof and four walls, yet with him at her side, it seemed like a mansion. It was going to be home…their home.

Suddenly, she could wait no longer. Clean or not, she wanted to lie in Dakota's arms, to feel his hands on her body and his mouth on her lips. She needed to hear the words he always whispered in her ear right before he took her over the edge of reason.

Sweet Mercy…have mercy….

She smiled to herself, picturing the look on his face when he said it, and dropped the rag into the basin. She turned with anticipation in her eyes. But the smile on her lips stilled before it became full-blown.

There was a look on Dakota's face that she'd never seen— a cold, deadly expression that stopped her breath and very nearly her heart. She inhaled sharply as fear sliced through her daydreams, rudely yanking her back to the reality of loving a man who lived by the gun.

"Dakota?"

He didn't answer. He didn't move.

Mercy darted toward the bed, forgetting her sponge bath and the fact that she was naked.

Oddly, her nudity did not raise Dakota's lust. Instead, it seemed to enhance the innocence of the blue-eyed woman coming toward him, as if she were proving she had nothing to hide.

Don't fall for this again, he reminded himself, but when she fell into his arms with tears on her face, he cursed the surge of protective longing that swept over him.

Even now, sweet Mercy, when I know you for what you really are...

"Sweetheart! What's wrong?" Mercy asked.

Angry with himself and with her, he took her and rolled, pinning her beneath him on the dusty, narrow bunk. But when he pressed the barrel of his gun against her temple, he broke out in a cold sweat, unable to pull the trigger.

Mercy was in shock. Never in the six months that she'd known Dakota had he treated her in such a fashion. Other men had, but she thought he was different, and because this was so unexpected, she couldn't stop her tears.

"Dakota! Talk to me! Tell me what's wrong! You know I love you! You know I'd do anything for you! Why are you treating me this way?"

Dakota shook his head, trying to clear his thoughts, but all he succeeded in doing was hazing his vision of her.

Mercy couldn't believe what was happening. Even though

there were tears in Dakota's eyes, she feared for her life. None of this was making any sense.

"Stop this!" she screamed, and began hammering on his bare chest with her fists. "You're scaring me! Whatever is wrong, I've got a right to know!"

Words ripped from his throat in harsh, angry grunts. "Why? Why did you do it?"

"Do what?" she cried. "I didn't do anything but love you!"

Dakota blinked, trying to clear his vision. The action did little except blur the fear he saw on her face.

Make her pay, he told himself, shifting his body so that she was completely immobile, pinned to the bed by his weight. With his last ounce of determination, he increased the pressure of the gun against her temple. Their gazes locked as he cocked the hammer. The small, metallic click echoed loudly in the sudden silence of the small one-room shack.

Mercy froze, her eyes widening in horror as she became aware of the desperation on Dakota's face.

"Dakota… My God…don't! I love you! Doesn't that mean anything to you anymore?"

Her words ripped through the pain in his chest, spilling the hurtful anger into every part of his body. With a cold, cruel smile, he leaned down, dragging his mouth across her face and ripping a kiss from her trembling lips. Even now, as brutally as he was treating her, he felt her respond.

Finally he tore himself away, only slightly satisfied with the small drop of blood lingering on the edge of her lower lip. With a low, guttural curse, he raked his gun down her cheek. As badly as he wanted to hate her, he caught himself regretting the fear he'd put into her eyes. But his heart wasn't the only thing breaking. His voice cracked as he spoke.

"I guess I didn't know you quite as well as I thought. You're quite a little soldier, aren't you, darlin'?"

Tears tracked down her face, only to disappear in the

thick black hair pillowing her head. Her voice was weak and shaking as she lifted her hands in supplication.

"My God, my God... I don't know what you mean."

With an angry swipe of his hand, he slapped her hands away, refusing the gesture of peace.

"Since you've ridden just about every man you ever met, I guess that earns you the title."

Mercy stiffened. Not once in their entire relationship had Dakota ever alluded to her life as a prostitute, and now, when she'd given it and everything else up for him, he had thrown it in her face. Hurt by an accusation she couldn't deny, her tears fell faster, in anger now.

"Damn you!" she cried, and then choked on a sob as she hit him full force on the side of the face with the flat of her hand.

The slap ricocheted from tooth to tooth, and still Dakota kept his gun aimed at her head.

"Either pull the trigger or get off me!" Mercy screamed, and began hitting Dakota with doubled-up fists. "If you hate me this much, then do it! I dare you!"

He neither moved nor answered as his dark, angry gaze continued to burn across her features.

Groaning with disbelief, she pushed at his chest with the flat of both hands, trying to get out from under his weight.

"My God! I was such a fool! I left everything I had to ride with you! I put my own life at risk to run with a man with a price on his head. I gave you something I never gave another living soul."

The rage in her startled him. He might have expected it from an innocent...but not from Mercy. She was anything but innocent. Though he knew that, it was still all Dakota could do to meet her gaze.

"Damn you, Dakota, I thought you were different, but I was wrong! You're no better than every other man who spilled himself in me. In fact, you're worse! At least they didn't tell me a lie to get me to spread my legs. If that's all you wanted, then why didn't you say so?"

When she shifted beneath him, blatantly offering herself up to his maleness with a look in her eyes he would never forget, all the rage in him died. He eased the hammer on the pistol down without firing the shot. Choking on sobs, she went limp with relief. Dakota buried his face in the curve of her neck and swallowed a sob of his own.

A silent moment passed while Mercy struggled to get past her shock and Dakota fought to regain his sense of purpose. He was the first to act. Without speaking, he rolled himself from her body and stalked to the other end of the room, where he'd dumped his gear. He turned once, looking back at her with a longing he didn't know how to hide, then began dressing to ride.

Mercy watched in disbelief, trying to figure out what had gone so terribly wrong. But when Dakota jammed his hat on his head, slung his saddlebags over his shoulder and picked up his rifle, she jumped out of bed in sudden fright. Dear God! He was leaving her behind!

"Wait for me!" she begged, and started pulling on clothes in wild abandon.

He paused in the doorway, staring long and hard out toward the valley below, then spun abruptly, as if making a sudden decision. Without giving himself time to change his mind, he tossed her his rifle.

"Here," he drawled. "I know you can shoot, so if you love me like you say you do, then don't let Schuler take me back to hang."

Mercy caught the gun in midair as the door slammed shut behind him. Her face paled as she clutched the rifle. Suddenly she understood. The posse must have found them, and if Dakota's behavior was anything by which to judge, he believed she'd betrayed him!

"Dakota! No!"

But it was too late. She heard him riding away.

Frantic, she began grabbing at her clothing, her entire
body in tremors. Buttons wouldn't go into holes, and fabric stuck to her still-damp body, hindering the haste she so
desperately needed. Finally she had everything on but her
boots. As she bent down to slip them on, the handgun she'd
begun carrying in the pocket of her skirt shifted against her
thigh. She shuddered and said a small prayer. Seconds later,
she was out of the cabin, with the rifle in her hand and the
handgun bumping against her leg as she ran.

Sensing her panic, her horse shied, dancing sideways,
nickering and tossing its head as she tried to mount.

"Whoa, whoa…easy, boy," she muttered, trying to calm
the horse, as well as her own racing heart, but it wasn't to be.

As she was in the midst of trying to get her toe in the stir-
rup, the sounds of gunfire echoed from the canyon below.
Startled by the abrupt and unexpected noise, the horse
reared, then bolted, dumping her in the dirt and leaving
her unable to ride to Dakota's aid.

"Oh, no," Mercy groaned.

Picking herself and the rifle up out of the dirt as the horse
disappeared, she started running down the long, winding
path, with the sound of gunfire slamming into her body as
it echoed from rim to rim.

She came to a sliding halt at the crest of the hill and
looked down into the canyon, staring in mute despair. She
was too late! Dakota was pinned down, with no way out.
Using his dead horse for a shield, he continued to fire at the
men in the posse with cold precision.

Mercy groaned. She had to help him!

With shaking hands, she dropped to one knee and aimed
the rifle, adjusting her shot to the downward slant in eleva-
tion. But when she realized the rifle Dakota had tossed her
had only two rounds remaining, hope died.

"Damn you, Dakota, why? You never carry unloaded guns. Why now?"

Her finger slid from the trigger as she lowered the rifle to her side. Even if she hit her target both times, it would not be enough to stop the posse from capturing him. And if that happened, then she would be helpless to do as he'd asked. He already believed she'd betrayed him. No matter what, she couldn't let him hang.

It seemed like hours, but it was only a matter of minutes before the shooting stopped, as abruptly as it had started. Even where she was standing, the smell of gunpowder filled the air, and the silence after the endless barrage was almost as frightening as the inevitable arrest she saw coming. She stifled a sob. Dear God, Dakota was out of ammunition!

She watched as Ab Schuler stepped out from behind a rock, calling for Dakota to surrender. When Dakota stood, Mercy's spirit sank. And when he tossed his empty gun in the dirt and lifted his arms above his head, she panicked.

This couldn't be happening! Only minutes earlier she'd been planning the rest of their lives, and now it was over.

But Mercy hadn't survived this long in the Dakota Territory by being weak, and she couldn't ignore Dakota's last request. She got to her feet. Still clutching the rifle Dakota had given her, she walked to the edge of the rim. Schuler was putting handcuffs on her man. Panic resurfaced.

"Nooo!" she screamed, and the sound of her voice echoed down into the belly of the canyon like the eerie wail of a she-panther that had just lost its mate.

Momentarily surprised by the sound of her voice, the men down below paused in their jubilant actions, then stared around in confusion. When they saw the woman standing poised on the rim above them with a rifle in her hands, to a man they began grabbing for weapons and scrambling for cover.

Dakota looked up. Forgetting the handcuffs that Schuler

had just placed around his wrists, he stared, fixing the image
of Mercy Hollister one last time within his mind. The distance between them seemed to shrink, and he almost believed he could see the tears on her face. He turned until he
was facing her squarely, offering her a full view of his chest.

Do it, girl. If you ever loved me, for God's sake, do it now!

Even from where she was standing, Mercy recognized
Dakota's move. But he was asking her for something she
wasn't sure she knew how to give. How could she end the
life of the only man she'd ever loved?

From the corner of her eye, she saw Ab Schuler grabbing
for his rifle. She shifted her stance. There was no more time.
She lifted the rifle to her shoulder, taking aim the way her
brother had taught her years ago.

God help me.

She cocked the hammer.

God forgive me.

Everything seemed to happen in slow motion. The sound
of the gunshot cracked like winter ice on a spring-thawing
river. Loud and clear, the echo bounced from rim to rim and
into Mercy's heart, piercing her as sharply as the bullet that
struck Dakota square in the chest.

Mercy watched as Dakota dropped, and from where she
was standing, it was like watching snow fall, soundless, and
so inevitably final. Pain tore through her body in waves
as nausea nearly sent her to her knees. With a wild cry of
ungovernable rage for what she'd done, she drew back the
rifle and sent it spinning out into the vast space below, then
thought about following it down. Sick at heart, and staggering from an onslaught of emotion, she fell to the ground,
unable to look at Dakota again.

It hurt to breathe and she wondered if he'd felt the same
pain when her bullet ripped through his chest and into his
heart. A wave of vertigo sent her grabbing for dirt, and as
she did, the handgun in her pocket slid between her knees.

Seconds later, she was clutching it in one hand and staring up into the wide expanse of the midday sky, remembering that only yesterday she and Dakota had made love beneath that same bowl of blue.

The steel warmed to her touch, offering comfort and the answer she needed. She took a deep breath, then lifted the gun.

Ab Schuler spun with gun in hand as the outlaw dropped at his feet. A surge of anger washed over him. He'd been cheated out of watching the son of a bitch hang. He looked up in time to see Mercy's rifle go flying into space. Along with his men, he stared in mute fascination as it seemed to hang in the air before spinning end over end, then shattering on the rocks below. But when Mercy dropped to the ground and pulled a pistol from her skirt, fear for her stunned him as he realized her intent. He started up the path, screaming her name as he ran.

The second shot came before he'd gone ten yards, and he paused, unable to believe what she'd done. As before, the single gunshot echoed, but when it had passed, an unearthly stillness seemed to come over the canyon. The men in the posse looked away, as if they felt guilt for having been a part of what had just taken place, despite being fully within the boundaries of the law.

Up until now, the day had been hot and still, but a sharp wind suddenly sprang up, wailing through the mouth of the canyon like the sound of someone crying. The high-pitched moan grew louder and louder as the wind continued in force. One man quickly dropped to his knees in prayer, while another scrambled for his horse and rode out without ever looking back. Years later, as the story was told and retold, one thing never changed. To a man, the posse swore they'd felt the hot wrath of God that day as He came sweeping through the canyon to reclaim the two lost souls.

Chapter 1

Present Day
The Kiamichi Mountains of southeastern Oklahoma

A small branch slapped Boone MacDonald across the nose, bringing quick tears to his eyes that he blinked away. Silently he cursed the thickness of the undergrowth through which he was creeping, as well as the weak light from the three-quarter moon filtering through the dense thicket of trees. Skulking in woods as heavy as those on the Kiamichi Mountains was next to impossible. Not even a possum could move through here without making some sort of noise.

A low murmur of voices from the men up ahead drifted on the air, reminding him of the urgency of his task. Working as an undercover agent for the Drug Enforcement Administration was nothing new for him, but working this deep under cover was not something he liked. It wasn't the first time he'd insinuated himself into a gang, but it *was* the first time it had taken him so long to find out who was running the show. He'd been living a lie for nearly six weeks, and he had yet to meet the man behind the money.

For the past half hour, success had been less than fifteen yards ahead. Each time the silhouette of a tall, well-built man was briefly outlined against the moonlight, Boone could almost see his face. But it never happened. They were moving too quickly for him to get close enough for an identification.

Frustration mounted. Intent on the task at hand, he unintentionally walked into a spider web and stifled a curse as he swiped at the sticky, clinging strands on his face.

Suddenly he froze, part of the web still stuck to his hand. They'd stopped! His instinct for survival was at an all-time high as he stood with one ear cocked to the wind while the hapless spider escaped up a branch. Boone slowed his breathing, concentrating instead on the sounds around him.

In his mind, there could be only two reasons for the quiet. Either he'd been made and someone was at this moment circling his position, or they'd reached their destination. Forced to wait for answers he might not like, Boone took a quiet step back, moving deeper into the darkness of the trees.

Above him, an owl suddenly took flight, and he cursed his luck in having stopped beneath its roost. If the men were on to him, the bird's flight alone would indicate his position. He pulled a .357 Magnum from the holster beneath his black denim jacket, then squatted within the dense undergrowth, making himself less of a target.

All his senses were keying on sound and movement, sorting what he recognized from what he did not. His face was a study in darkness, both in spirit and in fact. Black eyes glittered dangerously from beneath hooded lids, giving away nothing of what was going on inside his mind.

He was a man who lived on the edge—a man who played by his own set of rules and, by doing so, had kept himself alive. His friends were few, his family none. As far back as he could remember, he'd answered to no one but himself, which, as a child, had been the reason for his constant movement through the welfare system. The way he'd looked at it, no one had wanted him. In self-defense, he had refused to care.

But that attitude had put him on the wrong side of the law at an early age. When he was sixteen, he had watched his best friend die from a gunshot wound to the head. At that moment, something inside of him had snapped. When the shock of it was over, he'd made a vow that ultimately changed his life.

Becoming a cop might have been his salvation. But even if he was now on the side of right, he was still living on the wrong side of the law, and it had seared his soul. He'd run with the bad boys for so long that being an outlaw had become the norm. He'd forgotten everything about the real world, including how to trust. The only thing Boone trusted was himself, his instincts, and they were telling him now to stay still.

While he watched, the owl he'd startled flew silently out of sight. His grip shifted on the .357 as a sharp burst of laughter broke the quiet in which he was waiting. He frowned. From his point of view, there wasn't a damn thing funny about the situation.

As he continued to listen, the unmistakable sound of car doors opening and closing brought him to his feet.

"Damn it," he muttered, and bolted through the trees, hoping for one last chance to ID his man. All he saw was the disappearing taillights of two separate vehicles. Once again, he'd missed his chance!

His face mirrored disgust as he holstered his gun, reminding himself that there was always a next time. Peering at the luminous dial of his digital watch to check the hour, he started back through the trees. The way he figured it, he was a couple of miles from his truck, and it was all uphill.

Habit sent him up the mountain at a different angle from the one he'd come down. Like the men with whom he ran, he moved with stealth, searching shadows and choosing his paths with caution. Fifteen minutes later, he was telling himself that he was too far east when he heard an indistinct sound. Eyes narrowing, he felt for the bulge of his gun beneath his jacket. But when the sound came again, he knew what he'd heard, and he started running with no thought of stealth.

Bathed in moonlight, the woman stood without moving while the water from the creek in which she was standing tugged at the hem of her long, wet gown. Plastered to her trembling body, the pale, fragile fabric made her appear like alabaster, rather than a living, breathing soul, and yet Boone knew that she was real. No statue had hair that fluid and dark, or breasts that lifted and fell with each indrawn breath.

The soft, helpless sobs that he'd heard still wracked her body. Her beauty was haunting, but her pain was palpable, plowing into subconscious memories of his own that were better left alone.

Riveted by her presence, he hesitated, wanting to go to her, but afraid to interrupt something he didn't understand.

"I love you. I've always loved you," she whispered, then reached out in front of her, clutching at air.

Boone took a quick step back into the trees, using the shelter of darkness as he trained his gaze on the scene, searching for the man who must surely be there. To his surprise, no one came forward.

Again the woman swayed where she stood, choking on her own sobs, as if in terrible pain.

"Why?" she cried. "Why didn't you believe me before it was too late?"

When she went to her knees in the cold mountain stream, Boone stalked out of the trees, heading toward her with single-minded intent. It was September. At night, the water in that creek had to be freezing. He called out to her, anxious not to frighten her, but knowing he had to help all the same.

* * *

Rachel Brand groaned as the pain in her head shattered, spilling through her body and sending her into the same black, numbing void that always preceded cognizance. Yet when sanity came, she knew without doubt that she'd sleep-walked again. This time she was in the creek, wet and cold, with no memory of how she'd gotten there. All she knew was that the episodes were becoming more frequent and, if tonight was any indication, life-threatening. Pulling a stunt like this in the Kiamichis in autumn was risky; repeating it in mid-winter could be deadly.

She got up, thumping her knee in helpless frustration. Tossing back the braid hanging over her shoulder, then grab-bing at the wet, clinging fabric of the gown wrapped around her legs, she started to climb out of the water. But disgust gave way to terror when a deep, quiet voice broke the soli-tude of the night.

"Lady…are you all right?"

Horrified, Rachel froze. She was no longer alone! She spun, unaware of how the gown had plastered itself to her body, delineating a slender build, a fullness of breast, the gentle flare of slim hips and long, trim legs.

In fear for her life, she began backing up as a tall, dark stranger came out of the trees. When he paused within the pale glow of moonlight in the clearing near the edge of the stream, she took one look at the strength in his body and the length of his legs and knew she could not outrun him.

"Don't hurt me," she begged, taking several tentative steps backward, as if testing the man's intent.

Boone wished he could pull out a badge and assure her that he meant her no harm. He knew how she would per-ceive his appearance. The outlaw look was in vogue when you were running with a pack like Denver Cherry's.

"Lady, be careful!" he said, his voice low and urgent, as she stumbled on the rocks hidden beneath the cold, icy waters. "Don't be afraid. I don't mean you any harm. I heard you crying and came to see if you needed help."

"No, I'm fine!" she cried, motioning to him to stay back. "Just leave me alone. Please!"

Rachel's heart was thundering, and her legs were shaking. Frantic, raked the dense forest behind him with her gaze, wondering how many more like him might come creeping out of the shadows.

Boone winced at the panic in her voice. This was getting him nowhere. Instinct told him to get out while the getting was good. The longer he stayed here, the more likely it was that some man would show up, and then there would be hell to pay explaining why he was alone in the woods with a half-dressed and terrified woman. But she looked so lost, and something inside him couldn't let go. He took a deep breath and gave it one last try.

"I swear to God, I would never hurt you."

The sound of his voice…and those words… They struck a chord of memory in Rachel that she'd never known was there. Her gaze focused on the cut of his shoulders and the tilt to his head, and she forgot what she'd been about to say. She had the strangest sensation of having heard that voice say those same words before.

Good sense was telling her to run, but her feet wouldn't move. His presence frightened and at the same time compelled her.

As she stood there trying to make sense of it all, the sensation of numbing cold disappeared. Before her eyes, the night began to turn backward, and Rachel watched in quiet defeat as the brilliant rays of a pink-and-gold sunset suddenly framed a man standing before her. He seemed to be the same man as the one in the forest, and yet in the ways that mattered, he was not.

This is it, she thought. *I'm either losing my mind, or going to die.*

The man now standing before her smiled, and to her disbelief, she felt herself smiling back. When he started toward
her with a bounce in his step and a gleam in his eye that she
seemed to know all too well, everything spun out of control.

*He laughed. "God, woman, but you're too beautiful to
be believed."*

*She threw her arms around his neck and lifted her face
for his kiss. It came as she'd expected, hard and swift and
with an ever-present sense of urgency. "If you mean that,
I'll love you forever," she whispered.*

*Fear tied hard warning knots in his belly. He wasn't pre-
pared for her openness, or for the loving, trusting look on
her face. Now was the time to stop this madness before he
got himself in too deep.*

*"Women don't love men like me," he growled, as his fin-
gers dug into her arms.*

*She smiled up at him, flirting in spite of the hard-edged
glitter in his eyes.*

*"You don't mean that," she said. "There isn't a woman
in Trinity who wouldn't trade places with me right now if
they thought you'd give them the time of day."*

*He laughed, a short, brittle bark of self-deprecating mirth
that made her shudder. The smile on his face was just shy
of cruel, but the look in his eyes told it all. He was just as
scared of this thing between them as she was. Ordinarily,
men didn't love women like her, either. She gave nothing
away. They paid for what they got. At least, they did until
you, she thought, and reached up, tunneling her fingers
through the thick black length of his hair.*

*"And just what kind of a man are you, if not a man to
love?"*

*A bitter expression tore the smile from his face as he
turned her loose.*

"I'm a loser, darlin'. A man on the wrong side of the law.

I've killed before, and I'll very likely kill again. I'm a bad-lands desperado who's forgotten how to pray and you'd be well advised to leave me alone."

She laid her hand gently against the edge of his cheek. "I would if I could," she said, and then stepped into his embrace and rested her head upon his shoulder. "Besides, haven't you heard that a woman's love can make a bad man good?"

Pain drilled a hole through his heart, piercing all the way to his soul. He looked down, then tilted her chin until she was staring him straight in the face.

"Sweet, sweet Mercy, don't you understand? Once a des-perado, always a desperado."

A cloud passed between earth and the moon, casting everything on the Kiamichis into an abrupt darkness. At the apex of total density, Rachel gasped. Just like that, the sunset and the dream man were gone. She had no idea how long she'd been standing there watching the scene unfold inside her mind, but the world had shifted back to night-time and reality.

Her awareness returned to the cold, flowing water on her bruised and numbing feet, and then to the stranger who'd come out of the dark. The first thought in her head was that if she couldn't see him, he couldn't see her. Grabbing at the tail of her gown, she bolted from the creek and back up the hill, running away from a waking nightmare more horrible than those that haunted her sleep.

Boone heard water splashing. His heart sank. She was running away.

"Wait!" he called, afraid that she would hurt herself by running full tilt through the woods in the darkness. But when the cloud passed and the mountains were once again bathed in moonglow, he found himself standing alone at the edge of the stream.

With a sense of having somehow failed her, he turned and started back the same way he'd come. A long while later, he slid into the seat of his truck and then sat without moving, contemplating the sequence of events that had taken place this night.

He'd started out with one mystery and wound up with two. He still didn't know the identity of the man behind Denver Cherry's operation, and he'd found a woman who seemed as lost as he felt. Even worse, he didn't know her name.

"And that's the way you'd better leave it," he reminded himself. "You were out to catch a thief, not mess with someone else's woman."

Startled by a car's sudden appearance around a bend in the road below, he started his engine, then let it idle as the vehicle passed by. When it was gone, he turned on the headlights and pulled out of his place of concealment and drove away.

By the time he got into bed and pulled up the covers, it was past 3:00. The silent rooms of the dilapidated trailer that was his undercover home seemed to mock him. They were empty, just like his life.

Long after the lights were out, his jangled nerves were still rocking, on edge. Tonight was the closest he'd come to finding the brains behind Denver Cherry's operation. But he'd failed again, and until he knew all there was to know about this drug operation, he was still a man living a lie.

With a curse, he rolled over on his belly. Jamming his hands beneath his pillow, he closed his eyes and willed himself to sleep. But when sleep finally came, there was little rest. Instead, he dreamed of a tall, slender woman with long black hair who called out his name and then ran screaming from him in fright.

Chapter 2

Rachel twisted the band on the end of her braid and then tossed it over her shoulder. It fell between her shoulder blades with a thump. Dressed for the day, she headed to the kitchen as the welcome scent of fresh-brewed coffee wafted through the rooms.

Working as an emergency medical technician for the town of Razor Bend was often stressful and sometimes hazardous, but to Rachel, it was a fulfilling career. She couldn't remember a time in her life when she hadn't wanted to be in some field of medicine.

She hadn't really chosen the job of EMT. It had chosen her. Years ago she'd witnessed firsthand the dramatic difference that on-the-spot medical help could make in saving someone's life.

After seeing the quick wit and skill of an EMT bringing a nearly drowned child back to life, her decision was made.

While her vocation had been planned, settling in Razor Bend had not. That had been an accident. Two years ago, while driving back from Galveston, Texas, where she'd spent a summer vacation from her job in St. Louis, Missouri, her car had blown a head gasket. It had taken the mechanic in Razor Bend a day and a half to get the parts to fix it. By the time it was ready to go, she'd fallen in love with the small mountain community.

That day, when she drove out of town, she'd left behind the beginnings of some good friendships, as well as her résumé. Less than a month later, she'd gotten a call that changed her life. Now she was a full-fledged employee of the town of Razor Bend. And, except for the recent onset of her sleepwalking episodes, everything was just about perfect.

Rachel entered the kitchen, aiming for the coffee brewing in the pot, and poured herself a cup. What was left of last night's headache lingered at the base of her neck. Coffee in hand, she turned to look out the kitchen window, giving careful attention to the wide expanse of yard that sloped downward toward the trees surrounding the house. As she lifted the mug to her mouth, blowing gently before taking a sip, she took note of the weather, gauging what she was wearing against what she might need before her shift was over. The sun was coming up. The sky looked clear. After the rain they'd had all last week, they could use a picture-perfect day.

It didn't take long for the jolt of caffeine to settle Rachel's nerves, but as she let herself relax, memories came flooding into her mind, and with them a return of the fear and the panic that had come with the stranger who caught her sleepwalking.

With a groan, she turned from the window, her heart pounding, her hands trembling as she clasped them around the cup. She closed her eyes, remembering the sound of his voice coming out of the darkness, and with it the fear that had momentarily shattered what was left of her sanity. He'd seemed so big and menacing, yet he'd made no overture toward her that she could call threatening. His voice had been filled with concern, but Rachel had known such an overwhelming sense of dread that she'd lost all rational thought.

Tired of worrying over things she could not change, she pulled herself out of the past to focus on matters at hand. Such as a grocery list she needed to fill. Taking a jacket to work, just in case it would rain. Things that mattered. Things that she could control.

But even though her mind had moved on, her body was still in the same place, standing before the window with a cup of coffee held tight in her hand.

Why? Why is this happening to me?

She'd moved up the mountain exactly four weeks ago tomorrow. She'd never had an episode of sleepwalking in her life until a little over six weeks ago. That had been at the end of July. Now it was September, and their frequency was increasing by the week. If only she could remember what was going on in her head when they happened, then maybe she could figure out what it all meant—and, better yet, find a way for them to stop.

The first time she came to in her nightgown on a back street in Razor Bend, she'd panicked. The second time it happened, she'd woken up on the edge of town in a downpour and crept back to her bed, certain that she would be found out and fired.

Luck had been with her, but Rachel didn't trust her luck to hold and had decided that finding a secluded house to rent outside of town might be safer…at least until she could figure out what had triggered this behavior.

This house was about as secluded as it got. Her nearest neighbor was down the mountain and more than two miles away, with acres and acres of dense woods between them. But after last night, she wondered if she'd made a mistake. Last night she'd come close to losing more than a job. What if she hadn't gotten away from that man? What might he have done to her? Worse yet, was he still out there…watching?

A muscle in her arm jerked, sending coffee sloshing over

the side of the cup. It was only luck that kept her from spilling it on the navy blue pant legs of her last clean uniform.

With a sigh of disgust, she put her coffee on the counter and then reached for a paper towel to clean up the mess she'd made on the floor. Moments later, she tossed the towel in the trash and then glanced at her watch. Her shift started at eight. It was time to go.

Grabbing her purse and jacket, Rachel exited her house just as the sun was brimming on the horizon. She paused, inhaling the fresh, piney scent of cool, clean air as a squirrel took a flying leap from the edge of her roof to the overhanging branches of a nearby tree. Laughter was rich in her voice as she chided his daring, but the smile on her face stilled as she looked east, past the limbs of the tree, to the sunrise in progress.

Her mouth went dry, and she choked on a breath. Her face flushed, then blanched, as she stared at the rich, vivid hues spreading across the sky. She reached toward the porch railing to steady herself.

It was all coming back. Only now was she remembering what happened before she broke and ran. Last night, the world had shifted before her eyes. She'd watched time move backward from night to day and let a dark-eyed, dangerous man take her in his arms.

Last night she'd tried to convince herself that her encounter with the stranger had been had been part of the dream that had taken her from her bed and into the woods, but now, in the bright light of day, she had to face the truth. She hadn't been asleep. She'd been wide awake and begging a stranger not to hurt her.

Rachel stared at the sunrise, shaking with a sick kind of fear.

"I'm going crazy."

Without warning, she bolted for her car. After she was

safely inside, with the door locked and the engine running, she started to rationalize.

"I'm imagining things," she muttered. "Maybe it's because I'm so isolated up here. My mind is starting to play tricks on me, that's all."

She put the car into gear and started to work. A short while later, she turned the last curve on the mountain road and saw Razor Bend in the distance. Relaxing at the familiarity of it, she took her foot from the brake and accelerated. It wasn't until she passed the city-limit's sign that something else occurred to her. Something she hadn't let herself consider all through the night.

If the man who'd caught her in the creek was real, but the outlaw in her dream was not, then how had she known before the outlaw spoke that he was going to call her Mercy?

Late that same afternoon, Rachel was on her knees inside the ambulance, putting clean linen on the gurney and restocking supplies. Charlie Dutton, a resident paramedic and also her partner for the past sixteen months, was in the office, filling out the paperwork on the run they'd just made. The rollicking rhythms of country music were playing on a nearby radio, a welcome interruption to Rachel's train of thought.

All day she'd been haunted by last night's events—another sleepwalking episode—the fear she'd felt at being caught in the woods by a stranger, and then the dream that had become mixed up in it all.

Only when she and Charlie were on an actual call was she able to put the memory behind her. But there was something different about her work today. Though her hands were busy, it seemed as if her mind were moving in slow motion. On one level she was doing everything right, but on another, she felt out of place, as if she were seeing the world through someone else's eyes.

Replace gauze pads.
Dark eyes searched her face as he lowered his head.
Check oxygen level in tank. *Sweet, sweet Mercy.*
Need a new box of disposable syringes.
Once a desperado, always a desperado.

Her hands paused above a shelf as she let her mind roll
backward. The feel of the outlaw's mouth on hers had been
so real…so familiar. She shuddered, then sighed. None of
what was happening to her made any sense. She yearned
for someone to talk to, someone in whom she could con-
fide, yet there was no one she could trust.

She couldn't talk to Charlie. He would think she was
crazy. The idea of talking to a psychiatrist had already
crossed her mind, but not in a small rural community like
Razor Bend. It was asking for trouble. Someone would find
out, and then that same someone—or another like him—
would decide she didn't have what it took to work under
stress. It could very well cost her the job she loved so well.

She'd already faced the fact that telling her best friend,
Joanie Mills, wouldn't be smart. The old saying "Telegraph,
telephone, tell a woman" could be directly applied to Joanie.
She owned a beauty shop called Curlers, and it was a known
fact in town that her place was a better source for current
news than CNN.

Therefore, Rachel would not be telling Joanie that she
sleepwalked, and she would certainly not mention the fact
that, in her mind, the thin line of demarcation between fact
and fantasy was starting to fade. Frustration was turning to
anxiety. If only there was someone… She shoved the last
box of disposable syringes into place and frowned.

Oh, God, what am I going to do?

No sooner had the thought crossed her mind than she realized the light in which she'd been kneeling was gone. She
looked up as her heart took a nosedive. It was Griffin Ross.

She managed a smile. "I didn't hear you walk up."

Griffin Ross grinned and leaned inside, pulling her down from the ambulance.

"I know I should have announced myself, but when you're working, you get this intense, adorable expression on your face. I couldn't resist playing voyeur. I'm sorry I frightened you. Forgive me?" Before she could answer, he'd kissed her cheek. Uncomfortable with what he'd just done, Rachel took a quick step back and managed to smile.

"You're forgiven."

Griff wanted to shake her. She said one thing, but he could see another in her eyes. Frustration was mounting over their situation. He'd been dating her for months, and if he was honest with himself, he had to admit that the only way he'd gotten to first base with her was on a walk. Rachel hadn't given him a moment of encouragement. As always, she smiled nervously, then turned away.

Griff must have come for a reason, Rachel thought as she tugged at the edge of a sheet covering the gurney, tucking it in place. He wouldn't be here during business hours unless he wanted something. She kept telling herself that if she stayed busy, she wouldn't have to make small talk with a man she wished would leave her alone.

As president of Ross Savings and Loan, Griffin was Razor Bend's most eligible bachelor. He'd been relentlessly pursuing her for the better part of six months, yet she knew that when he kissed her just now, she'd flinched.

It wasn't the first time she'd objected to Griffin Ross's interest in her, though Joanie saw fit to remind her on a daily basis that he was handsome, well-to-do, single—and interested. If she had a brain in her head, Joanie claimed, she would already have snatched him up. But Rachel didn't want him.

There had been more than one occasion during the past few months when she wondered if something was wrong with her feminine radar. She knew she should be thanking her lucky stars that a man like Griffin was pursuing her so diligently, but she wasn't.

Griff frowned as Rachel turned away. By nature, he wasn't a masochist, but he was beginning to realize that the only relationship he and Rachel Brand had was the one in his mind. Yes, they dated, and on more than one occasion they'd shared what he liked to call a passionate kiss, but nothing more. And the passion that existed between them was definitely one-sided.

But Griffin Ross hadn't risen to his level of success with a defeatist attitude. As his father had always said, the show wasn't over until the fat lady sang. He laid his hand on Rachel's shoulder, ignoring the flinching of muscle beneath his palm.

"Rachel?"

She looked up.

"The Elks lodge is sponsoring a fund-raising dance this weekend. Would you like to go?"

The pause between his question and her answer was too long. Griff hid his impatience behind an open smile, but when Rachel's partner, Charlie Dutton, came out of the office calling her name, he fought the urge to wring the man's neck.

Thankful that she'd been spared from answering, Rachel turned. "I'm here!" she shouted. "What's up?"

Charlie Dutton's walk was closer to a bounce than a stride, but when he saw Griffin Ross standing at her side, he came to an abrupt halt. It was all he could do not to frown.

"Sorry. I didn't know you had company. You left your keys on the desk." He handed them to her with an easy grin. "What's the deal with putting nail polish on them?"

"The keys to the front and back door look alike, but they're not, so I painted an *F* on this one, for *Front,* and a *B* on this one, for *Back,*" she said.

Charlie grinned. "So, what's on the key to your car? *C* for *Car,* or *D* for *Drive?*"

"Very funny," she said, dropping her keys in her pocket. "Don't you have something else to do?"

"No."

Rachel rolled her eyes. When pushed, Charlie Dutton was impossible.

"I was going to tell you that I'm through with the paperwork and ready to go to lunch," he offered, purposely ignoring the fact that Griff was there.

Rachel felt torn. She was all too aware that Charlie's feelings for her went beyond friendship, and while she admired and respected him, she felt nothing romantic for him in return. But they were partners, and on the job, where one went, the other followed.

"Just give me a minute," she said.

Charlie nodded, then gave Griffin Ross another cool glance and walked away.

Rachel waited until Charlie was gone before addressing Griffin's request. "About the dance... I'm not sure about my schedule. Can I get back to you?"

Griff's smile felt frozen on his face. "Of course. I'll give you a call at home in a few days, okay?"

Rachel braced herself for the kiss she saw coming, but when Griff's mouth touched her lips, she had to hide her distaste. His lips were too hot, too soft, and too demanding. Out of nowhere came the thought... *The outlaw's lips had been cool and hard...but so beguiling.*

A car honked on the street and Rachel jerked with embarrassment and took a quick step back. Distinguished citizen or not, she shouldn't be letting Griffin Ross kiss her while she was on duty.

"Griff, please don't," she said quickly. "Someone will see."

But as she looked across the street, to her dismay, she

realized her caution had come too late. Three of the most disreputable-looking men she'd ever seen were coming out of the Adam's Rib Café.

One was short. Another seemed as broad as he was tall. They were unshaven and unkempt. Their clothing ranged from black leather to worn and faded denim. The short, skinny one actually had the audacity to grin at her, then wink. But it was the tall one wearing black, dusty denim and a three-day growth of whiskers who caught her eye.

He stood a head above the others in stature, and even from where she was standing, she felt his eyes raking her body from her head to her toes. Neither by word nor by deed did he reveal what he might be thinking, yet Rachel felt the impact of his gaze as if she'd been gut-kicked. Breathless, and more than a little bit nervous, she tried to break his stare, but instead found herself unable to move. Griff's presence was forgotten, and there was a fleeting sensation of having stood beneath this man's gaze once before.

Griff frowned, for once refusing to hide his displeasure. "Damn it, Rachel…"

But his comment was forgotten when he realized that Rachel was no longer looking at him but at a point past his shoulder. Her eyes were wide and fixed, and her mouth was slightly parted. Startled by the intensity of her gaze, he turned, following the direction of her stare.

"Oooh, Lordy, wouldya look at the tits on her?"

Tommy Joe Smith followed the direction of Snake Martin's stare to the couple who were standing in the doorway of the EMS station. Snake's grin was lost behind a thick brush of brown, curly beard, but his leer was unmistakable. Tommy Joe had to admit Snake seemed to have an eye for the finer things in life, but he kept thinking of Denver Cherry, sitting at home waiting for them to come back with his food.

"Now, Snake, we got more important things to do today. Denver's waitin' on us, remember?"

The mention of Denver Cherry's name was enough to suck the smile off Snake's face. He glanced back at Tommy Joe, then over his shoulder, to the third man in their trio.

"I still say she's got some real pretty tits. Ain't that what you say, Boone?"

Boone MacDonald stifled the urge to put his fist all the way down Snake's throat. Damn him, and damn this situation. To his dismay, the woman they were ogling was none other than the one he'd found crying in the stream. The one whose voice had trembled with fear at his arrival— the same one who'd chosen to take her chances by running through the woods in the dark rather than risk another moment alone with him.

For the first time since he'd taken his oath of office, he hated what he was doing. People judged by appearances, and he knew how he appeared. He'd worked long and hard at perfecting his image…and his cover. And should someone be inclined to check, they would find out that one Boone MacDonald had a very dirty rap sheet, that he'd done time in and out of state, and that, when riled, he had more than a tendency toward violence.

On the job, his real name and true existence were kept hidden in an unused part of his mind. For Boone MacDonald, decent women did not exist. It had been so dark last night, even with the moonlight, that he'd believed himself safe. But from the expression on her face, he feared she'd recognized him as the man from the woods.

The only thing he could think of doing was to move, and move now. The last thing he needed was for her to point him out to that fancy man beside her. He didn't want anyone knowing where he'd been last night. Snake and Tommy Joe believed he'd been in Kansas, just what he'd led them to think. Having someone accuse him of sneaking around up on the Kiamichis last night could get him shot.

"Damn it, Boone, I asked you a question," Snake muttered.

Boone blinked, breaking the stare between himself and the woman, then glared down at Snake.

"She's not my type," Boone drawled. "I like my women blond and crazy, with long legs and red nails."

Snake's grin broke through the thick bush of his beard, revealing a mouthful of yellowing teeth. The image Boone had put in his mind made him giggle.

"Yeah, yeah," he said, his head flopping up and down on his scrawny neck like a cork bobbing on water. "I know just the kind you mean."

Tommy Joe waved a greasy sack in Snake's face. "Oh, man, if Denver could hear you two, he'd puke. Now come on, we gotta be going. The boss is waitin' for his ribs, and you know how Denver gets when he's hungry."

Relieved that the conversation had taken a turn away from the woman, Boone started toward his truck without waiting for the motley pair to follow.

From the corner of his eye, Boone saw the man beside her take her by the arm, then heard him call her name aloud. He paused, letting the sound soak into his mind. As he slid behind the steering wheel, a small, satisfied smile spread across his face.

So her name is Rachel.

Chapter 3

In the fall, dark came early in the mountains. By the time Rachel got off work and picked up a few groceries, it was already night. As she drove home, the headlights of her car beamed brightly on the narrow blacktop road, scaring away a rabbit and spotlighting a deer that had just started to cross. The big buck froze in the oncoming glare, and Rachel hit the brakes, fishtailing slightly to keep from hitting it. But when the tires started squealing, the buck jumped as if someone had prodded it from behind, then bounded off the road and out of sight.

Rachel breathed a sigh of relief, her fingers curling around the steering wheel as she stared past the yellow beams of light, searching the darkness to make sure it was gone. But while she was looking, she thought of the man who'd walked out of the trees last night, and in a fit of panic she stomped on the accelerator, leaving behind a wake of flying leaves and burnt rubber.

A few minutes later, when she pulled into the driveway, anxiety was still with her. Grabbing her bag of groceries, she slung her purse over her shoulder and bolted for the door.

Only after she was inside, with the door shut and locked, did she start to relax. As she passed through the rooms, she turned on light after light. By the time she got to the kitchen, her nervousness was almost gone. After changing out of her uniform and into an old pair of jeans and a loose long-sleeved shirt, she began preparing her food.

Somewhere beyond the ring of trees that surrounded her place, dogs yipped and then bayed as they did when treeing prey. At that moment, an idea came that filled her with relief.

A hunter! That was probably who found me last night!

Pleased that she'd given herself an answer she could live with, she went on preparing her dinner.

Yet all during her solitary meal, and even afterward, she fought a lingering hint of anxiety. Disgusted with herself for being faint of heart, she started to turn off the lights to get ready for bed.

The first switch Rachel turned sent the living room into darkness, and for a moment, before reality returned, she felt just as disoriented as she had when waking up in the stream. Shadows seemed to shift before her eyes. She stared until the familiar shapes of her couch and matching chairs became more than hulking figures in a dark, quiet room.

"You're losing it, Rachel," she muttered, and went to turn out the light still burning in the kitchen.

The scent of supper lingered in the air, the tantalizing aroma of broiled ham, the homey scents of butter beans and thick, crusty yellow corn bread. She gave the room a quick last glance, making sure everything was neatly in place, then flipped that switch as well.

But when those lights went out, her throat tightened. She stood in the darkened room, glancing nervously toward the back of the house. The light from her bedroom spilled out into the hall beyond, marking a place on the floor. In her mind, the warm yellow glow spelled safety.

She had to stop this craziness. This was her home...her haven. But even as she was listening to the voice of her rational self, she found herself walking back to the kitchen windows for a last, lingering look.

Outside, the lawn was heavy with dew. Moonlight glimmered on the glistening water droplets holding fast to the grass, giving the yard the appearance of frost, although Rachel knew it was not cold enough to freeze. A slight breeze pushed and tugged at the empty swing hanging from the limb of a gnarled oak. Something clattered out on the porch, and she leaned forward, peering toward the corner of the house, where the racket continued.

Inner tension melted as an empty bucket rolled into view, its bail flopping from one side to the other as it bounced off the porch, then along the grass. Weak at the knees, she sighed with relief.

"Another big deal out of nothing," she mumbled, then frowned as the bucket continued to roll farther and farther away from the house. That was her best bucket! If she let it go until morning, there was no telling where it might end up if some animal got hold of it.

Darn it all.

Ignoring the nervous jerk of her heart when the tumblers of the door lock clicked loudly in the silence, she took a deep breath and stepped onto the porch, pausing on the broad stone steps to survey the scene before her. Glancing nervously at bushes, she looked beyond the obvious, to what might be waiting for her, unseen.

As she stood, the brisk breeze began playing with wayward bits of her hair that had escaped its braid. Satisfied that all was normal, she took a deep breath and closed her eyes, letting herself become one with the darkness, instead of fearing it.

Off to her right, the low, mournful call of a dove soon brought an answer from its mate somewhere up ahead.

I'm not the only one who feels lost and nervous tonight.
When she opened her eyes and looked up, a black-velvet

sky shot through with pinpoints of lights winked down at her with timeless persistence. She smiled. The panic was gone. As she started down the steps, a night moth fluttered past her hand.

"Watch where you're going, buddy. You're not the only traveler out here tonight."

Blithely unaware of anything except the backyard security light toward which it was heading, the moth rode the breeze, safely out of her reach.

Now that Rachel was out, she didn't want to go back. She retrieved the bucket, setting it safely out of the wind, then returned to the porch, loath to give up her unexpected rapport with the night.

As she sat down on the old stone steps, the lingering heat they'd absorbed during the day still felt warm to her hands. Absently she undid her braid and, in lieu of a brush, began combing her fingers through the thick, dark lengths. The weight of hair on her back was just a little bit less than the weight in her heart, and out of nowhere came a longing for someone with whom she could share this time.

Just not Griffin Ross.

The knowledge was sudden, but too sure to be denied. The image of his handsome, smiling face popped into her head. Ashamed, she buried her face in her hands.

I don't love him. I'm not even certain I really like him. But why? What's wrong with me? What's wrong with him, that I can't give my heart away?

Unbidden, the outlaw from her dream superimposed himself over Griff's face, changing light hair to dark and blue eyes to black. One man's smile died, becoming a solemn expression in another's face—a face filled with longing too strong to be denied.

Rachel gasped. The image was so strong, so sure! She was certain that when she looked up, the man from her dream would be standing before her. But when she looked, there was no one there.

Stifling an odd sense of disappointment, she gazed across the yard and down the slope to the trees below, almost holding her breath. Everything seemed normal. Nothing was out of place.

Again she thought of going to bed, and then feared that if she did, another sleepwalking episode might occur. She thought of last night and the state in which she'd returned to the house, long hair flying and dripping wet, wearing nothing but a nightgown stuck fast to her body, and groaned.

"I probably frightened that hunter as badly as he did me."

But the assumption didn't lighten her mood. Like a bad penny, her thoughts returned to Griff. She didn't know what she was going to do about him, but a decision needed to be made, and soon. It wasn't fair to keep leading him on, letting him believe that she felt something for him that wasn't there.

Saturday night was only days away, yet it loomed in her conscience like doomsday. A dance. Griff had asked her to a dance. It wasn't as if he'd asked to spend the night, although she'd seen that desire in his eyes more than once. And if Charlie hadn't interrupted, she also knew she would already have said yes to the dance, simply for lack of a reason to say no.

A swift gust of wind suddenly cornered the house, shifting the neck of her shirt and cooling the skin beneath like the urgent breath of an anxious lover. Sighing with pent-up longing, she finally accepted the truth of her life. She didn't know what her future held, but Griffin Ross did not belong anywhere in it.

Still on the steps and now one with the night, she wished for a man like the man from her dreams.

Outlaw or not, he was loving and gentle with me.

Rachel jerked. Mentally she'd just put herself in the shoes of a woman called Mercy. Panicked by a warning she didn't understand, she wrapped her arms around herself, shivering, though not from cold.

But Rachel was not the kind of woman to live in a dream world. Today the reality of life had metaphorically slapped her in the face. A real-life outlaw had been standing on the streets of Razor Bend, staring at her and making no attempt to hide his interest or apologize for the company he kept.

A shiver of warning came over her, and she wished he had not witnessed her kissing Griffin Ross. She could have dismissed the incident without thought if it hadn't been for him. But he'd seen, and she couldn't forget. In fact, he'd stared so intently that she'd begun to imagine his breath upon her face. In spite of his needing a shave, his dark, handsome looks had intrigued her...reminded her of someone...someone she'd once known. If only she could remember who...

She stood up with a jerk. Thoughts like that were dangerous for lonely women, and Rachel knew it.

"He didn't intrigue me. Not at all. It was...it was curiosity, and nothing more."

Aggravated at herself and at the flight of fancy her mind had taken, she stomped across the grass to the empty swing dancing alone in the breeze. Scooting onto the old board seat, she pushed off, setting sail in the moonlight with a satisfied sigh.

Thinking of her partner, Charlie, she chuckled. "If he could see me now, he'd call me crazy for playing in the dark."

But she didn't care. The wind felt good on her face. The feeling of weightlessness lifted her spirits, and before she knew it, she was flying up and back, her legs pumping with each swing, caught up in a wayward joy not unlike that of the night moth that had swooped past her hand.

While waiting for his call to go through, Boone watched a cockroach crawling up the wall of the tin can he called home. It was past time to check in with his contact, and while he had nothing new to report, he knew that Waco still wanted to hear her sweet boy's voice. That was the order given, tongue in cheek, by Captain Susan Cross, who was not only Boone's contact, but also his immediate superior.

The phone number Boone used was a dedicated phone line in the captain's office. And if she wasn't there in person, the message on her answering machine was as low and sexy and as atypical as the code name that hid her true identity.

The rings came, one after the other, and on the fourth ring, when the machine should have kicked on, Boone's expression lightened as Waco's low, husky voice purred in his ear.

"This is Waco. Talk to me. It's been a long, lonely night."

"Hey, sweetheart, what's happening?"

"Boone…darling, it's about time you gave me a call."

Waco's sweet, sexy voice was her only physical asset, in direct opposition to her thick, stocky body, her short, graying hair and the gold-rimmed half glasses she wore down on her nose.

In spite of the fact that she was his boss, Boone never had to fake a smile when he heard her speak. He was hearing her call him "darling," but in his mind, he could just see that intent bulldog expression she always got when business was at hand.

"Sweet thing!" Waco cooed. "You've been a bad, bad boy again, haven't you? Why didn't you call me last night like you promised?"

Boone grinned as he leaned over and picked up a dirty yellow tennis ball from the floor near his boot. With unerring aim, he drew back and threw it, nailing the cockroach on the first throw, then retrieving the ball as it bounced back his way.

Captain Cross frowned at the thump she heard over the phone.

"What was that?"

"Bug patrol," Boone drawled, and tossed the tennis ball into a nearby chair.

Ignoring his insinuating reference to the dive in which he was living, she focused on the business at hand.

"So, when are you coming to see me, handsome? It's been a long, long time since I've kissed your sweet face."

Boone grinned. "Yes, ma'am, I'd venture to say it has."

At the word *ma'am,* Susan Cross leaned back in her chair and then grinned. "I take it you're alone."

"Affirmative, Captain."

Her voice sharpened. "Okay, then the gloves are off. Why didn't you check in last night? I had visions of having to send out the troops to comb those damned mountains for your body."

Boone shifted his cell phone to the other ear and then leaned forward, staring at the floor as he sifted through what he could tell her, as opposed to what was better left unsaid.

"I started to, and then things changed. I almost got lucky."

Cross rolled her eyes. "Well, that's just dandy, but I don't want to hear about your prowess in bed. I need facts. You've been under too long now as it is. I'm considering pulling you out and coming at this bunch from a different angle."

Boone jumped to his feet, and when he spoke again, his voice was deep and demanding. "No way." And then he imagined Cross thrusting out her chin as she always did when readying for a verbal battle.

"No way, Captain...ma'am."

Cross sighed. She was all too aware of how determined this agent could be. He was one of her best, and yet she knew less about him personally than any agent on the force.

"Okay, then talk to me."

"Last night I trailed Cherry and two of his boys through the mountains. They had a meeting with a man I suspect is the real power behind Denver Cherry's tawdry little throne.

I think they'd been to the new lab, but I didn't get on their tail in time to find the location, or ID the man."

Cross doodled on a pad on her desk as she listened. The news was not what she needed to hear. Boone had been under cover in Razor Bend for more than six weeks, and still it seemed he hadn't made a close enough connection with this bunch to gain their trust. They kept moving their drug lab, and although he was technically in the gang, they kept him apart from the funny business they were conducting. The most he'd seen and could swear to was the chemicals they used to cook up the methamphetamine.

"Okay, you missed a chance, that's all. One missed chance does not a failure make."

Boone grinned. "Where did you learn that bit of wisdom?"

"Fortune cookies."

He laughed aloud, and realized it felt good.

And just because he couldn't see her, Cross allowed herself a wide grin in return. It wouldn't do to let the men know her heart of stone was actually made of glass.

"So, tell me what you're thinking," she barked.

Boone relaxed. He should have known she was just testing his frame of mind. Yet, when she asked, he realized he wasn't thinking of the job, but of a woman named Rachel and how she'd looked in wet white flannel.

"It wouldn't do to repeat it," Boone drawled.

Cross rolled her eyes. "Go get yourself laid, and call me when your head's on straight."

A crooked smile broke the angles of his face.

"I couldn't cheat on you, darlin' Waco. You're the love of my life."

A sharp snort prefaced the distinct click in Boone's ear. He grinned again. Although Captain Cross had hung up on him, she'd fueled the fire of a need Boone was trying to ignore. He knew damn good and well that getting laid was out of the question, but if he was careful, he told himself he could see Rachel again. Not enough to get himself in trouble—just enough to sleep on.

He was telling himself no even as he was getting into his truck. He wasn't going to do anything but look. She wouldn't see him again—not unless he wanted her to. In his mind, there was only one place to start—the stream where he'd seen her last night.

When he finally found the location, he stopped in the moonlight, remembering the way the wet white gown had molded itself to her body, picturing the gentle thrust of her breasts and the imprint of long, slim legs beneath the fabric.

Long minutes passed while he wrestled with his conscience.

Finally, with an undisguised groan of disgust, he stalked through the cold, shallow water and started walking uphill, in the direction she'd disappeared.

The house was shining in the darkness, lit from within like a church on Sunday. Her car, the same car he'd seen on the street near the EMS station, was now parked beneath a tree. A light in the house was on, and the warm, yellow glow bleeding through the curtains was a balm to his solitary heart. To Boone, it was a beacon inviting him to come in from the cold.

But he couldn't. This picket-fence, happy-ever-after life was not for him. Not now, maybe not ever, and especially not with a woman who feared the very sight of his face. Living a lie was easier for Boone than living with the truth of his own life. In reality, he was a lonely man. Under cover, he was simply a loner.

And then she came out of her house, and he forgot everything he'd told himself on the walk up the mountain.

Now, ten minutes later, he stood in the darkness, deep enough in the trees not to be seen, while he stared at the woman in the swing. Her head was thrown back, and her arms were straight and outstretched as she clung to the ropes, pumping her legs with each ebb and flow of her flight through the air. Her braid had come undone, and the long black hair now hanging down her back lifted and billowed around her face like a widow's veil blowing in the wind.

He ached with a longing he didn't understand. What he'd done tonight by coming here was way past stupid. He'd wanted to know her name, and now he did. Yet after he'd learned it, it hadn't been enough. Now he stood in the dark with his heart in his mouth, listening to her laughter ringing out in the night. Somewhere between ten o'clock and midnight, Boone fell quietly in love. It made no sense. He'd only seen her twice before. Once on her knees in a stream, crying for a man who was nowhere in sight, and again in another man's arms. But it didn't seem to matter. He knew her name was Rachel, and he knew he loved her.

Denver Cherry rocked back on his heels, absently rubbing his paunch with the flat of his hand as he paced the floor in front of his television, his cell phone held close to his ear. Nearing sixty, the aging biker still sported long, graying hair with a beard to match. The tattoos on his arms and his belly were all the remnants he had left of a woman he'd once known in Seattle. Just under six feet tall, he carried fifty pounds of excess weight on legs that had been broken more times than he could remember. It was only after the last set of casts had come off that he traded his hog for a short-bed pickup and his biker leathers for jeans. While Denver's mode of travel and appearance might have taken on a new look, his occupation had not. Denver lived by a motto he wouldn't give up: Life is greener on the wrong side of the law.

Ignoring the intermittent static from the police scanner on a nearby counter, as well as the traffic on the CB base in the nearby kitchen, he stared intently at the big-screen TV on the other side of the room.

In deference to the call he was taking, the television was on mute, yet he was still able to follow the play-by-play of "Monday Night Football." When the 49ers suddenly fumbled the ball, he winced, then cursed beneath his breath and grabbed an empty beer can from a nearby table. Crumpling it with one beefy hand, he threw it across the room, where it landed with a tinny-sounding clink. He had a twenty-dollar bet on this game, and now there was no time for them to recover. Added to that, the boss was bitching in his ear about stuff that was out of Denver's control.

"Look, I know what I'm doing," Denver muttered. "It's not my fault that big shipment you sent out went down in the ocean off Padre Island. I told you that pilot was a user and a loser."

There was a moment of total silence, and Denver wondered if he'd overstepped his bounds.

Over the years, he'd worked with plenty of men who considered the profits they made secondary to the power they could achieve. Denver wasn't picky about the jobs he took. Shy of murder, if it paid good, he'd do it. But there was something about the boss that made him nervous. Something that didn't set quite right. More than once, he'd had the feeling that the man would just as soon gut him as look at him. He swallowed nervously as a low, angry voice growled in his ear.

"I remember everything, Cherry, but you better remember something, too. I don't like screwups, and those two fools you've got working for you aren't pulling their weight."

Denver frowned. There was no denying the truth. After the mess Tommy Joe made of the last delivery, he'd been ready to shoot him himself. If Snake hadn't popped the watchman who caught them in the act, they would have gone down for sure.

"I've got a new man," Denver muttered. "Been breaking

him in all slow-like. If he shows up today, maybe I'll send him on the run with the boys."

"No way, Cherry. I don't like *new.*"

Denver dropped into a chair, gauging the depth of his daring against what he was about to say. Boss or no boss, he'd had just about enough. His voice lowered warningly. "Listen here—you hired me to run it from this end, so either fire me or get the hell out of my face."

There was a moment of complete silence, then a warning whisper sent shivers down Denver's fat back. "Fine. The new man is on your head."

The line went dead in Denver's ear. He shrugged. What was done was done. He disconnected, then traded the phone for the remote. The instant roar of the crowd drowned out the sound of Tommy Joe's arrival. It was only after a shadow crossed his television screen that he realized he was no longer alone.

Denver glanced over his shoulder, waving for Tommy Joe to take a seat. When he refused, Denver knew something was wrong. By the look on Tommy Joe's face, losing twenty bucks might be the least of his worries. He began to curse.

Once again the television was silenced as Denver got up from his chair. He wasn't sure what was wrong, but the absence of Tommy Joe's other half was a good place to start.

"Where's Snake?"

Tommy Joe shuffled his feet, then looked at the floor rather than face Denver Cherry's wrath. His voice was barely above a whisper when he finally answered. "Jail."

Denver's face turned red. "Like hell! Then get him out. We've got a delivery to make tonight."

"Can't. Judge is out of town till tomorrow. The cops said arraignment will be sometime Tuesday afternoon."

Denver doubled his fists, resisting the urge to slam one into Tommy Joe's face for nothing more than relief.

"What did he do this time?"

Tommy Joe shrugged, and for Denver, it was the last straw in a day long gone wrong. He grabbed him by the throat and shoved him hard against the wall.

"You talk to me, you piece of sh—"

"Looks like I'm too late for the dance."

Both men looked up in surprise, to see Boone MacDonald leaning against the doorway with his arms folded across his chest. The black denim he was wearing went well with the cold, taunting smirk on his face.

Unlike Denver, Tommy Joe was more than happy for the interruption.

Denver frowned. Seeing that hard-eyed loner lounging in his doorway as if he owned the place didn't set too well with him, especially with the boss's warning still ringing in his ears.

"Don't mess with me, Boone, I'm not in the mood," Denver warned, but the worst of his anger was already subsiding. With a curse, he shoved Tommy Joe aside and dropped back in his chair.

Pretending disinterest in the whole affair, Boone shrugged while breathing an inward sigh of relief. Tommy Joe was his ticket to this party, and had been from the start. Snake didn't make friends, only enemies. If Denver got mad enough to run one of them off, Boone wanted it to be Snake, not Tommy Joe. Mixing with this crew for the past six weeks had been bad enough, but having it all blow up in his face without identifying the man behind the money would play hell with his conscience.

But while Boone was counting his blessings, Denver was gauging Boone's cold expression with satisfaction. At least this man had something between his ears besides the hair on his head.

"What brought you over?" Denver asked.

Boone tilted his head toward Tommy Joe. "I was looking for him. He told me the next time I went to Oklahoma City, he wanted to go. I'm on my way."

Denver straightened in his chair. This could be the answer to his immediate problem. He'd already warned the boss he was going to try the new man, and now here he was, heading in the direction Denver needed him to go.

"What's so great about O.K. city?" he asked.

Boone shrugged. "My old lady. I check in on her every now and then, just to make sure she hasn't slipped somebody else into my spot on her bed."

Denver's eyes narrowed thoughtfully. "I didn't know you were married. I don't like none of my men too tied down."

Boone's pulse rate accelerated slightly. *My men? Am I about to get that break?*

Boone cocked his eyebrow and then smoothed his hand down the front of his fly, playing his part to the hilt. "I'm not. But a smart man doesn't leave a woman like Waco alone for too long. She starts getting ideas about being better off without me…and you can't be having a woman get too independent, if you know what I mean."

When Denver laughed, Boone relaxed, and then glanced at the man cowering near the far wall.

"So, Tommy Joe, you still itching to take a ride?"

Tommy Joe glanced at Denver, then slumped. He knew the responsibility of delivering the haul would fall on his shoulders, now that Snake was out of commission.

"Guess not. I promised Snake I'd come by tonight. Maybe next time."

Pretending disinterest, Boone nodded, but his senses were on edge. He'd already figured out that when Snake and Tommy Joe were "busy," there was a load going out or coming in.

"Whatever."

He was halfway off the porch when Denver's shout halted

his progress. He paused, then turned, watching the fat man hobble toward him.

"What?" he asked.

"How would you feel about doing me a favor?" Denver asked.

Boone stood his ground, giving nothing of his underlying excitement away.

"Depends," he said.

Denver's eyes narrowed as he watched Boone's face for signs of too much interest. To his satisfaction, there was nothing visible but an impatience the man made no attempt to hide.

"I've got a little shipment of goods to be delivered tonight. With Snake in jail, I might be needing someone to help me out."

Boone pretended to frown and glanced at his watch, then up at Tommy Joe.

"What about him?" Boone asked.

Denver Cherry's voice was a mirror of his disposition. He sounded out of patience and purely put out. "His license is still suspended. I can't take a chance on him getting stopped for some violation and having some gung ho cop confiscate my stuff."

Boone shifted his stance. "Look, Cherry, I'm no saint, and I'm damn sure not stupid. I don't do anyone a favor until I know what I'm hauling." And then he grinned. "I've done too much time as it is. If I'm going down, I want it to be my choice."

At that moment, Denver wished he hadn't started this conversation unarmed, but it was too late to pull back now. "Meth."

Boone nodded. "Then I want to know something."

"Yeah, what?" Denver muttered.

"What's in it for me?"

Denver laughed. It was a short bark of delight that

sounded more like a shout than a chuckle, but it was proof of the satisfaction he was feeling. He knew he'd been right about this man.

"Enough," Denver said, still chuckling beneath his breath. "So, you interested or not?"

"Where's the drop going to be?"

"I'll draw you a map."

Boone stood in the yard, glancing at his watch and playing his hesitation to the hilt.

"What's wrong?" Denver asked.

"Waco. She's going to give me hell for not showing up."

Denver grinned. "No she's not. The party is on your way."

Boone started back up the steps. "Okay, boss, you've got yourself a deal."

The word *boss* was setting real good with Denver Cherry as he hunted through a drawer for a pad and pen. He liked a man who was willing to stay in his place.

Chapter 4

Traffic was moderate to heavy on Interstate 35-A. Boone had his pickup truck set on cruise control, careful not to risk a stop by some ticket-happy highway patrolman. As drug deals went, the shipment Boone was carrying was small. If something went bad, Cherry wouldn't lose enough to hurt him. And if Boone did as he was told and the buyer came away happy, then so much the better.

But there was one thing about the trip that kept bothering him. Why hadn't Cherry sent Tommy Joe with him? It would have made sense, even if as nothing more than a gesture of good faith to the man he was supposed to meet. He shrugged, then relaxed. Cherry was probably testing him on this run.

He glanced up in the rearview mirror, absently checking the lights behind him, then hit the turn signal and moved into the fast lane to pass an eighteen-wheeler. Moments later, a vehicle several cars back did the same. He thought nothing of it until it happened again...and then again...and then again. Within the space of half an hour, Boone knew he was being tailed.

The first adrenaline surge quickly passed as he recognized a familiar feature about the car. One headlight beam was yellow and one was white. Boone grinned, remembering the day he'd watched Tommy Joe and Snake replacing the bulbs. Snake had put in one kind of bulb, Tommy Joe another. It wasn't until that night that they'd realized their mistake and, typically, they had left the lights the way they were, claiming they burned, which was really all that mattered. But at night it gave the headlights a wall-eyed appearance, not unlike that of an animal with one blue eye and one black.

"So, fat boy, you decided not to trust me after all," Boone muttered.

Cherry had launched himself a spy. Boone eased back into the right-hand side of the lane and picked up the cell phone in the seat beside him.

A few moments later, a low, husky voice growled softly in his ear.

"Talk to me, baby," Waco said.

"I'm in," Boone said, and heard a deep sigh of relief.

"How so?"

"I'm northbound I-35 with a load behind the seat. It's not big, but I'm being tailed."

"I assume you're alone."

"Affirmative, Captain, except for the tick on my ass."

"You think they're testing you?"

"Yes."

"And if not?" the captain asked.

"Then I'll tell them if they can't play fair, I'm going home to tell Mama."

"Damn it, Boone, don't get smart with me. None of this is worth risking your life for."

Boone's smile faded. "Better men have died for less."

"The point is not debatable," the captain barked. "If you suspect a trap, then get the hell out."

"Why, Waco, darlin', I think you really care."

"You heard me," Cross muttered, pushing her glasses up

her nose with the tip of her finger as she swiveled her chair to face a map on the wall behind her desk.

"Where's the buy going down?"

Boone mentioned a county road a few miles south of the city of Norman. Cross stood up and leaned forward, poking a red pin on the map to mark the drop, then calculating the time it would take to get some agents in place.

"It's too late for backup to get there ahead of you," she muttered. "You should have called sooner."

"I don't want backup, I want Cherry's boss. This deal needs to go through without incident."

Cross frowned and rubbed at a pain shooting up her temple. She already knew that. It just didn't make her job any easier.

"So what you're telling me is, you only called because you wanted to 'reach out and touch someone,' right?"

Boone grinned. His captain had a way with words. "No way, Waco. I called to tell you to put a light in the window. Daddy's coming home."

A soft snort that sounded suspiciously like a chuckle was all Boone heard before the line went dead. He disconnected, then, out of habit, punched in a few random numbers, then disconnected again. It was an old trick he'd learned early on. Even though his contact was supposedly secure, there was no way he was giving anyone a free ride to his source by letting them pick up his phone and hit redial to find out who he had called.

He looked into the rearview mirror again. White and yellow eyes were bearing down upon him. The smile on his face was deadly.

"Okay, Cherry, let's see how good your boy really is."

Boone stomped the accelerator, ignoring the needle on the speedometer when it moved past eighty, then ninety, then into the red. Climbing...climbing...then off the dial.

Everything to his right was a blur. The vehicles he was

passing became nothing more than a flicker of shape, light and color. His gaze was focused on the darkness ahead and the narrow beam of light cutting through it.

A short time later, he glanced up in the rearview mirror. The reflection of headlights from the cars he was passing ran together like a bright yellow ribbon, but the wall-eyed headlights of his tail were no longer in sight.

Only after he began to ease up on the gas did he realize that he was gritting his teeth against an impact that never came. His jaw was clenched, but his hands were steady, his nerves calm. With one smooth, easy motion, he moved back into the right-hand lane, sliding in between a bull hauler and an eighteen-wheeler, where he continued to ride until his exit appeared.

Again he moved to the right, taking the off-ramp like a bird going home to roost. With nothing but guts for backup, he took the county-road bridge that arched over I-35 and headed for the location of the buy.

Within the hour he'd found the place Cherry had marked on the map and pulled off the road and into the driveway of the abandoned farm house. Off to his right was a faint trail leading toward what appeared to have once served as a hay barn.

Just as Cherry had directed, Boone circled around behind the barn, coming to a stop out of sight of the road. He killed the lights but left the engine running.

Five, ten, then thirty, seconds passed while his eyes grew accustomed to the dark. An overcast sky kept moonglow at a minimum. Only now and then was he able to detect anything more than the subtle shapes of trees and bushes. He reached down, feeling for the butt of his gun, protruding above the holster at his waist. The hard, familiar shape was comforting to a man who had no one to depend on but himself. Another minute passed, and then another, stretching nerves already humming with nervous energy.

And then, without warning, three men emerged from the old barn and started walking toward him. Adrenaline surged. They were carrying guns! He took a deep breath, pulled out the .357 and got out of the truck with it ready to fire. It was time to party.

One man growled. "Where's Snake?"

"In jail," Boone answered. "Cherry sent me instead."

Someone cocked the hammer on a rifle, and Boone's senses went on alert. He moved a step closer, making sure they could see that they weren't the only ones armed.

He heard one man mutter, "Watch it, Slick. He's packin'."

"Who the hell are you?" Slick asked.

"Name's Boone MacDonald. If you got a problem doing business with me, then let's call the whole deal off now, before someone makes a mistake they can't fix."

Feet shuffled, voices whispered, one to the other. Boone stood with his back to his truck and his finger on the trigger. The rest of the deal was out of his hands.

A few moments later Slick lowered his rifle. "You tell Cherry if his plans change again, he'd better let us know. Strange faces make us antsy."

Boone snorted softly. "I'd say that just about makes us even. So...show me some green."

Again whispers cut through the silence. Finally one of the men split from the pack and headed inside the barn.

Guns lowered. The other men started forward. Boone still held his gun.

"Let's just wait on your buddy," he said softly.

They stopped. Still muttering, they waited. Moments later, the man returned, carrying a sack.

"Nothing personal," Boone said, "but I'd like to see what you brought for lunch."

Someone snickered as the sack was tossed to Boone. He caught it in midair and opened it. Moonlight revealed large stacks of the used twenties and hundreds he'd been led to expect. He started backing toward his truck, without taking his eyes off the trio.

"No fancy moves now," Slick warned.

Boone paused. "It's behind the seat. Help yourself."

Once again Slick was in control. "Go get it, Donny," he ordered.

Boone stepped aside, giving way to a tall, lanky man wearing baggy jeans and tennis shoes. The cap on Donny's head bore the Dallas Cowboys logo, and the chew in his mouth was bigger than his nose. Even in the half-light, Boone could see it pushing at the interior of his cheek. As Boone moved aside, the man spat before leaning in to retrieve the package, then handed it over.

"You don't mind waiting a bit longer now, do you?" Slick asked as he dug inside the package to make sure he had what he was paying for.

"No skin off of my nose," Boone said. "Just so everybody's happy."

He watched for smiles of satisfaction. When they came, he was ready to go. Lingering too long around a buy could get a man killed.

"It was real nice meeting you boys," Boone said, and slid behind the wheel of his truck. To his relief, the trio seemed as willing to part company as he did.

He watched while they disappeared into the barn. Less than a minute later, an engine started. Lights came on, and a dirty black four-by-four bounced out of the doorway, heading toward anonymity with speed.

Only after they were gone did Boone start to relax. At least the first half of this night was over. He pulled his truck inside the barn, using it for cover the same way Slick and his boys had done earlier, then settled down to wait for the long-distance burr still stuck to his tail.

More than ten minutes passed, and he was beginning to wonder if he'd guessed wrong about Cherry. Maybe he hadn't sent Tommy Joe after all. But no sooner had he thought it than his nerves went on alert.

A car on the road beyond was beginning to slow down. Boone sat up straight. When he saw the headlights turning into the overgrown driveway, he grinned. The car and its lopsided leer came toward the back of the barn. When it stopped, the lights went out with a drunken wink. And when Tommy Joe's familiar figure rolled out from behind the steering wheel, Boone eased out of his truck with Denver's money in hand, careful not to make any noise.

Tommy Joe was sick with worry. Denver was going to be real mad. Not only had he lost sight of Boone on I-35, but now he'd gotten here too late to see if the buy had gone down as planned.

He got out of the car and circled it twice, eyeing the surrounding countryside with a nervous stare.

Dang old Snake, anyway. If he hadn't gone and gotten himself tossed in jail, none of this would be happening.

Tommy Joe kicked at a tuft of grass and then groaned when his toe connected with a half-buried rock. It was a perfect ending to a washed-out night. There was nothing left for him to do but go back and tell Denver Cherry the truth. He was starting to get back in his car when he looked at the barn. In his mind, the black, yawning maw of the open doorway was like a big, wide mouth laughing at him for his mistakes.

The barn! He'd better take a look around. If he didn't and Denver asked him if he had, he'd catch hell again. Tommy Joe wasn't good at much of anything, not even lying. Cursing beneath his breath, he began heading toward the barn for a last-minute check.

The hand squeezing his windpipe moments later was only half as frightening to Tommy Joe as the voice whispering in his ear.

"Looking for something?" Boone asked.

Tommy Joe gasped, his hands flailing as his air flow began to shut down.

"Damn you, Boone," he squeaked. "Let me go!"

Boone turned him loose, but with a last, warning push. Tommy Joe slumped against the wall, rubbing at his neck and trying not to quake at the hard, angry glitter in Boone MacDonald's eyes.

"No need getting all riled," Tommy Joe grunted. "I was just following orders."

He started to duck as Boone tossed a sack in his face, then caught it in reflex. His good humor returned when he looked inside. But his grin died when he looked up. There was no mistaking that Boone MacDonald was thoroughly pissed.

"Damn it, Boone. Don't get all high-and-mighty with me! You know what Denver's like. He gives the orders. We follow."

The flat of Boone's hand slammed into the middle of Tommy Joe's chest, pinning him against the wall.

"Tommy Joe..."

"What?" he muttered, while wishing himself a thousand miles away.

"Since you're so damn good at following orders, then I've got some for you."

Tommy Joe nodded, then feared Boone might not be able to see in the dark and added a nervous "Okay."

"I want you to take Cherry his money, and I want you to tell him something for me when you do. You tell him that I don't lie...and I don't trust people who do. Now, when I leave here, I'm going to see my woman, and I'd better not see that damned car on my tail again."

"Sure thing," Tommy Joe muttered, trying to get free of Boone's grip. It didn't work. To his horror, he felt the cold end of a gun barrel pressing against his temple. "Oh,

God!" he muttered. "Don't shoot me, man! Don't shoot! It ain't my fault!"

"Shut up!" Boone muttered. "I'm not through with you. I also want you to tell Cherry I'll be back in a couple of days to get what's owed me."

"Will do," Tommy Joe said quickly, anxious to appease the big man's anger.

With a muffled curse, Boone spun and stalked out of the barn toward Tommy Joe's car.

Seconds later the gun went off, and Tommy Joe fell to the ground. When he found the guts to look up, he realized that it wasn't him that Boone had shot at, it was his right front tire.

He scrambled to his feet, crawling and then running, the sack of money clutched tight to his chest.

"Are you crazy?" he screamed, staring at the shattered rubber. The tire was ruined. Angrily he tossed the sack on the front seat before scrambling to open his trunk.

Boone shoved the gun into its holster and then turned.

"You'd better hurry," he said. "Someone might just get curious about that gunshot and come to look." With that, he walked away.

Tommy Joe was cursing loudly as he scrambled through the trunk, pulling out his jack and lug wrench. But when he went back for the spare, it was nowhere to be found.

"Boone! Wait!" Tommy Joe yelled. "A spare. I don't have a spare!"

Boone grinned, and even at that distance, Tommy Joe shivered. It was a cold, mirthless smile that made his guts knot.

"Denver told me you didn't have a driver's license, either, but that didn't stop you from driving. There's an all-night station about seven or eight miles back. Guess you'll have to drive on the rim, huh?"

Tommy Joe started to curse. "Wait, damn it. You can't leave me here like this." He was digging through his pockets in panic, well aware of the lack of cash in the wallet he was carrying. "I don't have enough money to buy a new tire."

Boone's smile broadened as he pointed toward the car. "Sure you do. There's a sack full of bills in the front seat of your car."

Tommy Joe groaned. Denver would kill him for sure if he spent a penny of unlaundered drug money. To add insult to injury, as the taillights of Boone MacDonald's truck disappeared, it began to rain.

The day dawned gray and gloomy. Rain threatened on an hourly basis, but a drop had yet to fall. Rachel hadn't been at work two hours when elation hit. She was handed a gold-plated excuse not to go to the dance with Griff, and she couldn't even bring herself to feel guilty that it had come at the expense of one of her fellow workers. Ken Wade's family emergency had changed the week's work schedule for everyone. After volunteering to take her co-worker's shift, she felt ashamed of the thanks that he heaped on her head.

"You would do it for me," she'd said swiftly, and then made herself scarce.

She bolted for the office and shut herself inside before heading to the phone. Now she had a good excuse to turn down Griffin Ross's invitation to the dance. She dialed his number, then counted the rings.

His secretary picked up. "Ross Savings and Loan."

"Hi, Lois, this is Rachel. Is Griff busy?"

The pleasant smile on Lois Klein's face froze in place. She knew it wasn't Christian to envy, but she envied Rachel Brant's place in her boss's life with every ounce of her being.

Glancing across the floor to the glassed-in walls of Griffin Ross's office, where he sat at his desk, deep in a mountain of paperwork, she toyed with the idea of lying, then relented.

"He's always busy," she said. "But he's alone...and, of

course, he's in to you. Just a moment, please, while I ring you through."

There was tension in Lois's voice, and Rachel felt sorry to be the cause. It was common knowledge that Lois Klein was very much enamored of her boss.

"Wait!" Rachel said, almost shouting into the phone to keep Lois from putting her on hold.

Lois frowned. "Yes, was there something else I could do for you?"

Rachel took a deep breath; she had to be careful not to say too much. "Uh…about the fund-raiser Saturday night."

Disappointment stilled the expression on Lois's face. "What about it?"

"Are you going?"

"No, I'm not," Lois said.

Her answer was too swift and abrupt. Rachel knew she'd been right about Lois's feelings toward Griff.

"Gee, that's too bad, but I know how you feel. Neither am I."

The secretary's eyebrows arched with interest as she glanced at Griff. "But I thought you and…"

"Have to work," Rachel said, and then pretended to sigh in disappointment. "It's too bad that Griff might have to go alone. Unless he can find someone who hasn't already made plans, I suppose he'll just have to go stag."

This time the corners of the secretary's mouth tilted up to match her eyebrows' arch.

"Indeed!" she said, unable to believe the underlying hint she was picking up in Rachel's conversation.

"Yes," Rachel said. "So…if Griff's not busy, I guess you'd better put me through. I've got to give him the bad news."

"Sure thing," Lois said brightly. "Please hold."

One small click sounded in Rachel's ear, and the next thing she heard were the deep, resonant tones of Griffin Ross's voice.

"This is Griffin Ross."

Rachel stiffened. Just the sound of his voice made her nervous. In the past, no matter how many times she tried to dissuade him from further pursuit, he'd outtalked and outmaneuvered her every time. But this time she had to be strong.

"Griff, it's me, Rachel. Sorry to bother you at work, but—"

"You're never a bother!" he said brightly, and kicked back in his chair, ready to chat.

"About Saturday night," she began.

"I'll pick you up around six. We can grab a bite to eat beforehand. Nothing too heavy, though. I expect they'll have—"

"I can't go."

He straightened, unaware that his secretary was eyeing him from across the room.

"I have to work," Rachel added. "Ken Wade had a family emergency, and everyone's shifts have changed."

Griff wanted to argue, but he knew it would be futile. He could hardly have a fit in front of the customers and staff of Ross Savings and Loan. The finality of her announcement was obvious, and he knew her excuse was valid. He'd already heard about the Wade family's trouble, yet he couldn't help adding, "This is unfortunate, Rachel. You know, if you'd consider *us* once in a while, and let our relationship grow instead of being so self-centered, you wouldn't have to be working at that damned gory job."

Ignoring the other slights to her character, Rachel frowned as she stood up for the thing she loved most. "Griff, you don't know me at all, or you wouldn't say that. I like my job."

Griff panicked. He'd never heard such authority in her voice. "Darling, I'm sorry. I was just disappointed. How about if I call you tonight, after you get home? We'll make plans for another—"

"No, I don't think so."

He started to sweat. "I didn't mean to make you mad," he whispered, and spun around so that no one in the outer part of the building could see his face. "Please, Rachel. You know how I feel about you."

She sighed. "Yes, I think I do," she said. "And that's why I think it's time to put a stop to this, before it goes any further. I *like* you, Griff, and that's as far as it goes."

"But in time, I'm sure, you'll come to—"

"That's just it," Rachel said. "I'm just as sure I won't."

Griff couldn't believe what he was hearing. Never in his entire privileged life had he been thwarted so royally, or turned down so succinctly.

The skin of his face turned pale, and when the color came back, it was a dark, angry red. It took him every ounce of his control to keep his voice calm and his thoughts collected.

"I can't say I'm happy about this," he said. "But, as I always say, life isn't fair. I suppose I have to understand your feelings as clearly as I understand mine."

Rachel went weak with relief. This had been easier than she'd imagined, and because the load of guilt was off her shoulders, her voice was lighter than she might have intended when she said, "I'm really sorry, Griff."

"Yes, so am I," he said.

"Thanks for being so understanding," she added, and when she disconnected, she practically danced a little jig of delight at having conquered something that had been weighing on her mind.

I don't understand anything yet, Griff thought, as he hung up the phone. *But before I'm through, I will.*

When Boone awoke, rain was hammering against the window. He yawned, then stretched, savoring the feel of clean sheets and his own king-size bed. Last night had been a close one. Walking cold into a buy where the odds were three to one wasn't smart, but it had happened just the same. His expression darkened as he faced having to go back to Razor Bend. He was sick and tired of that roach-infested trailer, of listening to Snake and Tommy Joe's incessant chatter, and, most of all, he was sick of being Boone Mac-Donald.

But leaving Razor Bend also meant leaving Rachel Brant, and he wasn't sure how he felt about that. As long as he worked under cover, he could never go back as himself, and even if he did, what would it gain him? She had a boyfriend and a life that didn't include him, and that was the way it would have to be.

Angry with himself and the fact that he'd let hormones interfere with business, he rolled over, then got out of bed, walking to the window to stare out at the busy traffic on the Northwest Expressway just visible beyond the rooftops below.

Water was running swift and deep on the pavement and in the gutters. Experience warned him that some streets were bound to be flooded. It was all the excuse he needed to stay indoors, rather than check in at the office with Captain Cross, and going in and out of DEA headquarters in his undercover guise was risky, at best.

The thought of coffee, strong and black, pulled him away from the window and sent him into the kitchen to start a pot brewing. A short time later, when he exited his shower, the fresh-brewed scent filled the rooms.

He took a cup with him to the desk and sipped as he thumbed through his notes, making corrections as he went, before he made his call. There wasn't a lot to tell the captain apart from what she already knew, but she was his connection with reality, and accepting his reality was what was keeping him alive.

Chapter 5

A night and two days had passed since Boone had sent Tommy Joe home on three wheels. The way he figured it, he'd given Denver Cherry something to think about and Tommy Joe time to get over his mad. If he'd guessed wrong and Denver kicked him out of the gang, he almost didn't care. He was tired of playing cat and mouse with the entire bunch.

And the weather wasn't any better than Boone's mood. A cool front had stalled over the entire southern half of the state. For the past two days it had seemed that every time the hour changed, so did the weather. He'd driven south out of Oklahoma City in sunshine, but for the past two hours he had been driving in and out of rain.

He glanced at the mile marker and frowned. Only minutes away from Razor Bend; it was time to crawl back inside the head of a drug runner. No more Mr. Nice Guy. Boone MacDonald was back in town.

Puddles shimmered in the uneven roadbed, splattering the underside of his truck as he drove through them. A slight mist still lingered in the air, enough for him to keep the windshield wipers on low. The day was gray and showed no signs of getting better. Low-hanging clouds, heavy with rain that had yet to fall, darkened the sky, bringing an early end to a miserable day.

Boone was driving on autopilot. His body was in perfect control of his truck, but his mind was sifting through possible scenarios for his coming confrontation with Denver Cherry. When a small compact car suddenly came out of nowhere, passing his truck at high speed, it startled him.

"Crazy kid," he muttered as the car sailed through a puddle of water, showering both sides of the road with displaced spray. "If he isn't careful, he'll hydroplane that thing."

The couple in the front seat were laughing and talking, seemingly unaware of any danger. Boone continued along behind, watching the way the young woman would reach out to the driver, as if talking to him weren't enough, as if she needed to touch him, as well. Although the couple were sitting apart, their affection for each other was impossible to miss.

It kindled a longing in Boone to have someone like that of his own. Someone who cared when he was sick. Someone who could laugh with him. Someone who was willing to wake up beside him every morning for the rest of their lives.

At that moment, an odd sensation came over him. He felt lost, as if the road he was on had nowhere to go. Yes, he was going to Razor Bend, where he had a meeting with Denver Cherry that he knew could get sticky. But after that... what came next? Another bad guy? Another gang to be taken down? Another town, another identity, another lie to be told? For the first time in his life, Boone thought past tomorrow, and he didn't like what he saw. He didn't want to wake up one morning and find out that while he'd been living his lie, life had passed him by.

Rachel Brant.

The woman's name came unexpectedly. Boone snorted softly beneath his breath and shifted in the seat.

What about her? Why did he persist in fabricating the

mere idea of a relationship with a woman who didn't know he existed? He'd never thought of himself as a masochist, but he was beginning to wonder. He'd either been under too long, or alone too many nights.

"Forget about a woman you can't have," he muttered. He had reached down to turn up the radio when everything before him began to come undone.

The first thing he saw was a quick flash of brake lights on the car in front of him, a bright red warning that something was wrong. In response, he tapped his own brakes and began to slow down, but unlike the driver in the car up ahead, he hit them easy to decrease his speed.

Boone had seen the aftermaths of plenty of wrecks and had even been involved in a couple himself, but he'd never been a witness to what he was seeing now.

The little car spun completely around more than twice before it started to roll, and when it did, Boone winced and then groaned. Even though his windows were up and he was still a distance away, he heard the small car literally coming apart. Metal crunched; glass cracked, then shattered. One wheel came off and rolled down into the woods, out of sight, as the car settled upside down. Smoke and steam began to boil from under the hood as hoses popped and wiring was torn.

Boone felt shock and then a fleeting sorrow that happiness could so easily be destroyed. But there was no time left for emotion, only a reaction to the tragedy he'd seen. He grabbed for the phone lying next to him in the seat.

Because he was a cop, he made it his business to always know the number of the police department within his undercover operation. For him, it was nothing more than a little added insurance, but right now he was thankful he knew who to call.

As he punched in the numbers, his mind began to focus.

When the dispatcher answered, Boone's words were clipped, but his information was concise.

"There's a wreck just off the highway about four miles northwest of Razor Bend. Two people inside. Need an ambulance and a wrecker, stat!"

The dispatcher's voice faded in and out as Boone came to a sliding stop. He repeated the information at the top of his voice as he left his truck.

"No, no other cars involved!" he shouted, and when the dispatcher signed off, he tossed the phone into the seat and leaped from the pavement to the grassy slope and started running and sliding toward the upended car.

By the time he'd reached the wreck, he'd already made a mental inventory of what he could possibly do before medical personnel arrived.

The car was on its top. The right front wheel was still spinning as steam poured out from beneath the hood, filling the inside of the car and eliminating what visibility Boone might have had. The silence was eerie. Except for escaping steam, the only sound he heard was the rapid pounding of his own heart.

"Hey in there, can you hear me?" he shouted.

When no one answered, he circled the car on the run, making sure that the steam he saw was coming from the radiator and not an impending explosion or fire.

At the passenger's side, he got down on his hands and knees and thrust a hand through a shattered window, remembering that they would very probably be upside down, and began feeling for the woman he knew should be there. At first he felt nothing. He scooted closer to the car, extending his arm farther into the space. Seconds later, his fingers touched fabric, then hair, then warm, damp flesh. In spite of his years of training, he jerked in reflex.

"Lady! Lady, can you hear me?" he shouted.

She didn't answer. He leaned forward, accidentally

thrusting his fingers into a mop of wet, matted hair. He shuddered. *Dear God. Seconds ago she was laughing.*

Gently he traced the curve of a cheek, then the slender column of her throat. To his relief, he felt a pulse, faint but sure. When he did, he jumped to his feet and began pulling at the bent and folded metal. Seconds felt like an eternity as he struggled, trying unsuccessfully to dislodge the door. It was no use. He gritted his teeth, then leaned down again.

"Help is coming," he shouted, then ran to the other side of the car, thinking maybe he could get to them from that side.

That window was gone, too. Steam billowed out of the opening in long, cloudlike puffs, sending a signals of peril spiraling up into the gray, misty sky. Boone dropped to his knees, trying to crawl inside, but the driver's inert and pinned body was blocking the exit.

It didn't take long to see that the driver was dead, pinned in place by a crumpled piece of the dash. Through the smoke and steam, Boone had a fleeting glimpse of the young man's face, of his eyes, wide open, frozen in the horror of his last sight on earth.

"Damn," he muttered. He had started to back out of the window when, out of the smoke and steam, a small hand emerged, locking onto his fingers in a surprisingly firm grip. A tiny bracelet slid down a fragile wrist, and Boone felt what seemed to be charms dangling against his skin.

Oh my God! There's a child in here...a little girl!

He wrapped his hand around her grasping fingers then gave an easy, reassuring tug. As he did, he realized that she was strapped into some sort of child seat, because she was hanging upside down.

"Hey there, baby," he said gently, trying to keep the urgency out of his voice. "Are you hurt?"

At the question, the child started to cry. Not a loud, frightened wail, but a soft, helpless sob that tore at Boone's heart.

"It's okay, sweetheart," he said quickly. "We're going

to get you out. I promise. Yes, we are, we're going to get you out."

"Mommy. Want Mommy," the little girl sobbed, and tugged even tighter on Boone's hand, as if trying to pull herself out of confinement.

Boone thought of the woman and her faint, fading pulse and prayed for the ambulance to get there in time.

"Mommy's resting right now," he said quickly. "Don't cry, sweetheart…we might wake her up…okay?"

"Daddy…want Daddy."

Boone's heart ached. She was so small. Chances were she would never remember the daddy who'd brought her into this world. He would be nothing more than a name and a face in some old family pictures. Damn it all to hell, he thought. There was no justice in any of this.

"Daddy's asleep, too, honey."

Her grip tightened, almost as if she sensed that this man was her only line to safety. He began to wish she would scream or shriek from the fear she was bound to be feeling. She was too passive, too quiet. At that point, he realized that she very well might have internal injuries. He didn't even know her name, but for him, her living had suddenly become paramount.

Please, God. Don't let her die.

To his overwhelming relief, he began to hear a siren. It was a distance away, but it was the first sign he'd had that help was truly on the way.

"Do you hear that, baby girl? They're coming to help us. Don't be afraid…. They're going to help us all."

Then the tiny fingers started to slip from his hand, and Boone knew a moment of panic.

"Hey!" he said loudly, and his fear eased when she tightened her grip. He didn't even mind that he'd made her cry again. As long as he could hear her, he knew she was still alive. Gently, so as not to hurt what might turn out to be a broken or dislocated bone, he gave her fingers a soft but urgent tug.

"What's your name, honey? Can you tell me your name?"

"Out. Want out," she sobbed.

"I'll tell you my name if you'll tell me yours," he urged. "My name is…" He paused. Lying at a time like this almost seemed unholy, but then he shrugged off the thought. Names didn't count. It was the sound of his voice that she needed to hear. "My name is Boone. Can you say that? Can you say, Boone?"

"Boo," she repeated.

He didn't bother to correct her. She could call him anything she pleased. Then he heard her choke, and his heart nearly stopped. He had no way of knowing if she was gasping for breath or just choking on sobs.

"Sweetheart…can you tell me your name?"

She didn't answer.

"Honey…it's Boone, remember? Can you tell me your name?"

And then she spoke, and to Boone it was the sweetest sound in the world.

"Punkin."

His throat swelled and his eyes began to burn.

"Punkin, huh? That's a real pretty name. I'll bet you're a real pretty girl. Are you, baby? Are you a real pretty girl?"

"Daddy's girl," she said softly, and Boone lowered his head on his outstretched arm, fighting back tears.

"Come on, come on," he muttered to himself, praying for the ambulance to hurry.

More than once he tried to crawl past the man to get to her. He needed to see her. He wanted to feel her breath on his face and know that she was going to live long past this rainy September day. But the car had caved in, and the man was wedged between them like a block in a vise. Without help, Boone had gone as far as he could go.

And then the ambulance was suddenly there, lights flashing red and blue atop the boxy white truck, while the dying sounds of a siren choked into silence.

For the past few minutes Rachel Brant had been the farthest thing from his mind, but now, suddenly, she was on her knees beside him, grabbing his arm and asking for information. He started talking in shorthand, wanting them to know everything he knew before it was too late.

"Driver's dead. Woman on the passenger side. Alive... or was when I first got here. Can't open the door. Child trapped between them."

Rachel put her hand on his shoulder, her eyes wide and fixed on his face. "Sir, I'll need you to move back," she said quickly, and started to move him aside.

Boone frowned, afraid to let go of that small, trusting hand. "She won't let me go."

"Please, sir," Rachel said, pushing her way past his bulk. "I can't get to her with you in the way."

Reluctantly Boone turned loose of the little girl's fingers, and when he did, he felt a part of himself going with her. And when he did let go, the scream he'd wanted to hear earlier came, and in full, panicked force. The baby's shrieks echoed within the confines of the small, crumpled cab, and Boone could only imagine how afraid she must feel, losing touch with her last and only lifeline, while hanging upside down in a world filled with smoke.

In spite of her smaller size, Rachel couldn't get past the driver's body, either, and despite several attempts, she couldn't communicate with the child, because she was screaming with every breath she took. Rachel backed out the same way she'd crawled in. Her touch on Boone's arm was brief, but her instructions were to the point.

"Sorry," she said quickly. "See if you can calm her down. We'll have to get to her from the other side."

Boone went to his knees and thrust his arm into the car, more than willing to reach out to a child in fear.

"Hey, Punkin, it's me, Boone. Don't cry, sweetheart. I'm here. I'm still here."

To his relief, the small, flailing arm came into contact with his hand. He caught her, feeling the bracelet, then the tiny fingers that had been clutching at nothing but smoke.

The child latched on to his hand in desperation, and moments later her shrieks had subsided to thick choking sobs.

"Boo...want out. Want out," she begged.

"Damn it, hurry up!" he shouted. "She's hanging upside down in here."

The tone of his voice was angry, but Rachel knew that came from fear. She was well aware of the little girl's position, and the danger she could be in. Neck and head injuries were always serious. In a child that small, dangling in an insecure position could easily make things worse.

She circled the wreck, running to where Charlie was working on the other side, trying to focus on the task at hand and not the fact that she'd recognized the man on the other side of the car. He was the man from the Adam's Rib Café.

"Can't get this door open," Charlie said between grunts, tugging at the frame.

"The rescue squad was right behind us," Rachel said. "They should be here any minute. I'll get the KED, and a collar. We'll have to stabilize her before we can pull her out."

"I'll get it," Charlie said, and ran to the ambulance.

Rachel thrust her hand past the shattered glass, reaching down toward the woman inside. Thankfully, the steam was starting to subside and the victims were becoming visible. She felt for a pulse. It was there, but faint.

Charlie came back with the small backboard to stabilize her for removal. "What about the driver?" he asked as he dropped to his knees.

Rachel shook her head. "There's a child in an infant seat

trapped between them. Can't ascertain her condition, other than that she's still alert enough to cry and has bonded with the man who stopped to help. He seems to be able to communicate with her. I sure couldn't."

To their relief, another siren was blasting around the winding curves. The arrival of the rescue squad was imminent. Seconds later, Rachel was on her feet and running to meet them.

"Bring the Jaws," she shouted, indicating the powerful Jaws of Life, which they would need to extricate the victims from the crumpled metal.

Men in uniform began swarming around what was left of the small car. Everything was being done that could possibly be done, yet Boone couldn't find it within himself to care about anything but the child who had, strangely, entrusted herself to him.

The steam was nearly gone, baring what was left of the cab to a clear view. There was a spilled juice box lying on a film of shattered glass. The scent of grape mixed with the smell of burning rubber and spilled fuel, giving added poignancy to the truth of how quickly a life could end. A rag doll dangled from what was left of a rearview mirror. A woman's purse and its contents were strewn all over the ceiling of the car. Boone made himself focus on something other than the condition of the young driver's body. He looked past him to the child beyond, and for the first time he had a clear, perfect view of her face.

Even upside down, with her cheeks flushed and her eyes swollen from crying, she was beautiful. Thick brown curls framed a face just starting to lose its fat baby shape. Tiny scratches on her cheeks and forehead, probably from flying glass, had already stopped bleeding. She had a turned-up nose and a rosebud mouth, and there were creases in her cheeks that he suspected just might be dimples. Boone tugged at her fingers and smiled.

"Hey there, Punkin. It's me, Boone."

Unbelievably, she tried to smile back. Then he watched as her gaze slowly moved to her father, then her mother, as if she, too, was seeing for the first time the aftermath of what had happened. He didn't know what to say. Could a child that small understand what she was seeing?

"Punkin...?"

She looked back at Boone. "Sleepin'," she said softly. "Daddy sleepin'."

Tears shattered what was left of Boone's view. "Yes, baby, your daddy is sleeping."

Rachel was rechecking the injured woman's pulse when she heard the little girl's voice. Her gaze shifted to the man on the opposite side of the car. He was smiling at the child, but there were tears shimmering in his eyes, eyes so black she couldn't even see the pupils. The grip he had on the baby's hand was gentle, so gentle. She took a deep breath and went back to her work, aware that this was no time to join him in grief.

And then Charlie tapped her on the back. "Rachel, you've got to pull back. They're going to use the Jaws."

Metal crunched and popped as the hydraulic claw did what it had been designed to do. Moments later, they had the door on the passenger side open. Rachel pushed her way past the firemen to the young mother inside. To Rachel's relief, the woman's eyelids began to flutter. Charlie was on his knees beside her, the neck brace in his hand. They began to do what they'd been trained to do.

Before Boone knew it, the ambulance holding Punkin and her mother was flying down the road, with lights flashing and the wail of a siren to accompany them home. He shuddered. It sounded too much like a little girl's scream. And while he watched, another vehicle arrived. The name emblazoned in gold paint on both doors said it all. County Coroner. They'd come for Punkin's daddy.

Oh, God.

His mind went blank. He looked down at his scratched and bloodstained hands. The pale blue T-shirt he'd put on this morning was blood-spattered. His black leather jacket was wet and muddy. And while he stood, rain started to fall again. The urge to cry was so close at hand that he couldn't focus on what to do next. He closed his eyes and lifted his face to the sky, wishing it would wash away the memories of what he'd just seen.

With weariness in every movement, he turned toward his truck just as the familiar black and white of an Oklahoma Highway Patrol car pulled up to the scene. In a gesture of defeat, he leaned against the fender, waiting for the officer to emerge.

Rain was coming down faster now, plastering his hair to his head and his clothes to his body. Impulsively he held out his hands, welcoming the cold, bulletlike droplets that fell upon his bloodstained skin. For once the thought of solitude inside that run-down trailer house in the Kiamichis seemed inviting, but he couldn't leave. Not now. He took a deep breath. It wasn't quite over yet.

He drove through Razor Bend in a daze, not stopping until he found himself in Denver Cherry's front yard. He'd come back to Razor Bend to finish a job. Either he would finish it…or it would finish him. He walked onto the porch and into the house without knocking.

One look at Boone MacDonald and Denver forgot any notion he'd had about putting him in his place. There was blood on his shirt, and his clothes were wet clear through. He didn't know what had happened to him, but the look in Boone's eyes made Denver nervous.

"I suppose you came for your money," he said, trying to maintain the upper hand.

Boone didn't have to pretend to be angry. Denver Cherry was a man who didn't care who he hurt or how it happened, as long as he got what he wanted. The world would be better off without Cherry's kind, and yet he lived and a young man had died. Boone swallowed his rage. He couldn't get the sound of a little girl's sobs out of his mind.

"We never did agree on how much," Denver said, then looked away when Boone's hands doubled into fists. He'd known sending Tommy Joe to tail Boone might tick him off, but he'd never figured Boone would take it so hard.

"Just pay me. I've got things to do," Boone said.

Denver shrugged, then handed over a wad of bills that Boone didn't even bother to count. He shoved them in his pocket and turned on his heel, aware that if he didn't put some space between them, someone was going to get hurt.

"Hey, Boone."

Boone stopped in midstride, without turning around.

Denver stared at the angry set to Boone's shoulders, wondering what kind of response he was about to get.

"You did a real good job. I might have some more work for you, if you're interested."

Boone swallowed, then closed his eyes, letting himself remember why he was here.

"Sure, why not," he muttered. "But next time, either send your bird dog with me, or keep him tied on a leash. Understand?"

Denver grinned. "You're a hard nut, aren't you?"

Boone blinked. Today he'd cried. Tonight he just might get drunk. That made him a nut, all right, but he wasn't hard enough to ignore the pain.

"You know where to find me," Boone said, and slammed the door shut behind him.

Hours later, he lay in bed, wide-eyed and sleepless, ignoring a line of cockroaches running up the wall, while he listened to the rain running off the tin roof. An unopened bottle of Jack Daniel's sat right where he'd put it hours ago. He'd taken one look at it and known that drowning this pain wouldn't make it go away. A notion was pushing at him, urging him up, moving past reason to a need he couldn't stop. He wanted to know what had happened to those people from the wreck…and he needed to see Rachel Brant.

Watching her in action today had intrigued him. The helpless, crying woman he'd found in the dark was not the woman who'd taken charge at the wreck. The woman she'd been today was cool, collected and competent. She'd done everything right, and with skill and ease. She hadn't folded once at the sight of blood and death, and he knew seasoned officers who wouldn't have been able to say the same.

It wouldn't take long, he reminded himself. All he had to do was just knock on her door and ask about the victims' conditions. She was bound to know something.

He rolled out of bed and reached for his boots. Before he slept, he needed to hear the sound of her voice.

Rachel puttered through the last of her evening chores, only half-aware that the rain had finally subsided. Water dripped from the leaves onto the roof, soft, gentle sprinkles hardly detectable from indoors. It was only after she went outside to toss coffee grounds beneath her rosebush that she became aware of the slight trickle running through the gutter and out the downspout at the end of the house. There was a much-needed gentleness to the night that the day had not held.

Pictures kept flashing into her mind. A young father, gone from this earth too soon. A young mother, hanging on to life. A small child who'd held even tighter to a wet rag doll, her only familiar object in a world gone awry.

Rachel sat down on the back porch steps and buried her

face in her hands. Losing a patient was the downside of her job. She'd thought she'd learned to live with the knowledge that sometimes, even when they'd done everything possible, it still wasn't enough. But tonight she wasn't sure.

Music drifted out through the screen door and into the night, blending man-made notes with those of Mother Nature. In a fanciful way, the raindrops sounded a little like teardrops, which fit well with the songs being sung. Her taste in music was eclectic, but tonight, sad country songs fit her mood.

She looked up just as the moon emerged from behind a cloud. There on the lawn, standing in the shadows next to her swing, was the tall, unmistakable, silhouette of a man. She gasped. Heart pounding, she jumped to her feet. All she could think was to get inside and lock the door.

"Please, lady, wait!"

She froze. She couldn't see his face, but she knew that voice and the straight set of those shoulders as he stood with his legs slightly apart, as if bracing himself for a blow. It was the same man who'd found her standing in the stream!

He'd come through the woods as he had before, telling himself with every step he took that he was doing this all wrong, that if he kept this up, he might as well put a gun to his head and pull the trigger. Everything he was doing was in direct opposition to what an undercover officer should do. Personal wanting was supposed to take a back seat to the job, but that wasn't happening tonight.

And then he'd seen her come out of the house, and while his mind was shouting, *No!* his feet had been moving ever closer to her house, to her. When she sat down on the steps, he'd wanted to join her, and when she buried her face in her hands, his heart had gone out to her in empathy.

So, he'd thought, *you do feel the pain.*

Music had drifted out of the house, coming to him on the

night. At first it had been nothing more than background to the woman who'd captured his focus. But somewhere between one breath and the next, he'd heard the voice, then the words, and they'd taken his breath away.

It was an old song from the Eagles. Once, years ago, he'd stood in the back of a crowded concert hall and heard them sing this very same song.

Desperado.

Then, the words hadn't meant anything more than any lyrics, but now they came to him as a warning that struck deep in his heart.

He swayed where he stood, as if wounded. Love somebody before it was too late? It was already too late for him. By virtue of his life-style, and in society's eyes, he *was* a desperado…an outlaw who didn't belong in a good woman's life.

"I'll call the police!" Rachel shouted.

Boone's heart hurt at the knowledge he kept putting that fear in her voice.

"Please don't. I came to ask you a question."

Rachel's hand was on the doorknob, and if the man had taken a single step farther, she would have been inside in a instant. But he never moved, so neither did she.

"What?"

"Today you worked a wreck outside of town."

To say Rachel was surprised at the man's choice of topic was putting it mildly. She'd been expecting something personal, even something sexual, that would fit the dark anonymity of his coming and going. She stood without answering, waiting for him to make a wrong move.

"There was a little girl who called herself Punkin."

Rachel's eyes widened. How had he known that?

"Is she all right?" Boone persisted.

She could see no danger in answering, but her voice was still shaking when she spoke. "Yes, I believe so."

"And her mother?"

Rachel's hand fell from the doorknob to her side. "We left her in good hands. Last I heard, she was stable."

Boone exhaled slowly in relief. "Good," he said softly. "That's good."

"How did you know?" Rachel asked.

But Boone answered her question with another of his own.

"The little girl…Punkin…was she still crying when you left?"

Rachel's eyebrows arched. *Still? How did he know she'd been crying at all? Unless…*

"No. Some of the family had arrived. When I saw her last, she was sound asleep in her grandmother's arms."

"Thank you," Boone said, and his voice was so quiet that Rachel had to strain to hear his answer.

"Who are you?" she asked, just as the last notes of the song faded into the night.

"No one."

The emptiness in his voice was unmistakable. In spite of herself, Rachel felt empathy instead of fear.

And then he moved. But instead of coming toward her, he turned and started back toward the woods. When he moved out from beneath the tree and into the moonlight, it fell upon his shoulders, enhancing their breadth and his height. Once again Rachel was struck by his strength and his size. But this time, as he walked, something struck her as familiar. Impulsively she ran to the edge of the porch and called out.

"Wait!"

Surprised, Boone turned before he thought, and then realized that he was no longer concealed by the shadows of night. Although the distance between them was real, there was no way he could hide the sight of his face.

Oh, God… Dear God… Rachel thought, as her hands curled tightly into fists.

Neither spoke. Neither moved. A lingering rain cloud passed between moonlight and earth. A few moments later, it was gone...and so was the man.

A nervous chill ran up Rachel's back. She turned and bolted for the door, shutting it and locking it firmly behind her. Yet even after she was safely inside and sitting in the dark with the phone in her hand, she couldn't get past the fact that the man who'd found her sleepwalking...the man who kept coming to her out of the dark...the man who'd cared about a small child's tears...was the same man who ran with that gang.

That night, when at last she slept, she dreamed. But not the same dream as before. This time she dreamed of a man with dark, laughing eyes, a man who killed with the same passion as he made love.

Chapter 6

When the alarm went off in Rachel's ear, she rolled over and out of bed in the same smooth motion. Only after she hit the button to shut off the alarm did she realize that she'd set it last night out of habit. She groaned in disbelief. She didn't have to go to work today or tomorrow. It was six in the morning, and she'd gotten up for nothing.

"Good grief," she muttered, and crawled back between the covers.

But habit was a hard thing to break. In spite of burying her nose in the pillow and squeezing her eyes tight against a burgeoning dawn, sleep wouldn't come.

Finally she flopped onto her back, scrunched her pillow beneath her neck and contemplated the luxury of two entire days to herself.

No one to answer to.

No sitting around waiting for an emergency to happen.

Today, she could make things happen for herself. She glanced toward the window. It wasn't raining, but wind was whipping the azalea bushes beneath the window near her bed. Every now and then, an elongated branch hit the pane with a thump, then a scratch, as if someone, or something, were begging to get in.

Goose bumps peppered the skin on her arms as her imagination took flight. And even though she knew she was safe, she got up and headed toward the kitchen.

Two cups of coffee later, she was still pondering the identity of the man who'd found her in the stream. For all she knew, he was a criminal. He certainly looked like one. At any rate, he was a man who didn't belong in her world. She shuddered, remembering the men he ran with and the way he'd watched Griff kissing her with no sense of shame.

Yet, even in her dismay, she was forced to give credit where credit was due. If he hadn't happened upon that wreck yesterday, more than likely that mother would have died, and God knew what might have happened to the baby before anyone found them.

She would never have believed a man who presented himself as a modern-day outlaw could be as empathetic and compassionate as he had been with that small, frightened child. But he had.

In fact, Rachel knew that if that had been their first meeting, she would have come away from that wreck with a completely different impression of the man. She'd seen him reluctant to move from danger, eager to go back to the child who was trapped. And not only that, he'd been concerned enough to come last night and ask about her condition.

"Oh, for Pete's sake," Rachel muttered, and dumped the last of her coffee down the drain. "I'm romanticizing about some probable felon, just because he hasn't lost the ability to shed tears for someone else's pain."

Angry with herself and what she considered "flights of fancy," she made a list of things she wanted to do today, then went to get dressed. Casual would be the order of the day.

But just as she was walking out the door, the phone began to ring. Conscience told her to answer. Instead, she stood, listening to the second, then the third, shrill ring. When it rang for the fourth time, her answering machine clicked on, and Rachel stood in the doorway, listening to Griffin Ross's voice.

An odd sensation of dread settled in the pit of her stomach as he rambled through his monologue, with a reason for calling that she didn't believe. He was still talking when she walked out the door, locking it behind her. As she drove away, she had the strangest sensation of having made an escape, then told herself she was being silly. Griff wasn't the man she should be worrying about. He wasn't the one who'd been showing up in all the wrong places.

After a long, enjoyable day in Broken Bow, Rachel entered the city limits of Razor Bend. It was fifteen minutes to four, and school was letting out. A line of yellow buses was at a stoplight, waiting for it to turn green, while teenagers barely old enough to drive were cruising the streets in their cars, honking and waving as if they hadn't seen one another in weeks, when they'd just spent the day together in class.

She turned off the main thoroughfare and pulled up to the self-serve pump outside Jimmy's Place. He sold diesel and gas and the greasiest made-to-order burgers in town. Saturday nights, when the town all but died, Jimmy's Place was usually packed. The draw? A well-worn pool table in a small back room, four video games, of which only three worked, and the only place in town that fixed flats. She didn't need a flat fixed, but she could use a tank of gas. It was the perfect excuse to get off the streets until the worst of the traffic had passed.

Rachel put her car in park and killed the engine, then glanced over her shoulder to the sacks of groceries sitting in the back seat. There was nothing inside that warranted refrigeration, so they should be fine. Shopping in Broken Bow had netted her more than a week's worth of groceries, plus a couple of rental movies she'd been wanting to see. She got out with a smile on her lips, thinking about solitude, popcorn and Patrick Swayze in drag as she unscrewed the gas cap and set it aside.

But when she turned toward the pump, she stifled a gasp. A weasel of a man with a brown, shaggy beard was blocking her path. He grinned, then winked, adding a slow, appreciative whistle to the leer he was wearing.

"Well, hello, now…" Snake said.

His audacity took Rachel by surprise, and then, to her dismay, she realized where she'd seen him before. He was one of the trio of men who'd ogled her and Griff from the street in front of the Adam's Rib Café.

She refused to be bullied. She would not be afraid. She lifted her chin, her eyes glittering with anger as she waited for him to give way.

"Excuse me, but you're in my way."

Snake Martin grinned. "Now…there ain't no need to be actin' that way. I see you're needin' you some gas. How 'bout lettin' old Snake do that for you, honey? You don't want to be gettin' your pretty self all dirty doin' man's work, do you?"

Her stare was unwavering, and her words were cool and clipped. "I don't need any help," she said, and tried to step around him to get to the pump.

But Snake wasn't through playing. He moved with her, once again positioning himself between her and the gas. When he saw her pupils widen, he took advantage of her panic and grabbed her by the arm.

The contact was so sudden, so abhorrent, that Rachel panicked and tried to yank herself free.

"Let me go!" she cried.

But Snake still wasn't done. He knew who she was. He made it his business to know things about beautiful women. He also knew she was no longer anyone's property. The way he heard it, the banker had himself another girlfriend, which, to Snake's way of thinking, made this one free game.

"Now, now, you need to take it easy, sugar," Snake whispered.

"A pretty thing like you shouldn't be alone. You need a man…a man like me. I'd take real good care of— Ouch! Ow…ow… Damn it, Boone, let me go."

Rachel jerked, then looked over her shoulder to the man who'd come up behind her…and to the rage on his face.

Now she *was* afraid.

Boone's hand tightened around Snake's bony wrist until he was forced to turn Rachel loose.

"What the hell are you doing?" Boone asked, and if Snake had had the good sense he'd been born with, he would have known to be scared.

"Mind your own damned business," Snake said, then doubled up his free fist and took a wild swing.

Boone didn't bother to duck. At the moment of Snake's swing, he turned him loose and stepped aside. With nothing to check the forward momentum of his own body, Snake fell to the ground.

But when he would have come up fighting, he found himself on the underside of a very large boot, staring up into the face of a cold, angry man.

"Keeping you out of jail is my business," Boone said softly.

Snake winced. That boot on his neck was beginning to hurt.

"Damn you, Boone. I wasn't hurtin' her none. Was I, lady?"

Both pairs of eyes turned to Rachel, one begging to be absolved of an intended sin, the other pinning her in place with a cold, dark stare. She had half a mind to get in her car and drive away, leaving the two toughs to fight it out on their own, but she feared her exit would be less than effective. With a gas gauge on empty and nowhere to go, she struggled to find an answer that would put an end to the entire fiasco.

A gust of warm air whipped a wayward strand of hair toward her face, bringing with it the scent of old grease from the french fries Jimmy's Place served, as well as the gas in the pumps. But before she could answer either man's unspoken plea, something started to change.

The awning beneath which she was standing seemed to melt in her mind. Instead of shade, she felt sun on her face and the sting of dust in her eyes. The sound of cars on the busy street behind her faded, and to her right a horse nickered, then stomped fretfully as it pulled at its tether.

Someone ran past her, shouting. She turned to look, and Razor Bend had disappeared. The paved streets had turned to dust. The busy downtown business district was nothing but an odd, ramshackle assortment of unpainted clapboard buildings and weather-worn tents, popping in the wind.

A man called out a name that made her blood run hot, then cold with fear.

"Dakota! I'm callin' you out!"

Dakota stood in the middle of the street, his legs braced, his fingers taut and curled above the butt of the gun riding low on his hip. His voice was low, his demeanor deadly.

"For the last damn time, I did not steal your gold," Dakota growled.

Mercy moaned. She recognized the miner who'd called Dakota out. It was Rufus Stampler. He'd been drinking and gambling for the better part of a week. If his gold was gone, chances were he'd wagered it and lost when he was too drunk to know.

And then the miner made his move.

She screamed. "Dakota, look out!"

She could have saved her breath. Rufus had announced his intent when he went for his gun.

Dakota's draw was as deadly as the look on his face. He'd already known that it would come to this. It always did. For him, there was no other way.

Fire spewed from the end of Dakota's gun. The sound of the shot was still ringing in the onlookers' ears when the miner fell. His gun had never cleared the holster.

Weak with relief, Mercy thought if a man had to die, thank God it hadn't been hers.

The wind lifted the skirt of her red satin dress, plastering it indecently to her slim, shapely body. But Mercy Hollister had long ago given up decency for a dry bed and a full belly. And if asked, she would give those up, too, for the love of this man who lived by the gun.

She needed to touch him...to feel the heartbeat still strong in his chest. Blindly she started toward him, but someone grabbed her by the shoulder, yanking her rudely around.

Sunlight hit the tin badge pinned to the front of Ab Schuler's shirt. Mercy's heart sank. Ab couldn't arrest him. It hadn't been Dakota's fault.

"It was a fair fight. Rufus called him out. We all saw it," she said.

Ab Schuler frowned. He'd never known it was possible to love a woman and hate her all at the same time, but that was what he felt now, knowing that a gunman had replaced him in Mercy Hollister's heart.

"What's wrong with you?" he snarled, twisting her arm in an effort to make her see sense, but his anger turned to fear when a cold, deadly voice called his name.

He turned, still holding her arm. Dakota was standing not six feet away, with his gun drawn and aimed at Ab's belly.

"Let her go," Dakota warned, and then cocked his gun. Mercy fell free.

Rachel staggered, then covered her face with her hands. *Oh, my God... Oh, my God...*

Boone saw her sway, and before she could fall, he caught her close. For a heartbeat—but no longer—he knew what it felt like to hold Rachel Brant in his arms. The instant she felt steady, he let her go. When he looked back at Snake, the threat in his voice brought Snake to his feet.

"Get!" he said hoarsely.

Snake didn't have to be told twice. What had started out as a little bit of fun had turned into a great big stinking deal. He glared at Rachel as he stomped past her.

Boone turned, noting Rachel's lack of color, as well as the odd, flat stare in her eyes. Something didn't set right. She was a woman who dealt with life and death every day; he wouldn't have expected her to react so emotionally to an act of sexual harassment. Punch Snake out? Yes, definitely yes! But pass out on him? No.

"Are you all right?" he asked, wishing he could take her in his arms again and make that fear on her face go away. But the man he was pretending to be could not be touching a woman like her. It would only make things worse.

Rachel shuddered. That voice. His voice. It was so like… She looked up. Reality checked in with a jolt as she realized she had a name to go with the face.

Boone. Your name is Boone.

For some reason, it didn't quite fit. There was a cold, almost cruel, expression on his face, but his eyes, those dark, fathomless eyes, had changed. If she hadn't known better, she might have believed there was love shining there.

Boone was getting nervous. Why didn't she answer? Was there something he was missing?

"Lady, are you all right?" he repeated.

It wouldn't do to let him know she was scared. Her hand was shaking as she lifted it to her face, smoothing away the windblown tendrils that had escaped from her braid. Her voice was as calm as she could make it. "I'm fine, thank you."

Stifling an urge to continue this fruitless conversation, he walked away before he could change his mind.

Rachel stared after him, once again wondering why she kept thinking she'd seen him before. Before Razor Bend. There was something about that slow, careless walk. He reminded her of someone, but she couldn't think who.

"Who in the world could I possibly know who would be anything like—?"

Her heart skipped a beat, and she had to steady herself by hanging on to the pump.

Dakota! Dear God, he walks like the man in my dreams.

"Hey, Rachel. Need any help?"

She turned. The owner of Jimmy's Place was leaning out the door, waiting for her answer.

And where were you when I needed you? "No. No, I've got it," she muttered, and pulled the hose from the pump.

The tank began to fill, and as it did, Rachel was forced to accept a fact that she should have acknowledged long ago.

Just now, when the world as she knew it and the one in her mind had separated, she hadn't been dreaming. She'd been wide awake and part of an ugly confrontation. Yet in the midst of it all, reality had slipped, just as it had that night in the stream. No longer could she tell herself it was the aftermath of sleepwalking. Something was happening to her that she didn't understand. Even worse, it was something she couldn't control.

Denver Cherry was sprawled in his favorite easy chair, with the television remote in one hand and his third longneck of the hour in the other. He squinted at the set, watching Debbie do Dallas, as well as several other men in between, all the while wondering if his satellite dish was as steamy as the show on the screen.

Right in the middle of him wishing he had a little female company, the front door of his house flew back with a bang, rattling nearby windows and setting his teeth on edge. He turned, then glared. This was not the company he'd had in mind.

"Don't you people ever knock?" he growled, giving Boone a hard-edged stare.

Boone pointed toward Snake, who, like his namesake, was slithering toward a chair on the opposite side of the room.

"I've had it," Boone said. "Either I'm in all the way, or I'm out for good!"

Denver frowned. He didn't like ultimatums. He was the boss. He made the decisions.

"Now you listen here…." he growled. But he never got a chance to finish what he'd been going to say.

Boone jabbed a finger in Denver's fat belly. "No, you listen. The whole lot of you are nothing but a bunch of penny-ante thugs. You told me when I signed on that I could work my way up in this organization…that there would be something for me if I was willing to wait." He took a deep breath. There was a lot riding on what he said next, and it had to come out just right. "But I just figured something out."

"Like what?" Denver said.

Sarcasm colored his voice. "Like I think I've been lied to. You told me you had backing. You said there would be big money in it for me. Well, hell, Denver, except for that run the other night, all I've done is pick up after your two stooges."

Denver glared, first at Boone, then at Snake. Something had happened to precipitate this explosion. He would bet money on it. And it was forcing an issue he wasn't ready to face, namely bringing an outsider into the fold. Yes, Boone had made an unplanned delivery for him with no hitches. But he was an unknown. Until six weeks ago, Denver hadn't known the man existed, and now he wanted in. Well, he didn't think so. He'd known Snake Martin and Tommy Joe Smith nearly all their lives. Granted, they were stupid, but they followed orders and kept their mouths shut.

Denver glared at Snake. "What the hell did you do?"

"Not a damned—"

"Shut up!" Boone muttered.

Snake did as he was told. Boone started to pace in a jumpy, nervous manner, as if he expected the cops to burst in on them at any moment. To add to the drama, static from the police scanner broke the momentary silence in the room as a dispatcher's voice came in loud and clear behind them.

"See the woman at 1022 Main about a disturbance."

Boone relaxed. That wasn't the address of Jimmy's Place, but it very well could have been. He pointed at Snake, but his comments were directed to Denver.

"He accosted a very unwilling woman in a very public place. I'd venture to say any number of people saw what he was doing. I yanked his ass away before he wound up back in jail, and left the woman standing by the gas pumps at Jimmy's Place. For all I know, she still might press charges."

Denver's face turned a mottled purple. He stared at Snake, wondering, if he killed him right now, how he could dispose of the body without being caught.

"You fool!" His voice was shaking with rage. The boss was already on his ass about the messes Snake was making. "Do you ever think?"

Snake glared, although he was starting to realize the implications of what he'd just done.

"I didn't hurt her none," he muttered.

Denver stalked toward Snake, who was scrambling to his feet and looking for the quickest way out. He grabbed him by the throat and slammed him up against the wall, stopping Snake's exit.

"She better not have been someone's wife."

Snake slapped at Denver's hand, trying unsuccessfully to free himself from the angry man's grasp.

"Hell, no," he grumbled. "She's free and legal. She ain't married, and she ain't nobody's girl. I know that for a fact."

"You're lying," Boone said softly. "You know as well as I do that she belongs to that banker. We all saw him kiss her at the EMS headquarters where she works."

Denver's face paled. He gawked at Snake, as if seeing him for the reptile he really was. There was only one banker who counted in Razor Bend, and only one female EMT. Boone had to be talking about Griffin Ross and Rachel Brant.

"Is Boone telling the truth? Did you mess with Griffin Ross's woman?"

When Snake looked away, Denver exploded.

"You idiot! You fool! You stepped out of your league, and I will not put my neck on the line for you with the boss this time. He's already on your case for offing that guard. If he finds out about this, too, you're gone! Get that?"

"That guard wasn't supposed to be there," Snake whined. "It's not my fault. He pulled a gun on me first."

Boone froze. Snake had killed a guard? What guard? Every lawman's instinct he had said he should arrest them now and forget the boss, whoever the hell he was. And yet he stood without moving, aware that he couldn't say a thing. He'd just witnessed a confession to murder and was unable to act upon it.

"That does it," Boone muttered, and spun on his heel. "I'm outa here. I've done time, and I'll probably do some more before I die, but I don't plan on lethal injection as my method of passing. You people are out of my league. I don't hire on with killers."

Denver paled. He couldn't lose Snake *and* Boone. There was no way he and Tommy Joe could handle the business alone. The boss had too many irons in the fire already.

"Wait!" Denver shouted.

Boone turned.

"You're in."

Whatever elation Boone should have been feeling was masked by a slow-burning rage. "In how?"

Denver didn't like to be put on the spot. He shrugged. "You haul, just like Snake and Tommy Joe. You get paid when I get paid."

"And if something goes wrong?"

Denver sighed. "We take care of our own. If you get caught, you'll be bailed out."

"Who do I call if that happens? You?"

"No! If it happens, just bide your time. The boss handles that."

"But how will he know?"

Denver shrugged. "He just knows, that's all."

"I like to know who I'm working for," Boone said, aware that he might be pushing his luck.

This time Denver balked. "It's not my story to tell. If the boss wants to meet you, then you'll be the first to know. Otherwise, do what you're told and keep your mouth shut."

"I'm not baby-sitting that fool again," Boone said. "I work alone, or not at all." He glared at Snake again to reiterate his point.

Denver held up his hands, as if in surrender. "Fine...fine. Just check back with me in a day or so. We've got a load of crystal meth that's overdue from the lab. When it shows, we've got to get rid of it fast, understand?"

Boone nodded, then left. When he was several miles down the road, he reached for his phone. Moments later, he was unloading what he'd learned to Captain Cross. They'd spread a net to catch some thieves, and caught a killer, as well.

Pain shattered the dream within Rachel's head. She woke up facedown in the yard. As always, she had a blinding headache and tears on her cheeks. She scrambled to her feet. Unaware of the rain-soaked ground coming up between her toes, she swayed slightly as she stared into the night. This time, to her relief, she was alone.

"Dear God, this has got to stop," she muttered, and staggered up the steps and into the house.

Once inside, she stripped off her muddy gown as she headed for the bath, anxious to wash away more than the mud clinging to her skin and clothes.

The water was warm and welcoming as she stepped beneath the spray. She lifted her face, letting the heat soak into her chilled, shaking body. Long after she was out and dry, wrapped in a clean robe, she was afraid to sleep, for fear it would happen again. But she'd been forced to accept a truth she'd been ignoring before. She needed help—professional help. She would deal with it tomorrow.

And then she looked at the clock. Tomorrow was already here.

Griffin Ross had a new suit. Lois Klein spotted it the moment he walked in. Her hand automatically went to her hair, checking to make sure it was all in place. She didn't want to rush things, yet she was determined not to miss her chance. One dance did not a relationship make, and although they'd had what she considered a wonderful time, there had been nothing between them since then but cordial smiles and polite conversation.

Griff walked like a man who knew his place on this earth. He had everything he'd ever wanted…except Rachel Brant, and he hadn't completely given up on changing that fact. He saw his secretary fidget, and knew that taking her to the dance had been a mistake. Lois was a nice woman, and more than attractive, but she wasn't Rachel. He nodded and smiled as he walked past her desk.

"Morning, Lois."

She preened. "Good morning, Griff…." She blushed, then glanced at the customers waiting outside his office. "I mean, Mr. Ross."

Griff winced. He'd been right. Taking Lois to the dance had been a great big mistake.

Lois handed Griff a file. "Mr. Dutton is waiting to see you, sir."

Griff glanced at Charlie Dutton and smiled. "Come in, Charlie." As Charlie entered the office, Griff closed the door and then took a seat behind his desk.

Charlie slid into the guest chair and then sat forward, leaning toward the desk.

Griffin Ross was of the opinion that body language told more about a customer than what they might say about themselves. From the way Charlie was behaving, he was expecting him to ask for an extension on his loan. He couldn't have been more wrong.

"I came to pay off my note," Charlie said, and pulled a cashier's check from his pocket, already made out and signed.

For a moment Griff was taken aback, but then he smiled broadly. "Well, now, that's fine, just fine! But that's quite a sizable amount, isn't it?"

Charlie grinned and slid the check across the desk to Griffin.

"Thirty-three thousand dollars and forty-four cents, interest and all."

"My goodness," Griff said. "You must have a whale of a second job." He grinned. "What are you doing, making moonshine on the side?"

Charlie's eyes narrowed, but his smile stayed fixed. "I just had myself a little luck," he said quickly. "I don't like to be in debt any more than the next man."

Griff nodded. "Good. That's good. Now you wait here while I have Lois pull your note. We'll have you free and clear in no time."

Down the street, Rachel pulled her car up to the curb, right in front of Curlers. Joanie Mills looked up, then waved at her through the window as she gave her client's hair a final pat.

The doorbell jangled as Rachel walked in.

"Be right with you," Joanie said, making change for Mavis Bealer, who was paying for her perm.

"Nice hairdo, Mavis," Rachel said, and was rewarded with a wide grin as Mavis prissed herself out of the door.

Joanie turned to Rachel, and her smile faded. "What's wrong?"

Rachel sat down and ran her hands through her long, dark hair.

"I need the ends trimmed."

Joanie frowned. "I wasn't talking about your hair. I haven't seen circles that dark under anyone's eyes since New Year's Day. Have you had a bad week?"

Rachel shrugged. She could lie and blame her mood on her job, and Joanie would believe her. Joanie all but fainted at the sight of her own blood, and considered Rachel something between an angel and a masochist.

"I've had better," she said.

Joanie patted her on the shoulder and then flopped a waterproof cape around her shoulders, fastening it firmly at the neck. "Let's get you washed. You close your eyes and relax." She wiggled her fingers in Rachel's face. "I give the best scalp massages in town."

Rachel grinned as Joanie angled her head beneath a flow of warm water. "That's because you give the *only* scalp massages in town."

Joanie pretended to leer, and then lowered her voice to a whisper. "That's not what I hear. Someone told me that ColaBelle Prather was doing all right for herself on Saturday nights."

Rachel laughed, then closed her eyes and started to relax. Her friend's outrageous gossip was just what she'd needed to hear. She shifted in the chair and then settled, letting her mind wander in and out of focus as Joanie washed and rambled. It was only when Joanie's hands suddenly stilled in the act of scrubbing that she started to listen more closely.

When Joanie groaned and then sighed, Rachel opened her eyes and looked up. The look on her friend's face was close to rapture.

"What?" Rachel asked, wishing she could see more than the flyspecks on the ceiling above.

"Oh…my…Gawd!" Joanie gasped. Joanie quickly washed the soap out of Rachel's hair, then swathed her head in a towel and sat her up. "Take a look out there!"

Rachel rolled her eyes and grinned, then looked in the direction Joanie was pointing. The grin froze on her face as Joanie continued.

"I'd say about a hundred and ninety-something pounds. At least two or three inches over six feet…and good grief, Granny, the longest legs and the cutest butt I've ever seen on a man."

Rachel had no comment to make about Joanie's raves. There was nothing to say. She'd been up close and personal with this man far too many times as it was. Even ogling him from behind plate glass seemed risky.

"Just look at that face!" Joanie gasped, and pretended to shiver with ecstasy. "Isn't he just to die for?"

Judging by who he hangs out with, you very well might.

Joanie elbowed Rachel. "Wouldn't you just love to get him alone in the dark?"

A nervous twinge pulled at Rachel's belly. What on earth would Joanie think if she knew that had already happened?

"I don't know," Rachel said, feeling her way through the unexpected conversation. "He looks pretty rough to me."

Joanie grinned. "The better to love you with, my dear." She giggled.

But Rachel wasn't laughing. She was too busy trying to hang on to the chair. In spite of the fact that she could see her own reflection in the window before her, another shape—another face—was again superimposing itself over hers. It was her…and yet it wasn't. She wanted to shriek.

She wanted to cry. But she couldn't move. By the time she took her next breath, her reflection was gone and Mercy Hollister had taken her place.

It was happening all over again!

An off-key piano was being played downstairs. Short bursts of laughter drifted to the floor above, floating down the hall and under the door of Mercy's private room. A coal-oil lamp burned on the washstand nearby, highlighting the passion on Dakota's face as he slid into Mercy's soft body.

Mercy sighed and wrapped her arms around his neck.

"Dakota...Dakota... I love you so. Promise you'll never leave me."

He stilled, his eyes black and glittering. Caught in sweet Mercy's warmth, he looked down at her, A smile broke the hard, embittered expression he normally wore as he leaned down and kissed the side of her face.

"Only when I die. Only when I die."

Rachel jerked and, to her horror, nearly pitched forward out of the chair. If Joanie hadn't grabbed her, she might have fallen facedown on the floor.

"Good grief, girl. I know he's gorgeous, but this is no time to be falling at his feet. Besides, he's not the type to take home to Mama. That's a look-but-don't-touch man. They're pretty... but way too dangerous for a good woman's heart."

Rachel wanted to cry. She felt an overwhelming urge to tell Joanie what had just happened. But how could she explain something she didn't understand herself?

"Sorry," she muttered, and closed her eyes, trying to come to terms with the transition she'd just made from one world to another. "I got dizzy, but I'm fine now."

Joanie frowned and pressed her hand against Rachel's forehead to test for a fever.

"I'm not sick," Rachel said, and managed a smile. "Maybe you just sat me up too fast."

Joanie wasn't buying it, but she had no explanation to replace the one Rachel had given her. Still frowning, she turned Rachel toward the mirror to begin the trim she'd asked for; the man on the street forgotten.

But Rachel hadn't forgotten him. More than once, as Joanie combed and snipped, Rachel's gaze drifted to the mirror, and to the reflection of what—and who—she could see on the street behind her.

Boone was still there, leaning against the front of his truck, obviously waiting for someone in a store nearby. His face was a study in repose; she had the oddest sensation she was watching two different men.

Whenever someone passed by, Boone's face underwent an odd transformation. His eyes narrowed, his mouth turned up at one corner in a cold, mirthless smirk, and his slouch went from careless to careful. It was only when he believed he was unobserved that he let down his guard. Only then did Rachel see the man who'd been at the scene of the wreck, the man who'd crawled into a wreck to hold a little girl's hand, the one who'd shed tears for a dead man and his child.

Something inside her started to hurt. It was a pain she couldn't locate and had no way to heal. Blinking back tears, she tore her gaze from his face and made herself watch what Joanie was doing.

She was getting scared. Every time she saw that man, she also saw Mercy and her outlaw. Why? What on earth was the connection between them? Or was it all in her head?

She closed her eyes and sighed, absorbing the pleasure of the comb gently biting into her scalp as Joanie combed through her hair. But try as she might, she couldn't get the words of an outlaw out of her mind.

Only when I die. Only when I die.

Chapter 7

Rachel stepped off the elevator and turned left, as she'd been instructed to do by the downstairs receptionist, then paused outside a door halfway down the hall.

Doctors of Psychiatry
E. G. Ealey
Steven Milam
H. A. Smith

Her fingers were trembling as she took a deep breath and entered. The receptionist behind the counter looked up, nodding a welcome. Rachel returned it with a shaky smile.

"Rachel Brant to see Dr. Ealey."

The woman handed Rachel a clipboard with a blank form attached. "We'll need some information for our records. Fill out this form and give it back to me as soon as you've finished."

Rachel stared at the page. If she took the next step, there would be no turning back. It would be the final admission that her life was out of control.

Choosing a chair in the far corner of the room, she ventured a quick glance at the other people waiting to be seen and hoped there was no one present she knew. To her relief, they were all strangers.

Before she could change her mind, she filled out the form, but when she looked up to return it, the receptionist was no longer at her desk. Leaning the clipboard against the leg of her chair, she reached for a magazine.

Two magazines later, and well into her third, she turned to a page that brought her from a slump to upright, her attention focused on the subject matter of the article before her.

"Dreams: Imagination or Reincarnation?"

Curiosity turned to interest, and interest to shock. The more she read, the faster her heart raced. There were too many similarities between what had been happening to her and the case studies mentioned in the article to ignore.

Yet as she finished the piece, she knew that what she was thinking was way off the wall. Granted, the article was in the doctor's office, but that didn't mean he would adhere to such farfetched theories. The doctors she knew preferred to deal in specifics; specific symptoms were treated with specific procedures. And while psychiatrists dealt with mental instabilities and stress-related problems, she knew the chances were slim of finding one who would easily buy into the idea that one of his patients had memories of having lived before.

So what do I do now?

Rachel set the magazine aside, then looked up. The receptionist was back, but busy at her desk. The longer Rachel sat, the more convinced she became that the answers to her problems would not come from a doctor. Without giving herself time for second thoughts, she got up and started out the door, then paused.

What am I forgetting?

She looked back at where she'd been sitting. The clipboard with the form with all her personal information on it was leaning next to the chair where she'd left it. She removed the sheet of paper from the clipboard and put it in her purse.

"Miss Brant, the doctor will see you now."

"I'm sorry, but I've changed my mind."

Rachel walked out without looking back. Her step was lighter, her mind already focused. She glanced down at her watch. *Good. There's still plenty of time for what I want to do.*

It was late in the afternoon when Rachel left Lawton and started home. The drive to Razor Bend was long and boring, but after the time she'd just spent in the Lawton Public Library, she had plenty to think about.

The articles and books she'd found on the subjects of past-life regression and reincarnation were verifications of her own situation. But while she was beginning to think there could be truth in the theory, she had no idea as to why it was happening, or how to fix it.

What she did know was that the single continuing thread between her reality and insanity was an outlaw called Boone. The first experience of déjà vu had come the night she woke up in the stream. He'd been mere yards away, reaching out to her. At that moment she'd lost her identity in what she thought was a dream. His reappearances in her life were always unpredictable, yet the end result was always the same. Every time she saw him, she slipped back into Mercy Hollister's world. And therein lay her dilemma. She couldn't live out the rest of her life slipping in and out of reality. There had to be a reason why this was happening to her now, and she was determined to find it.

Her medical training gave her no background support for a hypothesis such as the one she was considering. Medicine was based on cause and effect—symptoms and treatments for specific illnesses and diseases.

In Razor Bend, as well as in most of the world, past life experiences meant what had happened yesterday, or last week, or last year…not in another lifetime. But Rachel was beginning to believe that maybe—just maybe—she'd walked on this earth in another time…in another place… in another life…and with another man.

Mile after mile she drove, drawing closer to home. About five miles outside Razor Bend, she began to relax. The sun at her back was close to setting. But when she took the next curve in the road, it didn't take her long to realize her plans for the evening were about to change.

In the distance, Rachel could see a man standing at the edge of the highway beside an obviously disabled pickup truck. Even from here, she could see the lopsided angle at which the truck bed was leaning. He'd had a flat. A few seconds later, she jerked with recognition. It was Boone!

Her fingers tightened on the steering wheel. *Why does he keep turning up everywhere I go?*

Panic fought with conscience as she drew nearer. Only a day or so earlier, he'd stopped on this very same road to give assistance to the injured and dying. Did she have the nerve to pass him by? Even worse, was she so lacking in brains as to stop?

She came closer, all the while warning herself not to look, but as she drew even with where he was standing, her gaze locked with his, as if drawn by a magnet.

In spite of his obvious need for help, he made no move to try to flag her down. Instead, his dark, silent gaze tore through her conscience, bit by bit. And as she drove past, a relentless warning kept up a replay inside her mind.

If you want to find out what's going on in your head, now's your chance. Stop, stupid, stop!

But she didn't. Afraid of feelings she couldn't control, she looked away, unwilling to let him see her weakness. But it was too late. She'd already seen his face, and it was the expression he was wearing that helped her make up her mind. He didn't expect her to stop…and for that very reason, she did.

* * *

The blowout had come without warning. One minute Boone had been driving with ease, thinking of picking up some barbecue at the Adam's Rib Café to take home for supper, and the next thing he knew, he'd been skidding all over the road. It had taken all his skill to come to a halt without hitting a nearby stand of trees. And as he got out of his truck, he'd realized he was less than a mile from where the wreck had occurred.

"This stretch of road must be jinxed," he muttered as he circled his truck, checking for damage. Luckily for him, the only thing ruined was a tire.

But his disgust turned to anger when he realized his jack was missing, and not only that, his spare was flat. He glanced up at the setting sun, judging the time he had left before darkness set in, and faced the fact that he'd be after dark walking into Razor Bend. Yet no sooner had he looked up than a car came around the far curve, heading his way.

"Talk about luck," he said. He was about to wave the driver down when he recognized the car.

His luck had just gone from bad to worse. It was Rachel Brant, and judging from the way she looked at him each time they met, there was no way she was going to stop. He stood like a man waiting for the other shoe to drop, watching as she drove past.

And then her brake lights came on and, to his disbelief, she started backing up. Moments later, her window came down. With only a trace of a tremor in her voice, she spoke. "Need any help?"

He couldn't think what to say. He'd been so certain that she would leave him standing there that it took him a moment to gather his thoughts.

"Had a blowout," he finally muttered.

Rachel nodded. "Do you have a spare?"

"It's flat."

Rachel took a deep breath. "I have room in my trunk. Toss it in. I'll be glad to drop you off at Jimmy's Place. It's the only place in town that…"

Boone finished her sentence. "…fixes flats."

Rachel grinned, more to herself than at him, but it broke the ice. She got out of the car with her key in her hand while Boone turned to get the spare.

Before she could get the key in the hole, wind whipped around the curve where she'd parked, blasting grit and dust in her face and into her eyes.

"Oh!" she gasped, and covered her face with her hands, but it was too late. The damage had already been done.

At the sound of her cry, Boone spun, just as she covered her face. Seconds later, he was at her side. He had no way of knowing what had caused her to cry out, but he could see that she was hurting.

"What's wrong?"

"My eyes," Rachel mumbled, and then staggered up against her own car, disoriented by the pain.

"Let me see," he urged, trying to pull her hands away from her face.

At first Rachel wouldn't budge. She'd covered her face in reflex, and although it had been too late to prevent the damage, the dark felt better than the light. And then his soft plea broke through her resolve.

"Please, honey…let me see."

Rachel froze at the familiarity, but his voice compelled her to obey. When he laid his hands on top of hers, gently urging them aside, her legs went weak, but from want, not panic. He'd stirred a longing within her that she'd been trying to deny. It wasn't fear that he made her feel. It was fascination.

"Easy now," he said softly, as her hands dropped to her sides.

And when she tilted her head back, her eyes still closed,

awaiting his ministrations, it was all Boone could do not to kiss the invitation he saw on her lips. Then she started to speak, and he gritted his teeth, trying to remember what he'd been about to do.

"Dirt. In my eyes. My eyes."

To his dismay, healing tears were already seeping out from beneath her dark lashes.

"I'm sorry," he said. "This wouldn't have happened if you hadn't stopped to help. Will you let me help you?"

Her hesitation was momentary. She was already blinded and helpless. He'd had his chance to do her harm, and once again, all he'd done was offer her aid.

She nodded.

Boone exhaled, only then realizing he'd been holding his breath. "One eye at a time, okay?"

His hands were cupping her face. Gently…so gently. It was all she could do not to lean into them, into him. "Okay."

"We need to rinse that grit out. I've got a nearly full bottle of spring water in my truck."

"That will work," Rachel said, and when he turned her loose to go back to his truck, she felt adrift in a dark, empty sea. Only after she felt his hand on her arm did she feel rooted once again to the earth.

"I need you to tilt your head back. Easy now…a little more…a little more."

She did as she was told.

"That's good. Hold it there."

She felt him put something in her hand.

"Here's a handkerchief to catch the drip."

Her fingers curled around the fabric and, in doing so, caught the tips of his fingers with it.

Boone inhaled slowly, reminding himself of the business at hand, and slipped out from beneath her touch.

Rachel sighed. She had every reason in the world to distrust him, and yet the feeling just wasn't there. He was too gentle to be frightening.

"Pour away," she said, and when the tepid water began washing away the dirt, she knew an overwhelming feeling of relief. "That feels so good."

Boone's imagination hit overdrive. If things had been different, he could have envisioned her saying that very same thing in his ear as they made love.

"Easy does it," he cautioned, staying her hand as she started to scrub at her eye. "Let's do the other one. Then, if we need to, we'll give them both a second dose."

Again the water ran free, washing the last of the grit out and freeing her sight.

"Hallelujah! I was blind and now I see," she said, half laughing and half crying with relief as she opened her eyes fully. It broke the tension of the moment.

A smile tilted the corner of his mouth. "Would you believe in another life I walked on water?"

Rachel laughed. "No."

"I didn't think so," he drawled, and handed her the bottle of water. "Here, trade you this for your keys. You get back in the car before any more damage is done. I'll load the tire."

Gratefully she handed over the keys and reached for the door.

"Can you see okay to drive?" Boone asked.

Rachel turned, gazing intently past his hard-bitten look to the gentle depths of his dark eyes.

"I'm fine…thanks to you."

Time stood still. Neither moved, neither spoke, both of them absorbing the fact that, for the moment, they were the only two people in the world. And then, off in the distance, the sound of an eighteen-wheeler pulling up a distant steep grade could be heard. Boone was the first to look away.

"I'd better get this tire loaded, or we'll have to drive behind that rig all the way into town."

Rachel slipped behind the wheel. Seconds later the trunk lid shut with a thump, and Boone slid inside, bringing a new kind of tension with him.

The space inside the car suddenly shrank. Rachel fiddled with her seat belt and tried to pretend he wasn't there. But it was useless. His presence was overpowering, and it was all she could do not to stare. She took the keys from him and started the car.

She'd never known his legs were so long or his shoulders so wide. She hadn't noticed that his eyebrows were as black as his eyes, or that his eyelashes threw shadows on the planes of his cheeks. Afraid that he would catch her staring, she gripped the steering wheel like a hungover bull rider on an eight-second ride and sped away.

Silence had never been so loud.

Neither spoke, and then both spoke at once, stepping all over each other's conversation in the act of trying to end the ongoing standoff.

Rachel flushed and then shrugged, waiting for him to continue, but Boone had other ideas.

"Sorry," he said.

"No," Rachel said. "You first."

He looked intently at her face. "How are your eyes?"

She smiled. "Much better."

He nodded, then looked away to keep from revealing his feelings. Dear God, being this close without being able to hold her was driving him mad.

Rachel glanced at him as the car took a curve. "Have we ever met before? I mean, before the other night?"

He panicked. It was the last thing he had expected her to say, and it was an undercover cop's worst fear, that someone from his past would walk up and call him by a name other than the one under which he was living. It could not only blow his cover all to hell, it was what got people killed. His gaze was cool and fixed as he answered. "No way. I would have remembered."

Rachel flushed, uncomfortable with the entire situation. But she kept thinking of the mess she was in, and that it was getting deeper by the day. For that reason, she persisted.

"So the first time we met was the other night…on the mountain?"

"I didn't mean to snoop. I heard you crying, you know."

She knew she shouldn't, but she was starting to believe him.

After all, he would have had no way of knowing that she was going to wander around the Kiamichis in her sleep.

"I know that," she said quietly.

"But I frightened you."

A slight grin split the seriousness of her expression. "That you did."

Boone's tension started to ease. Damn, but she was pretty when she smiled. He gave himself permission to stare, and then almost wished he hadn't. Her hair was down, just as it had been the night he saw her in the swing. It reminded him of some black satin sheets he'd once seen, rich, glossy and shining. He remembered the ebb and flow of it against her body as she'd taken flight in the night. Her clothes were simple, nothing more than blue jeans and a thick white sweater, but they were the perfect foil for that slim body and beautiful face. He wasn't sure, but he didn't think he'd ever seen eyes that blue or skin so fair. And then she ended his musing with another pointed question he would have preferred to ignore.

"So, what brought you to Razor Bend?"

"A job."

She nodded. Obviously she'd opened a subject he would rather not discuss. And when she thought of his buddies, she decided *she* would rather not know. "Been in town long?"

This time, at least, he could answer with complete truth. "Six weeks or so."

Rachel's heart thumped. The timeline coincided with the onset of her sleepwalking episodes. Another clue to add to the mental list she was making. For lack of anything else to say, she started to introduce herself.

"I suppose I should have done this before. My name is—"

Boone finished the sentence for her. "Rachel Brant." And then he was the one to look embarrassed. "Someone told me."

She glanced at the scenery, aware that she was less than three miles outside town. If there was anything more to learn, she was going to have to act fast. "And you're Boone?"

He nodded.

"First name or last?

This time he grinned, and as he did, Rachel felt herself sliding back in time.

"No…no," she muttered. "Not now. Not now."

Boone frowned. She wasn't making any sense, but when her gaze went out of focus and the car began to swerve, he shouted, "Rachel, look out!" then grabbed the steering wheel and set the car back on track.

Rachel jerked. The sensation was gone.

"Sorry. I'm… I keep seeing… Uh, I guess I must be tired."

He sighed. Something was going on with her, and had been from the moment he saw her standing in the water, talking to someone who wasn't really there. Just like now.

"Boone MacDonald."

Rachel was still lost in thought. "What?"

"My name is Boone MacDonald."

"Oh."

As they stopped at a crossroads outside town, she gave him another long, considering stare, then decided that after what had just transpired between them, she owed him at least this much. "I'm pleased to meet you, Boone MacDonald."

If he hadn't been already sitting, he would be now. That was the last thing he'd expected her to say.

Stay cool, damn it. Stay focused...and for God's sake stay away from this woman.

But he'd wasted a good pep talk on himself. Instead of turning a cold eye, he found himself with a half-assed grin and a lighter heart. "Have mercy," he drawled. "But the pleasure is mine."

Rachel froze. The smile on her face tilted as her mind began to race.

Have mercy? Did he just say, 'Have mercy'? Oh, my God! Oh, my God!

She heard Mercy's outlaw saying the very same words.

Have mercy, sweet Mercy.

"It's your turn to go," Boone said, pointing out the clear four-way stop and the fact that no one else was in sight.

"Oh! Right!"

Rachel accelerated, shooting through the intersection and on into town. When Jimmy's Place appeared on her left, she signaled her turn, pulled to a stop between the building and the pumps, then popped the trunk lid and killed the engine.

"We're here," she said.

Once again, he grinned, and at that moment Rachel knew that she'd seen that same smile before—but on another man's face.

Boone leaned toward her, not much, but just enough to make Rachel's heart jump with an odd sort of longing.

"Thank you," he said softly.

"For what?" she muttered, lost in the depths of a pair of dark eyes.

He grinned again. For some reason, this very capable woman seemed incapable of following a single train of thought.

"For the ride," he said.

Rachel blinked, then sat upright. "Oh! Oh, yes! You're welcome, of course."

"You sure your eyes are okay?"

"Yes." *Just don't ask me about my heart.*

Boone nodded. "Then I'll just get my tire and get out of your life." He got out of the car and headed toward the trunk to remove the spare.

"If only," Rachel muttered, then jumped when Boone slammed the trunk lid shut.

"Thanks again," he called.

She watched as he rolled the tire toward the garage and once again was struck by the familiarity of his slow, careless stride. Before she could think to move, he suddenly turned and caught her watching.

Embarrassed, she looked away, only to come eye-to-eye with Charlie Dutton's inquiring stare. He was standing in the doorway of Jimmy's Place with a can of pop, a bag of chips and an expression on his face that might have been described as one of disbelief.

It struck a defensive chord in Rachel that she couldn't have explained. What she did on her own time was no one's business, and yet living in a town the size of Razor Bend, she was constantly subjected to everyone's scrutiny.

She waved at Charlie, then glanced once again toward the garage. Boone was nowhere in sight. It was just as well. She started her car and drove away.

The road home was long and winding, but the path was well marked by a sunset of remarkable hues. This evening, the heavenly artwork was wasted on Rachel. Her mind was still locked on the facts she'd unearthed. But were they real facts, she wondered, or just figments of a wild imagination? Or, worse—was she truly losing her mind?

Griffin Ross was coming out of the bakery as Rachel pulled into Jimmy's Place. Unable to believe his eyes, he stood with his mouth agape. There was Rachel—*his* Rachel—and she was with another man. They were smiling and talking as if they'd known each other forever.

He stepped back into the lengthening shadows before she could see him and watched as she parked in the drive by the self-serve pumps. He saw the trunk pop up, then saw the man get out and remove a flat tire. A long, telling glance passed between them before Rachel suddenly waved and drove away.

The whole thing seemed innocent enough. And it was just like Rachel to help someone out.

But it was the man himself who was giving Griffin such pause for thought. He wasn't exactly one of Razor Bend's most admirable citizens. In fact, he looked as if he'd stepped off a Wanted poster. And he was staring after Rachel like a starving man looking at a feast. Even worse, Griffin had seen something very near longing on Rachel Brant's face. That was what really galled him.

Jealousy turned to rage. *She didn't want me. How dare she yearn for a loser like him?*

He stared until the man had disappeared into the garage with the tire, then stomped to his car with new determination. He didn't know who the hell that man was, but he was going to find out.

By the time Boone got home, it was way after dark. He was tired. He was cold. And he was hungry. The message light was blinking on his answering machine, but the urge to ignore it was great. The scent of the barbecued ribs he'd brought home seeped from the sack in his hand, enticing him. But his training overcame everything else. He set the sack aside, then punched the button, listening closely as Denver Cherry's voice came into the room.

All he said was "Call me," but Boone knew who it was, and his adrenaline surged. There was only one reason for

Cherry to be calling him. He picked up the phone and made the call. Denver answered on the second ring.

Boone's words were as clipped as Denver's had been. "It's me," Boone said. "What's up?"

Denver muttered beneath his breath, then grumbled, "What time is it?"

Boone glanced at his watch. "Ten minutes until twelve."

Denver groaned, and Boone could hear the bed springs giving beneath his weight.

"Don't you ever sleep?" Denver grumbled.

"I had a blowout coming home this evening. My jack was gone, and my spare was flat, and I take better care of my gear than that. You can tell that son of a bitch Snake I want my jack back. I'll deal with him on my own about the spare."

Denver's eyes narrowed. "Damn it! I want you and Snake to make peace, not start another war. We've got our hands full as it is. Come by tomorrow evening. Got a job for you."

Boone grinned. He'd been right in assuming the gang was about to make another big move. The shipment must be in. Denver sounded antsy, the way he always did when the stuff was on hand.

"I'll be there," Boone said.

"You'd better," Denver muttered, then disconnected.

Boone set the receiver back in the cradle, then glanced at his late-night supper and knew it would have to wait a little while longer. The captain needed to know what was going on. He picked up the phone and started to dial, then paused and hung it back up. Cautious as ever, he used his cell phone to make the call. Ignoring the time, he listened as the phone at the other end began to ring. A few moments later, a low, husky voice, somewhat sleepy-sounding but nevertheless alert, answered. "This better be good."

Boone grinned. Obviously the captain was at home and had put a transfer order on the safe line.

"It's me, darlin' Waco," he drawled.

"Talk to me, good-looking."

"You better be sleeping alone."

In spite of the late hour and the tone of her agent's voice, Susan Cross grinned. The man was outrageous. "And you better have some sweet words to whisper in my ear," she retorted.

Boone felt himself beginning to relax, and knew that part of it came from being able to share the burden of what he knew with someone else.

"Something big is going down tomorrow night."

Cross sat up on the side of the bed, grabbing for her glasses and turning on the light, all at the same time.

"Like what?"

"There was a big shipment due. I think it's in. Cherry wants me over there tomorrow evening. Said he had a 'job' for me."

"So you think they're going to move it out?"

"Yes."

"Will the boss be there?"

Boone tensed. "I doubt it," he muttered. "I pushed my luck the other day by insisting that I meet the man I work for, and Cherry balked."

Cross frowned. "Okay, here's what I want you to do. See if you can find out the distribution points. And after you've got your load, call me. We'll decide where to go from there."

Boone frowned. "Damn it, Waco, don't mess it up for me by taking them in yet. I'm getting close.... I can feel it."

Cross sighed. She was walking a fine line between the law and her subordinate's renegade ways as it was. Knowingly letting a huge shipment of methamphetamine onto the streets didn't set well with her, but neither did pulling in a man before he'd done what he set out to do.

"Just call me," she said, and hung up.

Boone sat with his head in his hands, his food forgotten. The whole situation stank to high heaven. He felt like a bug caught between a hungry crow and a big flat shoe. Whichever way he turned, he was bound to be had.

The image of Rachel Brant's face drifted through his mind, and he groaned. "Not now, lady, not now."

Yet long after he'd gone to bed, his thoughts were still of her—the sound of her laugh, the way her eyes crinkled up at the corners when she smiled, the scent of her perfume... even the way her breathing quickened when she looked at him. She was eating him up from within.

He rolled over in bed, angrily punching his pillow and then burrowing his nose into it. Moments later, he tossed it aside. Smothering himself wouldn't accomplish a damn thing except to take himself out of the fray, and Boone MacDonald wasn't the kind of man to run.

Long after midnight had come and gone, Rachel was still awake, rereading the articles on reincarnation that she'd copied at the library, as well as excerpts from books that pertained to the same subject. She went to bed around 3:00 a.m., convinced that she was on the right track. But even though her instincts said yes, there was a common thread among the articles that she had yet to verify in relation to her own situation.

She needed to know if a woman named Mercy Hollister had ever existed. If she hadn't, then Rachel was facing an entirely different problem.

But where to start? Finding something as simple as a birth certificate was an easy task now, but back before the territories became states, births had rarely been recorded. It hadn't been unusual for a person to live out their entire life with no written record of having existed.

And then she thought of the outlaw, Dakota. Maybe he would be the link. If he'd been real, then history might have made note of his name and deeds.

Again her doubts returned. What to do first? All she

knew was what she'd seen in her dream...or whatever one called the state of losing one's mind. And then she remembered!

Trinity. Mercy had lived in a town called Trinity.

Find Trinity, or find out if it had ever existed. If so, she could start from there.

With a sigh of relief, Rachel rolled over on her stomach, shifted the pillow until it felt just right beneath her chin and closed her eyes. Sleep came, and with it the dream.

When she awoke, it was just before dawn, and she was facedown in the grass beneath her swing. Her head was splitting, and there were tears on her cheeks. She couldn't remember a thing about what she'd dreamed or what it was that had made her cry. Disgusted and disheartened, she crawled to her feet and staggered back indoors.

This had been the last straw. She'd made up her mind. When she went in to work today, she was going to ask for time off. Until this mess was cleared up, she didn't trust herself to care for anyone else, when she couldn't even take care of herself.

Charlie Dutton pulled up to the station just ahead of Rachel, giving her both front and back views of his shiny new car. As he got out, she couldn't help but grin as he took out his handkerchief and polished a spot on the lacquered blue surface.

She honked as she parked. Charlie turned, then went to meet her with a sheepish grin on his face.

"Wow, Charlie, you're going to have to beat the girls off with a stick."

His grin stilled. "So, are you telling me you might be susceptible?"

When Rachel flushed, Charlie hid his hurt behind a chuckle. "Calm down," he said softly. "It never hurts to ask, right?"

Just for a moment, she'd been afraid he was serious. Relaxing as he slipped back into his easygoing manner, she thumped him lightly on the arm as they headed for the door.

But Charlie had something else on his mind besides showing off his new car. He hadn't been able to get past the sight of Rachel and that modern-day outlaw riding together in her car. Charlie being Charlie, he circled the issue of what he wanted to know by making a joke out of the question.

"So, are you giving old Griffin a run for his money?"

Rachel stumbled, and Charlie grabbed her before she fell on her face.

"What did you mean by that?" she asked, fixing him with a cool, judging stare.

"Oh…not much. It's just that I never knew your tastes in men were so varied."

She gritted her teeth. "Not that it's any of your business, but Griffin Ross and I are old news. As for my passenger last night, all I did was give him a ride. He had a blowout, and his spare was flat."

"His kind is bad news, Rachel."

She flushed, angry because he wasn't saying anything she didn't already know. "I gave him a ride, not the key to my house."

"Little steps will take a man the same place big ones do. The only difference is, it just takes a little longer to get there."

"Just what are you saying?"

From the chill of her glare, Charlie realized he'd already overstepped his bounds. There was no use making the situation worse.

"Oh, nothing," he said, and looked back at his car, absently admiring the high-gloss sheen.

Rachel sighed. Charlie was her friend. She should have expected him to at least voice his opinion.

"It's okay," she said, and patted his arm. "I don't think

he's as bad as he's made out to be. Remember how he was with those people the day of that wreck. They were lucky he was there."

Charlie rolled his eyes. "I must have been out of my mind to complain about a hero. I keep forgetting how women love them."

Rachel hit him on the arm and pointed toward the car, determined to change the subject.

"That last raise they gave you must have been a doozie."

Charlie's expression underwent a dark metamorphosis, but Rachel didn't notice. As they entered the garage, they stopped short, staring in disbelief at the crumpled fender, missing bumper and shattered windshield of one of Razor Bend's two working ambulances.

"Oh, no!" she moaned, and grabbed Charlie by the arm.

"It's the new one, too," he said, eyeing the dented hood. "Because of an accident we'll have to make do with the old one until this is fixed. Man, I hope the good citizens of Razor Bend don't have themselves a run of bad luck."

As they entered the office, Rachel couldn't help thinking that while the ambulance's condition was unfortunate for the town, it was quite convenient for her. With only one ambulance to run, and two paramedics and three EMTs besides herself, she wouldn't be missed.

Chapter 8

The bass boat slid into the bed of Boone's pickup truck as if it had been made to fit. With Tommy Joe on one side and Boone on the other, they walked the length of the truck, tying the boat down as they went. As he tied the last knot, Boone gave the rope a sharp tug, just to make sure it was holding. The last thing he needed was to lose that boat and its belly full of meth along the highway.

The false bottom should work. Oklahoma was full of people who lived for the great outdoors. About half the residents of the state either owned or rented boats. And at this time of year, die-hard fishermen everywhere were making last-minute runs to the lakes, rivers and creeks, taking advantage of the good fishing weather before winter set in. There wouldn't be a cop on the road who thought anything unusual of his rig.

"I guess I'm ready to roll," Boone said, and looked around for Denver. "Where's Cherry?"

Tommy Joe shrugged. "He'll be here directly. Want a beer?" Without waiting for Boone to answer, he tossed him a cold, dripping can.

Boone's hard-ass mode was in place as he caught the can

in midair. "No thanks," he drawled, and tossed it right back. "Tonight I'm the designated driver, remember?"

Tommy Joe snickered, then popped the top, unmindful of the froth that spewed and spilled out of the hole and down the sides of the can, coating his fingers, then dripping onto his shoes.

Boone leaned against the bed of his truck and took a slow, deep breath as he settled down to wait.

Come on, come on, he fumed, wondering where Denver Cherry had gone. The man was like a caged cat until the meth was moved off his place, and now that the moment was at hand, he'd disappeared.

A short distance away, Denver was making last-minute plans with the boss. Their conversation ceased in midstream as the boss started to curse.

"What the hell is he doing here?"

"Who?" Denver asked.

"That *cowboy.*"

Denver winced. The derision in the boss's voice was impossible to miss.

"That's my new man, Boone MacDonald."

"You're not serious."

Denver nodded.

"Can you trust him?"

Denver nodded, then backed off, reluctant to be blamed should something go wrong. "Well, as best as I can tell, he's okay. You know, there's no surefire way to tell until a deal goes down."

The boss grunted, and Denver got nervous, watching the way his eyes narrowed and his jaw clenched.

"Something wrong?" Denver asked.

"No. Which route is he taking?"

Denver told him and when he made no comment, added, "I'd better get going. I need to send them on their way."

"Them?"

Denver shifted his stance, readjusting his belly above the

belt buckle poking into his soft flesh. "Yeah, Tommy Joe is going with him, just to make sure everything goes okay."

"Send him alone."

"But I—"

An ominous quality infiltrated the boss's voice. "I said... send him alone."

"Yes, sir," Denver muttered.

"Now. Do it now."

Denver scuttled away. He'd heard enough to know that the boss was mad; he just wasn't sure why.

"Hey, here comes Denver," Tommy Joe said, pointing off to their right.

Boone turned just as the old biker waddled out of a thick stand of trees. His eyes narrowed thoughtfully; he wondered exactly what the man had been doing in there besides taking a leak.

"We're ready," Tommy Joe said. He started toward the passenger side of the truck, but Denver stopped him cold.

"You're not going," he muttered, and waved him away.

Boone went from a careless slouch to a careful stance. Sudden changes in plans made him nervous. He gave Denver a calculated stare. "Why not?"

"Yeah, why not?" Tommy Joe echoed.

"Because I said so," Denver shouted. "Now get back inside."

Tommy Joe scuttled away.

"Are there any other changes I need to know about?" Boone asked.

Denver met him stare for hard stare. "No."

Boone glanced over Denver's shoulder into the darkness of the trees. Then he grinned. "You're the boss," he said softly, and crawled into his truck. "See you when I see you."

Denver shuddered as Boone drove out of sight. Something didn't feel right, but there was no way of stopping things now.

* * *

Boone wasn't wasting any time waiting to be shot in the back of the head. Instinct told him he was being tested again, only this time he sincerely doubted it was Denver who'd set up the test.

As he started down the mountain, he passed the road leading to Rachel's house and had a sudden urge to ditch the whole night and hide within the shelter of Rachel Brant's embrace.

But it was a wild, impossible thought, and Boone wasn't the type to waver from what he'd set out to do. Instead, he picked up the phone. He'd promised Waco a call.

"Talk to me, baby," Waco crooned.

Boone grinned. "You can turn off the heat, sugar. I'm all alone."

Captain Cross reached for a pen. "What do you know?"

Boone swerved to miss an armadillo waddling across the road and then glanced back at the boat, making sure it was still in place.

"I know I wish it was Christmas and I was under your tree, sweet thing."

"Shut up and get down to business," she muttered, then grinned in spite of herself. "Did the whole load go out?"

Boone sighed. She wasn't going to like this one bit. "Yeah, but I couldn't say where. Denver made a run earlier that I didn't expect, and Snake was already gone when I got there."

"Damn."

"My sentiments exactly," Boone said, knowing he hadn't been quite honest with her.

If the captain had known all three locations, chances were she would have opted for the busts, arresting him along with the perps. It wouldn't have blown his cover, but it would have ended his quest to find the man behind Denver Cherry's operation.

"Where is he sending you?"

"Dallas."

"Where in Dallas?"

"Some joint called ReBob's Boat Repair, just off I-35, on the freeway."

"I'll let the proper authorities know."

"Damn it, Waco, don't get me busted. I'm not ready to quit this town."

Susan Cross frowned. "What do you mean…not ready?"

Boone took a deep breath. He'd said the wrong thing, and like the bulldog she was, the captain had jumped on his slip of the tongue.

"I don't mean anything," he muttered.

"I told you to get laid and get over it," she said sharply. "You damn well better not be messing around with some woman. It'll all blow up in your face and you know it."

"I'm not." And then he muttered, more to himself than to her, "Besides, she's not the laying type."

The captain groaned. "Why couldn't you go find some bimbo? What on earth possessed you to get mixed up with Snow White?"

Boone sighed. "It wasn't by choice. I couldn't help myself."

"God help us all," she groaned. "I ought to pull you out now, before you ruin the entire operation, and send Wayland in instead."

"Like hell," he said sharply, disconnecting before she could make any more threats.

An hour passed. Boone guessed he was no farther than five miles from the state line when his cell phone rang. The sound startled him. The only person who knew this number was…

"Waco?"

"You've been set up."

Her words jolted through him like a bolt of heat lightning. Now it made sense. This was why Tommy Joe had been pulled off the run. But why would Denver risk losing this load?

"How did you find out?"

"Don't question me, just listen. Where are you now?"

Boone gave his location.

"Good," she muttered. "Then there's still time to make the switch."

"What switch?"

"You aren't listening," she said sharply.

He listened, and hours later, when he pulled into Re-Bob's Boat Repair, he was driving a rickety old Jeep with a canoe tied on top. The meth was in backpacks under a tarp on the back seat, along with a motley assortment of camping equipment. It took less than fifteen minutes to do what he'd been sent to do, and when he was finished, he lit out of Dallas without looking back.

Just across the border into Oklahoma, he switched back to his own truck, thanking the pair of sheriff's deputies who'd patiently waited for his return. But his truck wasn't the only thing they traded. He headed toward Denver Cherry's house with the payoff. A bag full of marked bills.

A new sun was just coming over the treetops as Boone pulled into Denver's front yard. Denver came to meet him, with a cup of coffee in one hand and a sausage biscuit in the other. For once, he seemed amiable, even jovial.

"Trade you coffee and a biscuit for what's in the case," Denver said, grinning around the oversize bite he'd just taken.

Boone set the case down at Denver's bare feet and then gave him a cool, studied stare.

"I think I'll pass."

Denver frowned. "Something wrong?"

"You tell me," Boone said, and started back to his truck.

"Hey, don't go off mad!" Denver shouted.

Boone turned, and the cold, hard glare on his face startled Denver enough that he sloshed hot coffee on his feet.

"What makes you think I should be mad?" Boone asked.

Having left that cryptic statement hanging in the air, Boone drove away, leaving Denver with scalded toes and a hundred thousand dollars in marked money.

Denver grabbed the money and then hurried inside. The boss wasn't going to like being called on the job, but Denver didn't much care.

Sunlight ricocheted off highly polished chrome, momentarily blinding the man behind the wheel as he came to a four-way stop just inside the city limits of Razor Bend. When the car phone rang, he answered without thought, unprepared for the sound of Denver Cherry's voice.

"Hello?"

"It's me," Denver said.

The driver's face underwent a dark change, from bland observation of the roadway to cold anger.

"What?"

"I just thought I'd let you know my new man did all right last night. Everything went off without a hitch. He just left."

A rough curse slipped out of the driver's mouth before he thought, but it was enough to let Denver know he'd been right in suspecting that something bad had gone down last night.

"Whatever you did, don't do it again," Denver warned. "You do, and I'm out." Having said what he'd called to say, he hung up, then dropped into the chair. "Hell's bells," he muttered. "Am I the only one left with any sense?"

While Denver was making his call, Boone was making a side trip of his own. Although he was exhausted and needed to sleep, there was something else he needed much more. Whatever the captain had averted last night could have cost him his life.

All the way back from Dallas, his thoughts had been about Rachel. If he had died, would she have cared? He'd held her but briefly. He'd touched her face, but he wanted to touch her soul. He needed to know if her lips were as soft as they looked. He'd made love to her, but only in dreams. The urge to know her in the true sense of the word was making him crazy. The thought of losing her was worse than losing his own life.

And yet, as he turned off the road and into the driveway leading to her house, he knew he was losing his grip. He couldn't lose someone he'd never had. Coming up here was wrong. It was dumb. It was dangerous. And yet, God help him, it had to be done. He wanted just to see her face, hear her voice. After that, maybe he could rest.

But when he got there she was gone.

Rachel boarded a plane in Oklahoma City and made a connection in Denver that took her straight into South Dakota. When she disembarked, instead of going for her luggage, she paused at the windows outside the skyline surrounding the terminal.

She stared until her eyes burned and the glare of the sun against the plate glass made her flesh damp with perspiration. As she stood at the window looking out on the horizon, a stocky middle-aged man in business attire paused beside her, noting her intense expression.

"I know how you feel," he said. "It's always good to get home, isn't it?"

Rachel turned, her eyes wide and a little stunned. "Oh, I don't live here," she said. "In fact, this is my first visit."

"My mistake," he said, and then added as he started to walk away, "You just had that look."

"What look?" Rachel asked.

"Oh...you know...the kind of look soldiers have when they get pictures from home. Like they've left a piece of themselves behind with those they love. I just assumed..." He shrugged. "Anyway, have a nice day, miss."

He walked away, leaving Rachel to wonder if what he'd said was true. On the surface, everything around her seemed foreign. But was there a part of her, a subconscious part, that was rejoicing in a long-awaited return? She shuddered. At this point, the thought didn't bear contemplation.

A day later, she learned one irrefutable fact: Trinity was no more.

But it had been there once, a small but thriving boomtown located somewhere between Lead and Deadwood. That it had ever existed was a shock in itself. She'd been braced for defeat, and instead she was getting answers she hadn't been prepared to find.

But her search for any sort of trail to Mercy Hollister or an outlaw named Dakota was fruitless, until the curator at a Wild West museum showed her into a room filled with memorabilia of Wild Bill Hickok and his days in Deadwood. Even then, she almost missed it.

An old, fragile and very yellowed newspaper had been put on display behind a glass frame. The headlines were all about Hickok and a gunfight he'd had. But it was an item in the lower right-hand corner of the paper that caught her eye. And it was the lead line that sent her to her knees, her nose pressed against the glass as she read.

Outlaw dies at lover's hands

When she was through, it was all she could do to get up.

"Dear, sweet Lord," Rachel whispered, and wanted to run as far and as fast as her legs could carry her. She'd come hundreds of miles for the truth, and now that it was staring her in the face, she felt nothing but panic.

Not only had Mercy Hollister been real, but, according to this article, she'd been responsible for the death of an outlaw called Dakota Blaine. It didn't make sense. The visions she'd been having were of a man and a woman in the deep throes of love, not a woman in fear for her life—or afraid of the man. How had this happened? What could possibly have changed between them to bring them to such a sorrowful end?

Rachel flushed, then turned pale as she fought to keep from passing out. Only the fact there were other people in the room kept her sane and silent.

"Okay, okay. So they were real. That doesn't tie me to them," she muttered, then went limp with defeat.

The very fact that she'd been reliving their lives tied her firmly to them, whether she liked it or not. When she finally trusted herself to walk, she went outside and caught a cab back to her hotel. It was time to go home.

And home she was. When Rachel landed in Oklahoma City once again, it was raining. The damp, dreary day went well with her state of mind. When she boarded the plane in Rapid City, she'd been in shock. The flight back home had been hell, as she struggled with what she had learned. The past three days had changed her perception of the world. She didn't want to be anyone but herself, but what she wanted might have to take a back seat to who she had been.

Granted, she was back in Oklahoma, but the facts she'd brought home still gave her no answers. Yet as she started the long drive to Razor Bend, there was one fact she couldn't ignore. Boone MacDonald's appearance in her life had triggered everything that was happening to her. Therefore, he must also be the key to making it stop.

The next morning she entered her boss's office with a letter requesting an indefinite leave of absence. Not only was her request granted, but his unexpected concern and offer of help sent her out of the office with tears in her eyes.

Which was exactly how Charlie Dutton first saw her. He grabbed her by the arm and spun her around as she started to pass him by.

"Hey! Is that any way to treat your partner?"

Rachel looked away, unwilling for him to see her tears, but she was too late.

"You're crying."

Rachel gave him a lopsided grin. "No, my eyes are leaking."

"Same thing," he muttered. "What's wrong?"

"Nothing. Really."

"The same nothing that prompted the three-day absence?"

"Sort of."

"Look, it's probably none of my business, so if you don't want me to butt in, just say so."

"So."

He glowered. "Damn it, Rachel, you're my partner. Consider yourself butted. I want to know what's going on."

His mangled grammar made her laugh. "Charlie, you sweet-talking charmer. You have such a way with words."

He glowered, refusing to be deterred. "What's wrong? And why aren't you in uniform?"

This was going to be rough. "I've decided to take a leave of absence."

"I knew it! Something is really wrong. You wouldn't be doing this if…" His face darkened. "It's a guy, isn't it?"

She flushed.

"It can't be that stupid banker, because you were the dump-*er,* and he was the dump-*ee.* It's not him, is it?"

"No, Griffin has nothing to do with my decision to—"

"Son of a—" Her grabbed her by the arm in sudden anger, pinning her until she had nowhere to look but at him.

Rachel struggled. "Charlie, let me go!"

"It's that man I saw you with. That...that...damned outlaw, isn't it?"

Rachel glared. She wouldn't answer, because she couldn't lie, and if she said it was true, Charlie would have Boone's head before she could explain what was wrong. And, dear God, how to explain what was going on?

"I'm going to kill him," Charlie muttered, and dragged Rachel out of the hall to a secluded part of the station. "Did he hurt you? Are you, uh... Is there any way you could be...?"

Rachel gasped, her eyes wide with shock. "Good Lord, no!"

Charlie flushed, then looked away. "Well," he muttered, "I had to know."

"He doesn't have anything to do with it," Rachel said, and then bit her tongue at the lie. "I've been having some personal problems. Until I get them all worked out, I don't feel it's in my patients' best interest that I be less than focused, do you?"

"Is that the best excuse you could come up with?"

"Just about."

He slumped, his hands shoved in his pockets. "I have a new car, a new haircut, I even have a new suit. Who am I going to impress if you're not here?"

Tears came again, and Charlie groaned when he saw them in her eyes.

"Well, damn it, I was just kidding," he muttered. "I already have too many girls as it is. Practically have to beat them off with a stick."

Rachel laughed, then caught her breath on a sob. "Take care of yourself," she said. "I'll be seeing you." Then she walked out the door.

"Yeah, right," Charlie muttered. "See you around."

Rachel exited the station with her head down, blinking

back tears with fierce intent. She needed a hole to crawl into and a shoulder to cry on, but she didn't think the pair would compute. Not unless she found a willing gopher or a very small man. Unfortunately for her, before she reached her car, she had her man—just not the one she wanted.

"Rachel, I've been trying to catch you for…"

Griffin Ross paused, at a sudden loss for words, when he saw the tears in Rachel Brant's eyes.

"Why, sweetheart, what on earth is wrong?"

His sympathy was her undoing. She shook her head and tried to duck into her car, but he would have none of it. To her dismay, he took her in his arms.

"Griff, don't," she muttered, and ducked out from under his grasp, then out of his reach.

"You've been crying!"

She rolled her eyes. The men she knew were *so* astute.

"People do that sometimes, you know."

"But why?" he asked.

"Frankly, Griff, it's none of your business," Rachel said, and got into her car and drove away, leaving him to think what he would of it all.

Boone came out of the auto supply store carrying a new jack. Snake had proclaimed an innocence that Boone didn't buy, but he'd made a believer out of Snake, just the same. Now, when the gang was all together at Denver's house, Snake gave him a wide, cautious berth, which was fine with Boone. The less he had to do with the man, the better off they would both be.

A flash of color caught his eye as he put the jack in the bed of the truck. He turned. Relief surged. It was Rachel. She was back!

He glanced at his watch, noting the time, and wondering why she wasn't in uniform. Then he shrugged and got into his truck.

I'm making a big deal out of nothing. Shifts change.

And yet, as he drove down the street to the Adam's Rib Café to have lunch, he couldn't help remembering the look on her face. She'd seemed upset.

Tonight I'll go see. She won't even have to know I'm there.

The night was clear and dark. The threat of rain had passed. Countless stars dappled the dense black sky as a breeze rustled leaves just starting to turn color.

Rachel slept warm and snug beneath her covers, unconcerned that, outside, an oncoming frost was dropping the temperature by degrees. Her sleep was deep and dreamless. She never knew when it began to change.

She rolled onto her back, her eyes wide open and fixed on a scene only she could see. Panicked, she shoved the covers aside and bolted from the bed, running through the house on bare feet, once nearly tripping on the tail of her white flannel gown. Her subconscious mind was in total control. Locks turned. Doors were opened, then closed behind her, as if someone else were performing the acts.

Rachel ran from the house, unmindful of the dew-damp grass or the growing chill in the air. She moved as a woman in terror, struck dumb by the sight of what lay before her. In her mind she was shouting, but no sound ever came from her lips.

All she could see was the man in the canyon below her. The scent of gunpowder filled her nostrils. The sun beamed down upon her head. She lifted her arm and screamed. It came from so far within her that it moved past her mind and into the present, breaking the silence of the Kiamichis. Moments later, pain shattered the dream. She fell to her knees in the grass, with tears streaming down her face.

Boone braked as his headlights flashed on a deer racing across the narrow ribbon of blacktop. Its magnificence was illuminated as it paused, momentarily stunned by the bright glare of the lights in which it had been caught. The rack of antlers spreading out from its head gleamed, a bejeweled crown on the king of the mountain. Then the animal moved and, like a shadow, was gone.

Boone accelerated carefully, cognizant of the fact that another deer could be waiting just around the next bend.

A mile farther up the mountain, that caution saved him from hitting the woman who ran from the trees and straight into the glare of his lights. She ran with eyes wide open and tears on her face.

It was Rachel.

He hit the brakes, jamming the truck into park as he grabbed for the door. Within seconds, he was out of his truck and running toward her with his weapon drawn. Convinced that she was fleeing for her life, he crouched with his gun aimed into the darkness behind her, aiming at an unknown foe as she let out a scream and fell onto her knees in the ditch at the side of the road.

Chapter 9

Gritting her teeth, Rachel clutched at her head, only vaguely aware of the cold and the damp and a blinding white light.

"Oh, God, make it stop," she begged, rocking back and forth on her knees and digging her fingers into her hair as the pain ripped through her brain like grasping tentacles.

But when she was lifted from the ground and held fast against a wild, beating heart, she went limp, absorbing the warmth of a body and the strength from the arms in which she was held.

She sighed as a low, urgent voice murmured near her ear. "Rachel! What happened to you?"

She couldn't focus, and even as she spoke, the sound of her own voice in her ears wracked her head with a fresh wave of pain. "Who—?"

"It's me. Boone."

She blinked, her head lolling against his arm. She tried hard to focus on the dark, shadowy face silhouetted above her, but the light from behind him was too bright and the pain in her head still too great. She clutched weakly at the front of his jacket, her voice barely above a whisper.

"Home...I want to go home."

Boone turned, holding her tight. Seconds later, she was

on the seat beside him. By the time he reached her house, tears were streaming down her face. In all his years on the force, he'd never been this scared. Hesitancy was in his voice as he reached for her, wanting to hold her. "Rachel?"

She leaned toward him, and it was all the invitation he needed.

"Come here, baby," he said softly. "Let's get you in the house."

She went into Boone's arms as if she'd been doing it all her life. As he carried her up the walk, something hard and cold and hidden way deep inside him began to unfold. And when he carried her into her house and kicked the door shut behind him, he had an overwhelming sense of having finally come home.

The rooms were warm, a safe shelter from the cold and the night. He sat her on the side of her bed, and she stayed, like a misbehaving child who'd been put in a corner. Then he tossed his jacket on a nearby chair and knelt down before her.

"Rachel...can you tell me what's wrong?"

Speech was impossible. All she could do was hang on to the bed as the light in her room changed from bulb to wick and the covers from patchwork and cotton to red velvet and white satin.

Dakota looked up at Mercy with a smile on his face and a promise in his eyes. His fingers were soft and gentle as his hand moved up her thigh.

Mercy shivered with longing and leaned back on the bed, waiting for this man to work his magic.

He hooked his forefinger in the top of her stocking and started pulling it down, inch by agonizing inch.

Mercy sighed and then groaned as he lowered his head, fervently kissing a dimple near the bend of her knee. Dig-

ging her fingers into his thatch of black hair, she urged
him back up until he was kissing her mouth instead.

Rachel blinked, as if refocusing her gaze, and for the first time since she'd been lifted from the middle of the road, she knew her rescuer for who he was. The dark eyes, the hard-edged features in a cold, handsome face. Black hair and leather, Levi's and boots.

"Boone?" Her eyes grew round. Her voice started to shake.

"Why...? How?" Helpless to say more, she waited for him to explain.

Tenderly he brushed the long black tangles of her hair from her face and ran his thumb lightly near a scratch on her chin, catching the small streak of blood running down before it dripped on her gown.

"You were out on the mountain. I almost hit you with my truck."

"Oh, my God," Rachel groaned, and hid her face in her hands.

"You need to get into something warm and dry. Will you let me help you?"

Only after he remarked on her condition did she begin to feel the cold. She shivered, then dropped her hands in her lap and looked up.

"Well?" he persisted.

"I have a robe in the bathroom. If you'll just give me a minute..."

Boone stood up and stepped away, but when she put her feet on the floor, she winced and dropped back onto the bed. He followed her descent. Back on his knees, he saw the deep, ugly gash in the arch of one foot.

"Damn, Rachel, you need to see a doctor."

"No!" she said, clutching at his arm as he reached for the phone.

"Why not?"

She didn't answer.

"Rachel?"

She turned away.

He cupped her face, forcing her to look back at him.

"Talk to me, woman. Why not?"

To his surprise, she seemed angry. "Because then I'd have to explain how it happened, and I don't have an explanation to give."

It didn't make sense. When he saw her, he would have sworn that she'd also seen him. After all, she'd been running toward him with her eyes wide open.

"So, you're telling me you don't remember what happened."

Her expression darkened. "That's what I said."

"I'm sorry. I didn't mean to sound so persistent." He laid his hand on her knee, waiting until she looked back at him. "It's happened before, hasn't it? That first time I saw you, in the creek, you were talking to someone who wasn't there."

She bit her lip.

Fear for her, coupled with a frustration he couldn't deny, sharpened his voice. "What, Rachel? Talk to me, damn it!"

This time her anger was real. "And say what, Boone? That I guess I'm losing my mind? Don't think it hasn't already occurred to me."

Regretting the way he'd raised his voice, he tried to smooth things over, but her temper had already been lit, like a short, burning fuse.

"I go to bed. I close my eyes. I sleep. But I don't always wake up in my bed!" The more she talked, the faster the words came, often harsh, sometimes shrill, as if she were on the brink of breaking down. "Sometimes I wake up standing in water. Sometimes I'm facedown in the dirt. It happens. I don't know why. I can't control it." Then she swayed and once again covered her face with her hands. "Oh, God...I can't control it."

"Damn."

It was all he could say. With a groan, he went from his knees to her side, then lifted her in his arms and set her down in his lap, holding her close until her shaking had stopped.

Rachel felt like a thief, absorbing his strength to replace her own. For some reason, she wanted to explain how destructive these episodes had become.

"I took a leave of absence from work."

Boone held her just that little bit tighter. "I noticed you've been gone. Figured you'd gone to visit your folks or something."

"No, I was on a...trip. My parents are dead. Have been for several years."

"Sorry."

She sighed. "Me too."

"Are you okay now?"

"Yes, just help me to the bathroom, will you? There's some peroxide in the medicine chest I can use on my foot."

The fluorescent lights were unkind to the damage she'd done to herself. In the bright white light, all was revealed, from the scratches on her face to the rip in her gown. Even more, her womanly shape was too easy to see beneath the soft white flannel.

Desire for more than her smile made Boone's hand shake as he held her foot over the edge of the tub. Following her instructions, he poured antiseptic on the wound, then applied a bandage. He gave her another long look as he put away the supplies.

"Now what?"

She almost blushed. "If you'll give me a minute..."

He walked out of the bathroom, shutting the door behind him. He clenched his hands as he stared around Rachel's room. The essence of her was everywhere, from a lacy slip hanging on a hook on the closet door to the tumbled covers of the bed she'd been sleeping in. He stared at the sheets and the pillow still bearing the indentation of her head until something inside him snapped. Gritting his teeth, he stalked out of the room. Not only had he reached the limit of his self-denial, he was pretty sure he'd passed it.

When Rachel came out, she was alone. Surprised, she stood for a moment, listening to the quiet in her small frame house. And then a pot banged somewhere down the hall. He was in the kitchen and, from the sounds of it, trying to cook something. Probably for her. She smiled to herself. For a bad boy, he had a remarkable bedside manner.

As she hobbled to the kitchen, it never once crossed her mind to thank him kindly and send him packing. Somewhere between the time she went to bed and the moment when she returned to consciousness in his arms, she'd come to terms with the fact that her life and Boone MacDonald's were somehow intertwined.

Even though she made no sound, Boone seemed to know he was no longer alone. When he turned, she was staring at him from the doorway. She'd gone from the white gown to a pink one with a robe to match. He didn't know whether to stand his ground or run for cover. Either way, he'd lost the last of his control. For better or worse, it was a given fact that he loved her.

Have mercy, he thought. "Feeling better?" he asked.

She smiled. "Yes, thanks."

"I'm making coffee."

She pointed. "Works better when it's plugged in."

He looked down. "Well, damn," he muttered, and shoved the plug into the outlet.

"Boone."

"Hmm?"

"Thank you."

He could see her out of the corner of his eye. All it would take was a couple of steps and she could be in his arms. He didn't move.

"You're welcome."

To his relief, the coffee started to brew.

She didn't budge from the doorway, continuing to stare at him for long, agonizing minutes, until Boone felt ready to explode. Finally he gave her an angry glare and pointed toward the table and chairs.

"Either sit the hell down or suffer the consequences."

She sat.

He poured coffee and joined her.

Another minute passed while she blew on her cup and Boone gulped from his. Silence grew. And grew. And grew. It was Boone who broke first.

"If you don't need me anymore, I'm out of here," he said, disregarding the fact that he sounded rude. But his patience had long since run its course, and desire for this woman was eating him alive.

Need you? I think I'll always need you, Rachel thought, and then it scared her so much that she didn't argue when he stood up to leave.

"Are you finished?" he asked, pointing to her half-empty cup.

Rachel nodded and shoved it aside. But before she could help herself up, he once again lifted her into his arms, then paused, giving her a look she was afraid to believe.

"What do you think you're doing?" she asked, and hated the nervous tremor she heard in her own voice. It wouldn't do to let him know she was scared.

"Tucking you into bed?"

It was the hesitation in his voice that gave her comfort. If she wasn't the only one unsure about the ground on which they were standing, then it helped to balance the confusion she was feeling. There was a tinge of despair in her voice as he carried her down the hall. "Maybe you should just tie me down while you're at it. I'm not real good at staying tucked."

He grinned, and once again Rachel was reminded that this was no altar boy she was messing with. The smile on his face was pure devil, the glitter in his eyes far too bright for her peace of mind.

To her relief, he kept quiet until he was in the act of pulling up her covers. At that point, he reached out and traced the arch of her upper lip with the tip of his finger.

"The last time I tied a woman up in bed, it was not with the intention of putting her to sleep."

Rachel gasped. The image was too vivid to ignore.

Desire for her was so strong that Boone couldn't deny himself any longer. Before he could talk himself out of the deed, he bent down.

She tasted better than he'd dreamed. Soft, slightly surprised lips parted beneath his demand. He groaned, and she sighed, and the pressure increased. At the point of lying down beside her, he drew back, his nostrils flaring, his eyes dark and wild with unfulfilled need.

"Don't expect me to apologize for that."

"I don't expect anything of the sort from a man like you," Rachel said, then could have kicked herself. After all he'd done for her, all she seemed able to do was hurt him, and she knew that she had. It was there in his eyes.

He grinned, but it was not a happy smile. "Well, darlin', it seems you've got me pegged, and that's a fact. If you value your sweet head and your hide, you'll keep yourself locked inside this house, where a desperado like me can't get to you."

Desperado!

The constant similarities she kept seeing between this man and Dakota gave her a chill of warning. Rachel shivered and pulled the covers up to her chin, her eyes wide and fixed in shock.

"Have mercy, Rachel, don't give me that look."

Have mercy. Once again, another echo of the long-dead outlaw. Rachel stared, searching for more than a familiar phrase to tell her that she was on the right track.

"I'll lock myself out," Boone said.

He had started toward the door when she stopped him with a whisper so soft it went almost unheard. "I'm not afraid of you anymore."

He froze, and when he turned, there was a look on his face that she knew she would never forget.

"You should be, sweet Rachel. You surely should be."

And then she was listening to the sound of his footsteps moving through her house and the soft, distinct click of the lock falling into place. He was gone.

She relaxed, then, moments later, leaned over and turned off the light by her bed. Only after the house was dark did she hear him start up his truck and drive away. She closed her eyes, wondering if he'd looked back, and then she slept. When she woke, it was morning and the sun was streaming in upon her face.

Joanie Mills darted into the bakery just as Rachel was in the act of going out.

"Rachel! Just the gal I want to see!" she cried. "Wait for me. We need to talk."

Rachel rolled her eyes and leaned against the wall. If only she'd been a little bit earlier, she might have escaped Joanie's third degree. A minute or so later, Joanie was back at the door, with a jelly doughnut in one hand and a soda in the other.

"Get the door for me, sugar, will you?"

Rachel obliged.

"Follow me," Joanie ordered, as she started down the street toward her shop. "We've got to hurry. Melvina Woodruff is due in fifteen minutes for her monthly rinse. I swear, that woman's roots grow faster than mold on bread."

In spite of the grilling she knew was forthcoming, Rachel had to laugh.

Joanie grinned, then noticed Rachel's limp and pointed with the straw poking out of her soda cup.

"What happened to you?"

"I, uh...I stepped on a root."

Joanie's painted-on eyebrows arched toward her bright red hair. "You were barefoot? Lord A-mighty, girl, it's too late in the year for such stuff." She opened her door by backing into it, using her blue-jeaned behind for leverage. "Get in here *now*. You've got some explaining to do."

Rachel knew she didn't have to go. But as she followed Joanie inside, deep down she knew she'd been wanting to do this from day one.

"Sit," Joanie ordered, and inhaled the last of her doughnut in one gulp, washing it down with a long slurp of soda. "You talk, I'll listen. I've got to get Melvina's rinse mixed before she gets here. She always wants it too black. I tried to tell her that a woman her age shouldn't have hair darker than the moles on her arms, but she just won't listen."

Rachel grinned. Melvina would hate to know her moles had been the topic of such a discussion.

"I'm waiting," Joanie said.

"For what?"

"For why you didn't see fit to tell me you've taken a leave of absence from work, and why you left the state and didn't bother to tell me you were gone. I had to hear it from Charlie." She frowned as she poured and measured, all the while keeping one eye on the clock and the other on Rachel. "You know how I hate hearing second-hand news."

"There's not much to tell," Rachel said. "I went to South Dakota to—"

Joanie shrieked. "South Dakota! Girl! What on earth

were you thinking? There's nothing up there but—" She took a deep breath and started over. "Sorry."

"As I was saying," Rachel muttered, "there were some things I needed to find out, and going there was the best way to do it."

Joanie paused, the bottle of rinse held tight in her hand. "So...did you find out whatever it was you needed to know?"

Rachel sighed and nodded. "Probably even more than I wanted to know."

"Rachel?"

"What?"

"You know you're the best friend I have in Razor Bend, probably my best friend in the entire world, don't you?"

Rachel looked a little embarrassed, although pleased by what Joanie had said. "I guess."

"Then know this. We both know I gossip a little, but I swear to God—even on my sweet mother's grave, and she's not even dead—that I would never, ever, reveal anything you told me in confidence."

This is it, Rachel thought. Now's my time. "Joanie?"

"Yeah?"

"Do you believe in reincarnation?"

Melvina Woodruff's rinse hit the floor with a splat, coating Joanie's white tennies in a dark, malevolent color, as well as a goodly portion of the floor on which she was standing. To her credit, she never looked down.

"Rachel Brant...are you just askin' for something to talk about, or are you serious?"

"Do you see me laughing?"

Joanie's eyes grew round with interest. "Tell me."

"You swear?" Rachel asked, reminding her of her vow.

Joanie nodded, then sighed. "Who would believe me, anyway?"

Rachel began to relax. It felt good to be able to talk, even if what she said made no sense.

"It's like this. Over the past six weeks I've come to a conclusion. Either I'm losing my mind, or my mind is no longer my own."

"Rachel...you're scaring me."

"*You're* scared?" Rachel's fingers curled around the arms of the chair as she leaned forward. "Joanie, you have no idea. I'm remembering things that never happened to me. I'm seeing things that aren't there. I wake up in the present, but right when I'm least expecting it, it's as if the world turns backward and I'm still in it, but I'm not me anymore."

To Joanie's credit, she didn't laugh or tell Rachel that she was crazy. Instead, she stepped over the black puddle on the floor and hugged her.

"I'm here, honey. You just talk away. Tell me whatever you want, however you feel like saying it, while I clean up this mess."

Rachel went limp, only then realizing she was still holding the sack of cookies she'd bought from the bakery. She set them aside and, to her dismay, felt a lump come into her throat.

Her chin quivered as she voiced her worst fear. "Do you think I'm crazy?"

Joanie's face crumpled as she gave Rachel a handful of tissues and then took one for herself and blew noisily before answering. "Lord, no, honey. You're the most together person I know. You have to be, to do the things you do."

"Then explain it to me," Rachel said. "Tell me why this is happening. Tell me how to make it stop."

"I can't," Joanie said, and then lowered her voice. "But I'll tell you one thing my granny used to say—and my granny knew about things that other folks made fun of. She always said, 'There's many a thing twixt earth and heaven that man's not supposed to understand.'"

Rachel grabbed for her purse as Joanie groaned.

"Darn, here comes Melvina."

"I'd better go," Rachel said, unwilling for anyone but Joanie to see her distress.

She had started out the door when Joanie called out. "Rachel, wait!"

She turned.

Joanie pointed to her sack. "Forgot your cookies."

Rachel rolled her eyes and managed a grin. "Oh, that. I thought you were about to say I'd lost my marbles."

Joanie was still laughing when Rachel walked out the door. All the way to her car, Rachel kept thinking that she shouldn't have said anything. Yet, even though she'd done little more than skim over the facts, she knew she would do it again. The relief that she felt was overwhelming. Secrets were a burden to carry and a good thing to share.

It was nearing noon. Rachel was sitting in a chair outside Jimmy's Place, waiting for an oil-and-lube job to be finished on her car before starting home, when Charlie Dutton and Ken Wade pulled the ambulance into the station to refuel.

Charlie jumped out, a wide grin on his face, as Ken winked and went inside to sign the charge ticket that would be billed to the city.

"Loafing already?" Charlie teased.

"I'm waiting for Stu to get through with my car."

Charlie snorted softly beneath his breath. "Hope you're not in any big hurry," he muttered. "Stu doesn't exactly set the world on fire."

"He may be slow, but he's sure," Rachel said.

"The only thing he's sure about is that he's going to get his five-fifty an hour, no matter how much work he puts out."

Rachel laughed. "Who put the bee in your bonnet?"

"You," Charlie said, and pointed at Ken as he came out

of the store. "Damn it, Rachel, I miss smelling your wild-flower perfume. *He* doesn't smell like wildflowers."

Ken laughed. "And may I say my wife is heartily thankful for that. You might also like to know I don't wrap bandages right, and I hit all the holes in the road, and I—"

Charlie threw up his hands. "So I've been griping a bit."

Rachel grinned. "Charlie always gripes. The trick is not to pay any attention until it matters." Her grin widened. "I know. Maybe you should just buy a bottle of my perfume. That way, when he gets testy, you can just sprinkle a little bit on him to sweeten him up."

"Okay, that does it," Charlie said. "Get in. We're taking you for a ride."

Rachel looked startled. "No, I think I'd better…"

"Oh, for Pete's sake," Charlie muttered. "We're only going to the Adam's Rib to eat lunch. You still eat, don't you?"

"Only if you're paying."

"You asked for that, buddy," Ken said, as he opened the door and crawled inside first, stepping between the seats and into the back, where the patients were transported, leaving the empty seat for her.

"Hey," Charlie said. "How come you're limping?"

"I cut the bottom of my foot. It's nothing."

"Want me to take a look at it for you?"

Rachel grinned as she slid into the seat. "No thanks, I still know how to doctor my own boo-boos, thank you. Besides, I know an excuse to play with my feet when I hear one."

"Can't blame a guy for trying," Charlie said, and took off for the café with a grin on his face and the wind in his hair.

Rachel glanced down at his hand, her eyes widening at the ornate gold ring he was wearing. Impulsively she started to remark about its sudden appearance, but Ken caught her eye and shook his head, warning her away from that tack.

She shrugged and let the thought go, but as they parked

and got out, it crossed her mind that her life wasn't the only one undergoing drastic changes. Lois Klein had told Joanie, and Joanie had told her, that Charlie had paid off the note on his house. Add to that the new car he'd just bought and the ring on his hand, and either Charlie had a fairy godmother he'd wasn't talking about, or he'd won the lottery and was hoping to hide the fact from the IRS.

They entered the café, laughing and talking as old friends do, only to come face-to-face with Griff and Lois having lunch. Griff's face turned red, while Lois's glowed. All Rachel felt was relief.

"Hi, guys," Rachel said brightly. "What's good today?"

"*We're* having the special," Lois said, adding extra emphasis on the *we*.

Griff stood and started pulling out an empty chair for her. "We'd be glad to share a table. It's pretty crowded in here today."

But Charlie was having none of that. "Thanks," he said, "but there's an empty one over there."

There was nothing for Griffin to do but watch Rachel disappear through the crowd with the two men. He sat down, his food forgotten, and tried not to glare at the woman sitting at his table. *Why? Why couldn't Rachel be as pliable as Lois?*

Lois beamed under his tense observation, unaware of the turn his thoughts had taken.

A little while later, the bell over the front door jingled again and, out of curiosity, Rachel looked up—and came close to choking. Hoping Charlie hadn't noticed, she looked down at her plate; then, like a magnet, her gaze was drawn up again, and she stared, unable to take her eyes from the men who'd entered.

Snake never saw her. Tommy Joe, too, was focused on food. But Boone seemed to know she was there before the door swung shut behind him. Like a heat-seeking missile, his gaze locked on hers, and a wry smile tilted the right-hand corner of his mouth. The look he gave her was intimate, the smile secretive.

Griffin Ross saw the whole thing, from Boone's entry into the café to Rachel's blush and smile. He stared in disbelief, clutching his table knife as if it were a switchblade and fighting the urge to plunge it into the big man's back as he passed their table.

My God, Rachel, how could you?

Rage shook him as he flung down the knife and a handful of bills and stalked out the door, Lois hustling along behind in mute confusion.

The three men came nearer, and Rachel caught herself holding her breath and watching the changing expressions on Boone's face. Once again their gazes met, and his moved first, from her eyes to her mouth. She felt hot and at the same time cold as she realized he was remembering their kiss. Embarrassed and a little bit panicked, she looked away.

As they neared the table where she was sitting, his footsteps slowed and then stopped. Certain he was about to make a big scene, she kept her eyes on her plate and clutched at the napkin in her lap. Moments later, she realized he'd stepped aside to let a busboy pass, and tried to relax. But with him standing only inches away, it was impossible.

Keep your eyes on your plate, she told herself. It was no use. She could no more have looked away than she could have stopped breathing. She raised her head and got caught in the dark, silent power of his gaze.

"Excuse us," he said softly, and then moved on, well aware of the flush he'd left staining her face.

Charlie saw enough to worry about, but never got a chance to inquire. At that moment, his pager went off. He and Ken started digging in their pockets.

"Sorry, Rachel, duty calls," Charlie said, as he and Ken

tossed their money on the table and bolted out the door, leaving her behind to finish alone.

She fiddled with her tea, sipping and stirring until the hair on the back of her neck started to rise. She didn't have to turn around to know Boone was staring. His spirit was all around her.

The urge to get out from under the weight of his presence was overwhelming. She stood up too fast, stumbling as she put too much weight too suddenly on her sore foot. All the way to the door, she kept reminding herself, *I'm not afraid. I'm not afraid.*

And, in a way, it was true. Alone, Boone MacDonald posed no threat, but when she saw him with the company he kept, she was reminded of who and what he really was—a man who undoubtedly lived on the wrong side of the law.

When she was halfway out the door, someone gripped her shoulder, and she didn't have to look back to know who it was.

"Need a ride?" he asked softly, glancing down at her foot.

She looked over his shoulder, expecting Snake and Tommy Joe to be at his heels.

"I'm alone," Boone said, answering her unspoken question as to the other men's whereabouts.

"Thanks, but I think I can—"

"You gave me a ride. I'm only returning the favor."

Rachel thought of the half-mile trek to get back to her car and the pain already throbbing in her foot.

"Okay."

It would have been impossible for Boone to describe his relief. It wasn't much, but it was a great big first step in trusting him. He hurried ahead to open the truck door for her.

In the act of trying to seat herself, Rachel was suddenly lifted and scooted inside before she could argue the fact.

"Don't fuss. Last night I carried you, and you didn't complain. You can't begrudge a small boost."

She refused to look at him all the way to Jimmy's Place. He pulled up and parked, then jumped out before she could move. In seconds he'd come around to her door and was helping her out.

"Easy does it," he said gently, taking both her hands and easing her out of the seat.

It was only after she was firmly standing on both feet that he realized they were still holding hands. This time he was the one who started to panic.

"Boone?"

Let her go, you fool. Mesmerized by the look in her eyes, he wasn't strong enough to follow his own advice.

"Hmm?"

"Have you ever been to South Dakota?"

Gut-shot by the question, and scared to death of why she'd asked, he froze. Boone MacDonald hadn't been there, but *he* was born there. It took everything Boone had not to panic. Instinctively he stepped back, putting some distance between himself and the shock. Shoving his hands in his pockets, he gave her a cold, questioning stare.

"No, I haven't. Why do you ask?"

Rachel shrugged. "No reason. It's just that while I was there last week, I saw some—"

He grabbed her by the arm, and this time he made no attempt to hide the anger in his voice. "You were there? Why?"

"You're hurting me," Rachel said.

The accusation shocked him. He turned her loose as quickly as he'd grabbed her, and wondered if he was losing his mind. He'd known better than to do this. Rule one in undercover work was to stay focused on the assumed identity. Never let a piece of your real self show through. Boone MacDonald wouldn't have had a damn thing to do with a woman like Rachel Brant. It was the man he was who'd been drawn to her. *I'm the one who keeps coming back, time after time. And I'm the one who will suffer if anything goes wrong.*

"As I was saying," Rachel said, "the state historical society has a wonderful display on Deadwood. You know… all the gold-rush stuff, and Wild Bill Hickok and—" she shrugged "—and things. I wondered if you'd ever seen it."

Too stunned to speak, all he could do was shake his head.

Accepting the disappointment, all Rachel could do was try to smile. "Then that's that," she said. "Thanks for the ride. I guess I'd better go see if Stu is through with my car."

She limped away, and he tried to tell himself that it didn't matter. People took trips. Trips to anywhere they chose. But why, he wondered? Of all the places in the world to see, why on earth South Dakota? Unless…

He got in his truck and drove out of town, leaving Snake and Tommy Joe to get back to their vehicles as best they could. He had a sudden need to find out all he could about Rachel Brant.

Chapter 10

Boone wasted no time in digging into Rachel Brant's past. To his relief, it seemed she was all she claimed to be. Orphaned at the age of twenty-one. A certified EMT. Dedicated to her work. And, up until a short time ago, rumored to be about to become Mrs. Griffin Ross.

But no more. Griffin Ross was dating his secretary, although some said it was more for show than for love, at least on his part. And Boone knew that Rachel Brant was combing the Kiamichi Mountains at night like a woman possessed, crying out to a man who wasn't really there. It made no sense to Boone that she'd taken a leave from her job, and even less that she seemed drawn to him, rather than afraid. While there were questions that remained unanswered, he wanted to believe her trip to South Dakota had been a coincidence. And because he wanted it so badly, he let it be so.

Two days passed in which Boone rarely went home. Instead, he prowled the streets of Razor Bend in the hope of seeing Rachel again, but it didn't happen. And while there was nothing going on at Denver Cherry's but the nightly drink-till-you-drop routine, Boone couldn't completely absent himself from the group, not when it had taken him so long to be called to the fold.

Never before had he wanted to call it quits as badly as he did now, and it was because of Rachel. He was beginning to think of this job as his last. Once an undercover cop began to think more of who he was, than of who he was pretending to be, things always went wrong. He wanted out before that started to happen.

It was midnight when Boone drove up to the trailer and parked. He sat in silence with the engine running and the radio playing, letting himself unwind before going inside to bed. And as he stared at the darkened windows and the rusting trailer, the solitude of his existence overwhelmed him.

He hit the steering wheel with angry force. "Why am I doing this? We lock them up, the system lets them go."

On impulse, he picked up his cell phone. Leaning his head against the back of the seat, he closed his eyes, waiting for the link to the outside world that kept his head on straight.

"This is Waco. Is this you?"

Boone exhaled in an angry grunt. "I don't know," he muttered. "You tell me."

Susan Cross hit the mute button on her remote and shoved her bowl of popcorn aside. Something was wrong. "Talk to me, darlin'," she said softly.

"I want this over."

"Has something happened?"

"Hell, no. If it had, we wouldn't be having this conversation."

"I don't understand," she said.

Boone sighed and shoved a hand through his hair, massaging the back of his neck as he did.

"Me either, Captain. I shouldn't have called."

It took Susan a moment to think, and when she did, the first thing that came to mind was the woman.

"It's her, isn't it?"

His heart sank as the futility of the situation struck him. *Dear God, it will always be her.* But admitting to his captain that he was losing his edge didn't come easy.

"I don't know what you mean," he muttered.

A short, succinct epithet rang in his ear.

He arched an eyebrow, then grinned. "Why, Waco, I didn't know you knew words like that."

"Say the word and I'll pull you in," she said.

Boone sighed. That wasn't why he'd called, and it damn sure wasn't what he wanted.

"Look, Captain, like I said, I'm sorry I called. Let's just call it a bad-hair day and let it go at that, okay?"

"I have some news that might cheer you up," she said.

Boone stiffened. "I'm listening."

"Marked drug money has been circulating in Razor Bend like flies on honey."

This was definitely good news. "Have you been able to trace it to the source?"

"We're working on it," she said. "One thing's for sure, if it showed up there, then our boy is there, too. We're checking to see if it's being laundered through a business or major purchases of some kind. Either way, I hope to know something within the week."

"Thanks, Captain," Boone said.

"No, Boone, thank you," she said quietly, and hung up.

Boone disconnected, then, out of habit, entered a series of random numbers and disconnected again.

It was warm inside his truck. The heater was working at a neat little clip. He glanced up at the trailer, thinking of cold sheets and the lonely bed waiting for him inside.

"Suck it up," he reminded himself, and was reaching to turn off the engine when a song on the radio stopped his intent.

To his regret, it was the same lonely song he'd heard playing once before at Rachel's place.

"Desperado."

And in that moment, he knew what he was.

A longing swept over him that he couldn't control. Blind as he was to everything but the words of the song hammering at his heart, the need to see Rachel was too strong to deny. He put the truck in gear and took off down the mountain.

Rachel couldn't sleep. Truth be told, she was afraid to close her eyes. She'd paced inside her house until she wore out the floors, as well as her patience. The night was cool, but calm. The Kiamichis beckoned, promising peace if only she would come. Rachel walked out her back door, then stretched and inhaled slowly. Like a piper playing a seductive, sweet song, the dark enfolded her. Even as she sat down on the steps, the tension inside her was beginning to unwind.

Long minutes passed as she sat there, one with the night, listening to an owl hoot from a nearby tree, watching a possum as it waddled to and fro beneath a nearby bush, feeling the moisture on her face as it came down through the air, soon to become dewdrops on the lush mountain grass. Crickets chirped; night birds called. And then, while she wasn't listening, everything went silent. It was only after the possum suddenly scuttled away that Rachel realized what had happened.

She stood, alert now to a presence that, at this point, she could only feel. It took several moments for her eyesight to penetrate the darkness beyond the perimeter of the security light outside her house, but when it did, her heart started to pound.

She could see him now, coming toward her like some dark mountain cat, long and lean, dressed in black, blending with the shadows through which he was moving. There was a purpose in his step that she'd never seen before, an intent that created an ache deep inside of her.

Oh, God.

Waiting…waiting…she felt her legs begin to tremble, and she reached out toward the porch post to steady herself.

He came on without words, his intention obvious in the tilt of his head and the rhythm of his walk. He was closer now. She imagined she could hear his heart thundering in his chest, feel the rush of his blood as it coursed through his veins. Somehow, before it happened, she knew what the weight of his body would feel like as he drove deep inside her. She shuddered, then swallowed a moan. The time was past for sampling. What was between them was ripe; about ready to burst.

When he reached the bottom of the steps, he looked up, blistering Rachel with a single dark stare.

"Turn loose of me, woman, or suffer the consequences."

His demand was raw, like the need on his face.

Rachel took a deep breath. "I can't. I don't know how."

"Then God help us both, because neither do I."

Seconds later, she was in his arms.

Urgently, desperately, Boone's mouth swept her face, then her lips, then down the curve of her neck, drinking in the essence of the woman called Rachel.

When she moaned against his mouth, he lost the last of his control. He pulled her off her feet and into his arms, shoving aside a screen door, then kicking the wooden one shut behind them.

"Turn them off," he ordered, tilting his head toward the lights.

Rachel reached for the switch. As it clicked, dark replaced light, and she was aware of the sound of his breath as it flowed against her cheek. How ragged, how deep…

As if she'd done this all her life, Rachel locked her hands behind his neck and pulled his head down until there was nothing between them but a hurt waiting to be healed.

Boone could hardly think, yet there were things that had to be said.

"I want you, Rachel. I'm going to make love to you, and once I start, I won't stop." He didn't want to do it, but he took a deep breath and gave her an out. "If you don't want the same thing, tell me now."

He could feel the tension winding in her body like the springs of a clock. Her whisper brushed past his face, settling deep in his soul. It was the last thing that either of them said.

"Oh, God, Boone MacDonald, just don't let me go."

There was a trail of clothing on the floor, scattered from the kitchen down the hall to the end of her bed. The covers were torn back, with fresh sheets exposed. Completely revealed, Rachel lay waiting, her skin burning from the fiery sweep of his mouth, as he tossed the last of his clothes aside. He came to her without words or excuse, wasting no time in foreplay or sweet whispers and lies. And when he moved between her legs and drove himself deep inside, there was an intensity of feeling Rachel couldn't deny. She'd known all along what this ride would be like.

Once he was inside her, Boone paused, his jaw clenched, muscles jerking in his arms as he raised himself up to look down at her face. He never wanted to forget the way she looked making love.

Passion gave a sultry expression to Rachel's face. Her eyes were hooded, as if she were waking from a deep, restful sleep. Her eyelashes fluttered like butterflies in the wind. Her neck was arched, her lips were slightly parted, and with each soft gasp of air she inhaled, she clutched him tight, for fear he would disappear like the man from her dreams.

He groaned, then bent down, his mouth only inches from her damp, swollen lips. Rolling his hips against her belly, he moved himself deeper inside.

"Look at me, Rachel. Look at *me*."

She sighed and then shuddered, trying to do as he asked, but his face kept blurring in and out of her sight. From Dakota to Boone, from Boone to Dakota, as if she were looking into a bad mirror in a carnival sideshow.

The urge to move was coming upon him like a powerful wave. But he wanted her to know, when she fell over the edge of reason, that it was because he'd sent her there.

Resting his weight on his elbows, he put a hand on either side of her face and pulled her focus toward him. Centering her gaze so that she saw nothing but his face, he started to rock. For a brief span, time stood still.

Thoughts tumbled, one after the other, from her to him, from him to her. They read them in each other's eyes. Saw them in each other's faces.

She was soft where he was hard, giving against his need to take, gentle when he was strong. She filled him, completed him.

Watching a man like Boone come undone in her arms was, for Rachel, more than a joy. It was at once a satisfaction and a pleasure, knowing that she'd been made for this… for him. And of that she had no doubt. In spite of what and who he was now, they belonged.

Flesh against flesh, their bodies hammering with an unfinished need, Rachel felt the end beginning and knew a quick moment of relief. Soon, soon, it would happen. It had to. A woman could withstand only so much sweet pain. Mesmerized by the power of the man above her, Rachel couldn't look away. Making love with him was unlike anything she'd ever experienced.

And then it came upon her, a rush of blood, a pounding heart, a blinding flash. When she would have closed her eyes from the pleasure, he wouldn't let her go to that place all alone.

And then it was over.

Spent and shaking, they lay in each other's arms and cherished the loving they had shared. Rachel exhaled softly and closed her eyes, only now aware that she'd been crying.

He heard her sigh and lifted his hand to her cheek. It came away wet. With a groan, he pulled her closer, pillowing his head on her breast. The security of her heartbeat, the satin feel of her skin, all were a balm to a lonely soul.

Just before his eyes closed in sleep, the last lines of the song he'd heard earlier drifted into his mind. It gave him comfort to think that maybe it wasn't too late for him after all. He'd let her love him…even better, he'd let himself return that love. Maybe he would be the exception to the rule. Maybe this desperado could find the way to a good woman's heart.

Dawn was imminent when Boone slipped out of bed. He dressed as he'd undressed last night. Room by room, item by item, taking his clothes from the floor as he went. His boots were the last to be put on. Last night they'd been the first to go. But when he was dressed, he found it wasn't as easy to walk out as it had been to come in. He went back to her room, then stood in the doorway, watching her sleep.

He'd made tangles of her hair. Her shoulder was bare, a reminder that he'd taken everything from her last night, including her clothes.

When she was asleep, the animation that was so much a part of her face was missing. Only now, while she was still, was he fully aware of her near-perfect features and heart-shaped face. He looked at her, and his breath caught from the intensity of his feelings.

Last night he'd been swept away by passion. Today his mind was clear, his focus intent. He'd thought he knew about love, but that had been before Rachel. He'd never known that love could hurt so deeply, or heal so completely. The bond between them was more than he'd expected, and not enough to count on. How was she going to feel in the bright light of day? Would she be sorry? And, what was worse…even if she was sorry, he couldn't wait around to see.

Taking a pad and pencil from her bedside table, he scribbled a note and dropped it on the pillow. Resisting the urge for a goodbye kiss, he walked out of the house without looking back.

By the time he got home, the sun was just coming up over the horizon. He entered the trailer with no small amount of regret. Going from her place to his was like walking out of the light into the dark. It was a rude reminder of who he still had to be.

Rachel woke up one eye at a time, stretching slowly as she rolled over on her back. She couldn't remember the last time she'd slept this soundly or felt as refreshed. She glanced at the clock and groaned. It was almost 10:00 a.m. She yawned, and as she did, she realized her lower lip felt tight. Tracing her finger against the edge, she winced, and then the reason for its condition slammed into her with force. Boone! Ravaging her mouth…her body…her soul.

"Oh, my God!"

She sat up in bed. Last night, and everything that had happened, came back to her in a rush.

Her pink gown was still hanging on the closet door by a hook. She'd never put it on. Her clothes were all over the floor. There was nothing between her and God but a white cotton sheet…and Boone was nowhere in sight.

The fact that he was gone was multiplied a hundredfold by the fact that he hadn't bothered to say goodbye. And then she saw the note lying on the pillow and picked it up. It was brief. But the message was more than she'd expected from a man like Boone.

Vaya con Dios, Rachel, till we meet again.

She fell back on her pillow, clutching the note to her breast.

Till we meet again. It was all she needed to know.

Rachel came down off the mountain with a purpose in mind. She wanted to know more about the man with whom she was falling in love, and that wasn't going to happen if they wound up in bed as quickly as they had last night. Not, she reminded herself, that she didn't want to be there again.

There were other things they could do in between. She desperately wanted to find out more about him and, in doing so, get some much-needed answers about herself, as well. But she had no idea how to go about finding him or finding out, so she let the thought ride.

Shopping. She could shop for food. She didn't know a man who wouldn't slow down for a home-cooked meal. Her mind was filled with thoughts of how she could get him to unwind.

Yet by the time she'd wheeled an empty shopping cart up and down the aisles for a good fifteen minutes without making a single choice, the headway she'd planned to make was nowhere in sight.

As bad luck would have it, Joanie came up aisle two as Rachel was going down. For some reason, she feared Joanie would be able to see the change in her. Rachel shifted gears, trying to think of meat and potatoes instead of Boone Mac-Donald, and hoped her expression wouldn't give her away.

Joanie parked herself near the canned peas and carrots and pointed to Rachel's empty cart.

"Hi, girl. I see you're just starting."

"Sort of," Rachel said. "I didn't make a list. Can't remember what I needed."

"Don't you hate it when that happens?"

Rachel nodded and started to smile, but the cut on her lip pulled, causing her to wince instead.

Joanie being Joanie didn't miss a thing, from the glow in Rachel's eyes to the small bruise Boone's loving had left on her lip. Her eyebrows rose as her eyes began to twinkle. "So…I guess it's pretty lonesome up there on the mountain all by yourself."

Joanie's drawl didn't fool Rachel one bit. *I should have known.* She gave her friend a cool, unwavering glare. "I don't suppose it would do any good to tell you to mind your own business?"

Joanie scooted closer until they were head to head. "I don't suppose it would," she drawled. "Now, fess up. Who's got your head in a whirl? Don't tell me you've made up with Griff?"

Rachel frowned. "We didn't ever fight, so we had nothing to make up."

"But I thought… Then, if you never…" Joanie sighed. "Just tell me this. He's handsome. He's solvent. He's single. What was wrong with him?"

"Nothing was wrong with him," Rachel muttered, and took off down the aisle.

Joanie cut her off at the milk case. For once, the giggle was gone from her voice. "Don't do this, Rachel. You're scaring me, okay? First you ask me if I believe in *you-know-what*…." She glanced over her shoulder, making certain there was no one in sight, although she'd never said the word *reincarnation* aloud. "You said nothing was wrong with Griff, which means you think something might be wrong with you, instead." Joanie grabbed her by the arm, her face full of concern, and all but pinned Rachel to the milk case as she waited for an answer. "Well…I'm waiting."

But Rachel didn't answer. She was looking over Joanie's shoulder to the aisle beyond, at the tall, dark man who was sauntering down the aisle with a loaf of bread dangling from one hand and a three-liter bottle of pop in the other. His hair was windblown, his black jeans were soft and faded. He wore a dark blue T-shirt and a black denim jacket. His boots were worn and dusty, as if he'd been out in the woods, and from the way he was walking, he'd seen her long before she spotted him.

It was Boone.

There was no expression on his face, but his eyes were alive with a message she couldn't misinterpret.

Remember last night?

How could I forget?

It didn't take Joanie long to realize that she'd lost her friend's attention. Rachel had a faraway look in her eyes, and a smile on her lips that shouldn't have been there.

"So, you think what I just said was funny, do you?"

To her surprise, Rachel still didn't answer, and judging from the way she was staring over Joanie's shoulder, she'd completely forgotten Joanie was here. She spun around, ready to attack.

"I'd like to know what's so all-fired interesting behind my—" Joanie took a deep breath. The answer was literally staring her in the face. "Oh…my…Gawd."

It only lasted a few seconds, but within that space of time, Rachel felt as if all the bones in her body had just turned to mush. Before she could think what to say, Boone turned a corner and disappeared up another aisle.

Joanie grabbed her by the arm, and this time she had Rachel's full attention. "Please, Rachel, tell me that didn't mean what I thought it meant."

Rachel winced at the fear in Joanie's voice. But what on earth could she say that would make any sense? "I don't know what you mean," she muttered, and looked away.

"Is he why you dumped Griffin Ross?"

"No," Rachel said. "He came after."

Joanie exhaled slowly. "Then there *is* something between you two?"

Rachel looked up, but she didn't have to answer. The truth was there for Joanie to see.

"Oh, honey, I hope you know what you're doing," she said softly.

Rachel sighed as she looked in the direction Boone had gone. "That's just it, Joanie," she said, her voice quiet and shaking. "I don't have a clue, yet in spite of how this may seem, it still feels right."

Joanie shook her head and started to walk away when Rachel called out, "Joanie, you won't say any…"

There was a look of high indignation on Joanie's face. "I can't believe you felt the need to ask."

You can't believe it? I can't believe I've put myself in the position of having to ask.

"Thank you," Rachel said.

"You're welcome," Joanie replied, and left Rachel standing.

Rachel shoved her cart forward, but didn't get very far. She was so shaken that for a few minutes all she did was stare blindly at a display of fruits and vegetables. She didn't know anyone was behind her until a low, husky voice whispered near her ear, "What's the matter, lady, can't you make up your mind?"

She jumped, but she didn't have to turn around to know who it was. Boone was back.

She glanced over her shoulder just long enough to confirm her suspicions. "You're making me crazy," she snapped.

He grinned. "Welcome to the club, darlin'," he said, and dropped a pint of out-of-season strawberries in her cart. "These look good, don't you think? Sweet and juicy…but not too soft. Just firm enough to sink your teeth right into."

A chill ran up Rachel's spine that had nothing to do with fright. She stared down at the strawberries, thinking of what he'd said—and the way he'd said it.

Ignoring Rachel's slight state of shock, Boone picked up

a long, dark green cucumber, hefting it in his hands as if testing it for length and weight.

"Hey, how about one of these? It feels just about right. Plenty long and smooth…and firm. They have to be firm, or the dish is ruined. Here, what do you think?"

Before Rachel could answer, he tossed it toward her. She caught the cucumber in midair, then looked up at him in shock. There was a grin on his face she couldn't believe.

"So," he asked. "Do you think it's hard enough?"

If it had been a rat, she couldn't have been any more shocked by it. She dropped it into the basket. It landed next to the strawberries, then rolled into a corner.

By now, her face was definitely flushed. Somewhere in the back of her mind, she knew she should make a run for the door, but there was a part of her that was far too intrigued by this man to do anything but see what came next.

Boone moved down the display case, sorting and feeling. "Say, the celery looks good. You know how to pick the best?"

Rachel had no idea, but from the way Boone was grinning, it was plain he was about to let her know.

"See the leaves on the end of the stalk?"

Her gaze moved up the stalk as if magnetized.

Boone held the stalk upside down, dangling the celery like a baited hook over a pond full of fish. Unbeknownst to her, Rachel's eyes were widening and her lips were slightly agape.

"What I always do is dangle this over my hand…sort of like a feather duster…see?"

Rachel saw.

"Sometimes the leaves will be all soft and limp. That means you need to put that stalk back. But if the leaves feel crisp, and the sensation makes your toes curl in your shoes, then that means…"

Rachel snatched the celery out of his hand and slapped

it in her basket. "For God's sake, Boone, what are you trying to—?"

"Oh, wow! Look here," he said, and grabbed her cart, pulling her farther down the aisle to the end, where a large display of oranges had been arranged.

These look safe enough, Rachel thought. She was wrong.

He took one off the top of the pile and tossed it up in the air a time or two, like a baseball, as if getting the feel of it in his hand.

"Now, choosing these is completely opposite of the rest of the stuff we have in the basket."

"Why am I not surprised?" Rachel muttered.

Boone looked at her and winked. "Pay attention, woman. You might learn something."

All I have to do is take control of this situation and he'll stop. But that meant she would have to leave him, and there was a great big piece of Rachel Brant that knew she didn't ever want to leave this man again.

"Unlike other fruits, which need to be firm to be good, an orange should have plenty of juice and plenty of flavor." He held it under her nose, offering it up to be smelled. "Even if it smells like an orange, it could still be a fake." There was an odd tilt to the corner of his lips. "You can't be too careful about fakes, you know."

Rachel couldn't have moved if she wanted to.

"The true test is to squeeze it."

She watched as Boone wrapped his long fingers around the fleshy orange globe and then, ever so slowly, began tightening them. Her heart jerked as she remembered last night and the feel of his hands as he'd cupped her hips, tilting her body up to meet his advance.

She swallowed nervously as his voice lowered. When it was just above a whisper, she caught herself leaning forward, anxious not to miss a single word of his lecture.

Boone continued, well aware that he had his one and only student…and the orange…in the palm of his hand.

"But you can't be sure with just one squeeze. Sometimes you have to squeeze it over and over and…"

Rachel groaned.

Boone swallowed a chuckle and dropped the single orange into her cart.

"Now that we've got salad and dessert out of the way, what kind of meat do you like?"

"Not wieners."

Boone threw back his head and laughed. And when he did, for a moment, Rachel saw Dakota's face slide between them. He, too, seemed to be laughing aloud, and she could almost hear a soft, indistinct giggle, as if Mercy were sharing his mirth.

"Oh, God," Rachel said, and grabbed the cart for support.

"Just when I think you're gone…you come back."

She didn't realize until she'd spoken that Boone could misinterpret what she said. But when the laughter died, she knew what had happened. Back came the old, angry Boone. The one with no smile and cold eyes.

"Wait," Rachel said, and took him by the arm as he turned. "I wasn't talking to you."

"Yeah, right," Boone said, and made a big pretense of looking around, although they both knew there was no one else in sight.

"You don't understand," Rachel said.

"Then make me," he said quietly. When she didn't answer, he walked away.

Rachel hurt too much to cry. *What have I done?* But there were no answers for her, and she'd suddenly lost her appetite for everything, including shopping.

Long, empty minutes passed while she stared at the oranges like a woman in mourning. When a lady with two noisy children headed her way, she reacted by pushing her near-empty cart to a checkout stand, then waiting with dull, lifeless eyes while the clerk rang up her groceries. She hadn't bought much as such things normally went—one small pint of strawberries, a long, smooth cucumber, the green, leafy celery and a single orange, slightly squeezed.

"Will that be all, Rachel?" the clerk asked.

She nodded, then dug out her money as the young boy who sacked groceries for the store began to bag her purchases.

"Wait! That's not mine," she said, as the boy dangled a large plastic bottle of lilac-scented bubble bath above the sack.

"Oh, yes, ma'am, it is," the kid said. "A man paid for it a few minutes ago and then left. He said you would be along to pick it up."

Bubble bath?

Weight lifted from the region of her heart. All might not be forgiven, but it would seem he was willing to give her another try at explaining…as well as washing his back.

Chapter 11

Evening came, and with it anxiety about the night that lay ahead. After the way Boone had walked out of the store, Rachel was scared to death he might not come back. The only thing giving her courage was the bottle of bubble bath he'd left at the checkout stand.

The strawberries had long ago been cleaned and bagged, and now they were chilling in the refrigerator. The celery and cucumber had gone into a salad. T-bone steaks were in the refrigerator, still thawing after having been removed from the freezer a few hours ago. The bottle of lilac-scented bubble bath was sitting on the side of the tub. The orange was on hold until breakfast.

She kept telling herself that she had to eat, whether he came or not, and that she'd been taking baths alone for a good many years. She didn't need the appearance of some modern-day desperado to make her wash behind her ears. She was perfectly capable of feeding and bathing herself. All she'd done was plan ahead. Just in case.

Rachel walked through the house one last time, checking to see if there was something she'd forgotten. Pale blue throw pillows were neatly arranged on her floral-print sofa; magazines were in place. Dark green easy chairs were turned at just the right angle for conversation, and there was a minibouquet of bright orange marigolds on the cherrywood coffee table in the center of the room. The table was laid, but not with good china. Something told her that Boone wasn't the kind of man to sit easy at a table with too much fuss.

There was nothing left to do but wait. Rachel passed the hall mirror, then stopped and went back for a last-minute check. Her slacks were old but neat, charcoal gray. Her sweater was a soft rose pink, matching the color on her cheeks. Her hair was down, but pulled back from the sides and fastened at the crown of her head. A cascade of long, loose curls tumbled from the clip holding it in place. Reluctantly she met her own gaze, comparing what she saw with the way her heart ached. Her eyes seemed to be a perfect match to her mood; dark and blue.

She turned away and walked out the back door as a heartfelt sigh escaped her lips. Glancing toward the sunset spreading across the western sky, she thought to herself that Mother Nature was rather fanciful tonight. Only a western sky in evening would dare wear such bold slashes of orange, or such vivid shades of hot pink coupled with the dark, somber hue of deep purple.

But not even the glorious sunset could hold her attention. Not tonight. Rachel's gaze turned toward the forest beyond her backyard. The shade it was casting was already turning from blue to darker gray. Before long, it would be impossible to tell where the trees started and shadow ended.

Please let him come, she prayed. She stood with her hands folded in front of her like a penitent child, but there was a tense, expectant tilt to her stance.

The sunset came and went.

Out on the road beyond her house, she heard the gears of a pickup truck shifting as the driver started up the steep, winding blacktop. That wouldn't be Boone. He would come when she was least expecting it. She never asked why he chose to appear and disappear in such secrecy, because she was afraid of what he might say. She was falling in love with a man who couldn't give her a future, yet she was willing to accept what he *could* give. If love was all he had to offer, then she would take it.

She stood without moving until the chill wind that came up began to seep through her clothes. When her teeth began to chatter and her eyes began to tear, she told herself it was because of the wind and not from disappointment. With a tilt of her chin, she turned to enter the house.

Her hand was on the doorknob when the skin on the back of her neck began to crawl. Her heart missed a beat as she turned around. She walked off the porch and then farther, moving past the glow of the security light, then past the old rope swing dancing in the brisk night wind.

With nothing but instinct to guide her, she kept moving toward the forest with swift, certain strides. And then she saw him coming out of the trees in a long, easy lope.

Joy surged. She went from a walk to a run, and seconds later found herself in his arms, her feet dangling from the ground as he enfolded her within his embrace.

Laughter mixed with tears as she pressed cold welcoming kisses all over his face. He smelled of pine, and of soap and a musk-scented cologne that made her senses swirl.

"You're here! You're here! I was afraid you wouldn't come!"

Boone could think of nothing but the feel of her breasts against his chest, the tiny span of her waist as he'd lifted her up, and the gentle swell of her hips beneath the palms of his hands as he held her close. She was everything he'd ever wanted, and he was the last thing that should have happened to her.

If the good people of Razor Bend knew she was consorting with a man like him, her reputation would be on the rocks. He couldn't live without her, but the least he could do was keep his distance until dark.

"Darlin', wild horses couldn't have kept me away," he whispered, and feathered a kiss near the bottom of her ear, then laughed when she shuddered and moaned.

"Oh, Boone, Boone…" Her voice was soft, and her words were broken.

She met his kiss in the dark, felt his hands in her hair, and accepted the fact that he made her complete. Desperation tinged her every thought, her every motion, until she was shaking with need. With her heart in her eyes, she took him by the hand and led him toward the house.

Boone went willingly, stunned by the way she'd run into his arms. He didn't know a thing about what made her tick, but he knew how to detonate the woman in her. He wondered if she felt as off balance in the face of the passion that hung between them as he did. It scared him to think how much she meant to him, and with that thought came the knowledge that he might be putting her in danger simply by associating with her. His stride slowed, and as they neared the old swing, he stopped.

Puzzled, Rachel turned. "What's wrong?"

"Slow down, darlin'," he said softly. "We're moving too fast."

His meaning was all too clear, and she knew it had nothing to do with the speed of their walk.

The smile on her face dimmed, and Boone felt it go out like a light in the dark.

"Have mercy, Rachel. Don't look at me that way." He took her hand and led her to the swing. "I've got eight hours to get this right, okay?"

She smiled but didn't really mean it. She'd been so happy to see him. What if he didn't feel the same way? What if he'd come to tell her it was over?

"I'm so stupid," she muttered, and was starting to turn

away when she heard him curse beneath his breath, then grab her by the hand. She had nowhere to look but at him.

"No! You're not stupid, but you're damn sure missing the point. I didn't say what I did to hurt you."

"Then why are you hesitating?" she asked, and hated the tremor in her voice. "Are you sorry for what we did last night? Because if you are, I can promise you I won't hold you to a—"

"Being with me could get you hurt."

She froze. Now it was out in the open. She could no longer ignore his life-style, because he'd thrown it in her face. Yet hearing it from his own lips couldn't change what she felt. She loved him.

She reached out, cupping the side of his face with the palm of her hand. A day-old growth of whiskers tickled her fingers as she traced the shape of his mouth. A muscle jerked at the side of his jaw as she brushed her thumb across his lower lip.

"Did you ever think of changing?" she whispered.

He groaned and dropped down to the swing, then pulled her onto his lap. Rachel tried to face him, but he stopped her, so she sat with her back to his front as he held her hard against him.

Boone buried his nose in her hair, inhaling the sweet, clean scent of Rachel's shampoo, as well as the woman herself. Dear God, what had he done? Part of him needed to tell her the truth…at least as much as he could.

"They say a nurse found me in a cardboard box on the doorstep of a hospital when I was less than a day old. It was snowing. I'd been wrapped in two army blankets, both old, both dirty. They also told me I was howling at the top of my lungs. When she took me inside and dug me out of the box, the only thing I had on was an adult-size T-shirt with a note pinned to it. There was a name. They had no way of knowing if it was my first name or my last, so the nurse improvised."

Rachel's heart began to break for the little boy he'd been and for the hurt she still heard in the man.

"Oh, Boone, I'm so sorry." She leaned against him, giving him her warmth and her strength.

He swallowed the knot in his throat and then hugged her tight. "I didn't tell you that for sympathy, but you've got to understand, I didn't grow up like you did. I didn't have anyone who gave a damn whether I lived or died… or cared if I stayed in school, or whether I got in trouble. It's not an excuse…but it's an explanation. Right or wrong, that's who I am."

"Surely you had friends while you were growing up?"

She felt him shrug.

"You don't make many friends when you're constantly being moved within the system."

The image of a little boy with big eyes and no smile hurt her heart. Rachel slid from his lap and turned. "I'll be your friend."

Before he could think to react, she'd run behind him as he sat in the swing.

"Rachel, wait," Boone said quickly, embarrassed, when she started to push.

"Pick up your feet," she chided. "Good grief, a body would think you'd never been in a swing before."

He did as he'd been told.

"Now hold on," she said, as his momentum began to build. "You're going to love this. Once you get going real good, it almost feels as if you could fly."

And there in the Kiamichis, on a dark September night, they fell the rest of the way into love. Boone MacDonald had taught Rachel Brant how to love; now she was teaching him how to play.

For a while time stood still as she pushed and he sailed

high off the ground. The muted sounds of laughter drifted into the quiet as the rope yielded to Boone's weight, squeaking and rasping on the massive limb over which it was tied. Leaves rustled overhead as he dipped and swayed, and somewhere in the middle of it all, Rachel quit pushing and stepped back to watch.

There were tears in her eyes, but the delight on his face was there to see. At that moment Rachel made herself a vow. His childhood might not have been worth remembering, but if he would let her, from this day forward she would give him a life he would never forget.

"I love you, Boone."

Right in the middle of an arc leading up toward the sky, Boone heard her. When he came down, he bailed out and walked into her arms. All he could do was hold her tight and pray that what he'd done wouldn't ruin them both.

"Love? God, Rachel, do you know what you're saying?"

"Only what I feel."

He took her hand and held it over his heart. "Feel that?" he asked.

Her eyes widened as the thunder reverberated beneath her palm.

"Yes…oh, yes."

"I don't have the words to explain what you mean to me, but I can honestly say that I would lie down and die for you and not ask why."

Dakota's face began to drift between them.

Don't let them hang me. Don't let them hang me.

Rachel choked on a cry of dismay and threw her arms around Boone's neck.

"No, no," she muttered, and hid her face against his chest as she held on tight. "Don't ever say that! Never, ever say die!"

Something inside him began to ache. He'd never felt a pain such as this before, but he was pretty sure it was regret. Their whole relationship was built on a lie. What scared him most was wondering, if she learned the truth, would she still feel the same?

He smiled, then hugged her close.

"Come on, darlin', you feel cold. I think it's time we went inside."

Rachel shuddered. She was chilled, all right, but only on the inside, and from fear, not the cold.

Rachel lay on her side, watching Boone as he slept. A lock of hair had fallen over his forehead, giving him a little-boy look. But that was as far as it went. There was nothing childish about Boone MacDonald, including the way he made love. She inhaled softly, and even in sleep, Boone seemed attuned to her every move. He reached out, pulling her closer against him, relaxing only when her head was beneath his chin and her cheek pillowed on his chest. Rachel let herself be snuggled. Tonight had been a long night of firsts.

Lesson number one: Real men *can* smell like lilacs and still drive a woman out of her mind.

Just thinking of the bubble bath they'd shared made her grin. Her bathtub was old and deep, but not nearly big enough to accommodate a man with legs as long as Boone's, especially with Rachel sitting between them.

They'd made hats with the bubbles, fake smiles with the bubbles, transparent bras with the bubbles, even large, bulbous noses with the bubbles, and they'd laughed so hard they accidentally swallowed some bubbles. When the water got cold and the bubbles began to go flat, there was nothing left to hide the circumstance they were in. Wet, naked, and yearning to belong to each other, Boone drained the water out of the tub and took her to bed with minuscule bubbles still clinging to her skin.

"I'm all wet," she cried as he pulled back the bedspread and laid her on the blue patchwork quilt beneath.

His smile was wicked, and his eyes were dark and dancing, as he slid between her legs and into her body like a well-oiled machine.

"That just makes it better," he whispered.

Rachel laughed. He'd deliberately misunderstood what she meant, but she didn't care. This playful side of him was an unexpected joy.

Lesson number two: Making love naked on patchwork quilts is highly erotic. Making love on the floor is plain cold.

Now Boone slept while Rachel gazed her fill, and sometime during her musing, her own eyes closed and she slept. And, God help her, she started to dream.

"You promised you'd love me forever, but you cheated... you lied. You never said forever would be over so fast."

Boone sat up in bed, wide awake and staring about in sudden confusion. He could have sworn he'd heard a woman's voice.

Rachel twisted and turned beneath the covers, reaching out to someone who wasn't there. But it wasn't her behavior that made Boone start to shake. Rachel was talking, but in a different voice. It was higher-pitched and had a different inflection.

"Oh, man," Boone muttered and reached out to her.

"No...don't go...don't go!" Rachel cried, and threw back the covers, unintentionally shoving his hand aside as she did.

Before Boone could think, Rachel was out of the room and running down the hall, moving through the darkened rooms as if they were swathed in full light. He reached for his jeans and pulled them on in a panic, grabbing a blanket as he followed her out of the house.

The front door was ajar. He stood on the porch, searching the night to see which way she'd gone. Already out of range of her security light, it was a flash of pale flesh in the distance that caught his eye. She was heading for the forest. He bolted off the porch in a flat-out run. If he didn't reach her before she got to the trees, he would lose her for sure.

Ignoring the pricking of the rough ground on his bare feet, he ran as he'd never run before, catching up with her just outside the boundary of the forest.

But when he tried to put the blanket over her chilled, naked body, she fought him like a woman possessed.

"Rachel, don't!" he begged.

When he was at the point of wrestling her to the ground, Rachel suddenly stilled, and the blanket he'd just put on her slid off her shoulders, pooling around her bare feet. Boone stared as she dropped to her knees, then cried out and fell facedown upon the ground.

"Have mercy," he whispered, and picked her up. This time, she made no move to stop him.

Like a baby, he wrapped her in the blanket and started back toward the house with her limp body dangling from his arms. Though the price had been the trauma of seeing Rachel in such a state, he now had an explanation for the strange behavior he'd been witnessing.

Rachel wasn't dreaming. She was sleepwalking. Up until the moment she passed out, her eyes had been wide open. It seemed as though she was reliving some incident out of her past.

Unaware of what she'd done, Rachel was inside the house and tucked in bed before she began coming around. When she did, two things brought her rudely awake. The lights were on, and the shock in Boone's eyes was something she'd hoped never to see. It must have happened again…and he'd witnessed it! She covered her face with her hands.

Boone crawled into the bed beside her and pushed her hands aside.

"Don't hide from me, sweetheart," he said softly. "What happened to you?"

"I think you can answer that better than I can," she said, and then winced at the sound of her own voice. Her head was throbbing.

Boone's touch was gentle as he rubbed at the frown on her forehead. "Have you seen a doctor?"

"No."

This didn't make sense. She was trained in the medical field. Surely she wouldn't have a reluctance to trust a fellow professional.

"Why not?" he persisted.

Oh, Boone. How can I make you understand? "Because pills can't fix what's wrong with me."

Rachel's face was filled with despair. He ached to make her better, and he had never felt so lost. This couldn't be fixed with his fists or a gun, and he feared not even his love was strong enough to make this go away.

"Then what will?" he asked.

Rachel's eyes widened, and her chin began to quiver. "I don't know."

"God," he muttered, and lay down beside her, holding her close. "You scared me, Rachel."

"I know," she whispered. "I scare myself."

Neither of them slept again. About an hour before dawn, Boone got out of bed and began putting on his clothes.

"I wish you didn't have to go."

In the act of tucking his shirt into his jeans, he turned. There was a calm, watchful look on his face that she'd never seen before. "Maybe one day I won't," he said.

She sat up.

"But today's not the day."

She flopped back down on the pillow with a mutinous look in her eyes. "Will I see you tomorrow?"

He grinned slightly. "Honey girl, it's already tomorrow."

"You know what I meant," she muttered, as he started for the door.

He turned. "Don't wait up," he said. "I might be late."

Rachel jumped out of bed. Unmindful of her nudity, she raced for the bureau. "Here," she said, and tossed him a key.

He caught it in midair, then looked down. "What's this?" he asked, pointing to the red *B* she'd put on it.

"Fingernail polish. The *B* stands for *Back,* as in *Back Door.*"

He grinned and slipped it on his key ring. "Why, Rachel, I thought you were giving me the key to your heart."

She threw her arms around his neck. "I already did," she said softly. "Don't you remember?"

Lesson number three: There is nothing quite as sensual as being completely naked and being made love to by a fully dressed man.

Charlie Dutton and Ken Wade were coming down the mountain after an early-morning run to Latisha Belmon's home. It wasn't the first time they'd been called out to put her back in bed, and it very likely wouldn't be the last.

Latisha was seventy-two and nearly four hundred pounds, and the strength in her legs was just about gone. And her husband, Clyde, at seventy-four and weighing in at 128, was no match for her weight or her girth. When Latisha went down, Ken and Charlie went up...the mountain, that is.

Sharing a sack of doughnuts and finishing the last of his cold coffee, Charlie came around a corner in the ambulance, taking his half of the road out of the middle.

"Son of a—!" He dropped the coffee in his lap and grabbed the wheel with both hands, narrowly missing the pickup that was in the act of pulling out of the trees and onto the road.

"Oh, man!" Charlie muttered, swiping at his lap and glaring in his rearview mirror at the same time. "Look what he made me do!"

Ken was still choking on the doughnut he'd been trying to swallow when the near accident occurred.

"Well, now, Charlie, you were a little bit too far to the left, and we weren't running lights or siren, so he couldn't have known we'd be coming. Besides, I'd a whole lot rather have to change uniforms than go back and explain to the boss why we just wrecked the last ambulance in Razor Bend."

Charlie paled. "You're right," he muttered, then stared thoughtfully as they passed the cutoff that led to Rachel's house. "Still, I wonder what he was doing up in there."

Ken shrugged and dug in the sack for the last doughnut. "Oh, who knows. Probably hunting or something."

"More likely something," Charlie muttered, remembering where he'd seen that man before. It was the same man who'd hitched a ride into town with Rachel. His stomach turned as a thought skittered through his mind. He frowned. He didn't like what he was thinking one bit. At that moment, he made up his mind—first chance he got, he was going to stop by and visit Rachel. Just to say hello.

Boone was still white-knuckled from the near miss with the ambulance when he pulled into the yard at his trailer. Seeing Tommy Joe sprawled out on the front steps didn't do his disposition one bit of good. He got out with a scowl on his face.

"Hey, Boone," Tommy Joe said, as he pushed his bulk up from the steps. "I didn't think you was ever coming back. Where you been?"

"None of your damned business," Boone muttered, and pushed his way past Tommy Joe and into the trailer, leaving him to follow behind at his will.

Tommy Joe grinned. "You got a girl? I bet anything you

got yourself a girl. I told Snake the other day, I think old Boone's got hisself a girl."

Boone turned around. All expression was gone. His eyes glittered angrily as he pushed a finger in Tommy Joe's chest.

"You and Snake stay out of my face, and I'll stay out of yours," he said softly.

Tommy Joe paled. "Hey, man, I didn't mean anything by it. I was just making small talk, you know."

"So you came for a *chat?*"

"No...no. I came to deliver a message. Denver wants all of us at his house tonight."

"What's up?"

"I don't know. I just follow orders, I don't give 'em."

Damn it, Boone thought. After what he'd witnessed last night, he didn't want to leave Rachel alone in a bed ever again. Now, here he was, faced with a choice between the job he'd been sent to do and being with the woman he'd come to love.

"I'll be there," Boone said, and looked at the door. "Don't let it hit you on the way out."

Tommy Joe scuttled out, leaving Boone alone with an ever-increasing sense of doom.

Chapter 12

Daylight had come and gone when Boone pulled into Denver Cherry's front yard.

"What took you so long?" Denver muttered as Boone walked in the door.

"You need to get your money back. The printer left the time off the engraved invitation," Boone drawled.

Denver grinned, revealing broken teeth through his brush of gray beard.

"You're a real wiseass, aren't you?" he asked, then chuckled. "Reminds me of myself in my younger days," he muttered, then scratched beneath his armpit as he pointed toward the kitchen. "Ribs and beer on the table, if you're hungry."

Boone frowned. "Not hungry. What's up?"

"No need to get in a huff," Denver said. "We're waiting on the boss to show."

Boone's heart went into overdrive, but, to his credit, he never blinked an eye.

"Maybe I'll get that beer after all," he muttered, and sauntered into the kitchen as if he didn't have a care in the world, when he really wanted to kick up his heels. *It's about time.*

Another football game was blasting from Denver's living room, and from the sounds of it, Boone decided, Denver must be raising the volume on every down. The noise was so loud that when he opened the can of beer he never heard it pop, although it fizzed over the top and down the side of his hand. A double order of barbecued ribs lay uncovered on the take-out tray, while a couple of flies ate their fill. Boone looked around the kitchen in disgust. He tossed the can of beer in the sink, wiped his hands on his jeans and stalked out of the kitchen just as Snake Martin walked into the house. He was muddy and winded and looked as if he'd been running.

"What's wrong with you?" Denver asked.

Snake ran a shaky hand through his hair, then scratched at his face where his beard began.

"Durn near had myself a wreck. Ran off in a ditch tryin' to miss a deer."

Boone could almost sympathize. He'd come close to having the same thing happen to him only days earlier.

"Well, you're here, and that's what counts," Denver said.

"I'm not here to stay," Snake said. "I need a jack." He shuffled his feet, unable to look Boone in the face.

"What happened to mine?" Boone asked.

"Someone stole it," Snake muttered, then flushed as he realized he'd finally admitted to the theft after all.

Boone grinned. "Well, well, what goes around comes around."

"My jack won't work on your four-by-four," Denver said. "Not big enough."

Snake cast a quick glance at Boone, who was grinning more broadly by the minute.

"You're going to have to ask," Boone said.

"Can I borrow your jack?" Snake mumbled.

"I didn't hear you say 'please.'"

Snake was livid. "Damn it, Denver, make him—"

"Oh, shut up and do as he says," Denver grumbled. "You got yourself into this mess. Now get yourself out."

If Snake had had a gun, he would gladly have emptied it in Boone MacDonald's belly, but since he didn't, he saved the image of the act for another day.

"Please, Boone, can I borrow your jack?"

"How about 'pretty please with sugar on it'?"

Snake's face mottled in anger. "I'm gonna…"

Boone laughed, then took the keys from his pocket and tossed them to Snake, who caught them just before they hit the floor.

"Here. You know where it is, so help yourself. Bring back my keys when you bring back my jack, or I'll take it out of your miserable hide."

"Ain't someone gonna take me back to my truck?"

Denver took one look at Boone and knew that ordering him to go wouldn't work. Not this time.

"Wait for me outside," Denver said. "I gotta get my shoes."

Snake was still muttering as he walked out the door.

"You better not mess with him," Denver warned as he pulled on some sneakers, minus their strings. "If he gets mad at someone, he can be real mean."

Boone didn't blink. "I've seen mean before." Then he picked up Denver's remote and hit the mute button. "That's too damned loud," he said softly, and walked into the kitchen and out the back door as Denver went out the front.

A mile and a half down the road, Denver saw Snake's red-and-yellow four-by-four nose down in a shallow ditch. He pulled over, then let Snake out, aiming the lights so Snake could see to set the jack.

At that moment a car topped the hill, then began slowing down. Denver squinted against the oncoming glare, waving his arms to alert the driver not to run over them.

"Hey, look," Snake said. "It's the boss."

The big car came to a stop, and Denver called back Snake as the door began to open, "I know who it is. Now get on with what you're doing. The boss won't like having to wait on us."

Snake went to his knees. Setting the lug wrench in place, he began loosening the bolts one at a time.

The man was nothing but a dark silhouette against the glare of his own headlights. "What's going on?"

Denver held out his hands, as if to say it was out of his control. It seemed the boss was in no mood to talk.

"Just get it over with and get on up to the house. I haven't got all night."

"You bet, boss. Be right there," Denver said. "I'll move my car so you can get by."

Snake suddenly remembered the borrowed keys in his pocket. While he wouldn't have admitted he was afraid of a thing, in truth, Boone MacDonald made him nervous. He saw Denver get in the car and panicked. He didn't want Boone coming after him alone in the dark.

"Uh… Hey, boss!" Snake yelled, and started running toward the long, shiny car. "Take these keys back to the house for me and tell him I'm not through with the jack." He dropped them in the boss's hand and hurried back to his truck.

The keys slid through the boss's fingers into the dust. Cursing, he leaned over to pick them up, then saw something he didn't want to believe. There, highlighted in the twin beams from his headlights and angling from the ring, was an oddly marked key. The letter *B* had been painted on it with red fingernail polish. He held it closer to the light, and as he did, shock began to seep throughout his system.

Son of a… It couldn't be! But it was, and it was marked just like the one on Rachel Brant's key ring. He'd seen her with it dozens of times in the past.

"Snake!"

The little man looked up from his work. "Yeah, boss?"

"Who do these keys belong to?"

"Boone MacDonald."

Rage struck him hard and fast. Unable to trust himself to speak, he clutched the keys until they left an imprint in the palm of his hand. He'd even seen Rachel and Boone together, and still he'd ignored the implications, choosing to believe the worst was all in his mind. But to know it had come to this! A cold smile broke across his face.

Now I know why the interest between us was never there. You little bitch, who would have thought your tastes ran so rough?

The importance of tonight's meeting had taken a back seat to revenge. Now he had another objective. One far more serious, far more deadly. Boone MacDonald was going to pay for messing with a woman out of his league. For that matter, Rachel needed to be taught a lesson, too. They wanted to be together? Fine. For all he cared, they could spend eternity in each other's arms.

"Denver!"

Denver came on the run. "Yes, boss?"

"I've changed my mind about tonight," he said.

"But I thought…"

"I said, I changed my mind." He slapped the keys in Denver's hand and drove off without another word of explanation.

"What set him off?" Snake muttered.

Denver shrugged, his mind locked on the football game playing on without him. "Who knows? Just hurry up, will you? I'm gonna miss the whole last half."

Last night had been the longest night of Rachel's life. She'd fallen asleep on the sofa waiting for Boone, waking up just before morning with cold feet and a crick in her neck. It was a far cry from lilac-scented bubble baths and a warm embrace.

In the back of her mind, she couldn't help thinking that her actions had scared him off. And in a way, she could hardly blame him. What man wanted to be saddled with a woman who went off half-cocked in the middle of the night, ranting and raving about something she couldn't explain?

Halfway through breakfast, Rachel made a decision. She couldn't spend the rest of her life hiding in a house in the Kiamichis, waiting for dark. What she needed was a little reorganization. She picked up the phone and punched in the numbers, hoping that her friendship with Joanie was still of good standing. She waited as the phone began to ring.

"Curlers."

Rachel grinned. From the abrupt manner in which Joanie answered the phone, she must have been be up to her elbows in shampoos and sets.

"Hi, Joanie, it's me. Got any free time today?"

"Rachel! I was going to call you when I had a minute. Are you wanting an appointment or a friend?"

Thank goodness Joanie didn't hold a grudge. "How about both?" she asked, and heard papers shuffling as Joanie leafed through her appointment book.

"Hmmm...Shirley Jo just called and canceled a perm, so I've got anywhere from eleven this morning until three this afternoon free. You name it."

"How about a manicure and then lunch?"

"Eleven okay?"

"Put me down," Rachel said. "We need to talk."

"It's a date," Joanie said. "See you later."

Rachel hung up, satisfied that she was moving in the right direction. Just because she'd fallen in love with a so-cial outcast, that didn't mean she had to remove *herself* from society, as well.

*   *   *

"Red is a good color on you."

Rachel frowned as she held her forefinger up to the light, squinting to judge the shade of nail polish Joanie was applying. "You think so?" she asked.

Joanie grabbed her hand and yanked it back down to the table. "I *think* you don't care what color I put on, just as long as I listen." She shifted the gum she was chewing to the opposite side of her cheek, cracking and popping it as she went. "Well? What's the big scoop?" she asked, as she bent to her task.

"Joanie, have you ever been in love?"

Joanie's jaw went slack. Red fingernail polish dripped unattended on Rachel's thumb.

"Oh, shoot, look what you made me do!" she said, dabbing at the blob with polish remover.

Rachel sighed. She should have known this wasn't a good idea.

Joanie couldn't bring herself to look up, but she had to ask. "Rachel?"

"Hmm?"

"Is it that man who runs with Denver Cherry's men... Are you in love with him?"

There was no way Rachel could deny the fact and ever face herself in a mirror again, but she was afraid. Afraid of being rejected. Afraid of losing her very best friend.

"What would you say if I said yes?"

Joanie jerked. When she looked up, what she saw in Rachel's face frightened her. "I don't know, sugar...maybe a prayer?"

Rachel's eyes teared, and when Joanie saw her reaction, she groaned and set the polish aside.

"Honey...don't cry," she said softly. "Look, I don't pretend to understand why people fall in and out of love, but you and him...I don't get it. What on earth does he have that

Griffin Ross didn't have, or, for that matter, Charlie Dutton? You know Charlie's got a big crush on you."

It took a moment for Rachel to find the words to explain, and even then, it was almost impossible to express how she felt. "It's not what he has, Joanie. It's what he gives me."

"Okay, so he's good in bed. I could tell that from looking at him." She rolled her eyes and then shivered. "Gawd…have you ever seen eyes like that on a man in your life? They just about look through you, don't they?"

"You don't understand. It isn't about sex. It's like… Oh, never mind." Rachel laid her hand down on the manicure table again. She should have known this would be a mistake. "Here, either take the stuff off or make me match. I can't go out of here with one hand done and the other bare."

Joanie sighed. It was obvious Rachel was hurt by her inability to understand. She dabbed the brush back in the polish, then paused.

"Look, sugar. If you love him, then there must be more to the man than good looks and a bad reputation, okay? All I'm saying is…be careful."

"Okay."

Moments passed, and just when Rachel thought the worst was over, Joanie started up all over again.

"Rachel, make me understand."

Rachel took a deep breath and then started naming reasons, as if she were reading from a list. "He makes me whole. He fills my heart. He makes me laugh."

"He'll make you cry."

Rachel frowned, then glanced up at the clock. "Are we nearly through? If we get to the café after twelve, the best tables will all be full."

Joanie wilted. "Sorry. I never did know when to keep my big mouth shut."

"That's okay," Rachel said. "Actually, you reacted just about like I thought you would."

"Then why did you tell me?" Joanie asked.

Rachel shrugged. "I don't know. Maybe I just wanted one person to know what was going on in my life, in case…"

Joanie paled. "In case of what?"

There was a strange look on Rachel's face as she spoke. "Just in case, that's all."

The subject was promptly dropped. A short time later, they entered the Adam's Rib Cafe just ahead of the noon-hour rush, and took a table toward the back, so that Joanie had a bird's-eye view of everything that went on.

"We're having the special," Joanie said, waving away the menus. "She's having iced tea. I'm having a cola with no ice and a slice of lemon."

Rachel grinned. Some things never changed.

Halfway into their meal, Rachel looked up in dismay. Griffin Ross was coming their way.

"Rats," she muttered.

Joanie glanced up, then back at Rachel. "Gee, honey, I'm sorry. If we'd thought, we could have ordered this to go and eaten it back at the shop."

"It's too late now," Rachel said. "The vulture's descending."

"Rachel! Darling! Long time no see!" Griff cried, and, without waiting to be asked, seated himself at their table. "You don't mind, do you? It's a little crowded in here, and I've got to eat and run."

There was little they could do but acquiesce with as much grace as possible.

"This is a bit of good fortune," Griff said, as the waitress hurried away with his order. He thrust his hand inside his suit coat. "I just picked these up at the drugstore. You and Joanie made quite a splash at the Labor Day picnic, remember?"

He handed over a packet of newly developed pictures, which Joanie began sifting through in delight. In no time at all they were grinning and laughing as they relived the memories of the day, the three-legged race, the marshmallow roll, and the sack race that had resulted in both Rachel and Joanie falling into the duck pond at the park. Even Rachel had to admit it had been a good day. Griff had been full of fun, and a very good sport.

The café was doing such a brisk business that Rachel never noticed when Boone walked in, pausing near the door. She never saw the shock, then the disbelief, spreading over his face, and even if she had, she would have been hard-pressed to find a way to explain without making a scene.

Without saying a word, Boone spun and walked back out the door the same way he'd come in—hungry and alone. He was still discouraged by the cancellation of last night's meeting with the boss, and this only added to the frustration he was feeling.

Just for a while he'd been convinced his time as Boone MacDonald was nearly over. Then Denver had come waddling into the house with Snake right behind him. All he'd gotten out of the night were his keys back and his jack intact.

He glanced at the café, then headed for his truck. *This doesn't have to mean a thing,* Boone kept reminding himself. *The room was full. They were just sharing a table.* But even though he thought it, he couldn't force himself to believe it. Betrayal was a hard image to lose.

Later that same day, Rachel was on her way home when, on impulse, she wheeled into the parking lot outside EMS headquarters. Ken Wade was in knee-high fireman's boots, with a hose in one hand and a soapy cloth in the other as he washed down the ambulance. He grinned and waved as she started up the sidewalk.

"Hey there!" he called. "Coming back to get your name in the pot?"

"Not yet," Rachel said. "But soon."

He grimaced. "Not soon enough for Charlie. He thinks you can do no wrong."

"And I suppose you can do no right?"

He laughed. "You said it."

"Sorry," Rachel said. "I didn't take him to raise. He was like this when we met, remember?"

In playful retaliation, Ken waved the spray of water in her direction. Not too close, but close enough to send her scurrying inside.

Because she was looking over her shoulder as she went, she ran full tilt into Charlie. Her purse went flying, spilling its contents all over the floor and under a chair near the door.

"Whoa!" Charlie said, laughter filling his voice. "I always knew you couldn't stay away from me, but you didn't have to run. I would have come if you'd called."

"Good grief," Rachel muttered as she went down on all fours, grabbing at a lipstick, then a pen, then her wallet.

Charlie bent to help. "What was the big rush?" he asked, as he handed her a comb.

"I was about to get hosed down."

Charlie grinned. "Yeah, Ken's mean with that soap and water."

"My keys…I can't find my keys," Rachel muttered as she looked around on the floor.

They both began to search. Seconds later, Charlie spied them beneath the front bumper of the spare ambulance, parked inside the station.

"There they are," he said. Before he handed them back, he fingered through them in a nosy but friendly sort of way. When he looked up, he was grinning. "Hey, Rachel, let me see the bottoms of your shoes."

She did as he asked without thinking why, assuming that she must have walked in grease or the like without noticing.

"No," Charlie muttered. "I guess I was wrong."

"About what?"

"Well, you mark your keys to tell which goes to the front door and which goes to the back. Thought you might have your shoes marked, as well. You know...one for the left and one for the right."

The grin on his face was too broad to resist. She laughed. "You worm. Give me my keys."

"It's gonna cost you," he teased, dangling them over her head.

"Like what?"

An odd expression spread over his face. "Like a kiss?"

Suddenly the fun had gone out of the game. Rachel froze, unable to find a way out of the embarrassment she was feeling. Charlie was her friend. He was her peer. But he would never be anything more.

"Oh, good grief," Charlie said, and dropped the keys in her hand. "I was just kidding."

"I knew that," Rachel muttered, and put the keys into her purse, along with everything else they'd retrieved.

"So, if you didn't come for a little loving, what's up? Please tell me you're coming back to work."

She shook her head. "Not just yet, Charlie...but soon."

He rolled his eyes in an overdramatic gesture of defeat. "I will not survive Ken Wade."

"That's funny. He says the same thing about you."

To his credit, Charlie grinned, and Rachel began to relax. The worst was over.

"I see they got the ambulance fixed."

"Yep."

Rachel eyed Charlie, trying to figure out what was so different about him. Suddenly, she knew.

"Your hair!"

Charlie flushed beet red and swiped his hand across the back of his neck.

"What's wrong with my hair?" he muttered.

"Odie Waters didn't cut your hair. It's been styled."

He thrust his chin out in a righteous show of defense. "So? Lots of guys do that."

"I know.... I didn't mean it didn't look good. What I meant was...it looks *good*. You know Odie. He's a dear, but he's been cutting hair the same way since the forties."

Charlie didn't answer, and his reticence made Rachel remember other changes in Charlie that had recently taken place.

"I wonder what will be next," she said, and poked him in the arm, trying to tease him out of his mood. "New car... fancy ring. New hairstyle. The next thing we know, Razor Bend will be too small for you."

"Well, a man's got to look to his future," Charlie said. "I might actually want to settle down one day. Can't do it on this salary alone, that's for sure."

It was the word *alone* that worried her. What else was Charlie doing to allow him such a major change in lifestyle? But as soon as she thought it, she let the thought go. Who was she to tell anyone what to do with his life? Hers was in chaos.

"Whatever you're doing, it must be right," Rachel said.

Charlie grinned, although a bit of guilt had started to rise within him. It *was* right, he thought. And it was no one else's business what he did with his money...no matter how he'd come by it.

"Well, I just came to say hi," Rachel said. "I'd better get out of here before the boss snags me and makes me feel guilty all over again."

"I'll walk you to the door," Charlie said.

"How about walking me past the madman of the car wash, instead?"

"Deal."

Together they walked to her car. As she was getting inside, Charlie leaned down.

"Hey, Rachel, if you ever want to talk about anything—

anything at all—I'm your man. I don't gossip. I don't judge. And I don't lie."

A wave of fear washed over Rachel, leaving her face shocked and pale. She didn't know how or why, but for some reason, she suspected he knew about Boone.

"Why…thank you, Charlie." It was all she could think of to say.

She looked up in her rearview mirror as she drove away. Charlie was standing right where she'd left him, watching her go.

Chapter 13

"He'll come tonight."

Rachel figured if she said it often enough, it would happen. But it was nearing sundown, and the time for hoping would soon be past. One thing had become clear to her after talking to Joanie. If she didn't trust her feelings for Boone, no one else would, and she'd come too far in accepting this relationship to quit on him at the first hint of trouble.

She walked out on the porch and sat down on the steps to begin her wait. But to her dismay, she realized that a thunderstorm was brewing. Heavy clouds were building in the southwest. And although the storm was too far away for her to hear thunder, the intermittent lightning strikes could be seen silhouetted against the navy blue sky above the Kiamichi peaks.

Shivering, she pulled her knees up to her chin. The wind began to quicken as she looked toward the forest beyond her back yard.

"Oh, Boone, hurry, please hurry!"

And as she waited, darkness swept over the land, lending an ominous quality to the oncoming storm.

Driven inside sometime later by blowing rain, Rachel finally gave up hope that Boone would come tonight. She sat in her living room with the television on, watching weather bulletins as they crawled across the bottom of the screen.

Half dozing in her chair, she was suddenly awakened by a loud clap of thunder that rocked the house on its foundation, followed by a bolt of lightning so close and so bright that she heard the crack as it hit. She hit the mute button on the TV and ran for the door.

All she had time to see was the gust of blowing rain as it hit her in the face. She ducked her head in reflex, and when she turned around, Boone was standing at the edge of the porch.

Startled more by his sudden appearance than by the man himself, she screamed. He ran toward her just as the second gust came, grabbing her close and propelling her backward into the house, out of the storm.

The door slammed shut behind them, and the silence of the room was overwhelming as Rachel looked up.

"You came!" she said, and threw her arms around his neck in a joyful welcome.

Boone told himself she wouldn't play games with him, but he couldn't forget how she she'd laughed and talked to Griffin Ross as if there had never been a break in their relationship.

Rachel caressed the side of his cheek, feeling the rough growth of a two-day beard and remembering how it felt on her skin.

"You didn't come last night. I didn't think you would come tonight, either."

Boone lifted his head, as if bracing himself for a blow.

Was that why you went back to Griffin Ross? Did a couple of nights in the sack with an outlaw satisfy your sense of adventure?

Rachel began to worry. He looked so lost and so hurt, and she didn't understand why. His hand was at the back of her head, as if cushioning it from an unseen blow, but he seemed locked in some silent war with himself that she didn't understand.

"Boone, if there's something you want to talk about, all you—"

He interrupted before she could finish. He seemed angry, and at the same time despairing. "I love you so damned much it scares me to death."

"Oh, Boone..."

He unsnapped his jacket and dropped it on the floor by the door. It fell with a sodden squish.

"My truck is parked on the far side of your house. If you don't want anyone to know I'm here, say so now and I'm gone."

Rachel didn't know why there was so much anger in the love he'd just professed, but she wasn't about to let him leave until he'd told her what was wrong. She pushed past him to the door, turned the lock and turned out the light. Except for the mute and flickering television, the house was now in darkness. She turned and faced him.

"Something is wrong, so don't insult my intelligence by lying. Besides, if I had my way, you'd never leave me again."

Boone came toward her, then quietly enfolded her within his embrace.

"God help us both, Rachel Brant, because I don't have the good sense to let you go."

Dakota's hands dug into Mercy's shoulders with painful intensity.

"Come away with me, Mercy. Come with me now, before it's too late."

Rachel shuddered, clutching at Boone's shirt in sudden desperation. Why did this keep happening to her? Was it some kind of warning? Was the past about to repeat itself in more ways than one? Fear gripped her as she tried to imagine her life without this man in it. She couldn't. Not anymore. She fisted her hands in the front of his shirt, feeling the cold, damp fabric give way to her demand.

"You can make the world go away. Make love to me, Boone. Do it now."

Passion shattered the last of his control. Right now he didn't care if she'd cheated and he wouldn't accept that she'd lied. She belonged to him in a way she would never understand. He couldn't give her assurances or promises of a happy-ever-after kind of life. All he could give her was love.

He lowered his head. She met him. His mouth was cold, the demand in his kiss almost frightening until she heard a soft, muffled groan.

With desperation in every movement, he shoved their clothing aside and himself inside her. With no promise of heaven other than the look in his eyes, he pinned her between the door and his heart and drove them both crazy with love.

Light flickered on the opposite wall as the television continued to play with no sound. Every now and then lightning shattered the darkness outside, just as Boone was shattering the last of Rachel's control.

The force with which he took her was gentled by each touch of his hand on her body, his lips on her face and his sharp, ragged breaths on her cheek. Rachel had long ago lost contact with reality. Boone was her anchor, her center of gravity. As long as his arms were holding her in place, she couldn't fall off the world.

In the midst of too much pleasure, it all came undone. One minute Rachel was living for the next thrust of his body, and then heat spilled within her, leaving her weak and limp and hanging on to his shoulders to keep from falling. But each breath Boone was taking was longer and deeper than the last. She could tell the end was near for him, as well.

"God, Rachel… Oh, God…" His voice was less than a whisper, more like a prayer.

Rachel buried her face against the curve of his neck and felt him tremble. There was little she could do to help the inevitable, other than bring him closer. With her last ounce of strength, she wrapped her legs around his waist and held on for dear life.

A short while later, when Boone could remember to think and breathe at the same time, he sank to the floor on his knees, with Rachel still in his arms. At a loss for anything to say that wouldn't give himself away, Boone held her close, showing her in the only way he could that she was loved.

Rachel rubbed her face gingerly against his whisker-rough cheek, then leaned forward, tenderly kissing a small scar she felt on his chin.

"What was that for?" Boone whispered.

"The boo-boo I suspect no one kissed."

Remembering the knife and the man who'd put the scar there, he tried to grin, but it just wouldn't come.

"I wish to hell I'd met you years ago," Boone growled.

Oh, but, my darling, you did. Rachel traced the scar with the tip of her finger and smiled.

"It's never too late for love," she said.

"You'd better be right," he said, as he rolled, pinning her beneath him on the floor.

She grinned. "First thing you should learn about loving a woman. When it counts, we're always right."

"Did you leave any bubble bath for me?" Boone asked.

"You liked that? My, my, have I created a monster? I don't believe I've ever known a lilac-scented, bubble-blowing monster before."

This time, Boone found his grin. It was right behind the tears in his eyes.

"So sue me," he said. "Thanks to you, I'm weak as a kitten and cold as a frog. Right now, I'll take smelling like a lilac bush over these wet clothes any day."

Once again, they left a trail of clothing from the front door to the back of the house.

It was getting to be a habit. The storm had passed. The air smelled fresh, and the bushes beneath the glow of the security light glistened as if they'd been dressed in white diamonds.

Somewhere in another part of the house, her clothes dryer rumbled as Boone's clothing tossed within the drum. Rachel stood at the window overlooking the back yard, listening to the runoff from the rain flowing downward toward the trees. Ultimately, she knew, it would wind up in the small creek far below her house. The one where she and Boone had first met.

"Come to bed, Rachel. You're going to freeze."

She turned. Boone lay sprawled upon her bed. Although there was a sheet covering the lower half of his body, the thin covering did little to hide the length of his legs or his underlying strength.

She bit her lip, hesitant to speak of what she was thinking.

"I love the way things look after a rain. Everything is fresh and clean and shining. It always makes me think of new beginnings."

She clasped her hands beneath her chin, then let them drop to her sides, and Boone could tell by the way she was standing that she hadn't said what she wanted to say.

"What are you thinking, honey?"

Her voice was soft and full of hope. "Of new beginnings."

He stifled a groan. God help him, no one would like that more than he would.

"Come here," he said gruffly. Rachel came without hesitation.

"Do you believe me when I say I love you more than my own life?" he asked.

Rachel's throat began to close. She couldn't discuss this with him without feeling an odd sort of panic. She kept thinking of the old newspaper clipping she'd found in South Dakota. The one claiming a woman named Mercy Hollister had been responsible for an outlaw's death.

"Well, do you?" Boone asked.

She nodded.

"Okay, then listen, and try to read between the lines. I wish to God I could tell you what's going on in my life, but I can't…at least, not right now."

"That's okay," she said softly.

"No, it's not okay," Boone retorted. "In fact, it's a great big mess. But if I promise you it will get better, will you wait for me?"

Her heart soared. It was the first hint of anything between them resembling a future.

"I've been waiting forever," she said. "A few more life-times won't make that much difference."

He laughed softly and held her close. But Rachel couldn't find much humor in what she'd said. What frightened her most was being pretty sure they'd already messed up once. She didn't want to think about going through all this turmoil only to find they'd failed again to get it right.

Just before daylight, she helped him dress. His clothes were still warm from the dryer.

"I could get used to this," Boone said, as Rachel handed him his shirt. He put it on, then absently tucked it into the waistband of his Levi's before sitting down on the bed to pull on his boots.

"So could I," Rachel said, combing her fingers through his thick black hair.

"So what are you going to do today?" Boone asked.

Rachel plopped down on the bed. "I don't know. I've thought about going back to work. I feel so useless just sitting up here waiting to run amok."

He frowned. "I know some people in Oklahoma City,"

he said, and then added, before she could bring up the fact, "They aren't anything like Snake and Tommy Joe, trust me."

She looked away, hating that he'd brought the reality of his life into their own little world.

He was already saying more about himself than he should, but he couldn't stop talking.

"I could ask around. Find out if they know a good shrink." It was obvious from the way she was behaving that she didn't want to hear what he was saying. "Please, honey…there's got to be a reason why this is happening to you. I just want you well. It scares the hell out of me when I think how close you've come to real danger."

"Do you think it doesn't scare me, too?" she said, and tried to pull away.

He pulled her onto his lap, kissing the side of her cheek and her chin until she was forced to look at him.

"We've never talked about life before *us,* have we?" he asked.

She shook her head. There wasn't much to tell about hers, and she'd been afraid to ask about his.

"Rachel…"

She wouldn't answer. He sighed. This was getting them nowhere, and it was almost daylight. Although her house was far enough from the road to hide his car, he didn't want to push his luck. He had to be out of here before sunrise.

"Never mind," he said softly. "Just remember, anything broken can always be fixed."

She threw her arms around his neck and then clung to him in fear. "No, Boone, you're wrong. Remember what I do for a living?"

He knew what was coming.

"I've seen too many broken bodies and too many broken homes. Sometimes life just isn't fair."

He held her tight and closed his eyes. If he didn't think

about losing her, then maybe it wouldn't happen. Moments later, he looked up and out the window. The thick brew of night was swiftly diluting.

"Rachel, sweetheart, I've got to go."

"I know," she said, and lifted her lips for one last kiss.

It came, and with it all the reluctance Boone was feeling. He tore himself away with a groan, then headed for the door. Yet in spite of the urgency, something kept pulling at him, warning him.... *If you leave, you may never come back.* He turned, wanting to remember her all soft from sleep, wearing a well-loved smile and little else.

He got what he wanted.

"If you love me...trust me," he said.

Rachel never saw him go. The last thing she heard was his plea, and then the air began to thicken and the light began to shift, breaking into refractions and angles that didn't make sense. She groaned and clutched the bed for support as Dakota turned and looked at Mercy from the doorway of a dusty cabin.

He tossed a rifle toward her as she sat on the bed. "If you love me like you say you do...then don't let me hang."

Mercy caught the gun in midair, then screamed out his name. It was too late. He was already gone.

Rachel came too with a groan, then looked around for Boone. He was nowhere in sight.

"Dear God, dear God," she muttered, and jumped to her feet.

The coincidence between Boone's parting and what she'd just seen was too much to bear. She ran through the house, calling his name. When he didn't answer, she ran out of the house, onto the porch. The taillights of his pickup truck were just disappearing around the bend in the drive.

She dashed into the yard, waving frantically at him. "Boone! Wait! Come back! Come back!"

It was too late. He was already gone.

* * *

Water dripped from the leaves and down onto the man's hooded coat. He hunched his shoulders against the cold and took a step backward, although he was well hidden behind the trees in which he stood. His purpose: watching the driveway leading to Rachel Brant's home.

Driven by a jealousy he could no longer contain, he'd followed Boone MacDonald out of town, then all the way up the mountain, taking care to stay at least a quarter of a mile behind him. But when the taillights of Boone's pickup suddenly disappeared, it meant either the driver had parked to wait out the storm, or he was taking shelter elsewhere in a lying woman's arms. To his dismay, when he topped the hill where he'd last seen the truck, it was nowhere in sight.

Now, as he shifted from one leg to the other, tired of the cold and of the hatred eating at him from inside, he waited to see if he'd been right all along.

The sun was minutes from the horizon when a dark blue pickup suddenly appeared at the end of the drive, the driver momentarily pausing to check the main road. Even from where he was standing, he could see the driver's face. Rage rattled the edge in his voice as he watched Boone MacDonald turn up the mountain and drive out of sight.

"I'll kill them both," he muttered. "So help me God, I will kill them both."

Boone paced the trailer with nervous intent. He'd been in this business too long not to trust his own instincts, and they were warning him that something was going to happen. He could feel it. But he was ready. He wanted this job to be over. What worried him was Rachel. If Denver's boys found out about her, he shuddered to think what they might do, especially after he'd called Snake down for making a pass at her. The little weasel was still holding a grudge. And because he knew better than to ignore his own intuition, he picked up the phone. It was time to confess—at least up to a point—about what he had done.

"This is Waco. Is this you?"

"It's me, Captain. I don't have much time."

Susan Cross shoved aside the file on which she'd been working, giving Boone her full attention. "What's up?"

"I need you to do something for me," he said quickly.

"Name it."

"There's a woman. Her name is Rachel Brant."

A soft curse slipped into the one-sided conversation, settling on Boone's nerves like a slap.

"Just listen," he muttered. "You can give me hell later."

"I'm listening," she said.

"If anything should happen to me, I want your promise that you'll make sure she's protected in any way necessary."

"Boone, what the hell have you done?"

"Fallen in love."

"Dear God," Susan said, and rubbed at a pain shooting up the back of her neck. "Does she know anything?"

"No, she loves Boone. She doesn't know I exist."

"Do you know what you've done?"

"Yes, ma'am," Boone said sharply. "Why the hell do you think I called you?"

Susan sighed. "To fix another one of your messes, I assume."

"I knew there was a reason I loved you," he said softly.

"Oh shut up," Susan said. "I'm immune to your charm."

"You love me and you know it," Boone said.

"I want your ass back here at headquarters in the morning, or I'll know the reason why," she ordered.

He sighed. It was to be expected. "I'll see what I can do," he said.

"No! You do what *I* said," Susan said.

The click at the other end of the line did not make her happy. She swiveled around in her chair and picked up her other phone.

"Bennet, get Wayland in here on the double, and tell him to pack a bag. He might be staying a while."

Susan Cross's angry voice was still ringing in Boone's ear as he walked into Jimmy's Place. The place was crawling with customers. It seemed as if every other citizen of Razor Bend had come to town all at once, and half of them were gathering here.

"What's going on?" Boone asked, as a man hurried by.

"Jimmy's having a drawing. Every hour, on the hour. You have to be present to win."

Boone looked around the room, absently fiddling with his key ring as he realized the impact of what was taking place. Jimmy was a smart man. If people had to wait to win a prize, they spent money while they waited. Candy and chips were flying off the shelves, and the door to the cooler was banging on a regular basis as customers reached for cans and bottles of pop to wash it all down. The air was thick with smoke from burgers cooking on the grill, and people were laughing and talking among themselves as they waited for the hour to come around.

Boone frowned. From the looks of things, it was going to take longer than he'd expected to buy a couple of quarts of motor oil, but it didn't really matter. His days were all the same. He felt as if he were caught in the middle of a long, dark tunnel and all he could do was wait for a light to appear and show him the way out.

He took a step back and knew it was a mistake by the body-to-body impact he made with the man behind him. The ring of keys slipped out of his hands, hitting the floor with a loud, distinct clink.

Boone reached down at the same time as the man he had bumped.

"Sorry, buddy," Charlie Dutton said, as he picked up the keys. "It's pretty crowded in…"

The keys were splayed, and one in particular stood out from the rest. It was shiny and new and marked with the letter *B* in red fingernail polish. The implication of that key on this ring stunned him, and the urge to put his fist in the big man's face was overwhelming.

I only gave him a ride, not the key to my house.

Rachel's words rang in Charlie's ears like a death knell. My God, girl, what have you done?

Boone straightened, his fists doubled, readying himself for the blow he sensed was coming. Instead, Charlie took a deep breath, then dropped the keys in Boone's hand.

Time seemed to stop. Eye-to-eye, they stood without moving, gauging each other's intent. Charlie was the first to speak. He pointed to the keys he'd just handed Boone.

"A man needs to be real careful about his keys."

Boone looked down at the ring in the palm of his hand. There, shining out from the others, was a small gold key with a bright red *B*. His heart stopped.

Rachel.

He looked at Charlie again. An intense stare passed between them again, and this time it was Boone who broke the silence.

"You don't need to worry," he said quietly. "I'm real careful about all my things."

Charlie wanted to hate him, but there was something about the look in Boone MacDonald's eyes that led him down another emotional path. "You take care now," Charlie said, and moved away through the crowd.

When the man was gone, Boone started to shake. He didn't have to wonder what that was all about. It had been obvious from the start. Rachel had worked with that man. He knew her habits, and he'd obviously seen her mark keys like this before. And with that knowledge came another thought, even worse than what had just occurred. Charlie Dutton wasn't the only one who might have noticed the marked key.

Without giving it a second thought, he'd handed his keys over to Snake Martin as if he were handing him a match.

What in hell have I done?

A middle-aged couple barreled past him, laughing and waving to a man on the other side of the room. Boone stepped aside to let them pass, and as he did, he felt a touch on the back of his hand. It was little more than a brush of flesh against flesh, but it was enough to get his attention. He looked down. His heartbeat jerked, then kicked back in at an irregular pace. He knew that face, those curls, those beseeching blue eyes.

He squatted down until he was level with her gaze.

"Well, hello, Punkin," he said softly and held out one hand.

She ducked her head, then looked back again, this time wearing a smile.

"Already learning to flirt, are you?" he asked.

Although his meaning was lost on her, she giggled, pleased to have been noticed.

Boone wondered if she could possibly remember him, and then decided she couldn't. All that smoke and steam, and then hanging upside down, it was a wonder she'd remembered her own name. He searched her face for remnants of the wreck. The bruises were gone, as were the scratches and cuts. The only visible sign of what she'd endured was a small red mark near her temple. The scar would fade with time, as would her loss.

He winked and started to tousle her curls. But Punkin had other ideas. She grabbed his finger, just as she had the day of the wreck. Her grip was firm, her jaw determined.

"Boo," she said clearly.

"So, pretty baby, you do remember me."

"Melissa Ann, you leave that man alone!"

Boone jerked as if he'd been slapped as the little girl was suddenly yanked away. The middle-aged woman staring down at him wore a fearful expression on her face. He couldn't blame her. Boone MacDonald wasn't the kind of man to trust with any woman, no matter their age. He stood.

"I'm sorry, ma'am. I wasn't…" he began, but Charlie Dutton suddenly appeared once again at his side.

"Hey, Esther, how are things going? I see you and Boone are finally getting to meet."

Esther Worlie looked puzzled. Losing her son-in-law had been shock enough, and her daughter was just now able to move about on her own. When she turned around in the crowd and realized the baby was nowhere in sight, her heart had stopped. Seeing Melissa with this man had set off a new kind of panic.

When Boone would have walked off into the crowd without explaining himself, Charlie halted his exit with an unexpected introduction.

"Esther, this is the man who witnessed Paul and Sally's wreck. He called it in and stayed with them until we got there." An odd look passed between Charlie and Boone, as if neither of them could believe they were still talking to each other. "Boone MacDonald, isn't it?" Charlie asked.

Wordlessly Boone nodded.

Esther Worlie looked back at Boone, seeing him in a whole other light. A dark red flush spread over her face.

"Why…I had no idea," she muttered, then looked down at her granddaughter, who was cowering behind her leg. "Come here, Melissa, it's all right." When the child didn't budge, she bent down and picked her up. "I guess I scared her," she said. "It doesn't take much these days to set her off."

Boone hurt for the fear on the little girl's face. "I'm very sorry for your loss," he said softly. "I hope Punkin's mother is doing all right."

Esther looked even more surprised by Boone's use of her granddaughter's nickname than by his concern for her daughter's well-being.

"Why, yes, she is…thank you."

Boone needed to get away. This conversation was becoming dangerous. It was too congenial—too ordinary—for a man like him to be having.

"I guess I'll get my motor oil another day," he said quietly, and started to walk away when Esther Worlie stopped him.

"Mr. MacDonald?"

"Yes, ma'am?"

"You called my granddaughter Punkin."

He frowned. "Yes, ma'am."

"That was what Paul called her. No one else in the family ever calls her that." She looked at her granddaughter again, hesitant about how much to say in front of the child. "How did you know?" she asked. "I mean…Paul was already…"

Suddenly Boone understood. Her daughter had been unconscious. Her son-in-law dead. Who'd told him?

Boone ran his hand over the top of the little girl's head, gently tousling the abundant and unruly curls.

"I asked this pretty thing her name…and she told me, didn't you, Punkin?"

Esther Worlie's face fell. Her eyes teared, and her lips began to tremble. "She told you her name was Punkin?"

Boone nodded. "Yes, ma'am, she did. I guess the wreck cost her more than a daddy, didn't it? If no one ever calls her Punkin anymore, then she lost her identity, as well."

Esther Worlie had a lot to consider as she walked away with her grandchild in her arms.

Boone watched until they disappeared in the crowd, then turned to Charlie, who'd remained a silent bystander during the odd conversation. Boone's eyes narrowed as he studied the intent expression on the man's face.

"I owe you," Boone said.

Charlie shrugged. "One of these days I'll collect."

There was too much tension between them for Boone to stay any longer. "I'm out of here," he said, and walked away.

Chapter 14

Although Boone was nowhere in sight, Agent B. J. Wayland wasn't bashful. He wasted no time in checking his old friend's messages. He'd been sent to find him and bring him out, and that wouldn't happen unless he knew where he'd gone.

A cockroach scuttled across the floor beside his tennis shoe as he considered his options. He stepped on the bug and replayed the message.

"Boone, Denver says come on over around eight. He's got someone he wants you to meet."

B.J. checked his watch and frowned. It was five minutes until eight. Having been briefed on the situation, he knew all about Denver Cherry, as well as his cohorts. He took a cell phone out of his jacket pocket and made a call.

"Captain, he's not here, but there's a message on his machine that leads me to think something's about to go down. Didn't you tell me he's never met the man behind the scenes?"

"That's right," Susan Cross said.

"I think he's about to," B.J. said.

"Do you know where?"

"Denver Cherry's…I think."

"You have the location," Susan said. "Get over there now. From the way Boone was talking earlier today, I think he expects trouble."

Wayland grinned. "Want me to go in shooting or wait for someone else to fire the first shot?"

Susan rolled her eyes. "You hotshots are all alike. You know the routine. I'm sending down backup...just in case. They'll have your number. You coordinate."

"All right," Wayland said.

"And, Wayland..."

"Yes, Captain?"

"Just get him out of there alive, okay?"

Wayland's smile turned cold. "Yes, ma'am...I'll do my best."

Boone's nerves were on edge. When he pulled up in front of Denver Cherry's house, he noticed Denver's vehicle was missing. Snake and Tommy Joe came out of the house as he parked and got out, and with every step he took, his gut instinct was to duck and run. This didn't feel right.

"Where's Denver?" he asked.

As always, Tommy Joe deferred to Snake, letting him answer.

"At the lab," Snake said, and then glanced at his watch.

Boone's hopes fell. Not only had he never met the boss, he'd been unable to find the new location of the lab. "Then the meeting is off?"

"Nope," Snake said. "You're coming with us. The boss is already there."

Boone felt torn. This was what he'd been waiting for, but it wasn't the way he'd wanted it to happen. "I'll follow you," he said, and started toward his truck.

"No way," Snake said. "We can't have no damned parade on the way up. You go with us. Boss's orders."

Tommy Joe was as nervous as Boone had ever seen him.

That alone gave Boone food for thought. While Boone was pretending disinterest in the entire affair, in reality his mind was in overdrive. Something was up besides a meeting, and as he slid onto the seat between Snake and Tommy Joe, he had a sudden sense of his own mortality. As they drove away, the last thought in his mind was of Rachel. He'd never gotten to tell her goodbye.

The narrow blacktop highway up this side of the Kiamichis was unmarked and unlit. At night, unless you were familiar with its twists and turns, it could be deadly. Snake drove with his usual disregard for oncoming traffic and the laws of gravity, while Boone took comfort in the small loaded handgun concealed inside the top of his boot.

The radio was blaring a sad country song with which Snake felt compelled to sing along. Tommy Joe rode with his left elbow in Boone's ribs and his other one hanging out the open window. The wind whipped through the cab, drowning out the worst of Snake's voice and easing the stench of sweat from the two men's unwashed bodies. Boone never took his eyes from Snake's hands. Of the two men, he trusted him the least. It was his first mistake.

Snake slammed on his brakes without warning and shot off the road to the right, barreling down the driveway leading to Rachel Brant's house before Boone had time to react.

"What the hell are you—?"

The familiar feel of a gun in his ribs ended his question. He looked at Tommy Joe with surprise.

"Sorry," Tommy Joe said. "Just following orders."

Snake hit the brakes near the front porch steps, coming to a halt right beside a dark, shiny car. Boone's heart stopped. He recognized the car, even knew the man who drove it, and at this point, he didn't even want to consider what all this meant.

"Get out," Snake ordered, and grabbed Boone by the

arm, dragging him beneath the steering wheel and out of the truck.

Boone didn't argue. Tommy Joe's gun was too close to the small of his back.

Their footsteps were loud on the old wooden porch, and Snake shoved Boone through the door first without bothering to knock.

From the first, Boone had faced the dangers of living life as an undercover cop. Over the years, he'd prepared himself for just about any situation that could possibly have occurred. But there was no way in hell he could have predicted he would find the woman he loved in another man's arms.

Despair gave way to a ballooning, white-hot pain, and for a moment Boone wondered if he'd been shot. But when he took a deep breath, he realized the only thing shot was his faith. The expression in his eyes went flat. A muscle jerked in his jaw as a cold, derisive smile spread across his face.

Rachel was still reeling from the shock of opening her door, expecting to see Boone, and finding Griffin Ross waiting instead. He'd asked to use her phone, but that had been three minutes ago, and he had yet to make a move toward it, or the table on which it was sitting. Instead, he kept glancing nervously out the window, then back at her, muttering things that made no sense.

Just when Rachel thought this night couldn't get any worse, more car lights suddenly appeared, and instead of curiosity about who it could be, Griffin Ross was all but jumping up and down in an odd kind of delight.

"Griff, what on earth…?"

He spun, grabbing her by the arm. She didn't know what shocked her most, the grip with which he was holding her, or the crazy grin on his face.

"What's wrong with you?" Rachel cried, trying to yank free from his hand.

Instead of being set free, she was attacked. He slammed her up against the wall, grinding his lower body against her hips and his mouth against her lips. Shock passed swiftly into disbelief. This couldn't be happening...not to her... and not with Griff.

She tried to scream, but when she opened her mouth, he thrust his tongue inside. All but gagging at the unexpected intrusion, Rachel hammered helplessly at his chest with her hands.

And then the front door opened. Her freedom was as sudden as her violation had been. Stunned, she watched Griffin turn, then smile at the men who came through the door.

"Oh, my God," she groaned, and wiped her hand across her face. Everything she'd been experiencing up to this point had prepared her for an understanding she wasn't ready to face. Something told her this was the beginning of the end.

The look on Boone's face broke her heart. She knew how this would look. Her first thought was to explain.

She started toward him, but Griffin grabbed her, yanking her roughly against him, then sliding his arm beneath her breasts and holding her fast.

The shock was so sudden and so rough that it left her momentarily breathless, and in that moment, when she couldn't speak, she realized that Boone had not come in of his own accord. There was a gun in his back. Her hesitation was just long enough for Boone to say what was on his mind.

"Well, hell, Rachel. You're quite a little trooper, aren't you? That must be some man you've got, to let him talk you into sleeping with his enemies."

"You're quite a little soldier, aren't you, Mercy? Since you've ridden every man you rode with, I guess you..."

"No!" she screamed, struggling to get free of Griffin's clutch. It *was* happening all over again, just as she'd feared, and unless she could figure out a way to change it, she was going to be responsible for another outlaw's death.

Griff splayed his hands across her breasts in a rude but possessive gesture. "What's wrong, little Rachel? Did you get a little too attached to this pig?"

"You're the pig!" she cried, and kicked backward at his shins, trying to free herself from his grasp.

"You can cut the play," Boone said. "You won, Rachel. I hope you and your socially correct boyfriend live a long and miserable life on other people's money."

Rachel didn't know what he was talking about, but she knew how this must look. Boone wasn't going to help her. It was up to her to save them both. Then, to her dismay, Griffin Ross pulled a gun out of his pocket and jammed it into her throat.

"Take him out back," he ordered. "Before we let these two lovers follow each other to hell, there's some unfinished business sweet Rachel and I have between us, isn't there, darling?"

Boone froze. Two lovers? Follow each other to hell? He stared at Rachel, at the shock on her face and the fear in her eyes, and wondered if he'd read this all wrong.

"Rachel, I…"

She moved like a wildcat thrown into a den of pups. Screaming at the top of her lungs, she spun and lunged, leaving claw marks down Griffin Ross's face before she kicked him in the crotch. He dropped the gun to grab his face, falling backward over the only light in the room. As if in answer to a prayer, the room went dark.

Snake never saw the kick coming. One minute he was in control; the next thing he felt was his supper coming up uninvited as Boone's boot hit him square in the belly. Tommy Joe ducked and fired the gun at the same time, and because he did, the shot went wild. It was all the chance Rachel needed. She grabbed Boone by the arm.

"Run!" she screamed, and started through the house,

moving on instinct and memory around furniture and walls, pulling him with her.

As they reached the kitchen, she paused long enough to throw the main switch on the breaker box. Boone yanked her by the arm.

"What are you trying to prove?"

"That I love you!" Rachel screamed. "Now run, damn it, run!"

He didn't have to be told twice. They bolted out the back door and into the yard, running past the shrubs and the swing, out into the wide-open space between her house and the woods beyond.

Just let me get her out of range of that damned security light and into the trees, Boone thought.

Gunfire suddenly erupted behind them. The lights were back on. Someone had found the switch. Boone heard the screen door slam and then a rash of wild, angry shouts.

He shoved Rachel in front of him, not wanting her to be an easy target at his side.

"Keep going!" he yelled.

She ran without looking back, confident from the sound of his footsteps at her heels that he would follow.

"There they go!" someone shouted.

Rachel winced at the sound of Griffin's voice. He must be crazy!

Fear lent speed to her steps, although she was getting winded. A stitch was pulling in her side, and her legs felt like rubber. No matter how fast they ran, the trees didn't seem any closer.

Gunfire came again, like firecrackers going off on the Fourth of July, and Rachel had a fleeting thought that she would never like fireworks again. She wanted to look back, to see if Boone was still behind her, but she was afraid that if she stopped she wouldn't be able to take another step.

Again the sound of gunshots shattered the silence, echoing from one side of the Kiamichis to the other, until Rachel couldn't tell where the shots had originated.

Then she looked up, and to her relief, the trees were right before them. Elation lent a fresh spurt of energy to her stride. Because she was so certain that they were safe, she didn't see Boone stagger and then pull himself upright. All she knew was that when they moved into the shelter of the forest, he was behind her all the way.

Wayland cursed his bad luck four ways to Sunday. He'd gotten to Denver Cherry's house just in time to see the tail-lights of a vehicle in the distance. Boone's truck was parked in the yard, but it didn't take more than a quick glance at the house to see that no one was there. Moving on instinct rather than knowledge, B. J. Wayland took after the tail-lights and hoped to hell he wasn't following some couple who were going off to the woods to neck. He would have some difficulty explaining if he caught them peeled down and going at it.

Twice he feared he'd lost them, but then he would catch a glimpse of the lights disappearing around another bend in the road.

"Damn roads aren't much better than a goat path," he muttered as he took a curve at high speed. Give him a flat road and a hot car any day over this hide-and-seek.

He flew past the small dirt road on his left like a blind bat coming out of hell with his tail on fire, moving with no sense of direction except fast and forward. It was pure luck and a good angle in the road that made him realize the car he'd been following had turned off. He glanced up in his rearview mirror just as Snake Martin hit the brakes in front of Rachel Brant's house.

B.J. stomped on his own brakes and went into a slide. The car spun sideways. When B.J. came to a stop, the smell of hot rubber drifted up through the heating system into the interior of his car, and the headlights were pointing in the direction from which he'd just come.

"Just like in the movies," he drawled, and gunned the car forward.

He parked in the trees at the end of the driveway and then got out, intending to go the rest of the way on foot. But he never made it past the front of his car before all the lights in the house went out. At the first sounds of gunfire, he grabbed his cell phone and hit redial as he started to run.

"Cross here."

"It's going down!" Wayland said as he ran. "Get me some backup, Captain. It doesn't sound pretty."

"What's your location?" she asked.

"Damned if I know!" Wayland yelled. "About five miles below Boone's trailer and into the trees. Just follow the sound of gunfire. You can't miss us."

"Wayland, don't do—"

"Gotta go, Captain. Catch you later."

The line went dead in Susan Cross's ear. She slammed the phone down as she bolted from the room. God save them all.

Boone hadn't planned on getting shot. But then, a sane man never actively searched for different ways to die. His shoulder felt numb, and the farther they ran, the lighter his head was getting. They had to find a place to hide, at least until he got his second wind. He hadn't come this far to fall flat on his face. And then he staggered as a tree suddenly jumped into his path. It was luck that kept him upright and moving...that and Rachel. To his overwhelming relief, she began to slow down and seemed to be searching the area for a specific location.

"Over here," she said, and took him by the hand.

He went where she led him, weaving around trees and staggering through bushes until they entered a tiny clearing, little more than six feet in diameter. Completely surrounded

by a dense stand of evergreens, their location seemed safe…
at least for the time being.

Rachel stopped, her heart pounding as she drew harsh,
aching breaths through burning lungs. She peered back
through the trees, unable to see anything beyond the
branches in front of her face, and exhaled slowly.

Safe. Now they were safe. She turned. Even in the darkness, the expression on Boone's face was too plain to conceal. Fear for what he'd seen…for what he'd so terribly
misunderstood washed over her.

"Boone…darling, you've got to understand. I didn't
know…."

He swayed, and she caught him. A new fear surfaced as
she steadied him where he stood. His breath came in short,
aching grunts. His shirt was wet with sweat. And then a terrible thought dawned. Despite their frantic race to safety,
it was too cold for him to be sweating to this degree. She
looked at her hand. Even in the darkness, the bloodstain
was impossible to miss.

"Dear God! Boone, why didn't you tell me?"

He went down on his knees to keep from falling.

Instead of an answer, he threw a question back in her
face.

"Why did you change your mind?" he muttered, and
dropped his head between his knees, trying desperately to
keep from passing out.

Rachel groaned. With all the medical skill in her head,
she had none of it at her fingertips.

"About what?" she asked as she undid his shirt, searching by feel, rather than sight, to test for damage.

"About your boyfriend. You already had me cold. What
made you change your mind?"

She attributed his rambling questions to shock as she felt
along his back for an entrance wound. And then she found
it and breathed a small sigh of relief. It seemed to be safely

away from his heart and spinal column, although she had
no way of knowing what the angle of the trajectory had
been. She closed her eyes, picturing in her mind the internal workings of the human body and what damage the
bullet could have done. There were too many variables to
assume anything.

"Oh, God, what I wouldn't give for Charlie Dutton now,"
she muttered.

"He's in love with you," Boone said, and then slumped
forward.

Determined to keep panic out of her voice, she eased
Boone down on his side. "And I'm in love with you," she
said. "That would make for quite an odd group, don't you
think?"

Shoving back the front of his shirt, she moved her exami-
nation to the front of his chest, searching for a point of exit,
and then groaned. There was none. She checked his back
again and stifled new panic. Blood was no longer seeping.
It was starting to flow.

Pressure. She needed packing and pressure. Without hesitation, she yanked off her shirt and began folding it up.

"Rachel, I…"

"Hush," she whispered. "I need to stop the bleeding."

She stuffed the thick pad she'd made beneath his shirt,
centering it on the hole in his back.

"Easy, sweetheart," she said as she eased him onto his
back, using his own body weight for pressure on her make-
shift bandage. For now, it was all she could do.

Boone looked up. Rachel's face was wavering in and out
of focus, as if she were a dark angel hovering above him.
Consciousness was slipping fast. He didn't know whether
he was just passing out or about to die, but there was something she needed to know. He grabbed her hand with surprising force.

"In my boot…there's a gun."

She gasped. "I don't know how to shoot."

"Get it," he said, and then groaned. "All you have to do is aim and fire. The bullet will do the rest."

"Oh, my God," she muttered, and pulled the thing out with trembling hands.

"Rachel."

She leaned down, her breath just a whisper above his face. "Yes, darling."

"I'm not who you think I am."

Tears blurred her vision of his face as she rested her forehead against his chest.

"You're going to get well," she said, focusing her energy on this man who'd stolen her heart. "I'll go anywhere with you. Live anywhere you say. I don't care who you are or what you do, just don't leave me, Boone. Dear God, don't leave me again."

He frowned. She wasn't making sense. He'd never left her before, so how could he leave her again? But one thing she'd said soaked into his fuzzy brain. She still believed he was an outlaw, and was willing to run with him if that was what it took for them to be together.

He went weak, and he didn't know if it was from lack of blood or the wash of emotion flooding him. He'd waited all his life for a woman like her, and now it might be too late.

"You don't understand," he kept saying. "I'm not the bad guy, Griffin Ross is the bad guy."

Though she still misunderstood what he was trying to say, she would have agreed with him about anything.

"I know that," she said softly, smoothing the hair away from his face, then clenched her teeth to keep from raging with helplessness. His skin was cold and clammy. Symptoms of shock.

She thrust her hand beneath his back to make sure the bandage was still in place, and then stifled a scream. It was already soaked.

"Rachel, I want you to leave me here. If you head toward the road, you can go for help."

She leaned forward until he could feel her breath on his face. "Just shut up and rest," she said. "We're in this together, and we're going to come out of it the same way."

He swallowed a groan. It was too damned ironic to believe. He'd thought for sure when he walked into her house that his cover had been blown. Rachel had gone to South Dakota. She'd told him so without blinking an eye. He'd been born in South Dakota. Rachel had dumped her boyfriend, then fallen for *him*. Then the boyfriend had turned out to be the man behind Denver Cherry's operation. Finally Rachel had turned up in the boyfriend's arms. It had all been so neat. And he'd been so very wrong.

He clutched at Rachel's hand, but she kept slipping away. Panic began to spread. This wasn't fair. He couldn't die. Not when he'd just found her.

"Denver Cherry wasn't the real boss. I never knew who my boss was," he muttered. "They were taking me to meet the boss."

Rachel groaned. She'd suspected that Boone was mixed up with drugs, but refused to consider the possibility. Hearing Denver Cherry's name confirmed her worst suspicions. His reputation had long preceded him, although the authorities had yet to prove a thing that could put him in prison. Now Boone was admitting what she'd refused to believe.

"Rachel...damn it, are you listening?" Boone said, and then broke out in a wave of cold sweat. "Hell," he muttered weakly.

Rachel pressed her hand above his heart; the beat was faint, almost too faint to be felt. Frantic, she thrust her fingers against his neck, searching for a pulse. It was there. Thready...but there.

His eyelids fell shut, and his head rolled sideways. In

that moment, Rachel knew true terror. Clutching the front of his shirt with both hands, she gave him a vicious jerk.

"Boone! Damn you, don't die on me, do you understand?"

His eyes came open. "What's it take to get a little sleep around here?" he muttered.

"You talk to me," she said.

"Where's the gun?"

She glanced around. It was by her knee, where she'd dropped it.

"Here," she said.

"Don't put it down again," he said, and for some reason the quiet authority in his voice moved past her panic to a reality she suddenly understood.

"I won't," she said, and set it in her lap, one hand on it at all times.

He started to talk, and at first Rachel thought he was rambling. But the longer she listened, the clearer it finally became.

"They were taking me to meet the boss. Denver wasn't the boss. They were taking me to meet the boss."

"Oh…my…God!" She leaned forward, cupping Boone's cheek until he finally focused again on her face.

"Rachel…I love you. Did I tell you I loved you?"

"Yes, darling, and you told me so much more, didn't you? You were trying to tell me Griff is the real boss, weren't you?"

A smile broke through the pain. He relaxed. She finally understood.

"I'm just going to rest now," he said. "Be right back, okay?"

But before Rachel could answer, sounds outside the trees in which they were hiding brought her to a new level of fear. Before she could react, the branches of the evergreens parted and Griffin Ross came staggering through, cursing as the thick branches slapped and stung at his face. She swallowed a moan. They'd been found!

If you love me, don't let me hang.

For Rachel, the message was loud and clear. She grabbed the gun from her lap and then stood with one foot on either side of Boone's prone body. Griff was going to have to come through her to get to Boone.

Griffin's gun was dangling from his hand as he shoved the last branch aside. When he saw Boone sprawled out on the ground, seemingly lifeless—just the way he wanted him—a smile of pure evil spread across his face. The fact that Rachel was only half dressed made it all the better.

There was still a cold smile on his face as he kicked at the toe of Boone's boot.

"Did I interrupt your little tryst?" Griff sneered.

Rachel's head started to throb.

"Get away from him!" she muttered.

"And what if I don't want to?" Griff asked, and started toward her.

Pain shafted from the back of her head and then spiraled down her neck. Her heart was racing, her hands were shaking, but there was a newfound resolve that she didn't understand. She didn't even know how to hold a gun, and yet she found it light, even comfortable in the palm of her hand.

"I know that you can shoot...so if you love me...don't let me hang."

Understanding dawned. That was it! She couldn't shoot, but Mercy could. *Okay, girl, you've been haunting my sleep, so help me now, or forever hold your peace.*

"Then I guess I'll just have to make you," Rachel said, and lifted her arm. Steadying the gun with both hands, she aimed at the biggest target she could see, which was the dead center of Griffin Ross's chest.

He stopped in midstep as shock spread across his face. He hadn't expected the gun. When it bloomed at the barrel, he wasn't prepared for the jolt of bullet to flesh, or for the numbness to spread so fast.

"You bitch!" he gasped, and tried to aim his own gun. But something was the matter with his arm. He stared down at his hand, watching in disbelief as the gun fell to the ground at his feet.

The ground was coming at him in waves. He looked up. "No fair," he mumbled.

"You already told me life wasn't fair, Griff. Don't you remember?"

He hated her for throwing his own words back in his face.

"I'll kill you," he said, and reached toward her.

The second shot knocked him flat on his back. "No, you won't," she said in a quiet, shaky voice. "Because you're already dead."

It might have been seconds. It might have been minutes. But a short time later, Rachel heard someone shouting as he ran through the trees. She didn't recognize the voice, but what he said sent her out to meet him.

"MacDonald! Where the hell are you, buddy? It's me. B.J.! Come on, man, answer me."

B. J. Wayland wasn't prepared for the woman who burst out of the trees. The gun she was waving made him nervous, but he took one look at her face, then registered the fact that she was minus a shirt, and decided to trust her.

"In here!" Rachel screamed, waving him to come inside. "He's been shot. We need an ambulance!"

B.J. blanched. Following her guidance, he pushed his way past the trees and stumbled on Griffin Ross's prone body as he entered the clearing.

"What the—?"

"He's dead," she said, and then her voice changed pitch as she let go of the panic she'd been holding in place. "Please! Oh, God, help me! Boone needs help!"

B.J. whipped out his cell phone and called for an ambu-

lance while Rachel sank to her knees, back at Boone's side.
Moments later, he knelt beside her, doing his own test run
on Boone's injuries and vitals. The weak pulse scared him.

"It won't take them long to get here," he promised. "The
ambulance and local authorities were already at the house."

"But…how?"

"I called them to come pick up those two losers in your
flower bed. I hope you don't mind. The fat one's in the yellow mums, and there's a skinny one who's taking himself
a last swing."

Rachel shuddered. The image of what had taken place
at her home was horrible. She'd believed it to be her haven,
and instead it had become a place of death.

"But who are you?" she asked. "And how do you know
Boone?"

B.J. shrugged. "Men like us stick together."

She didn't understand and, at this point, she didn't really
care. All she wanted was for Boone to wake up. She leaned
down, patting his cheek in a gentle, constant motion.

"Boone, can you hear me? It's over. All you have to do
is wake up and get well." Her voice broke. "Please, Boone,
don't leave me."

B.J. couldn't keep his eyes off her. Even in the darkness,
even with her hair disheveled and tiny scratches all over her
face and nearly bare upper body, the woman was stunning.
He took off his jacket and slipped it over her shoulders. She
hardly acknowledged the act.

"Are you Rachel?"

She nodded.

He looked down at Boone, remembering what the captain had told him about the situation. An odd grin broke the
somberness of his face.

"He won't die, honey," he said softly. "He's too damned
hardheaded to leave you behind for someone else."

Chapter 15

Rachel was hanging on to sanity by a thin, fragile thread. The halls of Comanche County Memorial in Lawton, Oklahoma, were well-lit and busy, but she couldn't see them for the darkness within her heart.

She looked up as Charlie Dutton slid into the seat beside her.

"Joanie sends her love. She says not to worry about a thing at your house. She'll get it all cleaned up before you get home."

Rachel blanched. Cleaned up? She'd forgotten the mayhem that had been done after she and Boone made a break for the door.

"Tell her thank-you," Rachel muttered, and couldn't bring herself to care if all four walls had fallen in. There was only one thing that mattered, and that was keeping Boone alive.

"Charlie?"

"Yeah?"

"Is he going to die?"

Charlie winced. Rachel looked so lost, so unsure, so unlike the Rachel he knew. She was wearing the blue long-sleeved shirt he'd had on under his uniform when they took Boone out of the woods. In a dark, selfish part of his soul,

Charlie had already let himself consider what might happen if Boone did die. Rachel would be free. But the thought hadn't been there long. When you cared for someone, you put her happiness ahead of your own all the way. He took her hand, squeezing it between his palms in a gesture of comfort.

"I don't know, honey. They're working on him now."

She shuddered, then swayed in the chair. Charlie slipped an arm around her shoulder and pulled her close.

"Lean on me, Rachel."

She accepted the offer. Silence stretched into endless minutes.

"Charlie."

"Yeah?"

"I'm sorry."

Her hair tickled the edge of his chin. Her shoulders were trembling. But what hurt most was the finality of it all. He couldn't kid himself any longer about her ever changing her mind. For better or worse, she was in love with another man. It was the tears on her face that broke his heart.

"I know, honey. So am I." *Oh, God...so am I.*

An hour passed, and then another. The sound of footsteps made Rachel look up each time someone passed, always hoping it was the doctor...and at the same time, afraid for him to come.

This time it wasn't the doctor. This time it was B. J. Wayland, and a middle-aged woman Rachel didn't know. Rachel straightened, slipping out from under the shelter of Charlie's arms as the woman stopped abruptly in front of where she was sitting.

"Rachel Brant?"

There was something in the woman's voice that demanded attention. Without asking herself why, Rachel stood.

"Yes, I'm Rachel Brant."

The woman held out her hand. "Captain Cross, DEA."

She glanced at B.J., then back at Rachel. Arching an eyebrow, she told Rachel, "*You* can call me Susan."

DEA?

Rachel wasn't the only one who was impressed. Charlie got to his feet and extended his hand.

"Charlie Dutton, paramedic out of Razor Bend," and then added, "Rachel is my partner."

Susan nodded. She understood about partners.

Rachel was afraid. If Denver Cherry had been running drugs and Boone had been working for Denver, then that meant these people were going to arrest Boone. She took a deep breath, lifted her chin and stared Susan Cross straight in the eyes.

"I don't know what Boone's done," she said quietly. "But I want you to know I plan to testify on his behalf as to the admirable qualities I had occasion to witness. Since I've known him, he's helped save a woman's and a child's lives, and he saved my life at the risk of his own."

Susan's eyebrow arched even farther.

"Told you, Captain," B.J. muttered. "She's the real thing. Blaine's a lucky SOB and that's a natural fact."

Susan Cross glared at B.J.'s slip of the lip and then gave Rachel a thoughtful look, although it seemed as if Rachel had missed the connection between Boone and Blaine. It was obvious to Susan that Rachel Brant was in severe distress about Boone MacDonald's health. It wasn't fair to let her think that if he lived, he would be imprisoned, as well.

"Come with me, Miss Brant. We need to talk."

Rachel hesitated.

"We won't go far," Susan said. "Just over there, by the windows. We can still see the doctor if he comes."

Rachel did as she asked. At this point, she would have done anything Susan Cross suggested.

But when they got there, instead of talking, Susan turned and stared out the windows overlooking the city of Lawton. She hadn't reached the age of fifty-five without facing some truths of her own. She was short, she was dumpy, and her hair was gunmetal gray. The only things she had going for her were her years on the force, her brains and her voice. That commanded authority. She demanded respect. For the most part, she got it. Her men trusted her, because she backed them one hundred percent.

She didn't want to lose the man in surgery, but when she saw Rachel Brant waiting with her heart in her eyes, she'd known the fight was already lost. She'd lost him to a woman who would never give him back.

Boone MacDonald was one of her toughest undercover agents. He would survive the surgery, of that she was convinced. But she'd taken one look at Rachel's beauty and heard her plea for clemency on his behalf and known that Boone would not survive losing Rachel Brant. And because of that, she divulged a truth she'd sworn to protect.

"He's one of ours, you know."

At first Rachel didn't understand. "He's one of your what?"

Susan turned, her eyes cool, always judging...constantly gauging.

"Boone—at least, that's the name by which you know him—is one of our best undercover agents."

The room started to spin. Rachel turned and leaned against the cold glass, relishing the coolness against her feverish forehead.

"Are you all right?" Susan asked.

Rachel closed her eyes, then swallowed a lump in her throat, remembering the things that had seemed so out of character for the man she'd believed him to be. He'd asked her to trust him. Offered her help when she was certain none was there. She caught her breath on a sob. He'd even told her at the last that he was one of the good guys, but she hadn't understood what he meant. Rachel took a deep breath, then let it out on a sigh.

"Yes, Susan, I'm all right. I'm very all right...now."

Susan Cross nodded. It felt good to break a rule. Maybe she should do it more often.

"Well, then," she said quietly, "you understand I'm telling you this under the strictest confidence. It wouldn't do to let some of his enemies know he was flat on his back and virtually defenseless, would it?"

The tone of Rachel's voice went flat, ominous in its lack of emotion. "No one will hurt him while he's defenseless, I promise you that."

To say that Susan was startled by Rachel's statement was putting it mildly, but then she remembered what B.J. had told her about finding Griffin Ross dead. It was obvious from the shape Boone had been in when they hauled him out of the Kiamichis that he couldn't have done it. That left Rachel as the triggerman. It was hard to look at her now and see a woman who'd drilled two holes into the front of Griffin Ross's shirt.

"Sometimes it's dangerous to make such a promise unless you're ready to back it up."

Rachel flushed but refused to admit to what the captain was implying. What had happened back there in the mountains was thanks to Mercy, not her.

There was no way a by-the-book kind of woman like Susan Cross would understand about a past life taking hold of the one happening now, and when Rachel thought about it, neither did she. All she knew was that, when it counted, she'd aimed and fired, just as Boone had told her to do, and hit a target she hadn't expected to hit.

Convinced that she'd accomplished what she'd set out to do, Susan started to leave, but Rachel caught her by the arm.

"Susan?"

"Yes?"

Shades of a Desperado

"What's his name?"

"Daniel Blaine."

Rachel nodded, trying to match the man she knew with a new identity. "What do they call him?"

Susan grinned. "Other than mule-headed?"

Rachel's heart lifted. The name might be strange, but the personality was not. "Yes, other than that."

"Just Daniel. He's not much for nicknames."

There was a note pinned to the T-shirt. Just one name. Didn't know if it was my first name or my last.

"No, I guess he's not," Rachel agreed.

"He's going to be all right," Susan said. "If you'd known him as long as I have, you'd believe me."

And then Rachel smiled. "It seems like I've known him forever."

Susan touched Rachel's arm. It was a brief, almost clumsy gesture. She wasn't used to showing her emotions.

"I'd better be going. We've got a lot of cleaning up to do. When he comes to, tell him we smashed the lab and took Cherry into custody. Griffin Ross had been laundering drug money out of his savings and loan, and with the aid of his secretary, who's agreed to cooperate fully by helping us with the paperwork to prove it, we can seize his personal assets. The rest of the bunch is history, thanks to you and B.J."

"Poor Lois," Rachel said, and then it dawned on her what Susan had just said. She gave the DEA captain a wary look. *Thanks to me and B.J.? So they know how Griffin died after all.*

"Don't worry," Susan said. "It was Boone's gun, and quite obviously self-defense. There will be no problem with who pulled the trigger."

Rachel lifted her chin. "I wasn't hiding the fact," she said quietly. "Put whatever you have to in the records. I just did what I had to do to keep him alive."

Susan's eyebrow arched again. "You know, there's something about you I didn't expect. Have you ever thought of going into law enforcement?"

Rachel didn't bother to hide her shudder. "No! I don't like guns. That was my first time to hold one, and I hope my last. I'm trained to save people's lives, not take them."

"I think you're looking at us from the wrong side of the road," Susan said. "We're trained to do the very same thing."

That was food for thought as Susan Cross walked away, taking B. J. Wayland with her. Rachel stared after them until the elevator swallowed them whole.

She turned and looked back out the window. It was almost morning.

Daniel Blaine. His name is Daniel....

Rachel straightened. A memory hovered at the back of her mind. There was something she needed to remember. Something about her trip to South Dakota. Something connected to the newspaper story about Dakota's demise.

"Oh, my God!" Blaine! That was it! Mercy Hollister had been responsible for the death of an outlaw named Dakota Blaine.

Charlie's reflection appeared in the glass as he came to stand behind her. "Rachel, is anything wrong?"

It was the last little link in her connection to the past that made a crazy kind of sense out of it all.

"No, oh, no. In fact, it's just the opposite. Everything is very all right."

Charlie didn't know what had made her so happy, but at this point, as he hugged her close, he didn't really care. He was willing to take what he could get, when he could get it.

Another half hour passed, and the earlier elation Rachel had experienced was beginning to pass. She was back to pacing and worrying, and Charlie was hard-pressed to find something to occupy her mind. A notion did occur to him, and as he considered telling her, he also considered the consequences if his secret went past her.

"Hey, Rachel, if I tell you something, will you swear not to tell a living, breathing soul, especially Joanie Sue Miller?"

Rachel nodded. "I promise, especially about Joanie."

"You remember Ida Mae Frawley?"

"Widow Frawley? The old recluse who died a few months back?"

"Yeah, that's the one."

"What about her?" Rachel asked.

"I used to mow her yard when I was a kid, did you know that?"

Rachel shook her head.

"Yeah, I did. As I got older, I did all kinds of odd jobs for her. She was almost ninety when she died. Someone had to help her."

"That was good of you, Charlie."

He ducked his head. "I guess she liked me a lot."

Rachel smiled. "You're an easy man to like, Charlie Dutton."

He gave her a long, judging look. "Remember, you promised."

"Oh, for Pete's sake. You'd think we were five years old and you just stole the last piece of pie. What are you trying to say?"

"Well, hell, how would you feel if you were minding your own business and then found out one day that someone had died and left you seven hundred thousand dollars?"

"Seven hundred thousand…" She gasped. "You're kidding!"

"No, I am not," Charlie said. "And keep your voice down."

Rachel was stunned. "That explains your ring and your car and your hairstyle," she said. "But not why you want to keep it a secret."

Charlie blushed, then looked away, and at that moment Rachel came as close to loving him as she ever would.

"I didn't want anyone to know because I want to be loved for who I am, not what I've got."

Rachel's voice trembled. "Oh, Charlie, I don't know what to say."

"Now, don't go all squishy-eyed on me. This is a secret, remember?" Then he grinned. "Besides, it's too late for you now, baby. Even if you swear, I won't believe you love me."

Rachel had to laugh, which was exactly what he had wanted, and before anything else could be said, Charlie grabbed her and spun her around. A doctor was coming toward them in surgery greens. Rachel went to meet him.

For the rest of her life, Rachel would remember the first sight she'd had of Daniel Blaine in ICU. She'd fallen in love with Boone, and she'd been prepared to love him in spite of himself. Now she was face-to-face with an unconscious man in a hospital bed and learning all over again what love and sacrifice were about.

She could only imagine the risks he'd taken by letting their relationship grow. Only now, since she'd learned his true identity, did she understand what he must have thought when he saw her in Griffin Ross's arms. She made a promise to herself then and there that she would never give him cause to doubt her again.

Four days later, Daniel Blaine was moved from ICU to a private room. When he moved, Rachel went with him. She'd been home only once, and that had been to get her own car and several changes of clothes. She wasn't letting him out of her sight until he was able to leave on his own. She knew now the selfless act of love he'd shown by shoving her in front of him as they ran through the night, putting himself between her and danger, willing to take the bullet that might have hit her instead. The doctors were doing their part in healing Daniel's body, but it was Rachel's quiet, steady presence that began the healing of a desperado's heart.

* * *

She thought he was asleep. Daniel could tell by the quiet
way in which she moved around the room, adding water to
the flowers the agency had sent, folding the extra blanket
at the foot of his bed, easing the sheet from beneath his arm
to keep from jostling the IV.

The sounds around him hadn't changed much in the past
five days. Nine altogether, taking into consideration the four
he'd spent in ICU. He didn't remember much from that time,
but he'd always known she was there. Her presence filled
some long-empty part of him.

Just outside the doorway, life went on, but inside his
room, his world consisted of Rachel. Doctors' and nurses'
intrusions were tolerated. Only Rachel was welcomed into
the private space of his heart.

The sounds of glasses and dishes being rattled told him
it must be suppertime. Food odors drifted amid the scents
of medicine and disinfectant, an unappetizing combination.

Daniel shifted slightly where he lay, easing the pressure
on the healing wound on his back, and as he did, he sensed
Rachel's instant appraisal.

His eyelids fluttered as he hid a smile. God help him,
but when he gave his heart to Rachel Brant, he'd also given
up the last of his secrets. The joke on her was that he didn't
mind at all. If they'd been his secrets to tell, he would have
shared them with her long ago.

He had but the vaguest of memories of what had happened after she took off her shirt in the forest and used it
to stanch the flow of his blood. They were little more than
flashes of images, of voices, of smells. The fear mirrored
on Rachel's face. The gun he'd put in her hand. The smell
of rotting leaves and cold night air...of pine and cedar...
and gunpowder.

But there was one image that had stayed sure and strong
in his mind, and that was Rachel standing over him like an

avenging angel with his gun aimed straight at Griffin Ross's chest. He remembered feeling hopeless and helpless, and he remembered a complete and total fear that he'd brought her to this end.

It had been days later before he learned what she'd done, and even then he had been unable to picture the Rachel he knew, the healer, the caregiver, as being able to shoot a man twice, point-blank. But he was living proof that she had.

"Daniel, darling..."

She'd had nine days to get used to the change in his identity, but it felt good to hear his name on her lips. Her hand was on his forehead. He felt her lips brush his cheek. He opened his eyes.

"They're bringing supper around."

"I don't want food. I want you."

Rachel stifled a smile. "Hmm...what was that word Susan Cross used? Oh yes, I remember...*mule-headed.* I believe she said you were mule-headed. Darling, are you? Mule-headed, I mean?"

Daniel grinned. "Probably, but that doesn't change what I want."

Rachel straightened his covers and stepped back just as a nurse entered the room with his meal. She leaned close and warned him in a none-too-gentle tone of voice, "What you want and what you're about to get are two entirely different things."

"Good evening, Mr. Blaine, how are we doing?"

Daniel glared. He hated the communal *we.* The last time he looked, he'd been the only one in this room stuck in a bed.

"You tell me. How are we?" he grumbled.

The nurse slid the tray onto the table and lifted the warming covers off the food, then hit a button on the bed that sat Daniel abruptly upright.

He cursed as the stitches pulled his skin.

"We're a little testy this evening, aren't we? That's always a good sign. We'll be ready to go home before we know it."

"You're damn sure not going with me," Daniel muttered, glaring at the food, which was sitting there on his plate in all its unappetizing glory.

"This looks wonderful," Rachel said, as she went to get him a warm, wet cloth so that he could wash before eating. Her voice was lower as she dropped the cloth in his hands. "Will one washcloth be enough, sweetheart, or should I get another one, with soap for your mouth?"

He got the message and took the washcloth without further comment.

"I'll be back later to get your tray, Mr. Blaine. Enjoy."

Daniel shoved the tray and table aside, then glared at Rachel, daring her to argue with his decision.

"You eat it," he said.

"No, thank you," she said brightly. "I had a snack while you were asleep." Then she picked up his fork and handed it to him without batting an eye. "Oh, look, darling, they've put cucumber in your salad. I seem to remember you're quite an authority on cucumbers."

His mouth quirked at one corner. The little witch! She was taunting him just as he'd teased her that day in the grocery store.

Rachel sat at the foot of the bed, with her hand on his leg, rubbing gently...but still, rubbing just the same. She leaned forward only slightly—but there was a definite and unexpected sexual tension in her voice.

"Is it good?"

He blinked. All sorts of images came to mind that might fit that question much better than the damned cucumber in his salad.

"Is what good?" he mumbled.

"The salad, sweetheart. Is it crisp? You know how you

like things to have a certain texture. None of that limp, floppy stuff for you, right?"

He had to grin. She'd won that round. He jammed the fork in the salad and took a big bite. To his chagrin, it didn't taste half-bad.

Rachel slipped off the bed and went to get her nail file. Moments later, she climbed back to her spot and began to file at a tear on her nail as if it were the most important thing she had to do. And because she wasn't paying attention, he finished his salad in spite of himself.

She looked up. "Ummm…the scalloped potatoes and ham smell good. How do they taste?"

Daniel stared at the conglomeration piled on his plate and wished for a greasy take-out burger instead.

Rachel wasn't to be deterred. "I *love* sauces, don't you? Especially cheese—the way it melts…and blends. It adds just that right touch to plain food. It's so…so…fluid, and warm, and…"

"Have mercy, Rachel. I'll eat the stuff, just give me a break!"

Rachel smiled and moved on to another nail while Daniel dug into his dinner.

"Would you look at that!" she said a little while later, when he'd finished the ham and potatoes. "There are strawberries in the mixed fruit! Remember when—"

"Don't even start," Daniel muttered, and picked up his spoon. "I'm eating. I'm eating."

Hours later, the hospital had undergone its daily metamorphosis. The shift had changed, and the nurses on duty were readying everyone for the night. Vitals had been taken; medicine rounds were over. The muted sounds of visitors taking their leave from other patients could be heard out in the hall.

Daniel was absorbing the quiet while absently watching

the television. After being coaxed to come up beside him, Rachel now lay on the edge of his bed, her back aligned with the length of his leg, dozing in snatches.

Every time she jerked, or sighed a little more than he'd expected, Daniel would lay his hand upon her hair, or stroke the softness of her cheek, anything it took to gentle her slumber and reassure himself that she was going to be all right. He'd had nightmares about Rachel sleepwalking off the edge of the world and him not being able to catch her. Even now, though she was wide-awake and within reach of his hand, the thought scared him to death. She was his life.

He heard her sigh and knew that she was awake again. That was good. There were things that needed to be said.

"Rachel?" he whispered. "Are you awake?"

She stretched. "Umm-humm."

"There's something I've been wanting to say."

She heard a tone in his voice that hadn't been there in days. She went still.

"Thank you for saving my life."

Horror flashed, then quickly disappeared. She would not let the memory of Griffin Ross's evil ruin their lives. She sat up to face him, wearing a small, unusual smile.

Daniel had no way of knowing that, for Rachel, the act had been twofold. Mercy Hollister had been responsible for the death of the man she loved. It had been up to Rachel to see that history did not repeat itself. She would have done whatever it took to keep this man alive—for herself, as well as for him.

"You're welcome."

His jaw clenched nervously as he debated with himself as to the best way to pursue what was on his mind.

"You know...we haven't known each other very long, although I feel as if I've known you all my life."

Oh, my darling, Daniel...if only you knew. Rachel smiled and reached for his hand. "I love you, sweetheart. Always have. Always will."

Daniel's eyebrow arched as a smile crooked the corner of his mouth. "You were scared of me, and you know it."

"Not of *you*. Never of you. Only what you represented."

He nodded. "I can accept that. What I'm trying to say is, I know in my heart how I feel, but I'm willing to wait as long as it takes until you're—"

"No."

He looked startled. "No, what?"

"I'm not willing to wait."

His grin widened as his black eyes glittered with promises he could hardly wait to keep. Then he took a deep breath, trying to remember where he'd been going with this thought. "I have a couple of things I need to tell you."

"Okay."

"This was my last undercover assignment."

She looked slightly startled. "Not because of me?"

A wry smile cocked the corner of his mouth. "Of course it's because of you. You think I'm going to go off half-cocked the rest of my life and leave you within reach of someone like Charlie Dutton?"

Rachel frowned. "I would never cheat on our love."

He caught her hand. "I was only teasing," he said quietly. "I knew this job would be my last one before you and I ever met. I've had enough of it, honey, and it's had enough of me."

Never in her life had Rachel wanted to throw herself into someone's arms as badly as she did right then, but they were too confined by tubes and needles to give it a thought. Instead, she leaned forward until mere inches separated their lips and whispered, "I'll never have enough of you. Just remember that."

Emotion came swiftly, blinding Daniel to all but the love shining out of Rachel's eyes.

"Rachel, if I asked you real nice, would you marry me?"

To his surprise, she started to cry.

He grimaced, swallowing a few tears of his own. "Come here, you."

She went willingly. Time passed as she settled in his good arm.

"Rachel."

"What, darling?"

"You never answered me."

She sighed. After all they'd been through, how on earth could he doubt? She moved, needing to look him in the eye when she said what she had to say.

"Yes, a thousand times yes, I will marry you. For the love we have now, and for all the love we once shared."

He groaned and pulled her back into his arms. What she'd said made no sense, but he was too happy a man to care.

"Daniel, be careful," she warned him, as he urged her into his lap.

"Now, darlin', I'm always careful, don't you remember?"

One last time, the image of Dakota's face slid between them. Black hair blowing in the wind as he mounted a horse in a flying leap. The laughter she could see on his lips as he yanked Mercy up behind him.

Rachel closed her eyes, waiting for the kiss to come, and when it did, there was no mistaking the man who was in control. Daniel's breath was soft against her skin. The touch of his hand ever gentle against her cheek.

"Open your eyes, Rachel. See who loves you, baby."

She complied, although she knew before she did as he asked.

Through the centuries, all kinds of men had walked the earth. Some of their spirits had been dark, their souls black and hell-bent against redemption before they were ever born. But not her Daniel. He *was* a desperado…but in a subtle shade of gray.

Epilogue

It was spring in South Dakota. When Daniel and Rachel landed in Rapid City, it was just after noon. The rental car was waiting, as they'd requested, and by the time they loaded their bags and headed toward Deadwood, Rachel's anxiety was at an all-time high.

It hadn't been until after their wedding that Rachel learned where Daniel was born. That surprised him. Up until that moment, he'd still believed that was why she'd gone to South Dakota in the first place.

But now they were here—together—and for reasons he still didn't understand. Rachel had been oddly reticent with explanations, and adamant that they should go, and so he'd come—because she'd asked.

She didn't sleepwalk anymore. She claimed the episodes had stopped as abruptly as they'd appeared. There were a lot of things Rachel didn't explain and Daniel didn't care to ask. As long as she was well, nothing else mattered.

They drove into Deadwood as the sun was setting in the west.

Tomorrow their mission would begin. Rachel walked among the tombstones, clutching a small plastic bag, her gaze focused downward, reading each epitaph, one by one. It was here. It had to be.

"Rachel, I know there's a real good reason why we came all the way to Deadwood for a belated honeymoon, and an even better one for dragging me through Boot Hill, but I have yet to figure it out."

"I love you, too," she said absently, and kept moving without looking back.

There was an abstracted look Rachel got on her face when she was concentrating real hard that made his toes curl in his boots. It always made him want to take her to bed and give her something else to think about. Daniel grinned to himself as he watched the sway of her hips in those tight blue jeans. These old outlaws would probably rise up and cheer if he followed his instincts right now.

"Hey, Rachel, don't you think it's sort of early on in our relationship for you to be ignoring me?"

Rachel paused and stifled a grin. Some of the verses on these tombstones were a hoot. This one in particular.

Red Fred
Died in bed

"What did you say?" she asked, suddenly realizing Daniel was a distance away and looking as if he were waiting for some sort of answer.

He laughed and threw up his arms. "Nothing, honey. Just wait for me."

Joy surged anew as Rachel stood in the warm Dakota sunshine while a cool spring breeze played with the ends of her hair. Love for this man...for her husband...was overwhelming.

His wind-tossed hair gleaming a sleek seal black, Daniel Blaine came toward her with a long, careless stride. His head was up, and his chin was thrust forward in the same way he met life: straight on. There was a power in him even clothes couldn't hide. The wide set of strong shoulders, the determination on his face that rarely wavered, and, always, a dark, carefree glitter in his eyes.

Rachel smiled as he drew near. In some ways he was like those who lay buried here, but in the ways that counted, he was so much more. He'd made the most of himself instead of letting life drag him down. She loved him, and her respect for him knew no bounds.

He swooped, lifting her off her feet and into his arms, kissing her grandly and with no sense of embarrassment for the dozens of other tourists who were sharing their day.

"Daniel Blaine! What will all these people think?" Rachel said, as he put her back down.

He threw his head back and laughed. "Honey, I don't care what they think. You're my woman. I'll kiss you any place I damn well please." He glanced down and then grinned. "Even in front of Red Fred."

She laughed and then took him by the hand. "You're impossible, but I love you. Now come help me look."

He rolled his eyes and let her lead him away. "I'd be glad to help, if I only knew what I was looking for."

Rachel ignored his complaint as, once again, her attention was focused on the tombstones scattered all around.

Few voices shattered the silence within the cemetery grounds as people walked about. Even though these men had been hell on earth, they'd been buried in hallowed ground. Preachers had spoken over their graves. Friends had shed tears for their passing. They'd gained a stature in death that they'd missed in life.

It wasn't until sometime later that Rachel paused, then dropped to her knees.

Daniel was a few feet ahead before he realized she wasn't behind him. He turned, a smile on his face and laughter in his voice as he started to chide her for dawdling again. But his jest was never voiced, because he saw her reach out and trace the letters on a gray, weathered headstone.

Her head was bowed, and even from where he was standing, he could see a tremor in her chin. Within seconds, he was at her side. Curiosity drew his gaze to the stone that had so captured Rachel's fancy, but curiosity changed to surprise when he read the name on the stone.

Dakota Blaine
Deserved No Mercy

"Well, I'll be darned," Daniel said. "We have the same last name."

Rachel's eyes were filled with tears as she lifted the tiny bouquet of flowers from the sack she'd been carrying. When she'd seen them displayed among the florist's array, she'd picked them up without a second thought.

They were bluebells, tiny bell-like flowers that grew on fragile-looking stems that even the strongest of winds could not break. Their pure blue was also the color of Mercy Hollister's eyes. As she laid them on the grave, Rachel knew Dakota would have approved of her choice.

"How did you know this was here?" Daniel asked, as he watched Rachel place the flowers with care.

She looked up at him. Tears shimmered on the surface of her eyes—blue eyes, just like the bluebells she'd laid on the grave.

"I guess you could say I saw it in my dreams."

Daniel gave her a sharp, studied look. "Are you all right?"

Rachel smiled and held out her hand. "Let's go. I've done what I came here to do."

He helped her up without pressing her further. Rachel had loved him without question; the least he could do was return the favor.

They walked away without looking back, but Rachel felt no need to linger. Only one more stop and her mission in coming this far would be over.

* * *

The day was drawing to a close, but Rachel had been firm in her convictions that this stop was truly necessary. The church was old and long since abandoned, yet the tiny nearby cemetery was well kept and mowed—proof to passersby that, while the parishioners had moved on, the care of those left behind still continued.

Daniel was beginning to worry. Combing cemeteries seemed an unhealthy pastime. The tension on Rachel's face was showing, and her actions seemed frantic, as if she were racing against some deadline of her own. This behavior was too symptomatic of her sleepwalking episodes for his peace of mind.

But she wasn't talking, and he didn't know how to intrude. For the time being, he stayed at her side, keeping careful watch over the lady who was his wife.

Months earlier, Rachel had enlisted the aid of a service designed for genealogists in search of missing ancestors. The letter she held contained the name of this church and the approximate location of the grave marker she'd come to find. One fact had come out in the search that she hadn't expected. Mercy Hollister had taken her own life. She had not been buried in hallowed ground.

For Rachel, it was the last piece of the puzzle she'd been trying to find. Maybe this was why Mercy Hollister's search for love on earth had not ended with her death. By taking her own life, she'd lost her chance to follow Dakota Blaine into eternity.

Rachel stumbled. Daniel caught her, then pulled her to him, caressing the side of her face with his hand as he gauged the fever of her intent.

"Rachel, darlin', you're beginning to scare me. Can't you tell me what's wrong? I promise you, there's nothing you can say that I won't understand."

Rachel was tired. She'd been fighting this thing alone for

so long. She caught his hand, feathering a gentle kiss upon the palm, then looked up, searching the beloved features she'd come to know so well.

How to tell you, my love? How to explain where we've been...what we've done? She sighed.

"It's almost over," she said, pleading with him to persevere with her a while longer.

He bowed his head and then held her close, feeling her tremble with fatigue. He fought with himself and his instincts, but his love for her won out.

"Tell me what to do," he said.

"Do you have my flowers?"

He held up the second small florist's sack. She nodded in satisfaction.

"Then come with me. It should be right over here."

She took him by the hand, and together they traversed the neat, narrow rows between headstones, to a small section of markers set aside from the rest. They were outside the old picket fence, beyond the neat rows and well-clipped grass.

The grass was taller here, obscuring the stones that were less prominent in height. A small brown rabbit suddenly darted from behind an old tombstone, while tiny wildflowers, only inches high, blew to and fro with the breeze. Rachel leaned down to read the names.

"Help me," she said.

Daniel came to her side. "Who are you looking for?" he asked.

"Mercy. Her name is Mercy."

A chill of foreboding swept across Daniel's senses, almost the same sensation as when a bust was about to go down. A sense of knowing that within moments everything was going to come apart and there was no way of knowing the outcome until it was over and done. But then it passed, and he took her hand.

Together they walked, stooping every now and then

to brush away leaves and read names, to toss away brush caught against the stones.

It was Daniel who found it. And, as Rachel had done at Boot Hill, he found himself down on his knees, tracing the weathered, hand-carved letters in an old piece of stone.

But as he touched it, he rocked back on his heels, startled by an overwhelming wave of sadness. He shook his head in disbelief and chalked it up to the fact that they'd been in too many graveyards.

"Rachel."

She was at his side in moments. She knelt beside him, and as his finger traced the letters in Mercy's name, her throat swelled with the ache of unshed tears.

"Oh, Daniel," she said, and laid her head against his shoulder.

Mercy Hollister
1853–1877
Dakota took her
Gone but not forgotten

Only Rachel knew the subtlety of the Dakota reference. It wasn't the Dakota Territory that had taken her away; it was the man who'd taken his name from the land.

Rachel began pulling grass and weeds away from the stone, clearing a small place for the flowers to go. But when Daniel handed Rachel the sack, she rejected it with tear-filled eyes.

"No, sweetheart, I think this would be better if it came from you."

He shrugged. "Whatever makes you happy, darlin'."

No, Daniel. It's you...or who you were...that will make Mercy happy, wherever she is.

The nosegay was small and round and tied at the bottom

with baby-fine ribbons. White ones. Purple ones. Sky-blue scalloped ones.

"Put it there, I think," Rachel said, pointing to a sheltered spot against the small stone.

Daniel leaned the flowers there, firmly shoving the end of the bouquet into the soft, loamy earth until they appeared to have sprouted on the spot.

The blossoms dipped and bounced with the South Dakota breeze. Rachel reached out and touched them, testing the fresh, tender petals with the palm of her hand. They felt cool and soft, like Daniel's lips on her face when they made love in the dark.

And as they knelt, a feeling of peace settled deep in Rachel's heart.

"It's over…isn't it?" she said softly.

"What did you say?" Daniel asked, and then realized Rachel wasn't talking to him.

His nerves skittered, reminding him suddenly that they were a long, long way from home. He put his arm around her and urged her to stand.

"Rachel, honey. It's getting late."

She looked up at him. "No, Daniel. We were just in time."

They stood, looking down at the flowers on the shamefully small grave.

"The flowers are pretty," Daniel said. "Wonder what kind they are?"

"Forget-me-nots."

He nodded, rereading the verse on the grave one last time.

"They seem to fit real well, don't they? You know…gone but not forgotten?"

There was a hard knot in her throat as Daniel took her by the hand. *Rest in peace, Mercy Hollister.*

Just for a moment, the steady blowing breeze seemed to stop, as if God were holding his breath. A small cloud passed between the earth and the sun, casting the place in which they were standing into sudden shadow. And then, slowly, as clouds have a way of doing, it moved on and, as it did, left sunlight behind to mark its passing.

Rachel watched the small shadow moving across the face of the land, across the cemetery beyond, and then along the road on which they'd traveled.

It was a fanciful thought, and one she knew had no real foundation, but she could almost believe the receding shadow was Mercy Hollister's spirit, going home to rest.

"Daniel?"

"Yes, darlin'?"

"Take me home."

* * * * *

THE WORLD IS BETTER WITH

Romance

Harlequin has everything from contemporary, passionate and heartwarming to suspenseful and inspirational stories.

Whatever your mood, we have a romance just for you!

Connect with us to find your next great read, special offers and more.

f /HarlequinBooks

🐦 @HarlequinBooks

www.HarlequinBlog.com

www.Harlequin.com/Newsletters

⬧HARLEQUIN®

A *Romance* FOR EVERY MOOD™

www.Harlequin.com

HARLEQUIN®

A *Romance* FOR EVERY MOOD™

JUST CAN'T GET ENOUGH?

Join our social communities
and talk to us online.

You will have access to the latest
news on upcoming titles and special
promotions, but most importantly,
you can talk to other fans about your
favorite Harlequin reads.

Harlequin.com/Community

Facebook.com/HarlequinBooks

Twitter.com/HarlequinBooks

Pinterest.com/HarlequinBooks

HARLEQUIN®

A *Romance* FOR EVERY MOOD™

**Stay up-to-date on all your
romance-reading news with the
Harlequin Shopping Guide,
featuring bestselling authors, exciting new
miniseries, books to watch and more!**

The newest issue will be delivered right to you
with our compliments! There are 4 each year.

Signing up is easy.

EMAIL

ShoppingGuide@Harlequin.ca

WRITE TO US

HARLEQUIN BOOKS
Attention: Customer Service Department
P.O. Box 9057, Buffalo, NY 14269-9057

OR PHONE

1-800-873-8635 in the United States
1-888-343-9777 in Canada

Please allow 4-6 weeks for delivery of the first issue by mail.